CRAMMING FOR DEATH

"Sir, if I'm going to be sent openly to Yata-kang, why was I told to come to Boat Camp?"

"It's the best place to eptify you for your mission."

"Major Delahanty told me about that," Donald said slowly. "It's still not quite clear to me."

"Eptification is derived from an acronym—EPT stands for 'education for particular tasks.' "

Confused, Donald said, "I seem to have missed the point somewhere. When you said lack of experience as a reporter didn't matter, I naturally assumed . . ."

The colonel regarded him with mingled amusement and contempt. "That's not what you need eptification in."

"What, then?"

"In four short days you're going to be epti-fied to kill."

"Brunner is a past master at bringing to life the backgrounds against which his characters play out their parts. In *Zanzibar* he has surpassed himself. Two young men provide the focus of the book . . . the destiny of each is a part of the crowded, hysterical world in which they live . . . provocative and fascinating."
—*Kliatt*

STAND ON ZANZIBAR

John Brunner

A Del Rey Book

BALLANTINE BOOKS • NEW YORK

FOR MARJORIE

of course

context (0)

THE INNIS MODE

"There is nothing wilful or arbitrary about the Innis mode of expression. Were it to be translated into perspective prose, it would not only require huge space, but the insight into the modes of interplay among forms of organisation would also be lost. Innis sacrificed point of view and prestige to his sense of the urgent need for insight. A point of view can be a dangerous luxury when substituted for insight and understanding. As Innis got more insight he abandoned any mere point of view in his presentation of knowlege. When he interrelates the development of the steam press with 'the consolidation of the vernaculars' and the rise of nationalism and revolution he is not reporting anybody's point of view, least of all his own. He is setting up a mosaic configuration or galaxy for insight . . . Innis makes no effort to 'spell out' the interrelations between the components in his galaxy. He offers no consumer packages in his later work, but only do-it-yourself kits . . ."

—Marshall McLuhan: *The Gutenberg Galaxy*

CONTENTS

the happening world

STAND ON ZANZIBAR

SCANALYZE MY NAME

Stock cue SOUND: "Presenting SCANALYZER, Engrelay Satelserv's unique thrice-per-day study of the big big scene, the INdepth INdependent INmediate INterface between you and your world!"

Stock cue VISUAL: cliptage, splitscreen, cut in bridgemelder, Mr. & Mrs. Everywhere depthunder (today MAMP, Mid-Atlantic Mining Project), spaceover (today freeflysuiting), transiting (today Simplon Acceleratube), digging (today as every day homimage with autoshout).

Autoshout cue: "It's happening it's happening! SCANALYZER SCANALYZER SCANALYZER SCANALYZER SCANALYZER SCANALYZER—"

Stock cue VISUAL: cliptage, wholescreen, planet Earth turning jerk-jerk-jerk and holding meridians for GMT, EST, PCT, Pacific Conflict Zone Time.

Live cue SOUND: "And it's six poppa-momma for the happening people keeping it straight and steady on that old Greenwich Mean Time—how mean can time get, you tell me, *hm?* Zee for zero, bee for base, counting down to one after ess ee eks—sorree—ess EYE eks! We know what's happening *happening* HAPPENING but that piece of the big big scene is strictly up to you, Mr. and Mrs. Everywhere—or Mr. and Miss, or Miss and Miss, or Mister and Mister, take your pick, hah-hah! Counting down to one after one poppa-momma for that good old Eastern Standard tie-yum, one after ten anti-matter for the Pacific Coast, and for all of you fighting the good fight in lonely midocean one after seven anti-matter—PIPS!"

Clock cue: 5×1-sec. countdown pips on G in alt., minute signal on C in alt.

Plug cue: "No time like the present for things to happen in, no better way to keep time straight and steady than by the signal from General Technics' critonium clock, so accuright it serves to judge the stars."

Script cue VISUAL: cliptage, splitscreen, excerpts from day's news.

Live cue SOUND: "And no better way to keep abreast—pardon—than with SCANALYZER!"

Cut autoshout cue. (If they haven't made it by this time they've switched off.)

Plug cue: "SCANALYZER is the one single, the ONLY study of the news in depth that's processed by General Technics' famed computer Shalmaneser, who sees all, hears all, knows all save only that which YOU, Mr. and Mrs. Everywhere, wish to keep to yourselves."

Script cue: the happening world.

the happening world (1)

READ THE DIRECTIONS

For toDAY third of MAY twenty-TEN ManhatTEN reports mild spring-type weather under the Fuller Dome. Ditto on the General Technics Plaza.

But Shalmaneser is a Micryogenic ® computer bathed in liquid helium and it's cold in his vault.

(DITTO   Use it! The mental process involved is exactly analogous to the bandwidth-saving technique employed for your phone. If you've seen the scene you've seen the scene and there's too much new information for you to waste time looking it over more than once. Use "ditto". *Use* it!
—*The Hipcrime Vocab* by Chad C. Mulligan)

Less of a machine, more of a human being, but partaking of the nature of both, Georgette Tallon Buckfast is largely supported by prosthetics in her ninety-first year.

When the strain becomes TOO MUCH it's because Hitrip of California bred it to have less stalk per ounce, more clean-queen leaf. Ask "The Man who's Married to Mary Jane"!

Eric Ellerman is a plant geneticist with three daughters

who's scared because his wife has developed a permanent pot-belly.

". . . and Puerto Rico today became the latest state to ratify the controversial dichromatism provision of United States eugenic legislation. This leaves only two havens for those who wish to bear disadvantaged children: Nevada and Louisiana. The defeat of the baby-farming lobby removes a long-time stigma from the fair brow of the Junior-but-One State—a congenital stigma, one may say, since the J-but-O State's accession to hoodness coincided almost to the day with the first eugenic legislation concerned with haemophilia, phenylketonuria and congenital imbecility . . ."

Poppy Shelton has believed in miracles for years, but now there's one happening right inside her body and the real world is leaning on her dreams.

THE DIFFICULT WE DO AT ONCE. THE IMPOSSIBLE TAKES A LITTLE LONGER.
                        —Base version of General Technics motto

Norman Niblock House is junior VP in charge of personnel and recruitment at General Technics.

"One fraction of a second, please—participant breakin coming up. Remember that only SCANALYZER's participant breakin service is processed by General Technics' Shalmaneser, the more correct response in the shorter quantum of time . . ."

Guinevere Steel's real name is Dwiggins, but do you blame her?

Do your slax sufficiently convey your natural power—at a glance?

If you're wearing MasQ-Lines, the answer's yes. Tired of half measures, we at MasQ-Line Corp. have put the codpiece back where it belongs, to say to the shiggies not kidder but codder.

Sheena and Frank Potter are all packed ready to leave for Puerto Rico because a green and a red light are just lights to him.

"*Two* participant breakins! Number one: sorree, friend, but no—we are not wrong to say Puerto Rico's decision leaves a mere two havens for the dissident. Isola does enjoy statehood, but the whole area of the Pacific its islands occupy is under martial law and you don't get a pass for other than martial reasons. Thanks for asking us, though, it's the way of the world, you're my environment and I am yours, which is why we operate SCANALYZER as a two-way process ..."

Arthur Golightly doesn't mind not being able to remember where he put things. Looking for them, he always finds other things he'd forgotten he had.

THE DIFFICULT WE DID YESTERDAY. THE IMPOSSIBLE WE'RE DOING RIGHT NOW.
> —Current version of General Technics motto

Donald Hogan is a spy.

"Number the other: dichromatism is what's commonly called colourblindness, and it is sure as sidereal time a congenital disability. Thank you, participant, thank *you*."

Stal (short for Stallion) Lucas is a yonderboy, weighed, measured, and freeflying all the way.

(IMPOSSIBLE   Means: *1* I wouldn't like it and when it happens I won't approve; *2* I can't be bothered; *3* God can't be bothered. Meaning 3 may perhaps be valid but the others are 101% whaledreck.
> —*The Hipcrime Vocab* by Chad C. Mulligan)

Philip Peterson is twenty years old.

Are you undermined by an old-style autoshout unit, one that needs constant reprogramming by hand if it's not to call you for items that were descheduled last week?
GT's revolutionary new autoshout reprograms itself!

Sasha Peterson is Philip's mother.

"Turning to a related subject, rioting crowds today stormed a Right Catholic church in Malmö, Sweden, while early mass was in progress. Casualty lists suggest a death toll of over forty including the priest and many children. From his palace in Madrid Pope Eglantine accused rival Pope Thomas of deliberately fomenting this and other recent uprisings, a charge vigorously denied by Vatican authorities."

Victor and Mary Whatmough were born in the same country and have been married twenty years—she for the second time, he for the third.

What you want to do when you see her in her Forlon&Morler Maxess costumelet
Is what she wants you to do when you see her in her Forlon&Morler Maxess costumelet
If she didn't, she wouldn't have put it on
Maximal access is no exaggeration when you spell it MAXESS
Style illustrated is "Courtesan"
But you should see "Tart"
What there is of it

Elihu Masters is currently United States Ambassador to the one-time British colony of Beninia.

"Speaking of accusations, Dixierep Senator Lowell Kyte this anti-matter charged that dicties were now responsible for nine-tenths of the felonies committed per anum—sorree!—per annum in his home state of Texas and that Fed efforts to quell the problem were a failure. Privately, officials of the Nark Force have been heard to express concern at the way GT's new product Triptine is catching the dicties' fancy."

Gerry Lindt is a draftee.

When we say "general" at GT we mean GENERAL. We offer the career of a lifetime to anyone interested in as-

*tronautics, biology, chemistry, dynamics, eugenics, ferromag-
netism, geology, hydraulics, industrial administration, jet pro-
pulsion, kinetics, law, metallurgy, nucleonics, optics, patent
rights, quarkology, robotics, synthesis, telecommunications,
ultrasonics, vacuum technology, work, X-rays, ylem, zool-
ogy . . .*

*No, we didn't miss out your speciality. We just didn't have
room for it in this ad.*

Professor Doctor Sugaiguntung is head of the Tectogenetics Department at Dedication University in the Guided Socialist Democracy of Yatakang.

"The incidence of muckers continues to maintain its high:
one in Outer Brooklyn yesterday accounted for 21 victims
before the fuzzy-wuzzies fused him, and another is still at
large in Evanston, Ill., with a total of eleven and three
injured. Across the sea in London a woman mucker took out
four as well as her own three-month baby before a mind-
present standerby clobbered her. Reports also from Rangoon,
Lima and Auckland notch up the day's toll to 69."

Grace Rowley is seventy-seven and going a bit weak in the
head.

*Here today and gone tomorrow isn't good enough for us in
this modern age.*
Here today and gone today is the pidgin we pluck.

The Right Honourable Zadkiel F. Obomi is the president
of Beninia.

"Westaway a piece or two, a stiff note was received in
Washington this anti-matter from the Yatakangi government,
claiming naval units working out of Isola had trespassed into
Yatakang's territorial waters. Officials will be polite, but it's
an open secret Yatakang's hundred-island territory gives
refuge all the time to Chinese aquabandits who sneak out
from so-called neutral ports and ambush U.S patrols in mid-
ocean . . ."

Olive Almerio is the most successful baby-farmer in Puerto Rico.

You know the codders who keep one, two, three shiggies on the string. You know the shiggies who every weekend blast off with a different codder. Envy them?
Needn't.
Like any other human activity this one can be learned. We teach it, in courses tailored to your preferences.
Mrs. Grundy Memorial Foundation (may she spin in her grave).

Chad C. Mulligan was a sociologist. He gave it up.

"Last week's State Forest fires on the West Coast that laid low hundreds of square miles of valuable timber destined for plastics, paper and organic chemicals were today officially attributed to sabotage by Forestry Commissioner Wayne C. Charles. As yet it is uncertain to whom the guilt belongs: treacherous so-called partisans among our own, or infiltrating reds."

Jogajong is a revolutionary.

The word is EPTIFY.
Don't look in the dictionary.
It's too new for the dictionary.
But you'd better learn what it implies.
EPTIFY.
We do it to you.

Pierre and Jeannine Clodard are both the children of *pieds-noirs,* unsurprisingly as they are brother and sister.

"Tornado warnings are out in the following states . . ."

Jeff Young is "the man to go to" anywhere west of the Rockies for the rather specialised goods he handles: time-fuzes, explosives, thermite, strong acids and sabotage bacteria.

"Turning to the gossipy side: once again the rumour goes the rounds that the small independent African territory of Beninia is in economic chaos. President Kouté of Dahomalia in a speech at Bamako warned the RUNGs that if they attempted to exploit the situation all necessary steps to counter ..."

Henry Butcher is an enthusiastic proselytiser for the panacea he believes in.

(RUMOUR   Believe all you hear. Your world may not be a better one than the one the blocks live in but it'll be a sight more vivid.

—*The Hipcrime Vocab* by Chad C. Mulligan)

It is definite that the man known as Begi is not alive. On the other hand, in at least one sense he isn't dead either.

"Also it's noised that Burton Dent is bivving it again, in that he was seen scorting former fuel supply Edgar Jewel into the particulate stages of this anti-matter. Meantime, Pacific time, it looks like Fenella Koch his spouse of three years may be turning spousiness into spiciness with cream-dream Zoë Laigh. Like the slogan says—why not equals why ker-not!"

Mr. & Mrs. Everywhere are construct identities, the new century's equivalent of the Joneses, except that with them you don't have to keep up. You buy a personalised TV with homimage attachment which ensures that Mr. & Mrs. Everywhere look, and talk, and move like you.

(HIPCRIME   You committed one when you opened this book. Keep it up. It's our only hope.

—*The Hipcrime Vocab* by Chad C. Mulligan)

Bennie Noakes sits in front of a set tuned to SCANALYZER orbiting on Triptine and saying over and over, "Christ what an imagination I've got!"

"And to close on, the Dept of Small Consolations. Some

troubledome just figured out that if you allow for every codder and shiggy and appleofmyeye a space one foot by two you could stand us all on the six hundred forty square mile surface of the island of Zanzibar. ToDAY third MAY twenty-TEN come aGAIN!"

tracking with closeups (1)

MR. PRESIDENT

The Right Honourable Zadkiel F. Obomi could feel the weight of the night pressing on his grey-wire scalp like the oppressive bulky silence of a sensory deprivation tank. He sat in his large official chair, hand-carved into a design that recreated without copying the sixteenth-century style of the master craftsmen some of whom had been his ancestors ... presumably. There had been a long interval when no one had time to care about such things.

Both his hands lay on the edge of the desk before him, as lax as vegetables. The left one showed its pinkish palm to the ceiling, with the creased lines that once, when he was a very small boy, had led a woman of half-French and half-Shango breeding to predict he would be a great hero. The other was turned to show its mahogany back, its tree-knot knuckles, as though poised to rap out a nervous fingertip rhythm.

It did not stir.

The deep intellectual forehead and the arch of his nose were probably Berber. But below the bridge on either side the nostrils flared out and the broad flat lips matched the plump cheeks and round chin and heavy pigmentation. That was all Shinka. He had often said jokingly in the days when his life had room for jokes that his face was a map of his country: invader down to the eyes, native from there on south.

But the eyes themselves, that made the dividing line, were simply human.

The left one was amost hidden under its drooping lid; it had been useless since the assassination bid of 1986, and a long scar still puckered the skin of his cheek and temple. The right one was bright, sharp, darting—at present unfocused, for he was not looking at the other occupant of the room.

The dead night suffocated him: Zadkiel F. Obomi, seventy-four years old, first and thus far only president of the former British colony of Beninia.

Not seeing, he was feeling. At his back, the huge empty nothing of the Sahara—the best part of a thousand miles away, yet so monstrous and so dominant it loomed in his brain like a thunderhead. Before him, beyond the walls, beyond the busy city, beyond the port, the early-night breeze of the Bight, smelling of ocean salt and spices from the ships standing to at the harbour bar. And to either side, forming the shackles that anchored his wrists on the desk against his half-formed desire to move them and turn the next page of the sheaf of documents awaiting his attention, the deadweight of the prosperous lands on whom fortune had smiled.

The population of the planet Earth was numbered in many billions.

Beninia, thanks to the slashed-on-a-map boundaries of the colonial government, had only nine hundred thousand of them.

The wealth of the planet Earth was inconceivable.

Beninia, for the same reason, had a little less than enough to save its people from starving.

The size of the planet Earth was . . . large enough, so far.

Beninia was pitted and pendulumed, and the walls were closing in.

He heard in memory the soft wheedling arguments.

With a French accent: *Geography is on our side; the lie of the land indicates that Beninia should logically join the Daho-malians; the river valleys, the hill passes, the . . .*

With an English accent: *History is on our side; we share the same common language; in Beninia Shinka speaks to*

Holaini, Inoko to Kpala, in the same tongue as Yoruba speaks to Ashanti; join the Republican Union of Nigeria with Ghana and be another RUNG . . .

Abruptly rage claimed him. He slapped the pile of papers with his open palm and leapt to his feet. The other man in the room jumped up also, face betraying alarm. But he had no time to speak before Mr. President strode out of the door.

In one of the palace's four high towers, on the inland side where one could look towards the lush green of the Mondo Hills and feel the bleak desolation of the Sahara far beyond, there was a room to which only Mr. President had the key. A guard at the intersection of two corridors saluted him with a quick wave of his ceremonial spear; he nodded and went on by.

As always, he closed and locked the door behind him before he turned on the light. He stood a few seconds in total darkness; then his hand fell to the switch and he blinked his one good eye at the sudden glare.

To his left, resting on a low table adjacent to a flat padded hassock, a copy of the Koran bound in green leather and tooled by hand with golden Arabic script listing the nine-and-ninety honourable names of the Almighty.

To his right, a *prie-dieu* in traditional Beninian carved ebony, facing a wall on which hung a crucifix. The victim nailed to the wood was as dark as the wood itself.

And facing the door, black masks, crossed spears, two drums, and a brazier of a type only the initiates of the Leopard Claw Brand might see without its disguise of leopard's fur.

Mr. President took a deep breath. He walked to the low table, picked up the Koran, and methodically shredded each of its pages into confetti. Last, he ripped the leather binding down the spine.

He turned on his heel, removed the crucifix from its peg, and snapped it across. The crucified one fell to the floor and he ground the doll-shape underfoot.

He dragged from the wall each in turn of the masks. He tore away the coloured straw hair from them, poked out the jewelled eyes, broke loose the ivory teeth. He stabbed through the sounding heads of both the drums with one of the spears.

The task complete, he turned off the light, left and locked the room, and at the first disposall chute he came to throw away the one and only key.

context (2)

Stock cue VISUAL: cliptage, wholescreen, atmospheric-type, orchestrated, first favouring copter views and MCU's New Jersey Turnpike Jam 1977 (¾ million cars o/w 16,-000-odd had to be crushed in situ) intercut w crush-hour shots Fifth Ave., Oxford St., Red Sq.; later favouring cretins, morons, phocomeli.

Live cue SOUND: "Today we congratulate Puerto Rico on the defeat it's inflicted on the baby-farming lobby. People who have celebrated their twenty-first find it hard to believe that a mere thirty years ago highways and cities were choked to strangulation point with masses of allegedly moving metal that got in each other's way so much we finally saw sense. Why worry about two tons of complicated steel gadgetry you won't need when you get where you're going—that won't even get you there in reasonable time? Worse yet—which measurably shortens your life through cancer or bronchitis thanks to the stench it emits!

"Like living creatures, automobiles expired when their environment became saturated with their own excreta. We ourselves *are* living creatures. We don't want the same to happen to us. That's why we have eugenic legislation. Praise the J-but-O State for joining the majority of us who have

15

seen the danger coming and resolved to put up with the minor inconveniences it entails when we decide to control the human elements of the big scene we inhabit.

"This has been a Greater New York Times editorial slot."

continuity (1)

THE GUILT-EDGED SECURITY

Everything about Norman Niblock House was measured: as measured as a foot-rule, as measured as time. *Item* the degree to which he allowed himself to lighten his skin and straighten the kinks in his hair and beard, so that he could exploit the guilt-reaction of his colleagues while still managing to get next to the shiggies who did most for his cod. *Item* the soupçon of eccentricity he manifested in his behaviour, as much as could ordinarily be tolerated in a junior VP of a big corporation and that much over the limit which said he was not a man to trifle with. *Item* the amount and nature of the work he arranged to have channelled to his office, selected so the visits of other zecks found him engaged in vastly important transactions.

He had been recruited to the company under the provisions of the Equal Opportunity Act which bound corporations like General Technics to employ the same ratio of whites to Aframs as was found in the country at large, plus or minus five per cent. Unlike some of his intake, he'd been welcome with a sigh of relief by the then vice-president in charge of personnel and recruitment, who had almost given up hope of finding enough Aframs willing to accept the standards of their host society. (A doctorate? What's a doctorate? A piece of paleass's toilet-paper.)

17

Norman N. House, D.Sc., was a prize. Knowing that, he'd made the race to win him long and hard.

Perceptive for the third time in his life (the first time: picking his parents; the second: sideswiping the only other contender for the post he now held down), the VP noticed that his new subordinate had a talent for impressing his personality on people he had never met before and was unlikely to meet again. They said later that he had House style. It meant that while he could bear to forget others he hated the idea that they should forget him.

The VP, envying this talent, took to cultivating Norman House in the hope that some of it might rub off on him. The hope was unfounded. Either a man is born with the gift or he learns it by conscious application over twenty years. Norman was then twenty-six and had been applying himself for the requisite two decades.

But the VP was tossed a few glib, helpful snippets.

"What I think of him? Well, his papers are good" (spoken judiciously, willing to make allowances) "but to my mind the man who has to wear MasQ-Lines is basically unsure of his own competence. They pad the frontal area, you know."

The VP, who had six pairs, never wore them again.

"What do I think of her? Well, she profiles okay on the testing sheet, but to my mind any girl who wears a Forlon&-Morler Maxess top over a pair of impervious slax is the type who won't go through with what she starts."

The VP, who had invited her to dinner and expected to be paid in the current contemporary coin, excused himself on grounds of imaginary illness and went grumpily home to his wife for the night.

"What I think of the annual report? Well, the graphing is up on last year's, but the noise level generated by this operation suggests it could be fifteen to eighteen per cent higher than it is. I'm wondering if it'll last."

The VP, who had been dithering, decided to retire at fifty with the Grade One bonus stock issue instead of hanging on to collect the Grade Three entitlement, double the size, due at sixty. He sold the stock as soon as he acquired it and chewed his nails while he watched its value creep up month by month. Eventually he shot himself.

It was his suspicion that the rise of GT stock might be due to his own replacement by Norman which killed him.

Norman walked briskly towards the general elevator. He declined to use the one that led directly from street-level to the wall behind his desk: "It's ludicrous for someone who deals with people not to mingle with the people he's dealing with, isn't it?"

At least one of the senior VP's had lately stopped using his private elevator too.

But in any case, he was going up.

Waiting, there was one of the company shiggies. She smiled at him, not because they were acquainted—he preferred to let it be felt that someone who relied on the firm to get him shiggies was less of a man than Norman House—but because the time and effort he invested in trifles like not using a private elevator paid off in the common belief that of all the twenty VP's in the company the most approachable and sociable was Mr. House. Stockboys toting crates in GT's West Virginia electronics plant shared the opinion, never having set eyes on him.

The smile he automatically returned was forced. He was edgy. An invitation to take lunch on the presidential floor with the senior zecks might be accounted for in two main ways: there might be promotion in the offing, although the grapevine he assiduously cultivated had brought him no hint of it; or, far more likely, they might be planning yet another review of the staffing system. He had endured two such since inheriting his present job, but they were a nuisance, and sometimes he could not hang on to people he had schemed for months to slot into influential posts.

The hole! I can cope with these paleasses. I did it before.

The descending light of the elevator showed and a soft chime rang out. Norman returned his attention to the here and now. A clock over the door, keyed like all those in the GT tower to the famous critonium master clock, indicated 12–44 poppa-momma. If he let the shiggy take the car down, he'd be a measured minute late for lunch with the Highly Important Personages.

That should be about right.

When the car arrived, he waved the girl past him. "I'm going up," he told her.

Promotion in the offing or not, he meant it.

The predicted few moments behind schedule, he emerged on the presidential floor. Synthetic grass hushed under his feet as he walked towards the group gathered alongside the swimming-pool. Four of the shapeliest of the company shiggies were disporting themselves nude in the water. He thought of the recurrent joke question—"Why doesn't GT pioneer company codders?"—and had trouble masking his amusement as he was greeted by Old GT herself.

Merely by looking at Georgette Tallon Buckfast one could not have guessed she was both an extraordinary person and an extraordinary artifact. One had to be told that she was ninety. She looked at worst sixty: plump, well-favoured, crowned with enough of her own brown hair to belie the old charge that she was more male than female. True, close study of her bosom might reveal the inequality which betrayed her use of a cardiac pacemaker, but nowadays many people wore such accessories by the time they were seventy or even younger. Only intensive prying had led Norman to knowledge of the lung-tissue transplant, the plastic venous valves, the kidney graft, the pinned bones, the vocal cords replaced because of cancer.

According to reliable estimates she was somewhat richer than the British royal family. Wealth like that could buy health, even if only by instalments.

With her were Hamilcar Waterford, the company treasurer, much younger than Old GT but looking older; Rex Foster-Stern, senior VP in charge of projects and planning, a man of Norman's own height and build who affected Dundreary whiskers and what the Children of X sneeringly termed a "non-partisan tan"; and an Afram whose features had a tantalisingly familiar cast, though he was not someone Norman had seen around the GT tower before—fiftyish, stocky, bald, Kenyatta beard, looking tired.

Norman considered a new explanation for his having been invited to this luncheon. Last time he had encountered a middle-aged stranger at such a function it had been a retired admiral GT was thinking of adding to the board for the sake of his service contacts. He had gone to a hovercraft manufacturer instead, so nothing had come of it. But if this was another of the same, Norman was going to be as insolent as he could manage without jeopardising his career. No kinky-knobbed Uncle Tom was going to be slotted into a high board chair above Norman House.

Then Old GT said, "Elihu, let me introduce Norman House, who's our VP i/c personnel and recruitment," and the world shifted to a different axis.

Elihu. Elihu Rodan Masters, career diplomat, U. S. Ambassador to Beninia. But whatinole could GT want with a snake's-tongue scrap of land like that, stuck wedgewise into Africa with neither skills nor natural resources to be exploited?

There was no time for speculation, though. He put out his hand, cutting short GT's introduction with the gesture. "No real need to introduce anyone to Mr. Masters, ma'am," he said briskly. "Someone with his kind of personal distinction is environment-forming for all of us, and I feel I know him well though I never had the chance to shake with him before."

In Old GT's face—for a woman who had built herself both a giant corporation and a huge personal fortune, she was surprisingly bad at controlling her expression—Norman could see annoyance at being interrupted struggling with satisfaction at the prettiness of the compliment.

"Drink?" she said finally, the latter winning out.

"No thanks, ma'am," Norman answered. "It's against the word of the Prophet, you know."

Beninia, hm? Something to do with opening an African market for MAMP? Over half a billion bucks tied up in that, and no place to sell the produce of the richest mineral strike since Siberia—it can't go on. But Beninia can't even afford to feed its own population from what I hear . . .

Plainly embarrassed at having forgotten or not known that one of her own VP's was a Muslim, Old GT took refuge in testiness. The House style was proof against that. Pleased with the turn the talk was taking, extremely aware of Master's eyes on him, Norman thoroughly enjoyed the ten minutes of conversation which preluded their adjournment to table. In fact he took it so much for granted that the buzz of the phone a minute or two after one o'clock was to herald the serving of the meal that he continued with the story he'd been telling—a mild anti-Afram joke suitable for mixed company, well salted with the derogatory term "brown-nose"—until GT shouted at him the second time.

"House! *House!* There's trouble with a gang of visitors being shown over Shalmaneser! On your orbit, isn't it?"

Preserving his exterior calm by reflex, Norman rose from his polychair.

If this is something they've laid on to screw me, I'll give them dreck for dinner. I'll—

"Forgive me, Mr. Masters," he said in a slightly bored tone. "I'll only be a minute or two, I'm sure."

And headed for the elevator, seething.

tracking with closeups (2)

YONDERBOY

"Talk about launch windows all it means some pudding-hole zeck knotted his strings Shalmaneser-pizzleteaser why-inole waste the time come all this way to New York better weather even without a dome fit to freeze your cod off in here better shiggies wearing less and better pot to cap the lot eight today already here it is not yet one poppa-momma and hardly a heist in a haywagon"

Inside the vault housing Shalmaneser: cool. Waiting for the launch window, which is a decorative way of saying when the GT guide is good and ready to start, this fact has already decided several of the crowd one hundred nine strong (some of whom are tourists some of whom are genuine potential recruits lured by the handouts and TV plugs of the GT Corp. some of whom have seen themselves here so often in the personae of Mr. & Mrs. Everywhere that they couldn't tell you why they bothered to make the visit in reality and some of whom are GT's own plantees primed to speak up at the right moments and give the impression of Things Happening) that they aren't going to be interested in what they're shown. Cold! In May! Under the Manhattan Fuller Dome! And clad in Nydofoam sneakers, MasQ-Lines, Forlon&Morler skirtlets and dresslets; strung about with Japind Holocams with Biltin g'teed Norisk LazeeLaser monochrome lamps, instreplay

SeeyanEar recorders; pocket-heavy with Japind Jettiguns, SeKure Stunnems, Karatands to be slipped on *as easily as your grandmother drew on her glove.*

Uneasy, watching their accidental companions on this guided tour.

Well-fed.

Shifty-eyed, slipping tranks into their chomp-chomp jaws.

Damned good-looking.

Thinking that any one of these crowding-near neighbours could be a mucker.

The New Poor of the happening world.

Stal Lucas didn't like the way the guide looked over the party when he finally deigned to show. Someone looking over that many people wouldn't notice Stal Lucas, individual: age twenty, height six, wearing SirFer S-Pad-Drills, Mogul slax and a freeflying Blood Onyx shirjack with real gold fastener tags.

He'd see, rather, a vaguely milling bunch of misfits, vagabonds and pseudos, out of which some subgroups could be separated. Like Stal and his sparewheels from California, in New York on a two-night-one-day Jettex Cursion for the lift and not getting any. The world shrunk so tight you couldn't pull it on over your shoes and still this distancing effect between the coasts . . .

On the entire one hundred and, there were four shiggies to fine-focus: one orbiting, probably by now ignorant not only of what building she was in but of what astral plane she was inhabiting; two with codders they hung to the arms of undetachablike; one like she just blew in from RUNG with African hair and bilberry skin which it wouldn't do for Stal to be seen counting down with.

The rest were so drecky it was hard to believe, going right down to one in a shapeless brown bag of a garment toting a big heavy sacking purse, hair cropped to a crewcut, nervous face shiny except where it was chapped or spotted—a Divine Daughter, probably. Nothing short of religion could persuade a normal girl to make herself look so awful.

"Whereinole the shiggies?" Stal said half under his breath. In company jobs, of course. Of all the megalopoli New York ate most and paid best. Same problem Ellayway, though there the hirer was government, drecking the draftees to the Pacific Conflict Zone, but who's richer than a government?

So kill time. So put up with this sheeting notion of being dragged around a cold vault. So wait until tomorrow antimatter when the plane will take Stal and sparewheels back to love on her and oh Bay.

"Where they keep Teresa, say?" muttered Zink Hodes, sparewheel nearest to Stal. He alluded to Shalmaneser's legendary girl-friend, source of endless dirty jokes. Stal didn't deign to reply. Zink had gone storehopping last night and was wearing a Nytype outfit. Stal was unpleased.

A couple up ahead with not one or two but count 'em three prodgies trailing along: embarrassed at the attention they attracted from envious neighbours in the crowd, explaining in loud voices that the three weren't all theirs but they were taking a cousin's appleofmyeye out for the day as well as their own two, mollifying the people around them but not so readily that they weren't the last to shush when the guide finally called the visitors towards him.

"Good afternoon and welcome to the General Technics tower. I don't have to tell anyone about GT—"

"So why you don't get the mouth sewn shut?" whispered Zink.

"—because it's environment-forming for everyone in this hemisphere and even beyond, from Moonbase Zero to the Mid-Atlantic Mining Project on the deep ocean floor. But there's one element of our manifold operations which always fascinates you, Mr. and Mrs. Everywhere, and that's what you're going to be shown."

"He should fascinate good and tight, such as weld it," Zink said.

Stal cracked fingers at the two other sparewheels a pace distant and gestured they should shut Zink in from both sides.

"Leave you behind," Stal said. "Nylover. Or get on that plane we put you out at thirty thousand, no ass-padding for you land."

"But I—"

"Fascinate," Stal said, and Zink complied, eyes round with dismay.

"Notice the granite slab you're passing under with the lettering engraved by GT's high-precision explosive forming process. They said nobody could work natural stone explosively so we went ahead and did it, thus bearing out the company motto at the head of the list."

A dropout near Stal moved lips in an audible whisper as he struggled to interpret the obliquely viewed writing.

"Underneath are listed prime examples of human short-sightedness, like you'll see it's impossible for men to breathe at over thirty miles an hour, and a bumblebee cannot possibly fly, and interplanetary spaces are God's quarantine regulations. Try telling the folk at Moonbase Zero about that!"

A few sycophantic laughs. Several places ahead of Stal the Divine Daughter crossed herself at the Name.

"Why is it so sheeting cold in here?" yelled someone up the front near the guide.

"If you were wearing GT's new Polyclime fabrics, like me, you wouldn't feel it," the guide responded promptly.

Drecky plantees, yet. How much of this crowd are GT staff members hired by government order and kept hanging about on makeweight jobs for want of anything better to do?

"But that cues me in to another prime instance of how wrong can you be? Seventy or eighty years back they were saying to build a computer to match a human brain would take a skyscraper to house it and Niagara Falls to cool it. Well, that's not up on the slab there because they were only half wrong about the cooling bit—in fact Niagara Falls wouldn't do, it's not cold enough. We use liquid helium by the ton load. But they were sheeting wrong about the sky-scraper. Spread around this balcony and I'll show you why."

Passive, the hundred and nine filed around a horseshoe gallery overlooking the chill sliced-egg volume of the vault. Below on the main floor identical-looking men and women came and went, occasionally glancing upwards with an air of incuriosity. Resentful, another score or so of the hundred and nine decided they weren't going to be interested no matter what.

Stal remained in two minds. His eyes darted across the equipment laid out below. There was eighty or ninety feet of it, at least—cables, piping, keyboards, readins and readouts, state-of-action banks, shelving loaded with gleaming metal oddments.

"It's pretty big even if it doesn't use a whole skyscraper," someone called. Another drecky plantee, doubtless. Stal refrained from objecting when Zink scuffed his feet noisily.

"Wrong," the guide said, and swivelled a spotlight head-high beside him. The beam leapfrogged over machinery and people and came to rest on an unimpressive frustrum of dull white metal.

"That," he said solemnly, "is Shalmaneser."

"That thing?" the plantee exclaimed dutifully.

"That thing. Eighteen inches high, diameter at the base eleven inches, and it's the world's largest computer thanks to GT's unique patented and registered system know as Micryogenics. In fact it's the first computer estimated to fall in the megabrain range!"

"That's a damned lie," someone up the front said.

Thrown out of orbit, the guide hesitated.

"What about K'ung-fu-tse?" the someone went on.

"What? I'm afraid I don't—" The guide gave a meaningless smile. This wasn't an interruption by a plantee, Stal concluded, and raised on tiptoe to see what was happening.

"Confucius! You'd say Confucius! At the University of Peking they've had a megabrain computer in operation since—"

"Shut his hole! Traitor! Dirty lying bleeder! Throw him over the side!"

The yells were instant, reflex, automatic. Zink pushed forward and shouted with the others. Stal's eyes narrowed as he drew a pack of Bay Golds from his pocket and set one at the corner of his mouth. Only four left in the pack, spin them out with some of this Nytype dreck, this son-of-Manhattan-green which was what you could get on this coast. He bit down hard on the automatic aerating tip.

What was so important about what the Chinese did, unless the draft got your balls? Nothing to shout about, for def.

Corporation police dragged the little red brother out before anyone had a chance to do more than punch his head, and the guide, relieved, went back into his standard flight pattern.

"See where I'm focusing the light now? That's the SCANALYZER input. We feed all the news from every major beam agency through that readin unit. Shalmaneser is the means whereby Engrelay Satelserv can tell us where we are in the happening world."

"Yes, but surely you don't operate Shalmaneser just for that," another plantee said loudly, making Stal squirm in his shirjack.

"Of course not. Shalmaneser's main task is to achieve the impossible again, a routine undertaking here at GT." The guide paused for effect. "It has been shown theoretically that with a logical system as complex as Shalmaneser consciousness, self-awareness, will eventually be generated if enough information is fed it. And we can proudly claim that there have already been signs—"

Commotion. Several people pressed forward to get a sight of what was going on, including Zink. Stal stood his ground with a sigh. Another planted distraction was the likeliest. Whyinole should these blocks believe people couldn't tell a fake event from the real?

But—

"Blasphemers! Devilspawn! Consciousness is the gift of God and you can't build a soul into a machine!"

—a GT plantee wouldn't be invited to scream *that*.

There was a block in his way: some elderly codder inches shorter and pounds lighter than Stal. He shoved him aside and put Zink between himself and recriminations while he leaned over the balcony's rail. Clambering hand over hand down one of the twenty-foot pillars supporting the gallery was the shiggy in the shapeless brown outfit, jumping the last five feet now and rounding on the alarmed staff as they hurried to intercept her.

"It's Teresa!" someone shouted, attempting wit, and was answered by a few half-hearted chuckles. But most of the people on the gallery were at once showing signs of fright. Nothing like this had ever happened during a visit by Mr. & Mrs. Everywhere. People who wanted a better view started shoving against people who wanted out, and almost immediately tempers began to rise and voices with them.

Interested, Stal considered and rejected possibilities. No Divine Daughter would carry anything that would work at a safe distance—no bolt-gun, no firearms, no grenades. So the blocks who were shrieking towards the exit or hurling themselves flat on the floor were wasting their energy. On the other hand, there was room in that sack affair slung from her shoulder to hold quite a—

A telescopic axe with a blade the full length of the folded handle. Hmmm!

Screaming: "Devil's work! Smash it and repent before you're damned to all eternity! Don't presume to infringe God's—"

She flung the bag in the face of the nearest machine-tender and charged at Shalmaneser. Some mind-present codder threw a heavy service manual at her and it struck her on the leg, making her stumble and almost fall. In that instant defenders grouped, arming themselves with handleless whips of multicore cable and shelf-struts awaiting installation which made six-foot bludgeons.

But, cowardly, they only circled and didn't close in. Stal curled his lip in contempt.

"Go it shiggy!" whooped Zink, and Stal didn't comment. He might have said the same but that it was unbefitting.

A clash of metal on metal resounded through the vault as the girl squared up to the boldest of her opponents, wielding one of the shelf-struts. He yelped and dropped it as if it had stung him and she followed through wildly with the axe.

His hand—Stal saw it clearly in mid-flight—looped free in the air like a shuttlecock and there was blood on the axe's blade.

"Hey-hey," he said under his breath, and leaned another two inches over the balcony rail.

From behind her someone else lashed out with a length of cable, leaving a red brand across her cheek and neck. She flinched but disregarded the pain and slammed the axe down on one of the readin tables. It shattered into fragments of plastic and bright little electronic parts.

"Hey-*hey*," Stal repeated with a little more enthusiasm. "Who next?"

"Let's us all go out this evening and raise a little whaledreck," Zink proposed excitedly. "I didn't see a shiggy with this much offyourass in years!"

The girl dodged another onslaught and seized something from a trolley with her left hand. She hurled it in the direction of Shalmaneser and a flurry of sparks marked the impact.

Stal considered Zink's proposal thoughtfully, inclined to agree. The blood from the axe had spattered the girl's brown clothing and the injured man was lying howling on the floor.

He sucked at the tip of his Bay Gold, feeling decision gather as the smoke automatically diluted with four parts of air swirled into his lungs. But he was still holding it there—he could hold it for ninety seconds without trouble—when the sceneshifter moved in.

context (3)

YOU HAVE TO PUSH HIM OVER

"It's no coincidence"

(COINCIDENCE   You weren't paying attention to the other half of what was going on.
                                          —*The Hipcrime Vocab* by Chad C. Mulligan)

"that we have muckers. Background: 'mucker' is an Anglicisation of 'amok'. Don't believe anyone who says it's a shifted pronunciation of 'mugger'. You can survive a mugger, but if you want to survive a mucker the best way is not to be there when it happens.

"Prior to the twentieth century the densest concentration of human beings was almost certainly found in Asian cities. (Except Rome and I'm coming to Rome later.) When too many people got in your way you armed yourself with a panga or a kris and went out to cut some throats. It didn't matter if you were educated in their use or not—the people you came up against were in their normal frame of reference and died. You were in the berserk frame of reference. Background: the berserkers developed from communities who for a large part of the year sat on their asses in Norwegian fjordal valleys with an unclimbable mountain range on each side, a lid of horrible grey cloud on top, and you couldn't get away by sea either because of the winter storms.

31

"There's a saying among the Nguni of South Africa that you didn't only have to kill a Zulu warrior—you had to push him over to make him lie down. Background: Chaka Zulu made it a policy to take his assegai-fodder from their parents in early childhood and raise them in barrack-like conditions owning no possessions bar a spear, a shield and a sheath to hide the penis, with absolutely no privacy. He made independently the same discovery the Spartans made.

"Also it was when Rome had already become the world's first million-city that the Eastern mystery religions with their concomitant self-privation and self-mutilation took hold. You fell in behind the procession honouring Cybele, you seized a knife from one of the priests, you cut your balls off and ran through the streets waving them till you came to a house with the door open when you threw them over the threshold. They gave you an outfit of women's clothing and you joined the priesthood. Reflect on the pressure that drove you to think that that was the easy way out!"

—You're an Ignorant Idiot by Chad C. Mulligan

THE DEAD HAND OF THE PAST

Norman strode out of the elevator door prepared to let go one of his rare, always calculated blasts of temper, under which any of his subordinates would cringe into guilt. He had hardly seen the interior of Shalmaneser's vault when his toe struck something on the floor.

He glanced at it.

It was a human hand severed at the wrist.

"Now my grandfather on my mother's side," Ewald House said, "was a one-arm man."

Age six, Norman looked up at his great-grandfather with circular eyes, not understanding everything that the old man told him, but aware that this was important in the same way as not wetting his bed or not getting too friendly with Curtis Smith's boy of his own age but white.

"Not sort of neat and tidy like you see nowadays," said Ewald House. "Not an ampytee. Not done surgical in a hospital. He was born a slave, see, and . . .

"He was a lef'-handed man, see. What he did, he—he raised the fist of wrath against his bawss. Hit him ears over ankles inter the crick. So the bawss called up five-six field-han's chain him to a stump they had in the forty-acre field and just natcherly took a saw and . . .

"And sawed it. 'Bout here." He touched his own scrawny pipe-stem of an arm three inches below the elbow.

"Nothing he coulda done about it. He was born a slave."

This time, very still, very calm, Norman *looked* at the interior of the vault. He saw the hand's owner writhing and moaning on the floor, clutching his wrist and trying to find pressure points on the leaking bloodvessels through a fog of intolerable agony. He saw the smashed readin table whose fragments were crunching under the feet of the panicky, mind-absent staff. He saw the light in the eyes of the pallid white girl, breathing orgasmically deep, who was standing off her attackers with her bloody blade.

Also he saw, up there on the balcony, more than a hundred idiots.

He disregarded what was happening in the middle of the floor and walked over to a panel set into the wall of the vault. Two quick twists of the fastenings and it fell away, revealing a network of heavy insulated pipes as tangled as the tails of a king rat.

He hauled on a quadrant valve; struck a union a sharp blow with the side of his hand, too quick for the chill of it to penetrate his skin; and put one of the hoses under his arm so he could lean on it and drag it after him. There would be enough free length for his purposes.

He stared at the girl as he approached her.

Divine Daughter. Probably called Dorcas or Tabitha or Martha. Thinking of killing. Thinking of smashing. A typical Christian reaction.

You murdered your Prophet. Ours died old and full of honour. You would kill yours again, and cheerfully. If ours came back I could speak to him like a friend.

Six feet from her, the pipe scritching across the floor like the scales of a monstrous snake, he stopped. Uncertain about this man with the dark skin and the cold, dead stare, she hesitated, poising the axe to chop at him, then having second thoughts and thinking: this must be a distraction, a trap.

She glanced wildly about her, expecting to find someone preparing to take her from the rear. But the staff had recognised what Norman had brought with him, and were sidling away.

"Nothing he coulda done about it . . ."

Convulsively he opened the valve on the end of the pipe and held it to a count of three.

There was a hiss, and snow fell, and something laid white ice on the axe, and the hand holding it, and the arm above the hand. There was an endless instant of nothing happening.

And then the weight of the axe broke the girl's hand off her arm.

"Liquid helium," Norman said briefly for the benefit of the watchers, and let the pipe fall clang to the floor. "Dip your finger in it, it snaps off like a dry stick. Don't try it is my advice. And don't believe what you hear about Teresa, either."

He didn't look at the girl, who had keeled over—fainting or possibly dead from the shock—but only at the frosted form of the hand still gripping the axe's haft. There should have been some sort of response, if no more than pride in his own quick thinking. There was nothing. His mind, his heart, seemed as frozen as that meaningless object on the floor.

He turned on his heel towards the elevator again, aware of a terrible disappointment.

Zink moved closer to Stal.

"Hey-hey!" he said. "Made it worth coming, huh? Let's go raise a bushel of whaledreck tonight, clear from the floor of the ocean. That put me square on the proper orbit!"

"No," Stal said, eyes fixed on the door through which the brown-nose had disappeared. "Not in this town. I don't like the kind of enforcement they keep here."

the happening world (2)

THE SOFT CELL

"It has been more than a decade since the contents of the New York Public Library were actually in New York. Their exact location is now classified, but this has not reduced—rather, it has enhanced—user-access."

The most versatile copying system ever developed is East-man Kodak's Wholographik. Turn the print over, cut along the lines with ordinary scissors, distribute the pieces—and each of up to 24 sections will return up to 98% of the base information!

Donald Hogan sat among 1235 other people any or all of whom might be consulting the same book or magazine as he was at any given instant.

It was highly improbable, though, that anyone else would consult two consecutive items the same as his choice. His search pattern had been scrambled by Shalmaneser, and as an added precaution the transcript of it he carried with him had been copied out in Yatakangi—a difficult and unpopular language resembling Japanese in that it combined a welter of Chinese ideograms with two complete syllabaries, not, however, home-grown like the Japanese katakana but a bastard offshoot of Arabic script imported to the islands of South-East Asia in the late middle ages by Muslim proselytisers.

SUMMARY The authors describe a number of cases of debatable genealogy encountered by the New Jersey State Eugenic Processing Board. A successful method of detecting the genes responsible for recessive dichromatism is

CELL STRUCTURE ABSTRACTS
REVIEW OF BIOCHEMICAL ABSTRACT JOURNALS
PROCEEDINGS OF THE INSTITUTE FOR CEREBROCHEMICAL STUDIES

If you're looking for a tailored bacterium capable of turning those low-grade slurries into a profitable source of sulphur, ask Minnesota Mining for a sample of their strain UQ-141. Your first million organisms: $1000 postage paid.

SUMMARY Computer testing of a tentative formula for the egg of *Nannus troglodytes*. The evaluation indicates

The most useful one-volume reference work available to the contemporary student of addiction is Friberg and Mahler's DEFORMATION OF SUBJECTIVE PERCEPTS. It covers: opium and derivatives; coca and derivatives; peyote and derivatives; cannabis and derivatives; pituri, caapi, etc.; synthetics from lysergic acid to Yaginol ® and Skulbustium ®. Includes a specially written appendix on Triptine ®. One spool micro: $75 to the medical profession only.

SOMATIC ECOLOGY JOURNAL
SPORTS AND MUTATION REPORT
REPTILIAN HEREDITY REVIEW

SUMMARY A case is presented for the interpretation of cross-economic relationships in a Bolivian mountain village as a manifestation of Mergendahler's Syndrome with the energising factors deweighted by religious, nutritional and

Isolated genetic material is now available from GT for Rana palustris as well as Rattus norvegicus albus. Cross-sexual contamination g'teed held to less than 0.01%.

SUMMARY Occasionally when orbiting Bennie Noakes punches an encyclopedia connection on his phone and marvels at what it tells him, saying, "Christ what an imagination

COMMUNICATIONS SYSTEMS
TECTOGENETICS DIGEST
ABSTRACTS OF SUMMARIES OF BIOCHEMICAL PAPERS

SUMMARY Susceptibility to the carcinogenic effect of commercial-grade carbon tetrachloride is shown to be correlable with the known sex-linked heritable ability to detect by taste, in solutions of less than 1 ppm, the presence of

Nothing is more frustrating in the modern world than to be entitled to bear children and yet lack the capacity. We specialise in the reimplantation of externally fertilised ova.

BULLETIN OF THE SOCIETY FOR ABSOLUTE ORGASM
GRAUNCH::prosoversepix
ANT, BEE AND TERMITE SOCIOLOGY JOURNAL

SUMMARY   When ugly, frustrated dropout HANK OGMAN raped his mother and made her pregnant with what was almost certain to be a phocomelic foetus owing to her Yaginol addiction, things looked pretty black for responsible blockfather WALT ADLESHINE. However, thanks to nick-of-time intervention by gorgeous passion-panted surgeon IDA CAPELMONT, the tragedy was averted. "How can I ever repay you?" Walt demanded, and she named a price that

Donald Hogan, yawning, vacated his chair. It never took him more than three hours to get through the day's assigned schedule. He pocketed the notebook in which he kept the search pattern and wandered towards the elevators.

context (4)

Developed	Developing	Underdeveloped
U.S.A., Common Europe, U.S.S.R., Australia (e.g.)	China, Yatakang, Egypt, Repub. Union of Nigeria w. Ghana (e.g.)	Ceylon, Beninia, Afghanistan, Mozambique (e.g.)
Govt. by public apathy	Govt. by "revolutionary parties"	"Broken-backed" govt.
Currency subject to frequent revaluation through inflation	Artificially supported by official action	Subject to arbitrary fluctuations
Employment by private contract	Controlled by state	A matter of luck
News and entertainment media support govt. owing to patronage and political inertia	Directly controlled by govt. agencies, monolithic viewpoint	Run on amateur basis and subject to lapses of taste and reliability
Diet varied but factory- or battery-produced, requiring expensive supplements	Less varied but distributed by efficient rationing system ensuring balanced quality	Below subsistence level, rationing inefficiently administered
Medicare: some free (maternity, child welfare, old age), rest paid for but of high standard	All medicare free irrespective of nature but of generally lower quality	All paid for but of minimal standard; some states employ witch-doctors

Developed	Developing	Underdeveloped
Military service by draft; selective, much evasion; loyalty of inductees reinforced by psychol. techniques	Universal draft, negligible evasion, loyalty enforced by social climate	Army and navy escape routes for poverty victims, subject to revolutionary outbursts and largely indep. of govt.
Apts universal in cities, houses in low-density areas, street-sleeping permissive though discouraged	Apts universal, houses for those in govt. favour, street-sleeping punishable	Houses, shacks, hovels, no relevant legislation, much overcrowding
Expressplane, acceleratube, rapitrans, copter, fuel-cell taxi, flywheel bus, etc.	Expressplane, fly-wheel bus, fuel-cell taxi, pedal-cab, bicycle, etc.	Bus, truck, bicycle, draft animals, etc.
Phones efficient with viewscreens	Efficient in towns but not outside, some circuits sound only	Unreliable
Eugenic legislation agst. idiocy, phenyl-ketonuria, haemophilia, diabetes, dichromatism, etc.; enforcement strict	Idiocy, phenylketo-nuria, haemophilia, etc.; enforcement limited by lack of resources	None enforced or enforceable
Clothes subject to fashion, many disposables for cheapness	Clothes state-chosen and made, disposables regarded as luxury	Robes to rags; 1 garment often has several wearers
Homosexuality tolerated, ambivalence taken for granted	Extreme intolerance; bivving punishable and socially discouraged	Attitudes dictated by tradition and custom
Tobacco banned owing to carcinogenic effects	Tolerated subj. to exclusion of carcinogens	Smoked
Marijuana legal, becoming socialised	Tolerated	Traditionally socialised
Liquor socialised irresp. of legality	Legal in many countries but discouraged	Made at home
Psychedelics illegal, tolerated	Illegal, fierce enforcement	Too expensive

Developed	Developing	Underdeveloped
Resources running low	Vigorously exploited	Sold abroad or incompetently handled
Population human	Population human	Population human

HUMAN BEING   You're one. At least, if you aren't, you know you're a Martian or a trained dolphin or Shalmaneser.
(If you want me to tell you more than that, you're out of luck. There's nothing more *anybody* can tell you.
    —*The Hipcrime Vocab* by Chad C. Mulligan)

tracking with closeups (3)

NO YOU DON'T!

"So what do we do?" Sheena Potter demanded for the umpty-fourth time. "And don't take another trank—it's all I can do to get through to you as it is!"

"You're trying to give me ulcers," said her husband Frank.

"You sheeting liar."

"Then you're doing it inadvertently, and that means you're not fit to be allowed loose on the street, let alone breed your species." Frank spoke from the elevated, almost Olympian level of dispassion due to the five tranks he'd taken already this anti-matter.

"You think I want to breed? That's a different song you're singing from the usual, isn't it? Let's have you carry the little bastard—they can do that now, pump you full of female hormones and implant in the visceral cavity."

"You've been watching *Viewers' Digest*. No, that's wrong. You must have taken it off SCANALYZER. That's even more sensational."

"Dreck! It was Felicia who told me when I was last down at the night-school—"

"Lot of good your classes are doing you! You're still as stiff as Teresa! When do they progress you to elementary Kama Sutra?"

42

"If you were more than half a man you'd have taught me yourself—"

"The lack of response is in the patient not the agent, which is why I—"

"Now you're quoting ad copy, not even a news programme but a plug put out by some dribbling—"

"I should have had more sense than to marry a block who'd only had a few clumsy highschool—"

"I should have had more sense than to marry a man with colourblindness in the family—"

There was a pause. They looked around at the apartment. On the wall between the windows there was a pale patch, the same colour as the paint had been originally when they moved in. The picture which had occupied the pale area was in the red plastic crate near the door. Next to the red plastic crate were five green ones (may be tubed with padding); next to them were a dozen black ones (may be tubed without padding); and there were also two white ones which were a moderately convenient height for sitting on—the purpose Frank and Sheena were putting them to.

There was nothing in the drinks cabinet. Except a little dust and some dried spilt wine.

There was nothing in the icebox except a thin frosting on the deepfreeze section which would automatically be melted off the next time the comptroller cycled to "defrost."

There were no clothes in the bedroom closet. The disposall was grinding quietly to itself, half-choking on a batch of disposable paper garments and the twenty-odd pounds of unused perishables from the freeze.

The auto-seals had clicked across the power sockets; no child had ever lived here, but it was against the law for any socket not to be auto-sealed when the appliance connected to it was removed.

There was a file of documents lying on the floor at Frank's feet. It included a two-person tourist-class ticket for Puerto Rico; two ID cards of which one was stamped HEREDI-CHRO and the other SUSTOHEREDICHRO; twenty thousand dollars' worth of travellers' cheques; and a report from the New York State Eugenic Processing Board which began

"Dear Mr. Potter, I regret to have to inform you that inception of pregnancy by your wife with or without you as the father is punishable under Para. 12, Section V, of the New York State Parenthood Code as at present enforced . . ."

"How did I know the J-but-O's were going to ban me? The baby-farming lobby must be worth trillions of dollars and that amount of money talks!"

He was a vaguely good-looking man, rather lean, rather dark, his air and bearing older than one would expect from his chronological age of thirty.

"Well, I've always said I'd be willing to adopt! We could get on an adoption list and have an unwanted child in less than five years for sure!"

She was an exceptionally lovely natural blonde, plumper than her husband, dieted to the currently fashionable dimensions, and aged twenty-three.

"What's the point of going?" she added.

"Well, we can't stay here! We've sold the apt and spent some of the money!"

"Can't we go somewhere else?"

"Of course we can't go somewhere else! You heard about the people they shot last week trying to sneak into Louisiana—and how far would twenty thousand bucks go in Nevada?"

"We could go there and get pregnant and come home—"

"To what? We've *sold the apartment,* don't you understand? And if we're here past six poppa-momma they can *jail* us!" He slapped his thigh with his open palm. "No, we've got to make the best of it. We'll have to go to Puerto Rico and save up enough to make it over to Nevada, or maybe bribe someone to give us a passport for Peru, or Chile, or—"

There was a clang from the front door.

He looked at her, not moving. At last he said, "Sheena, I love you."

She nodded, and eventually managed a smile. "I love you desperately," she said. "I don't want somebody else's second-hand child. Even if it didn't have any legs, I'd love it because it was yours."

"And I'd love it because it was yours."

Another clang. He rose to his feet. On the way past her, to let the moving gang in, he kissed her lightly on the forehead.

continuity (3)

AFTER ONE DECADE

Emerging from the library, Donald Hogan looked first north, then south, along Fifth Avenue, debating which of half a dozen nearby restaurants he should go to for lunch. The decision seemed unreachable for a moment. He had been holding down his present job for ten years, almost; sooner or later he was bound to go stale.

Perhaps one shouldn't have one's greatest ambition realised in full at the age of twenty-four . . . ?"

He had, very probably, another fifty years to go; he had a calculable chance of a decade beyond that. And when he accepted the offer they'd made him he hadn't raised the matter of retirement, or even resignation.

Oh, they'd have to let him retire eventually. But he had no idea whether he'd be permitted to resign.

Lately, several of his acquaintances—he made a policy of not having friends—had noticed that he was looking older than his age and had developed a tendency to lapse into brown studies. They had wondered what on earth could be the matter with him. But if someone had been in a position to say, "Donald's wondering if he can quit his job," even the most intimate of all those acquaintances, the man with whom he shared an apartment and an endless string of shiggies, would have looked blank.

"Job? What job? Donald doesn't work. He's a self-employed dilettante!"

Approximately five people, and a Washington computer, knew otherwise.

"Sit down, Donald," the Dean said, waving an elegant hand. Donald complied, his attention on the stranger who was also present: a woman of early middle age possessed of delicate bone-structure, good taste in clothes and a warm smile.

He was a trifle nervous. In the last issue of the university's student journal he had published some remarks which he later regretted making public, though if pressed honesty would compel him to admit that he had meant them and still did mean them.

"This is Dr. Jean Foden," the Dean said. "From Washington."

The alarming possibility of having his post-graduate grant discontinued on the grounds that he was an ungrateful subversive loomed up in Donald's mind. He gave the visitor a chilly and rather insincere nod.

"Well, I'll leave you to get on with it, then," the Dean said, rising. That confused Donald even more. He would have expected the old bastard to want to sit in on the discussion and giggle silently—here's one more intransigent pupil up for the axe. His mind was therefore barren of possible reasons for summoning him when Dr. Foden produced and displayed the student journal in question.

"I was very struck by the article of yours in here," she said briskly. "You feel there's something wrong with our teaching methods, don't you, Don? Mind if I call you Don?"

"Not if you don't mind my calling you Jean," Donald said in a sullen tone.

Musing, she looked him over. Four-fifths of the contemporary population of North America counted as handsome or beautiful; balanced diet and adequate inexpensive medical care had finally seen to that. And now that the first eugenic legislation was beginning to bite, the proportion was liable to increase. Nonetheless, there was something out of the ordinary about Donald Hogan. His women usually said it was "character". Once an English exchange student had told him it was "bloody-mindedness", and he had accepted the term as a compliment.

He had brown hair and beard, he was a little below average height, he was well-muscled, he wore the typical clothes of a turn-of-the-century student. Externally, then, he conformed. But somewhere underneath . . .

Dr. Foden said, "I'd like to hear your views."

"They're on the page for you to read."

"Rephrase them for me. Seeing something in print often helps one to make a fresh assessment."

Donald hesitated. "I haven't changed my mind, if that's what you're getting at," he said at length. The stench and crackle of burning boats was vivid to him.

"I'm not asking for that. I'm asking for maximum concision instead of this—this rather rambling complaint."

"All right. My education has turned me, and practically everyone else I know, into an efficient examination-passing machine. I wouldn't know how to be original outside the limited field of my own speciality, and the only reason I can make that an exception is that apparently most of my predecessors have been even more blinkered than I am. I know a thousand per cent more about evolution than Darwin did, that's taken for granted. But where between now and the day I die is there room for me to do something that's *mine* and not a gloss on someone else's work? Sure, when I get my doctorate the spiel that comes with it will include something about presenting a quote original unquote thesis, but what it'll mean is the words are in a different order from last time!"

"You have a fairly high opinion of your own ability," Dr. Foden commented.

"You mean I sound conceited? I guess I probably do. But what I'm trying to say is I don't want to take credit for being massively ignorant. You see——"

"What are you going to do for a career?"

Diverted from his orbit, Donald binked. "Well, something which uses up a minimum of my time, I imagine. So I can use the rest to mortar up the gaps in my education."

"Ah-hah. Interested in a salary of fifty thousand per to do—essentially—nothing *but* complete your education?"

There was one talent Donald Hogan did possess which the majority of people didn't: the gift of making right guesses. Some mechanism at the back of his mind seemed ceaselessly to be shifting around factors from the surrounding world, hunting for patterns in them, and when such a pattern arose a silent bell would ring inside his skull.

Factors: Washington, the absence of the Dean, the offer of a salary competitive with what he could hope to earn in industry, but for studying, not for working ... There were people, extremely top people, whom specialists tended to refer to disparagingly as dilettanti but who dignified themselves with the title "synthesist", and who spent their entire working lives doing nothing but making cross-references from one enclosed corner of research to another.

It seemed like too much to hope for, coming on top of his expectation, moments back, that his grant was to be discontinued. He had to put his hands together to stop them trembling.

"You're talking about synthesis, aren't you?"

"Yes, I'm from the Dilettante Dept—or more officially, from the Office of Research Co-ordination. But I doubt if you have in mind exactly what I'm going to propose. I've seen the graphs of your scholastic career, and I get the impression that you could make yourself into a synthesist if you wanted to badly enough, with or without a doctorate." Dr. Foden leaned back in her chair.

"So the fact that you're still here—griping, but putting up with things—makes me suspect you *don't* want to badly enough. It'll take a good fat bribe to make you opt for it. I think nonetheless you may be honest enough to stay bribed. Tell me, given the chance, what would you do to round out your education?"

Donald stammered over his answer, turning crimson at his own inability to utter crisp, decisive plans. "Well—uh—I guess ... History, particularly recent history; nobody's taught me about anything nearer to home than World War II without loading it full of biased dreck. All the fields which touch on my own, like crystallography and ecology. Not omitting human ecology. And to document that I'd like to delve into the written record of our species, which is now about eight thousand years deep. I ought to learn at least one non-Indo-European language. Then——"

"Stop. You've defined an area of knowledge greater than an individual can cover in a lifetime."

"Not *true!*" Donald was gathering confidence by the moment. "Of course you can't if you've been taught the way I have, on the basis of memorising facts, but what one ought to learn is how to extract *patterns!* You don't bother to memorise the literature—you learn to read and keep a shelf of books. You don't memorise log and sine tables; you buy a slide-rule or learn to punch a public computer!" A helpless gesture. "You don't have to know everything. You simply need to know where to find it when necessary."

Dr. Foden was nodding. "You seem to have the right basic attitude," she acknowledged. "However, I must put on my Mephistopheles hat at this point and explain the conditions that attach to the offer I'm making. First, you'd be required to read and write fluent Yatakangi."

Donald blanched slightly. A friend of his had once started on that language and switched to Mandarin Chinese as an easier alternative. However . . .

He shrugged. "I'd be willing to shoot for that," he said.

"And the rest of it I can't tell you until you've been to Washington with me."

Where a man called Colonel—Donald was not told if he had a name of his own—said, "Raise your right hand and repeat after me: 'I Donald Orville Hogan . . . do solemnly declare and attest . . .'"

Donald sighed. Back then, it had seemed like the fulfilment of his wildest dreams. Five mornings a week doing nothing but read, under no compulsion to produce any kind of results—merely requested to mention by mail any association or connection he spotted which he had reason to believe might prove helpful to somebody: advise an astronomer that a market research organisation had a new statistical sampling technique, for instance, or suggest that an entomologist be informed about a new air-pollution problem. It sounded like paradise, especially since his employers not only did not care what he did with the rest of his time but suggested he make his experience as varied as possible to keep himself alert.

And in under ten years—he had to face the truth—he was getting bored. He could almost wish that they'd pull the second string attached to his work, the one which had caused him so much heart-searching.

Lieutenant Donald Orville Hogan, you are hereby activated and ordered to report immediately repeat IMMEDIATELY to—

"Oh, no!"

"Something wrong with you, blockbottom?" a harsh voice rasped inches from his ear. A sharp elbow jostled him and a scowling face stared into his. Confused, he discovered that without realising he must have made his decision about what restaurant to patronise today, and wandered down into the milling crowd that streamed the whole length of Fifth Avenue.

"What? Oh—no, I'm all right."

"Then stop acting like you're off your gyros! Look where you're going!"

The angry man he'd collided with pushed past. Mechanically, Donald put one foot in front of the other, still rather dazed. After a few moments, he concluded that the advice was worth taking. Perhaps part of his trouble was that he'd fallen into such an automatic routine he had lost the alertness and interest in the world around which had attracted Dr. Foden to him ten years back, in which case he was unlikely to get the option of resigning his job. More probable was what he'd half-feared when with a flourish of trumpets and a ruffle of drums they declassified Shalmaneser, and he'd foreseen automation making even synthesists obsolete.

And if he was going to give up his job, he wanted it to be on his own terms, not because he'd been fired for incompetence.

With a slight shudder he surveyed the avenue. Buildings tall as canyon walls closed it in, channelling the human traffic under the diffusely bright cover of the Fuller Dome. Of course, that didn't protect the whole of Greater New York, only Manhattan, which it had re-endowed with its former

attraction and enabled to win back more inhabitants than it
had lost in the late-twentieth-century rush to the suburbs.
Doming the entire city would have been out of the question
on grounds of cost alone, though engineering studies had
shown the feasibility of the project.

New York with its thirteen million people, however, was
falling further and further back from the status it had once
enjoyed as the world's largest city. It could not be compared
with the monstrous conurbations stretching from Frisco to
Ellay or from Tokyo to Osaka, let alone the true giants
among modern megalopoli, Delhi and Calcutta with fifty
million starving inhabitants apiece: not cities in the old sense
of grouped buildings occupied by families, but swarming
antheaps collapsing into ruin beneath the sledgehammer
blows of riot, armed robbery and pure directionless vandalism.

Nonetheless, though it had shrunk to medium size by
contemporary standards, this was still as large a city as
Donald felt he could stand, and it still possessed a certain
magnetism. The biggest employer of them all, State, domi-
nated the West Coast; here were the next biggest, the super-
corporations that were countries within a country. Ahead
loomed the colossal ziggurat of the General Technics tower
bridging three complete blocks, and it filled him with a sense
of gloom. If he did quit—if it were possible for him to quit
when they had pumped going on three-quarters of a million
dollars of public money into him—his only future would lie
in just such a mausoleum as that.

And look what it's done to Norman House!

Across the hugely enlarged sidewalks the people thronged
like insects, milling at the access points to underpasses and
the subway. On the central, official-business-only emergency
lane prowl cars cruised or paused, occasionally pulling over
to make way for ambulances and fire trucks. Either side of
the centre, the huge humming buses without engines—
drawing their power from flywheels spun up to maximum
revolutions when they turned around at the end-points of
their journey—hauled their loads of up to two hundred
passengers, sliding at two-block intervals into pickup bays
and allowing the electric cabs to overtake. No internal com-

bustion engine had been legal in the city since they put up the dome; the disposal of CO_2 and anthropotoxins from the people themselves was as much as the ventilation system could handle, and on warm days their exuded moisture sometimes overloaded the conditioners, precipitating a kind of drizzle underneath the dome.

How do we stand it?

He had chosen to live in New York because he had been born here, and because it headed the short list of suitable residences they gave him to choose from—cities possessing the kind of library facilities needed in his job. But this was the first time he had looked at it, really looked with both eyes and full attention, in perhaps as long as seven years, and everywhere he turned he found that another straw had been piled on the camelback of the city. He had noticed the street-sleepers when he came back from college, but he hadn't noticed that there were hundreds of them now, pushing their belongings on little makeshift trolleys and being moved on, moved on by the police. He hadn't noticed the way people, when they were jostled, sometimes spun around and shot their hands to bulging pockets before they realized it wasn't a mucker on their heels. And speaking of muckers: he hadn't really connected with the world he knew when the news reports described one who'd taken out seven victims in Times Square on a busy Saturday night . . .

Panic clawed at him, the same kind of panic he'd experienced on the only occasion when he ventured to try Skulbustium, the sense that there was no such person as Donald Hogan but only one among millions of manikins, all of whom were versions of a Self without beginning or end. Then, he had screamed, and the man who had given him the drug advised against a repetition, saying he *was* his persona and without it would dissolve.

In other words: there was nothing inside.

Just ahead of him, two girls paused to examine a display in the window of a store. They were both in the height of fashion, one wearing a radio-dresslet whose surface pattern formed a printed circuit so that by shifting her buckled belt to right or left she could have her choice of broadcasts fed into the earpiece nestling under her purple hair, the other in a skintight fabric as harshly metallic as the case of a scientific instrument. Both had chromed nails, like the power terminals of a machine.

The display that had caught their attention was of genetically moulded pets. Processes that already worked well with viruses and bacteria had been applied to their germ-plasm, but on this more complex level the side-effects were excessively random; each pet on show probably stood proxy for five hundred that never left the lab. Even so, the solemn, over-sized bushbaby in the window looked miserably unhappy for all the splendour of its purple pelt, and the litter of bright-red Chihuahua pups below staggered continually as though on the verge of epilepsy.

All that seemed to concern the girls, however, was that the bushbaby's colour almost exactly matched the hair of the one in the radio-dresslet.

First you use machines, then you wear machines, and then . . .

Shaking all over, Donald changed his mind about a restaurant and turned blindly into a bar to drink instead of eat his lunch.

In the afternoon he called on an out-of-work poetess he knew. She was sympathetic, asked no questions, and allowed him to sleep off his drunk in her bed. The world looked a little better when he woke.

But he wished desperately that there could be someone— not this girl necessarily, not even a girl at all, just *a person*— to whom he could explain why it was he had been moaning in his sleep.

DOMESTICA

Straight well-pos'ned Afram seeks roomie view long Ise luxy 5-rm apt Box NZL4

"*Yes* I do have three rooms but *no* you can't even if you have been evicted. Whatinole would I do with that gang of sheeting lizzies you tail behind you? I don't care if you are equipoised! I don't share with anyone who's not flying my strictly straight-type orbit!"

In Delhi, Calcutta, Tokyo, New York, London, Berlin, Los Angeles; in Paris, Rome, Milan, Cairo, Chicago . . . they can't jail you any longer for sleeping rough, so it's no use hoping.

There just isn't that much room in the jails.

Afram girl seeks lodg'g. Versatile. Box NRT5

LUXY APTS IDEAL FAMILIES ONLY $100,000 MINIMUM 3 RMS ALL DIVISIBLE!

Acceleratube Commuterservice makes it possible for YOU to work in Los Angeles, reside in the fresh-air expand-your-chest atmosphere of Arizona, transit time ninety minutes!

"This is Laura. Natural blonde, of course—honey, slip 'em down and demonstrate. Ah—the sharing bit *is* understood, presumably?"

"I hope so."

"So do I."

Laura giggled.

Jettex is practical as well as luxy—ask the folk from the Mountain States who can hold down city-centre jobs thanks to our five-minutely crush-hour service!

"Just a formality, if you don't mind. Young lady, hold out your hand ... Thanks. It'll take five minutes. Hang on ... Sorry, we can only give you a transient's pass for this state. Congratulations, though—hope it's a baby."

WHEN THE PRESSURE GETS TO THE BLOWOFF POINT YOU'LL BE GRATEFUL FOR GT'S KEYS TO EASIER LIVING. TRANKS, PROPHYLACTICS, ARE ONLY THE START OF THE STORY. OUR AIDS TO NORMAL FEMALE BIOLOGICAL FUNCTIONING ARE APPROVED BY ALL STATE CODES.

"Prophet's beard, Donald, if I'd known you had a thing about dark meat I could have had my pick of—"

"Then why don't you try a brunette some time, say an Italian type? Someone who's fed nothing but stark white sliced-and-wrapped is apt to want some wholemeal granary now and then!"

But in any household problems like this are bound to arise.

Olive Almeiro Agency offers you the chance of a lifetime. We have a wider range of good-heredity adoptables than any other agency in our field. Offer not good in following states: New York, Illinois, California ...

BE IT ENACTED THAT: carriage of the genes listed in Appendix A below shall *ipso facto* be grounds for abortion upon presentation of the mother at any Eugenics Processing Board in the following ...

"Who are you going to get in to replace Lucille?"

"Don't know. Haven't thought about it yet."

POPULATION STRETCHING TO LIMIT. Reports to-day from official sources hint that immigrants to this state with residents' qualifications more recent than 30th March last will be given choice of sterilisation or removal.

We've celebrated our twenty-first. Have you? Liberal association seeks broadminded couples, triples, to enlarge the scope of our activities. We have FOURTEEN children in the group already!

"Prophet's beard, Donald . . . !"

"I'm sorry, I've said I'm sorry! But can I help getting bored with your line of shiggies? Laura was Scandahoovian, Bridget was Scandahoovian, Hortense was and Rita was and Moppet was and Corinne was. I think you're in a rut, to be frank."

Reliable couple seek babyminding opportunities, one or several days p.w. (Certificates avlble. Webtoe only drawback) Box NPP2

BE IT ENACTED THAT: carriage of the genes listed in Appendix B below shall *ipso facto* be grounds for sterilisation of any male child achieving the age of puberty after . . .

"Ah, go to hell!"

"That's a remarkably Christian attitude, Donald. Both meaningless and barbaric."

"Stop trying to play on my WASP guilt feelings. Sometimes I wonder how you'd make out in a genuinely nonracial society."

"There aren't any. Give you another generation, you'll add the genes for dark skin-pigment to the list of—"

Leo Branksome! Come home! Being sterilised isn't going to make us love you any the less! You're our boy, our only son,

*and running away was a stupid thing to do! And you're only
fourteen, remember! Your adoring but miserable parents.*

"Thirty-four? And you have a clean genotype? My God, I
ought to push this glass in your face! All we've got is a
suspicion, not even proof but a suspicion, that Harold's mother had sickle-cell anaemia and I'd give my right arm for
children and you smug bastard can stand there and—"

tracking with closeups (4)

MASKER AID

Conscious that she was a walking advertisement for her own processes, conscious that not even the brilliant lights of the video technicians would reveal a flaw in her cosmetic garb, conscious with particular pleasure of the fact that the woman they had sent to interview her was conspicuously less well turned-out, Guinevere Steel cooed at the microphone.

"Why, the success of my Beautiques is due to two factors: the ability of my customers to recognise who does and who doesn't keep that quantum-jump ahead of transient fashions, and equally their ability to judge what does and what does not offer real value for money!"

She preened.

Indeterminably aged, she wore a bluzette of shimmering yellow because her complexion was in the Goyaesque-tan range; it moulded her bosom into almost perfect cycloidal curves, peaked on either side with a pair of her own remote-controlled Nipicaps—activated at the moment because they would show to excellent advantage on a video screen. They were always at the wearer's disposal; should she be interested in the man—or woman—she was talking to, she could dilate them without doing more than press her arm to her side; conversely she could deflate them, and there were few more ego-undermining things a woman could do to a block than let it be seen how her erogenous tissue lost intesrest.

She wore a skirtlet that was no more than an overgrown belt because she had extremely graceful legs. They tapered to jewelled slippers because she had high, springy arches, but not to bare feet because those arches had been reconstructed and on the left foot one of the scars still showed.

She had her hair in four parallel rolls, dyed silver; her finger- and toe-nails were chromed more brilliantly than mirrors and flashed back the light of the lamps at the camera's lens.

About seventy per cent of her skin was revealed, but none of it was bare except perhaps among the roots of her hair. Apart from the pearly masking on her face, she wore whole-body matting, a personal blend of her own Beautique's skin tinter, and altogether nearly thirty other products which left a detectable deposit on the epidermis. As a final touch her surface veins had been delicately traced in blue.

"Why, I think it's contemporary in the way it ought to be," she told the microphone. "We don't live in the world of our ancestors, where dirt, and disease, and—and what one might call general randomness dictated how we lived. No, we have taken control of our entire environment, and what we choose by way of fashion and cosmetics matches that achievement."

"But the current trend towards a more—more natural look," the interviewer ventured.

"What counts is how the person looking at you is affected," Guinevere said complacently. "It affects you, too, of course—to be totally confident, as we make our clients, of the impression you're going to create is the only thing that really matters."

"Thank you, Miss Steel," the interviewer murmured.

That much out of the way, Guinevere marched back into her private office. With the door safely shut, she could drop into her chair and let the bitterness leak out into the set of her mouth, the narrowness of her eyes.

Lighting a Bay Gold, she stared at her reflection.

Totally confident? In this business, where tomorrow the man in the case or the girl-friend, whichever, might decide to get to closer quarters? The more elaborate and fragile and lovely the cosmetic job, the greater the effect—and the worse the letdown when it had been kissed, and caressed, and wrestled with. There were seventeen Beautiques now, one for every year she had been in the business, each licensed after careful appraisal to a manager who had to have worked for three months directly under Guinevere herself, who was trained to exacting standards and had contracted to pay a fat commission for the privilege of using the name. Every rational precaution had been taken, but who should know better than a cosmetician that human beings are less than rational creatures?

Got to distract myself. Got to have some new ideas.

She thought for a while.

Eventually she scribbled a list and reached for the switch of the phone, after another quick glance at herself to make sure the image on the screen would be fitting.

A forfeits party. Always a good way to make other people look small. And at the head of the list that haughty brown-nose Norman House—which meant having his dismal roomie along. Plus everyone else who had failed to fall down and worship lately.

Forfeits for what? Twentieth century, how about that? Ancient Rome or somewhere a bit more exciting would be better, but that was the sort of area where you'd expect people like that drecky Donald Hogan to know more than the organisers about what was and what wasn't correct for the period. Hire a professional arbitrator, some nose-in-book student maybe specialising? No. Tried that once, didn't work. Glummy boy was shocked by some of the forfeits and caved in—correction, avoiding forfeit: *chickened* in—not that, either. Out? Up? Check a dictionary of twentieth-century usage.

And if let's say Mel Ladbroke could be persuaded to come, and bring some of that fascinating new stuff they're experimenting with at the hospital . . .

With a sort of savage delight she stabbed at the buttons of the phone.

You say one word, make one gesture, even, that's not in the context and I'm going to make you piss your pants, you horrible black bastard.

continuity (4)

ROOMIE NATION

When Donald reached home at six poppa-momma, Norman was there already, sitting in his favourite Hille chair, feet up on a hassock, scanning his day's mail. To his roomie's hello he returned merely a distracted nod.

By this time Donald was sufficiently recovered from the fit of depression he had experienced at lunchtime to note the various clues to Norman's state of mind which the visible evidence afforded. Being a Muslim, Norman refused to touch alcohol, but marijuana was traditionally socialised in the Muslim countries of Africa and he permitted himself to unwind the day's accumulated tension with a few reefers. Despite the excessive cost—every state which had legalised pot discriminated against that grown outside its own boundaries with a fierce tariff—he smoked the brand appropriate to a junior vice-president of GT: the acknowledged field-leader, Bay Gold. One rested in an ashtray at his side, but its smoke was winding up unheeded.

Furthermore, on the floor at his feet, as though tossed aside in a moment of impatience, there lay a Wholographik picture, an endless flowing series of echoingly rhythmical light and dark lines, along the edge of which was printed the colophon of the Genealogical Research Bureau.

Donald had long ago learned to accept as a foible his roomie's susceptibility to the various gimcrack Genealogical

Research outfits that catered, in this progeny-obsessed age, for people worried about their genotype. It was the first time he had ever known Norman not to fetch his monochrome reader immediately and study the latest come-on they had sent him.

Conclusion: something had disturbed Norman very badly, shifted him clear off his regular orbit.

Accordingly he made no attempt to start a conversation, but carried on with his own arriving-home routine: check the phone for personal calls recorded while he was out—there were none—collect the mail, which was as ever bulky and mainly commercial, from his delivery slot, and pour himself a little whisky from the liquor console before settling down in his own chair.

But he did not at once proceed to read the mail. Instead, he looked over his surroundings with a shadow of nervousness as though expecting this familiar setting too to take on the kind of strangeness he had experienced out on the street at lunchtime.

The open living-area reached directly from the entrance door was the section of the apartment they used in common. Even so, it bore little trace of Donald Hogan. It had been decorated and partly furnished before Norman agreed to accept him as a roomie; on moving in, he had contributed certain items like this chair, and a few ornaments Norman approved of, and the liquor console—not being a drinker, Norman had previously owned nothing but the kind of small wine-frame bottle-holder imposed by convention on a house-holder entertaining non-Muslim friends. Those things did not, on inspection, add up to a paradigm of Donald Hogan. Moreover, all of them were to be found on the same side of the room, as though an undefined boundary ran between the occupants of the apartment.

On the other hand, one could hardly say the place reflected Norman's personality, either. The realisation was a minor surprise to Donald. But all of a sudden he saw that there was a pattern implicit in Norman's choice both of furnishings and of colours. The shimmering russet of the walls, the facsimile William Morris design of the carpet, the Picasso, the Pollock and the Moore—even the worn Hille chair—seemed calculated, as though without warning a high corporation zeck might walk in and look around, then nod over the impression derived from the layout and decide that Norman House was a good steady type, worthy of promotion.

Donald repressed a shudder, wondering if the attempt to convey an aura of solidity and reliability might be aimed at himself as well as other, more influential, visitors.

Exactly one thing in the room jarred—his own possessions, that could be seen, were too neutral to matter, which was presumably why Norman had allowed them to remain out here on public display—and that was the polyorgan standing behind Norman's chair in the extreme corner of the room, the property of his current shiggy Victoria. It was marginally too modern, too gaudy, to fit in with the rest of the décor. But that, inevitably, would be transient.

Perhaps Norman's bedroom was a more honest reflection of him? Donald concluded that was unlikely. His own was not, because in theory at least, if not at present in practice, it was shared by a visiting shiggy. Additionally each of them had another small room for total privacy. Donald had never set foot over the threshold of Norman's, though he had glimpsed it through the open door. He had seen too little to judge if that was genuinely personalised. His own—probably not. It was more of a library than anything else, and half the books had been chosen on orders from his employers, not to suit his own tastes.

If the consequences of having to share an apartment were as negative as this, he thought, how would he justify his and Norman's preference for it and the widespread incidence of the habit, to a foreigner from a less healthy—hence less crowded—country, or to an old man who remembered when the first aspiration of a successful bachelor was a place entirely of his own?

Well . . . there was one obvious advantage, plus a number of minor additional ones. The easiest to see was that sharing enabled both of them to enjoy a standard of accommodation which for spaciousness and comfort exceeded what either could have afforded alone. Even on his GT salary Norman would have been hard put to it to live this well otherwise, what with the way prices had rocketed since the Fuller Dome was erected.

Some of the additional inducements were almost equally plain, like the shiggy-trading which was taken as a matter of course. Others were subtler, like the convenience of being able to let strangers assume that they were not just living together but living *together*. It grew so tiresome to be asked over and over again, "But if you're allowed to be a father, why aren't you?"

There was nothing in his own mail to attract his interest; Donald dumped the whole lot into the disposall. Sipping his drink, he grew aware that Norman had glanced at him, and he forced a smile.

"Where's Victoria?" he inquired, for lack of any other subject.

"Showering down. She smells, and I told her so." Norman's tone was absent, but behind the words Donald could detect all the inverted snobbery of the modern Afram.

You dirty black bastard . . .

Since Norman was apparently disinclined to prolong the exchange, he let his attention wander back to the Wholographik picture on the floor. He remembered the latest come-on he'd seen, one which Norman had left lying around in this room; it had claimed accurate genetic analysis given nothing more than one nail-paring from each of the subject's parents. That was such a flagrant lie he'd considered reporting it to the Better Business Bureau. Even in this year of grace you had only a sixty-forty chance of proving who your father was on such slender evidence, let alone of tracking back into the Caucasian side of what was predominantly an Afram heredity.

But he had changed his mind about making the complaint, for fear of infringing his cover.

God, if I'd known it was going to be such a lonely life I think I'd have . . .

"Hi, Donald," Victoria said, emerging from Norman's bathroom in a veil of steam and Arpège *Twenty-first Scentury*. She walked past him and threw one leg challengingly across Norman's lap. "Smell me now! Okay?"

"Okay," Norman said, not raising his head. "Go put some clothes on, then."

"You're a bleeder. Wish I didn't like you."

But she complied.

On the sound of the bedroom door shutting, Norman cleared his throat. "By the way, Donald, I've been meaning to ask you. Are you going to do something about—?"

"When I find someone suitable," Donald muttered.

"You've been saying that for weeks, damn it." Norman hesitated. "Frankly, I've been thinking I might be better off if I took in Horace in your place—I know he's looking for a spare tatami."

Suddenly alarmed, but concealing his reaction, Donald gazed directly at his roomie. Overlaid on his image he saw, as brilliantly as if she had still been in the room, Victoria: a high-Scandahoovian natural blonde, the only type Norman had ever brought into the apartment.

Does he mean it?

His own last steady, Gennice, had been his favourite: not one of the shiggies working the executive circuit like most of the ones they'd had in, but a woman with a strongly independent personality, almost forty and born in Trinidad. The reason he hadn't replaced her was partly lack of inclination, partly the impression that he wouldn't find her equal in a hurry.

He felt bewildered all over again, almost nauseatingly confused—the last thing he would have expected in his own home. He had imagined that he had made an accurate assessment of Norman, identified and typed him as the sort of self-conscious Afram who was uneasily balanced between insistence on having a white roomie and ill-concealed annoyance at that roomie's preference for Afram girls. But Horace, to whom he'd referred a moment previously, was shades darker than Norman himself.

He was relieved when the phone went. Answering the call, reporting over his shoulder to Norman that it was Guinevere Steel inviting them to a forfeits party, he was able to complete in his mind, privately, the conclusion he had come to. Norman must have undergone a traumatic experience today.

If he'd come right out and said so, though, he'd have

risked Norman putting his threat into effect; the Afram hated anyone to see beneath the calm mask he usually maintained.

And I don't think I could face adjusting all over again to a stranger the way I've adjusted to Norman. Even if I can't claim that we're friends.

"What's the theme of this forfeits party, by the way?"

"Hm?" Pouring himself another slug of whisky, Donald turned his head. "Oh—twentieth century."

"Talk and behave in period, is that the idea?" On Donald's nod: "Sort of stupid thing you'd expect from her, isn't it?"

"Of course it's stupid," Donald agreed, only half his mind on what he was saying. "She lives so obsessively in the here-and-now she probably thinks the twentieth century was a solid arbitrary chunk of thought and behaviour. I doubt if she remembers she was in it herself a decade ago. So we'll have people going around saying 'twenty-three skiddoo!' and 'give me some skin daddy-o!' and wearing niltops with New Look skirts all in one hopeless, helpless bungle."

"I wasn't thinking about that," Norman said. "You make it sound even worse than I imagined."

"What were you thinking of?" Donald said. Half-sensed at the back of his mind there was a need to talk—it didn't have to be about the shock he'd experienced earlier. Any kind of talk would do provided he could open out and feel he wasn't being secretive. The strain of never really communicating with anyone was getting on his nerves.

The corners of Norman's mouth turned down to hint at bitterness. "Why, I'll wager I'm the first Afram on her guest-list, and since I've accepted I'll remain the only one, and someone's going to be programmed to make like—let's say—Bull Clark. And she'll get a bunch of her entourage to gang together and claim a forfeit off me for not Uncle-Tomming."

"You really think so? Whyinole did you accept, then?"

"Oh, I wouldn't miss it for the world," Norman said with a trace of grim satisfaction. "A lot of other things happened last century besides what Guinevere likes to remember, and I shall take pleasure in stuffing them up her aristocratic nose."

There was a silence. Both of them felt it as intolerably

long. Norman had smoked barely half his Bay Gold, not enough to elasticate time for him, but because he had trespassed to the edge of the subject above all others where people like himself preferred not to be too open, he could not continue, a fact of which Donald was well aware. For him, though, the grouped references to the twentieth century had started his mind working on a train of association which forked and forked until he could no longer tell which point was relevant to what had been said at the beginning and which was not.

Perhaps I shouldn't have made that remark about putting Donald out and taking in Horace. One thing about keeping company with a WASP, especially a worrisome intellectual type like Donald: our private problems are far enough apart not to reinforce and multiply each other.

Wonder what did happen to Norman today? Something's shaken him, no doubt of it. What does it feel like to be inside his skull? The Children of X can't approve of codders like him, and his obsession with blue-eyed blondes. The company probably laps it up, of course; that big turnover in the eighties and nineties still casts its shadow. "The ideal company wife nowadays is an extremely ugly member of another racial group with no known father and two Ph.D.'s!"

But a company is no substitute for kinship.

Like to ask why he dislikes Guinevere so much. I can take her or leave her and she always has useful people to her parties, so I don't give a pint of whaledreck. Footnote: I must try to discover when that phrase leaked into common parlance; it was the sludge left when you'd rendered blubber down for oil, if I remember right. Maybe it was public guilt when they found it was too late to save the whales. The last one was seen—when? 'Eighty-nine, I think.

I envy Donald the element of detachment in his makeup. I'd never dare tell him, though. Could be it's only what mine is: a mask. But Guinevere is such a . . . and he hardly notices. What annoys him about her proposed party is like he said, the anachronism of treating the twentieth century as a lump. And it wasn't. Who should know better than one of us?

I'm behind the times. Prophet's beard, I'm practically obsolete. So I'm a VP for the world's richest corporation—have I succeeded in terms personal to myself? I've just chopped my way through the soft rotten feelings of ancestral guilt these WASPs suffer from till I've reached my nice cosy comfortable den. And here I am.

How long till sunset prayer this evening, by the way?

But the Guineveres of our world are no more than the spray on the top of the wave. It forms spectacular transitory patterns, but the ground-swell is what alters the coastlines. I can feel currents of it from where I'm sitting.

Imagine a VP of a big corporation sharing an apartment, forty years ago, with an alleged independently wealthy dilettante. They'd never have promoted him to the job in the first place. They'd have looked around for some type with a presentable wife, wouldn't have cared that the couple ate each other's hearts out in private and shipped their kids off to boarding-school and summer camp and any other place they could to get them out of the way. Nowadays they wouldn't give a pint of whaledreck even if we were sleeping together. It doesn't breed, and that's good. Everybody boasting about their children, complaining about not being allowed children—but they couldn't have pushed the eugenics laws through if people hadn't secretly felt relieved. We're at the precipice where even our own children add intolerably to the task of coping with our fellow human beings. We feel much more guilty these days about resenting other people's children than we do about the existence of people whose impulses don't involve propagating the species.

Come to think of it, there's a psychological as well as a physical sense in which we reproduce our kind. And we've tended to push the physical one further and further back in our lives. A lot of us have given it up altogether. We owe our intelligence—what there is of it—to having stretched the cub-period, the dominance of the *Lustprinzip*, beyond all reasonable bounds. Wonder if this is another way of stretching it still further. That would account for the development of the shiggy circuit, the fact that the world's big cities are alive with women who've never had a permanent home, but live out of a bag and sleep a night, a week, half a year wherever there's a man with an apartment to share. I must see if Mergendahler has published anything about this— it sounds like his field. I wish to God Mulligan hadn't quit; we need him to tell us where we are, we need his insight like we need food!

No, it's not Donald I should show the door to. It's Victoria. He's told me a score of times about my preoccupation with paleass shiggies, and I never listened, but he's right. Prophet's beard, all this talk about emancipation! Just one of the shiggies who've been in and out of this apartment like doses of aperient was stunningly beautiful and solid-ground sensible and marvellous in bed *and* a whole, rounded, balanced sort of person. And that was Gennice, that Donald brought home, not me, and I was unappreciative because she was a brown-nose. I must be off my gyros. I must be busted clear out of my nappy old plantation-bred skull!

Emancipated! Allah be just to me, I'm a worse prisoner of historical circumstance than the oldest Red Guard in Peking!

I wonder if we've been around each other long enough for him to think of me as Donald-a-person instead of Donald-a-WASP. I wonder if his impression of me is accurate. For the sake of absolute security I guess I should take him up on the threat he made, and move away. Being exposed for such a long time so intimately to one person is what the Colonel would call erosive. Funny how that one word he used has stuck in my mind so long . . . Still, no doubt they keep their eyes on me. They'll tell me if they think I'm endangering my cover.

If I were to come straight out and tell Norman: "I'm not a lazy slob parasitising off inherited wealth and making like a poor man's cousin to a synthesist because I haven't any creative talent—I'm a spy . . . !"

I'd be stupid.

Wonder if I'm going to get nightmares again, like in the early days, dreaming of a call in the middle of the night and a plane tomorrow to God knows where. Oh, surely they're not likely to pull me out of cold storage now? It's been ten years, and I'm adapted, and even if I sometimes get depressed I like things as they are. I'd prefer not to have to adjust to someone else as I've done to Norman. I used to imagine I could manage without friends so intimate it would be cruel to keep up the lie where they were concerned. I don't think I can. But at least in Norman's case I can excuse not telling him the truth on the grounds that it's too late; we've shared too much already. If I had to get this close to someone else I don't think I could maintain my pretence.

Lord, I hope the forecast of their needs was wrong when they sent Jean Foden and enlisted me!

It's all breaking loose at once. Someone's stirred my mind with a stick. Anybody would think I'd been ingesting Skulbustium instead of just my regular brand of pot. I have to hitch on to something fast, or I'll break to bits.

I've never really talked, like you'd say *talked*, to that codder in the other chair. I wonder if I can. Because if I can, that'll mean something did happen to me today, it wasn't just a momentary shock.

But I can't approach it cold. Work up to it by a roundabout route.

The quickest way to find out what he thinks about me, of course, might perhaps be to ask him . . . ?

"Donald—"
"Norman—"
They both laughed a trifle uneasily.
"What were you going to say?"
"No, no—you go ahead."
"All right, I will. Donald, what can you tell me to refresh my memory about Beninia??"

THE GRAND MANOR

"Rather painfully, we managed to digest Darwinian evolution so far as physical attributes were concerned within half a century of the initial controversy. (I say 'we,' but if you're a bible-thumping fundamentalist I expect you at this point to take the book by one corner at arm's length and ceremonially consign it to the place where you put most sensible ideas, along with everything else you decline to acknowledge the existence of, such as mainly shit.)

"We still haven't digested the truth that evolution applies to mental functions, too—that because a dog is a dog, a dolphin a dolphin, it has an awareness and sense of personal identity distinct from ours but not necessarily inferior. Is an apple inferior to an orange?

"But I'm trying to tell you what's happening to you, not what's happening to Crêpe Suzette your neurotic poodle. A good veterinary psychologist can probably be located by calling Information. You wouldn't believe him if he started telling you how much you have in common with that pet of yours, and likely you won't believe me. But if I annoy you sufficiently you may at least try to think up arguments to demonstrate how wrong I am.

"Basically, then: you have two things in common. You're a pack-animal; so is a dog. You're a territorial animal; so is a dog. (The fact that we mark our manors with walls instead of urine is irrelevant.)

"The depiction of Man the Noble Savage standing off the wolves at the cave entrance, all by himself with a club, while his mate and their young cower in the background, is so much whaledreck. When we were at the stage of taking refuge in caves our habit was almost certainly to congregate in troupes the way baboons still do, and when the dog-baboons move in everyone else—note that every*one!*—moves out. I mean like lions will shift the scene, and a lion is not what you'd call a defenceless creature.

"Lions are rather solitary, tending to work by couples over a manor which affords them adequate game for subsistence. Or not, depending on outside pressure from other members of the species. (Try owning a whole tomcat and you'll see the process in miniature.) Pack-animals have the evolutionary edge—in combination they're deadly. Lions learn this as cubs and then ignore the practice, which is why baboons can cave them in.

"NB: I said 'everyone', not 'everything'. You wouldn't recognise your ancestors as people, but they were, and you still are. Those ancestors were arrogant bastards—how else did they become boss species on our ball of mud? You've inherited from them just about everything that makes you human, apart from a few late glosses such as language. You got territoriality along with the rest. If somebody trespasses on it you're liable to turn killer—although if you don't like the idea you can kill yourself, which is among our few claims to uniqueness.

"Territoriality works this way. Take some fast-breeding animals like rats—or even rabbits, though they're herbivorous rodents, not carnivores as we are—and let them multiply in an enclosure, making sure at all stages they have enough food and water. Early on you'll see them behaving in the traditional rat fashion when conflicts arise: the quarrellers will square up to one another, feint, jab, charge and with-draw, the victory going to the more efficient braggart. Also the mothers will take good care, rat-style, of their young.

"When the pen becomes crowded past a certain point, the

fights won't be symbolic any more. There'll be corpses. And the mothers will start to eat their young.

"It's even more spectacular in the case of solitary creatures. Put a female ripe for mating into too small a cage that's already occupied by a healthy male, and he'll drive her out rather than give way to the reproductive urge. He may even kill her.

"Very baldly, then: shortage of territory, of space to move around and call your own, leads to attacks on members of your own species in defiance even of the normal group-solidarity displayed by pack-animals. Lost your temper with anyone lately?

"However, being a member of a species that's nothing if not ingenious, you've figured out two directions in which you can abstract your territoriality: one is to privacy, the other is to property.

"Of the two, the former is more animal and more reliable. Your base need is to have a manor defined against a peer group, but you don't have to do as dogs, tomcats and sundry other species do—mark it out with a physical trace, then patrol it constantly to scare away intruders. You can abstract to a small enclosed area where no one else trespasses without your permission, and on this basis you can operate fairly rationally. One of the first concomitants of affluence is a rapid raising of privacy-standards: someone from a comparatively low-income background has to accept that his childhood will be lived in a crowded, busy environment—in contemporary household terms, one room of the dwelling (if it has more than one) will be a family-room and that's the centre of operations. Someone from a more prosperous home, however, will take it for granted from about the time he learns to read that there's a room where he can go in and shut the door against the world.

"This is why (a) men from wealthy backgrounds make better companions under privative conditions such as a Moon voyage—they don't feel that their human environment is a permanent infringement of their right to a manor, no matter how thoroughly it's been abstracted from the original referent of a piece of terrain (b) the standard route out of the slum or ghetto is crime—equals getting your own back on other members of your species who trespass continually on your manor; (c) gangs develop primarily in two contexts— first, in the slum or ghetto where privacy as a counterpart of the manor can't be had and a reversion takes place to the wild state, with pack-hunting and the patrolling of an actual physical patch of ground; and second, in the armed services, where the gang is dignified by being called a 'regiment' or some other hifalutin dirty word but where the reversion to the wild state is deliberately fostered by deprivation of privacy (barracks accommodation) and deprivation of property (you don't wear the clothes you chose and bought, you wear a uniform which belongs to US!!!). Fighting in an army is a psychotic condition encouraged by a rule-of-thumb psychological technique discovered independently by every son-of-a-bitch conqueror who ever brought a backward people out of a comfortable, civilised state of nonentity (Chaka Zulu, Attila, Bismarck, etc.) and started them slaughtering their neighbours. I don't approve of people who encourage psychoses in their fellow human beings. You probably do. Cure yourself of the habit.

"We are breeding so fast that we cannot provide adequate privacy for our population. That might not be fatal—after all, it wasn't until as a species we discovered affluence that the demand for it became overwhelming. But we're undermining the alternative form of abstraction of territoriality, and deprived of both we're going to wind up psychotic in the same way as a good soldier.

"The point of abstracting to property is that the manor forms an externalised aid to self-identification. Put a man in a sensory deprivation tank, he comes out screaming or shaking or . . . We need continual environmental reassurance that we are who we think we are. In the wild state, the manor provides such a reassurance. In the state we've been describing a few paragraphs back, the ability to shut ourselves away from the continually fluctuating pressure of our peers enables an intermittent reassessment of our identity. We can lean on a group of objects—a clever surrogate for a patch of ground—but only if they have (a) strong personal connotations and (b) continuity. The contemporary environment denies us both. The objects we possess weren't made by ourselves (unless we're fortunate enough to display strong creative talents) but by an automated factory, and furthermore and infinitely worse we're under pressure every week to replace them, change them, introduce fluidity into precisely that area of our lives where we most need stability. If you're rich enough you go and buy antiques and you like them as a pipeline into the past, not because you're a connoisseur.

"The classical slave system survived for a long while despite the paradoxical discontinuity of pan-human identity which is implicit in any such social pattern. The American slave system was already breaking to pieces before the Civil War. Why? The answer is in the Code of Hammurabi, among other places—the first truly elaborate legal code we have any record of. It lays down fines and other punishments for personal injury. Although it's true that the penalty for injuring a free man is heavier than for injuring a slave, *the slave is always there*. Under the Romans, a slave had a certain inalienable minimum both of property (NB!) and of civil rights, which not even his owner could infringe. It was thinkable for a debtor to sell himself into slavery and pay off what he owed, in the rational—maybe far-fetched, but not lunatic—anticipation of recouping his fortunes. The first successful banker we know about was a Greek slave called Pasion who made himself a millionaire, bought his freedom and went into partnership with his former bosses.

"In the case of the American negro slave this possibility was not inherent in the system. The slave had the same human rights as a head of cattle—nil. A good master might conceivably manumit a slave who'd done him a good turn, or pension him off with his freedom as a favourite horse would be put out to pasture to spend his declining years in peace. But a bad one might decide to maim the man, brand him, or flog him to death with an iron-tipped cat-o'-nine-tails, and there was no one to call him to account.

"True, you're not a slave. You're worse off than that by a long, long way. You're a predatory beast shut up in a cage of which the bars aren't fixed, solid objects you can gnaw at or in despair batter against with your head until you get punch-drunk and stop worrying. No, those bars are the competing members of your own species, at least as cunning as you on average, forever shifting around so you can't pin them down, liable to get in your way without the least warning, disorienting your personal environment until you want to grab a gun or an axe and turn mucker. (This is in essence why people do that.)

"And there are more of them than ever before—*and* you've grown to expect privacy so that every now and then you can take the pressure off, but that privacy is becoming more and more expensive so that it's considered normal for even well-paid businessmen to share their apartments in order to enjoy luxuries their own salaries won't stretch to, such as rooms large enough to hold their private possessions as well as themselves—*and* you're being commanded by today's aggressive advertising to throw out those cherished belongings and get others which are strange to you—*and* you're being told day and night from authoritative official sources that people you don't know but who adhere to some mysterious quasi-religious precepts known as Marxist-Leninist-Maoist dogma and communicate in a language whose characters you can't even recognise as real writing are trying to trespass on your national gang's manor—*and* . . .

"In the last decade of the twentieth century sales of tranks soared a whopping thirteen hundred per cent. Unless you've been living in a country too poor to furnish the supplies, the odds are that two of every five of your acquaintances are dicties—perhaps on some socially acceptable drug like alcohol, but quite likely on a trank that by way of side-effect depresses orgasmic capacity and compels the user to resort to orgies in order to stimulate flagging potency, or on a product like Skulbustium which offers the tempting bait of a totally, untrespassably private experience and entrains senile dementia rather more certainly than tobacco entrains cancer of the lung.

"In short: your life from birth to death resembles the progress of a hopelessly drunk tightrope walker whose act has been so bad up till now that he's being bombarded with rotten eggs and broken bottles.

"And if you fall off, what they will do is broadly this: they'll take you out of the environment you're used to—you don't like it much, but at least it's not totally strange—and put you somewhere else you've never been before. Your key deprivation is of territoriality; they will shove you in a cell which has nothing whatever about it to help identify *you* as an individual. Your secondary lacks are of abstracted territoriality-equivalents; they will take away the clothes you chose yourself and give you tattered second-or twentieth-hand garments, and you will have no privacy whatever because on the basis of a time-schedule deliberately randomised so that you can't even brace yourself for the impact by the clock of hunger you carry in your stomach they will fling open the door and stare at you to see what you're doing.

"You will wind up inventing a private language because there's no other way of isolating yourself; you'll scrawl on the walls with your excrement because nothing else in the place belongs to you except the products of your own body; and they will call you a hopeless case and intensify the 'treatment' you're receiving.

"Don't say that it won't happen to you. The odds in favour have been going up daily for a hundred years. You know at least half a dozen people who have been in mental hospitals, and of that half-dozen at least one was related to you, even if no more closely than as a cousin. Again, if this is not the case, that's because you've been living in a country too poor to afford enough mental hospitals for its population on the generally accepted scale.

"Thank heaven for such countries! You might do worse than emigrate to one if what I've been saying worries you."

—*You: Beast* by Chad C. Mulligan

SCENESHIFTER

A little shamefacedly, because of official hostility towards such superstitions, students on their way to the fine tall modern buildings of Dedication University were apt to dodge into a shrine gay with paper streamers and gold leaf, there to light a volcano-shaped cone of incense paste as a propitiation, and concentrate a trifle more fully on their studies as a result.

There had been many changes in Yatakang, but the man who had been personally responsible for most of those which counted shunned publicity. Moreover there was one highly significant factor which had not altered: in Yatakang perhaps more than anywhere else on the face of the globe men felt a sense of divine arbitrariness.

The richness of the country's vaunted hundred islands was almost incredible. Alone of the nations of Asia it had an exportable surplus of food, mostly sugar and fishmeal. (The particular strain of *Tilapia* which provided the latter in thousand-ton batches had been modified by Professor Doctor Lyukakarta Moktilong Sugaiguntung.) Its mines made it self-sufficient in products like aluminium, bauxite and petroleum—for plastics, not for fuel. (A bacterium tailored by Sugaiguntung cracked the sticky aboriginal tars into pumpable light fractions all by itself and a mile below ground.) It was the largest country in the world without a single synthetic rubber

factory. (Its plantations had been ruthlessly stripped of twentieth-century stocks and re-sown with a strain Sugaiguntung
had developed to yield twice the quantity of latex every
season.)

But all this, with hardly more warning than the tremor of
a needle on a paper tape, might be shattered by the fury of
Grandfather Loa, who slumbered beside the Shongao Strait.
He had not lost his temper since 1941, but the market in
incense volcanoes flourished nonetheless.

"Now what I want you to do," Sugaiguntung said to the
orang-outang, "is this: go to the room with the door painted
blue—blue, yes?—and look through the drawers of the desk
until you find the picture of yourself. Bring it to me. And be
quick!"

The orang-outang scratched himself. He was not a very
prepossessing specimen. An unlooked-for side-effect had
afflicted him with alopecia, and his belly and half his back
were bald. But, having thought over the instructions, he loped
obediently towards the door.

The most important of Dr. Sugaiguntung's four visitors,
and the only one sitting down, was a heavy-set man in a plain
off-white jacket and trousers, his close-cropped scalp lidded
with the traditional black skull-cap. In the hope of an immediately favourable comment, Sugaiguntung addressed him.

"You'll appreciate, I'm sure, that this demonstrates his
ability to follow spoken commands, as well as to distinguish
colours not normally perceived by his species, and moreover
to identify his own image among a number of others—an
achievement which in the time available and considering the
complexity of the problem we . . ."

The visitor carried a short cane. When he wanted the
subject changed he slapped the side of his boot with it. He
did so now, with a noise like a cracking whip. Sugaiguntung
fell silent with Pavlovian responsiveness.

The visitor rose and for the fifth or sixth time made a tour
of the laboratory, his attention lingering on the two framed
items decorating the wall. There had been a third, and a
patch of unfaded paint still betrayed its former location, but
it had been intimated that even a citation for the Nobel prize
in chemistry was an unpatriotic thing to put on show. What

remained were a map of the world and a portrait of Marshal Solukarta, Leader of the Guided Socialist Democracy of Yatakang.

The visitor said abruptly, "You've looked at this map lately?"

Sugaiguntung nodded.

The cane flicked up to become a pointer, rapping on the glass overlying the map.

"It remains like a sore on the body of Yatakang, this ulcer of American imperialism, this memorial to their barefaced rapacity! I see," he added with marginally more approval, "that your map at least does not perpetuate the name of Isola."

It was a pre-Isolan map, but Sugaiguntung did not feel he could claim credit for that. He remained silent.

"And"—the pointer swung to the north-west—"while our friends and neighbours the Chinese are as Asian as we are, it is to be regretted, don't you think, that they have been for so long the victims of a European ideology?"

Sugaiguntung expressed vigorous agreement. That was not the official line, because the pullulating mass of the Chinese was much too close and much too powerful to offend, but it was one of the permissible inner-party attitudes.

The visitor's cane described a banana-shaped loop which encompassed the sprawling islands of Yatakang. "It is coming to be accepted," he murmured, "that the time is ripe for a genuinely Asiatic contribution to the future of this part of the planet. Within our boundaries we have two hundred and thirty million people who enjoy a standard of living, a standard of education, a standard of political enlightenment second to none. What's happened to that monkey of yours?"

With a sinking sensation Sugaiguntung dispatched one of his assistants in search of the orang-outang. He attempted to point out that all the animal's experimental predecessors had killed themselves, so that merely to have the creature alive at this stage would be an achievement, but the visitor slapped his boot again. There was an ominous silence until the youth returned, leading the ape and scolding him.

"He'd found the picture of himself," he explained. "Unfortunately there was a picture of his favourite female in the same drawer and he'd stopped to look at it."

From the orang-outang's physical condition—distressingly obvious owing to the baldness of his belly—it was clear he had developed a strong sense of two-dimensional image identification, an advanced talent which many human groups such as Bushmen and Bedouin had had to be taught by outsiders. But Sugaiguntung decided it was small use trying to impress that factor on his visitor.

The latter snorted. He said, "Why are you working with such unpromising material?"

"I don't quite follow you," Sugaiguntung ventured.

"A monkey's a monkey whether you adjust his chromosomes or not. Why not work on a level where much of the work has already been done for you?"

Sugaiguntung still looked baffled.

The visitor resumed his seat. He said, "Listen, Professor Doctor! Even enclosed in this laboratory you remain aware of the outside world—don't you?"

"I do my duty as a citizen. I devote part of every day to a study of the world situation, and I attend regularly at information meetings in the area where I live."

"Good," the visitor approved with sarcasm. "Moreover you have pledged yourself to our national goals, the incorporation of the American-dominated Sulu Islands into our country where they rightfully and historically belong, the establishment of Yatakang as the natural pathfinder of Asiatic civilisation?"

"Naturally." Sugaiguntung clasped his hands.

"And you've never flinched from contributing to those goals?"

"I think my work testifies that I have not." Sugaiguntung was growing annoyed, or he would never have trespassed so close to bragging.

"In that case you'll fall in with the suggestion I'm about to make, especially since the Leader"—a sketched salute towards the picture on the wall—"has personally selected it as the most promising path out of our present *temporary* difficulties."

Later, having lost the argument, Sugaiguntung found him-self wishing—not for the first time in recent months—that the tradition of honourably joining the ancestors had not been outlawed as inappropriate to a twenty-first-century state.

context (6)

ONE COMES OUT WHERE . . .

Beninia (ben-IN'-ya): country W. Africa, N. of Bight of Benin. 6330 sq. mi. Est. pop. (1999) 870,000. *Port Mey (127,000). Fishing, agriculture, handicrafts.

Brit. crown col. & protectorate 1883–1971. Indep. repub. 1971–date.

85% Shinka, 10% Holaini, 3% Inoko, 2% Kpala, 30% Xian, 30% Muslin, 40% misc. pagan.

". . . and remains today one of the cruellest legacies of colonial exploitation, a country which owes its present gross overpopulation to an influx of refugees from tribal conflicts in adjacent territories and almost completely lacks the natural resources to support itself. Recipient of endless UN aid, it has been reduced to the status of a beggar in the comity of nations despite President Obomi's proud rejection of Chinese 'technical assistance'. With the unfortunate fate of some of the former French colonies before him, possibly he was wise in the long term, but the long term is not yet here and the short term promises famine and plague . . ."

(NEGRO   Member of a subgroup of the human race who hails, or whose ancestors hailed, from a chunk of land nicknamed—not by its residents—Africa. Superior to the Caucasian in that negroes did not invent nuclear weapons, the automobile, Christianity, nerve gas, the concentration camp, military epidemics, or the megalopolis.

—*The Hipcrime Vocab* by Chad C. Mulligan)

"Old Zad's been in that job for going on forty years and I can't help wondering whether the reason he sticks it is because he wants to or whether there simply isn't anyone else in the whole benighted country fit to take over his chair!"

continuity (5)

HEAR HEAR

Victoria came out of Norman's bedroom wearing a white lei and Maxess lounging pants—two tight tubes of shimmering gold to thigh-height, ornamented behind with frills that were gathered into a bobbing rosette at her bottom, and a heavy gold fringe three layers deep hanging from a cord stretched hipbone to hipbone. It wasn't, obviously, getting dressed that had taken her so long, but perfecting the rest of her appearance. Her almost white hair was spindled into the fashionable antenna style, her veins were traced with blue—what some wit had nicknamed "printed circuit-lation"—and her nails, nipples and contact lenses were chromed.

Glancing at the men only long enough to determine that they were deep in conversation, she crossed the room to the corner where her polyorgan was set up. Using the earphones so as not to disturb them with her pracising, she began for the uncountableth time to rehearse a simple exercise with three beats in the left hand and five in the right.

As always when someone asked him about a subject outside his speciality, Donald was embarrassingly aware of the extent of his ignorance. However, when he had summed up what he could recall of Beninia—privately wondering all the time why Norman didn't simply go to the phone and punch for an encyclopedia connection—the Afram looked honestly impressed.

"Thanks. You've reminded me of several points I'd forgotten."

"Why the sudden interest in such an insignificant country?" Donald probed.

Norman hesitated. He glanced at Victoria, decided that with the unheard booming of the organ in her ears she could not be eavesdropping, and gave a wry smile.

"You don't have any in GT's company secrets, do you?"

"Of course not," Donald said with a trace of huffiness, and prepared to rise and collect another drink.

On the verge of anger—*trust a paleass to misunderstand me!*—Norman controlled himself.

"Sorry, that's not what I meant." He swallowed hard. "I meant: you don't mind if I mention something which strictly I ought not to?"

"I promise it won't go any further," Donald assured him, settling into his chair again. What could all this be leading up to? Norman was unprecedentedly nervous, twisting his hands together as though he could wring out the sweat that moistened their palms.

"Tell me why you think old GT, plus the corporation treasurer and the senior VP in charge of projects and planning, should invite Elihu Masters to lunch, put me on display like a—like a cabaret turn, and then discuss nothing repeat *nothing* but generalities."

He uttered the words with a kind of fierceness, for they symbolised what might be an important breakthrough.

Donald was startled at being taken into Norman's confidence after so long a period of mere mutual politeness—shading occasionally into acrimony. Careful to conceal his reaction, he mulled over the name.

"Elihu Masters? . . . Oh! He used to be our ambassador in Haiti, didn't he? Then they sent him to Beninia, and there were a lot of rumours about a demotion—hints of some kind of scandal."

Norman sighed. "We Aframs are as touchy as flayed skin, aren't we? There were accusations of prejudice, too, and all sorts of sinister machinations. I doubted the rumours about a scandal, because I'd followed his career with some interest and everyone I knew who'd met him spoke very highly of his integrity, but as to the rest of it ... Well, the idea of him being sent off to ferment in some quiet backwater didn't fit."

"You think there was a deeper reason behind the transfer?" Donald suggested. "I guess that's possible, but—well, would it have anything to do with GT? I don't see how, on the face of it, but of course you're the one who'd be in a position to judge that."

After a momentary hesitation, Norman said, "My first idea was that it might have a connection with MAMP."

"The Mid-Atlantic Mining Project?" Donald thought that over for a few seconds, then shrugged. "I did hear on the grapevine that GT was getting frustrated about having tapped a mineral treasure-trove which it can't afford to exploit—is that the case, in fact?"

"Pretty well," Norman admitted. "The point is, it would cost just about as much to bring usable ore to the surface from MAMP as it does to produce it from more conventional sources; they've tried and tried and they've failed to figure out a way of cheapening their methods. Current prices represent irreducible rock-bottom for anything from MAMP, but competing producers would cheerfully slice their profits to make GT look silly by undercutting them. GT would have to compete at a loss, and that's a crazy way to exploit a rich strike of ore, isn't it?"

"So what connection could Beninia have with MAMP?"

"None that I can see. It's not a market. It's too poor to buy even at a discount. Which leaves GT out of the picture and apparently brings in State."

Donald rubbed his chin. "How? Of course, it's an open secret that both the Dahomalians and the RUNGs are after Port Mey. It has potentially one of the finest harbours on the Bight of Benin. Right now, I gather, it's not much more than a fishing-port, but if it were properly dredged ... Hmmm! Yes, I suppose State *might* have an interest in maintaining Beninian independence."

"What's in it for State, though—Port Mey as a naval base?"

"We have our—uh—pocket republic of Liberia just around

the corner. In any case, it's too vulnerable; a well-trained army could isolate the city in half a day, and occupy the whole country in forty-eight hours."

"On the general principle of the thing, to keep it out of the hands of its expansionist neighbours?"

"I doubt if State would meddle to that extent even if President Obomi came and begged them on bended knee. Look what happened over Isola! That was twenty years ago and the storm of protest still throws up ripples occasionally, even though the union was made on the basis of a plebiscite."

Norman's jaw dropped suddenly, as though inspiration had struck him. Donald waited to see if he was going to voice it, then ventured a guess of his own.

"Are you wondering whether Masters approached GT, rather than the other way around?"

"Prophet's beard, Donald, are you developing a latent psi faculty? That is *precisely* what I was wondering! You wouldn't expect a man like Masters to be thinking of leaving the diplomatic service for a luxy boardroom job with more prestige than honest work. He's a good deal too young to retire, and a good deal too successful to be bought out of his chosen career. Nothing was said during lunch, either, to suggest GT was trying to recruit him—though actually, like I told you, nothing much was said about anything."

Silence fell anew. Donald's mind was busy with the implications of what Norman had told him, and he was prepared to wait for more to follow rather than risk diverting the conversation by making a remark of his own. However, Norman had fallen to staring at his own left hand, swivelling it back and forth on the wrist as though he had never seen it before. If he did propose to say something else, it was taking him a long while to put it into words.

And when at last he did seem about to speak, Victoria forestalled him, tugging off her earphones and swinging to face him.

"Norman! Are we going to do anything this evening?"

Norman started and checked his watch. He jumped to his feet. "Excuse me! I'm overdue for evening prayers. I'll be back in a moment, Donald."

"I don't get an answer?" Victoria prompted.

"Hm? Oh—no, I don't feel in the mood. Ask Donald."

She did so with a cock of one cycloidally arched eyebrow. He hesitated before replying; not having a shiggy of his own to offer Norman at the moment, he had enjoyed little of Victoria's company these past two weeks. But the sight of her flawless artificial perfection irritated him by reminding him of Guinevere Steel and the products of her celebrated Beautique.

"No, thanks," he muttered, and went to collect the drink he'd set out for several minutes ago.

"In that case you won't mind if I go out for a while," Victoria said pettishly, opening the door.

"Stay out as long as you like," Norman said over his shoulder, heading for his bedroom and the prayermat laid out facing Mecca.

The door slammed.

Left to himself, already half-regretting the fact that he had declined Norman's offer, Donald wandered about the wide living-room. Only part of his attention was on his surroundings; the rest of his mind was taken up with puzzled reflection on Norman's uncharacteristic behaviour.

Shortly, his random strolling brought him to the polyorgan. He had never inspected it closely since Victoria moved in. Of the very latest design, it folded up seat and all to the size of a suitcase and was light enough to lift on two fingers.

He admired the sleek changeochrome finish of the exterior, within the millimetre thickness of which light was split into its spectral components, making the material seem to have been dipped in rainbow paint. Idly, he put one of the headphones to his ear and tapped the keyboard.

A blasting discord threatened to shatter his eardrum.

He withdrew his hand as though the instrument had burned him and looked along the ranked controls for a volume switch. One instant before adjusting it, he was struck by a thought.

Victoria couldn't have been playing with the volume at that level. She'd have been deafened. Why would she have set the volume to maximum before leaving the instrument to go out?

For no better reason than that this sort of petty inconsist-
ency in his environment always piqued him—for the same
reason, in fact, that he had been sufficiently dissatisfied with
his education to attract the Dilettante Dept—he sat down at
the console and began to explore the operation of the instrument.

It was less than five minutes before he discovered the
spring-loaded switch activated by a little more pressure than
the player would normally apply to the vibrato control lever
resting against his right knee.

Wondering what he ought to do, he sat quite still until
Norman emerged from the bedroom. As usual, his few minutes of ritual obeisance seemed to have restored his calm and
good humour.

"You can't play that thing, can you?" he inquired, as
though perfectly prepared to discover Donald had been keeping the secret of his musical talent ever since his arrival in
the apartment.

Donald came to a decision. There was something underlying Norman's earlier unprecedented desire to confide in his
roomie. One more slight shock might shake loose the last of
his defensive barriers and open him up completely.

"I think you'd better come here and listen to this," he said.

Puzzled, Norman complied, accepting the headphones
Donald handed him.

"You want me to put them on?"

"No, just hold one to your ear. Now listen." Donald
pressed down a single key and a pure musical tone sounded.

"That seems to be—"

"Wait a second." Donald pushed his knee hard against the
vibrato control. The pure tone began to waver frantically
until it was cycling a semitone up and down from its basic
pitch. Harder still—

The musical tone ceased. A voice said, faintly but distinctly, "—precisely what I was wondering. You wouldn't expect
a man like Masters to be thinking about—"

Donald released the secret switch and the wavering tone
returned, continuing until he took his finger off the key.

For long seconds Norman remained statue-still. Then, beginning with his hands, his whole frame began to tremble, more and more violently until he could barely stand upright. Donald rescued the headphones from his nerveless grasp one moment before he let them fall, and guided him sympathetically to a chair.

"I'm sorry," he muttered. "But I thought you should know right away. Let me get you a trank, shall I?"

Eyes wide, fixed on nothing, Norman gave an abbreviated nod.

Donald fetched the pill and a cup of water to wash it down. He stood by until, from the cessation of the trembling, it was clear the drug had taken effect. Then he said, "Come now—they're not going to hold it against you at GT, surely! They must know that anyone in your position is a prime target for indesp, and a gadget that clever isn't something you'd stumble on except by accident, the way I did it."

"I'm not worried about GT," Norman said stonily. "Gt is big enough and bastardly enough to look after its sheeting self. Leave me alone, will you?"

Warily Donald drew back, watching Norman with taut concentration. He ventured, "Two major shocks in the same day is—"

"Is none of your drecky business!" Norman snapped, and jumped to his feet. He had taken three strides towards the door before Donald found his voice again.

"Norman, you're not going after Victoria, for goodness' sake! There's no point in—"

"Oh, shut up," Norman said over his shoulder. "Of course I'm not going after that sheeting shiggy. If she has the gall to show her face here again I can shop her for industrial espionage, can't I And it'll do my heart good, believe *me*."

"Where *are* you going, then?"

On the threshold, Norman spun around to face Donald squarely. "What's it to you? You're a bloodless featureless zombie, as measured as a yardstick and colder than liquid air! You've never bought the right to know what I'm doing— with your dilettante's detachment and your nonstop paleass politeness!" He was breathing in violent gasps despite the impact of the tranquilliser he had swallowed.

"But I'll tell you anyway—I'm going to try and track down

Masters so I can put right some of the damage I've done today!"

And he was gone.

Eventually Donald discovered that the pain he could feel in his palms was due to the way he was digging his nails into the flesh. He straightened his fingers with deliberate slowness.

That dirty son of a bleeder—what right has he to . . . ?

The anger paled like a dying fire, and left behind a sour feeling of self-contempt. He swallowed his new drink at a gulp, hardly tasting it.

It couldn't just be the revelation of Victoria's treachery that had shifted Norman off his gyros so violently. He must have known that his invariable habit-pattern of bringing in three or four new shiggies a year to the apartment—and always the same physical type—was setting him up for industrial espionage. It was risky for a company shiggy to accept such assignments, but when the target was a VP of General Technics the pay was bound to be tempting.

I wonder what corporation hired her.

But that was irrelevant. Somehow, everything seemed irrelevant, except one wholly incongruous central point: Norman had been on the verge of making a confidant of his roomie for the first time ever, and instead he had been driven into a shouting rage and gone storming away in search of one of his fellow Aframs.

Donald stood in the empty room and thought of the thirteen million people all around him, the population of Greater New York. The idea made him feel fearfully, intolerably alone.

the happening world (4)

SPOKEN LIKE A MAN

Confidential: Cases have been reported of the term "little red brother" being used by units of the marine and naval forces deployed from Isola. Officers are instructed to remind their men that the officially-approved terms are "chink", "slit-eye", "yellowbelly" and "weevil." Use of softass civilian terms is to be severely punished.

"What they could not hold by force of arms they are trying to win back by the power of their foreign money! We must drive out these parasites, these immoral bloodsuckers who corrupt our womanhood, mock our sacred traditions and scoff at our prized national heritage!"

KEEP OUT!

Allships urgentest allships urgentest following storm Thursday night mines are loose and drifting at approaches to Bordeaux Roads stand by till daylight and await go signal from units of Common Europe Navy.

"What I want to know is, how much longer is that damned government of ours going to take this lying down?"

PRIVATE!

"Our enemies skulk on every side, waiting for us to relax our vigilance. But we shall not give them the chance they seek to fall on and devour us. We shall stand firm, and our nation shall be purged of dross in the pure fire of self-sacrifice."

TRESPASSERS WILL BE PROSECUTED

To all Party bureaux: Revisionism and backsliding has been noted with concern in the following Departments . . .

"Yeah, but what I mean, even if he does have a clean genotype a guy with a proper sense of social responsibility just doesn't *have* five kids in this day and age! I don't care if he does get the Populimit Bulletin in his mail—that could be a cover, couldn't it? No, I say he must be one of these Right Catholic bleeders. And I want him out!"

BEWARE OF THE DOG

"What rightfully, legally and historically belongs to us lies groaning under the heel of a foreign tyrant!"

THESE PREMISES PROTECTED BY SAFE-T-GARD INC.

"It is not enough that we ourselves should enjoy freedom. We shall not be truly free until everyone alive can make the same sincere and honest claim."

NO RIGHT OF WAY

"It is not enough that we ourselves should enjoy freedom. There are those in our very midst who extol the virtues of an alien way of life which we know to be evil, hateful and wrong!"

NIGGER DON'T LET THE SUN SHINE ON YOUR HEAD

"Dirty Reds—"
My country 'tis of thee
NATIONALS RIGHT LANE   ALIENS LEFT LANE
"Capitalist hyenas—"
There'll always be an England
BLANKES NIEBLANKES
"The wogs begin at Calais—"
Vive la France!
FLEMING WALLOON
"Bloody nignogs—"
Deutschland über Alles
YORUBA IBO
"Goddamn people next door—"
Nkosi Sikelele Afrika
YOURS MINE
"They're all mad bar thee and me and thee's a little queer—"
MINE!
MINE!!
MINE!!!

PATRIOTISM   A great British writer once said that if he had to choose between betraying his country and betraying a friend he hoped he would have the decency to betray his country.

(Amen, brothers and sisters! Amen!

— *The Hipcrime Vocab* by Chad C. Mulligan)

tracking with closeups (6)

WHICH SIDE AM I ON?

In New York Elihu Masters preferred not to stay at a hotel, nor even at the home of one of his many friends, though he knew some of them were hurt by his repeated refusals. Instead he took a room at the United Nations Hostel, and if—as on this visit—the premises were so crowded that all they could find for him was a poky over-grown closet where the bed folded back to the wall so the occupant could get at the bathtub underneath, that was cool.

He was afraid of falling in love with his own country as his old friend Zadkiel Obomi had done, to the point where his precariously fostered, deliberately chosen commitment to the species man would cave in under pressure from the plight of his fellow Americans. Today he had come perilously close to doing exactly that. The spectacle of that youthful VP at General Technics had made him so indescribably sad . . .

He had not yet brought into the open the reason for his approach to General Technics, but he didn't doubt that they would have submitted the facts to Shalmaneser and received an assessment that was very close to the truth. Too much of his life was a matter of public record: his personal request for transfer to Beninia, for example, when in the normal course of events he should have been the next ambassador to Delhi and afterwards reaped one of the real plum jobs—Paris, perhaps, or even Moscow. There had been such a clamour about his going to Beninia, especially from the Children of X . . .

He sat in the room's only chair, facing but not seeing a wall-flat TV screen on which the marvel of holographic signal transmission presented images that seemed solid and changed their appearance and perspective if one moved from side to side of the picture. The set had recently shown him a SCANALYZER programme, and the details of Pacific fighting and vandalism, of anti-Right Catholic riots and muckers at large, had depressed him into a near-stupor.

Lax in one hand he held a book recommended to him by a friend, one which had appeared a few months after his departure for Beninia. He'd heard the author's name before, naturally; he was rated by those who should know as among the handful of truly great sociological *vulgarisateurs* in the tradition of Packard and Riesman.

But he'd announced this book as his swan-song, and true to his promise—according to the friend who'd loaned it to him—since its publication he had vanished. Rumour said he was dead by his own hand. Indeed, the despair that breathed through his mocking definitions reminded Elihu of nothing so much as Wells's *Mind at the End of its Tether*, that grim epitaph for human aspiration, and suggested that the rumour might be right.

He stirred now and looked at it afresh. The cover showed a barrel of gunpowder with a train fizzing across the floor. Doubtless that design had been chosen by the publisher, not by Chad Mulligan himself—he was aware of the twenty-first century and would never have permitted anything so archaic if he'd been informed in time.

In fact, Mulligan . . .

Elihu gave a slow nod. He had to concede that he was impressed, as one might be by a doctor who declined to mislead his patients with false reassurances. Mulligan might have understood the motives which could take the bright star of the U.S. Diplomatic Corps to the shabby, run-down slums of Port Mey instead of the clean modernity of Moscow. He might even, though himself a Caucasian, have comprehended the choice such a man felt was facing him: either to give himself up to the crying needs of his own people, who in this brave new century were still the trapped ones, spawning the majority of the muckers (though the newscasts by policy never mentioned their colour), the majority of the dicties (though most of them couldn't afford Skulbustium or Triptine and poisoned themselves on kitchen-brewed Yaginol or scraped poppy-juice from the slit pods with the backs of dirty knives), the ones who said, "I don't have to ghetto where I'm going because I was born here!"—or else determinedly to give love only to friends, and loyalty only to the entire human race.

Black or not black, this man Elihu Masters could not identify any better with the greedy bosses in Bamako and Accra, alternating between wheedling overtures to Beninia and shrieks of rage at each other designed to distract their own people from inter-tribal squabbling, than he could with the board of General Technics. Let the Dahomalians and the RUNGs fight their shadow-wars, utter their rival boasts about which country was the more industrialised, the more powerful, the more ready to spring to the defence of its national integrity; for him, the fact that Zadkiel Obomi could juggle four language-groups—two of which were intruders anyhow, descendants of refugees from twentieth-century tribal massacres in adjacent territories—and keep them singing under circumstances which might have been expected to lead to civil war, was the grand achievement of all Africa.

And perhaps . . . of the whole world.

He could hear that singing in memory now, over the thump-thump beat of pestles in mealie mortars because there were no surplus hides for luxuries like drumheads. To that insistent rhythm he found himself speaking aloud.

"It's not that it's good to live in squalor!" he exclaimed, and slapped the book on his palm for emphasis. "It's that they haven't been taught the ways we more sophisticated folk know to hate each other!"

He knew that was nonsense the moment he had said it. Human beings were deluding themselves when they claimed that hatred was something they had to be taught. Hatred of rivals, of intruders on private property, of the more powerful male or the more fertile female, was implicit in the psychological structure of mankind. And yet the fact remained: he had sensed in Beninia a sort of happiness in face of poverty he had never detected anywhere else.

Possibly it's due to Zad himself? No, that's equally nonsensical. Not even Jesus, not even Mohammed, not even the Buddha, could have made such a claim. Yet I'm sure it's an objective phenomenon! Maybe, when GT moves in, they'll put the facts to Shalmaneser and come up with the explanation.

But that was more ridiculous than ever, a pure piece of self-excusatory rationalising. The only facts available to be fed into a computer were public knowledge: Beninia was a small country, assailed by famine, run by its president and a handful of talented subordinates long past the point where its larger neighbours had given up and federated into colonial-language groups. In the background loomed certain curious historical problems, such as the reason why the Arab slave-traders ignored Shinkas when assembling parties for sale to European purchasers, why despite an unwarlike tradition that tribe had never been subjugated by its neighbours, why under the British colonial government there had never once been a revolutionary party set up, why . . .

"What the hell is the *good* of worrying about it?" Elihu said, once more addressing the walls of the room. "I love the place, and when they get love down to a bunch of factors you can analyse with a computer there'll be nothing left of whatever makes it worth being human!"

context (7)

BULL FIGHT

Scene: a cathedral during morning service.

Cast: Bishop and congregation.

Detail: a smear along the front rim of the pulpit. It was applied with a paintbrush and consists of a vesicant (formula related to mustard gas but a sight more efficient) and a hallucinogen (GT's catalogue reference AKZ-21205 converted by boiling with dilute sulphuric acid into the product nicknamed "Truth or Consequences").

Prediction: when the Bishop closes his hands, as he invariably does, on the pulpit rail ...

Truth: "I take my text from the Book of the Revelation of St. John the Divine, from the seventeenth chapter, and from the first verse of that chapter. Hr-*hm!* 'I will shew unto thee the judgment of the great whore that sitteth upon many waters.'

"Now I have no doubt that some of you—(*ouch! What in the name of ...?*)—will have been a trifle shocked (*what can possibly have made my hands smart like this?*) at the choice of text which I've made—quite deliberately, I assure you (*perhaps it'll wear off if I try and ignore it*)—in order to dramatise in the most violent possible fashion a truth which some people, professedly Christians like ourselves, have closed their eyes to. (*It burns like hellfire!*)

"The point which I want to make, which I hope to convince you needs to be made, is this—and it's quite a simple one. Because the Book from which I took my text is that among all others which is relevant to everyday human experience, it does not shun some of the less palatable aspects of our lives. It does not express approval of them, naturally, but it certainly does not censor, as it were, the home truths about us which we have to face squarely if we are to lead the kind of lives it's our Christian duty to attempt. (*Ah, that's better, it's coming down to a sort of warm glow like gloves.*)

"And because Man has a spark of the divine in his nature, the founders of our Church did not shrink from using very human—one might almost say crudely human—analogies in their teaching.

"The analogy of the prostitute, who sells her body for gain, is one which a few generations ago might have been regarded as distasteful by a great number of people. But the fact that our society called such people into existence was itself a shame—a disgrace, one might call it, using the strict technical aspect of the term 'grace'. Fortunately we have come to recognise some concomitant aspects of the responsibility with which we have been charged by being created in material bodies, and among these is a recognition of the fact that the fact that the choice of the symbol of marriage between our Lord and His bride the Church was no accident—that, in short, the union between man and wife is an expression of love, an expression of love, in other words—ah—an expression of *love*. (*I hope they won't notice if I lean back against the pillar behind me!*)

"Of course, prostitutes are becoming harder and harder to find these days. When I was a young man, there were some among my fellows who—ah—resorted to such persons, and I thought they were to be pitied, because clearly they had not come to terms with the built-in, as it were, faculty for expressing affection which is implied in the act which has not only the perpetuation of our species as its goal but also the giving of delight by one person to another or others.

"(?)

"When I say 'others', of course, I have in mind the regrettable fact that we human beings are far short of perfect and in a sense the full achievement of this heaven-sent faculty for pleasing one's life's partner is, like other human activities, one requiring testing and practice before the ultimate skill is achieved, and thus and therefore we find people who marry and genuinely regret that they chose this particular partner to whom in the upshot they are not after all suited and from whom with regret we part them regretfully because . . .

"Well, anyway. (*Never realised before how heavy and sweaty these idiotic robes can become!*)

"Lots of people don't get this point, as you very well know. I mean, ever since the great schism of the late twentieth century, we've been treated to the nauseating spectacle of some head-in-the-sand bigots over there in Madrid bombarding what are supposed to be their fellow Catholics with a succession of bulls and encyclicals and what-not just because the Church of Rome cottoned on to the basic truth that there's more to making love than manufacturing a series of babies who can be splashed with a bit of holy water and sent off to heaven to keep the hallelujahs flying and recognised the need for the contraceptive pill. But here's this Pope Eglantine going on about how you mustn't interfere with divine ordinances and give your other kids a chance to grow up in comfort so they can become rounded adult human beings, oh no, you must never ever enjoy yourself with anybody else except to procreate as though there weren't enough of us around treading on each other's heels and getting in the way all the time and taking away the bread from our mouths practically because they're so greedy and selfish and Christ it's enough to make you want to turn Muslim, really it is, because they're promised a string of perpetually virgin houris when they die and what else is the contraceptive pill except a here-and-now counterpart of that no mucking about when your wife gets her belly full and night after night lying alone and unable to sleep for the pressure and you know literally it gets to be an *ache* after a while and all those sheeting idiots like Augustine who had his fun when he was a kid with the women of the streets and then turned around and forbade it for everyone else I think he had the pox and it got into his spinal fluid and brought on GPI and if it weren't for the fact that he's probably impotent anyone would think the same thing had happened to Pope Eglantine and his gang of Right Catholics. Why don't I shut up and stop stuffing your ears with nonsense when you ought to be stuffing some other organ entirely?"

Consequence: the congregation was extremely disturbed.

continuity (6)

AUCTION BLOCK FOR ME

"Mr. House." The tone absolutely neutral. "We met earlier today. Sit down, won't you? It'll have to be on the bed, I'm afraid—or perhaps you'd rather we adjourned to one of the public lounges downstairs?"

"No, this is fine," Norman said distractedly, lowering himself on the very edge of the narrow bed. His eyes roamed randomly from point to point in the small room.

"May I offer you some refreshment? I recall that you don't take alcohol, but perhaps coffee, or—"

"No thanks. I'll smoke, though, if you don't mind."

"Ah, Bay Golds! That's the brand I used to favour—no, I won't, thank you. I gave it up. I was using it as a refuge from clear-headedness, and once or twice I nearly visited disaster on myself in consequence."

Skirmishing. Abruptly Norman found the words to speak his mind. With the reefer in his hand still unlit, he said, "Look, Mr. Masters, let me say what I've come to say and then get out and stop bothering you. Mainly, it's that I know I didn't make a very good impression on you at lunchtime."

Elihu leaned back in his chair, crossed his right leg over his left, put the tips of his fingers together, and waited.

"I'm not talking about the kind of impression old GT and the rest of the high muckamucks brought me in to make on you. That has nothing to do with me as a person—it's all the

106

corporation image bit, here's an enlightened employer with coloured VPs, and it's stale news. The big companies have been doing it for fifty or sixty years and all it's done is assuage a part of their guilt. What I'm apologising for is the impression *I* set out to make."

He looked at Elihu squarely for the first time. "Tell me honestly: what did you think of me?"

"Think of you?" Elihu echoed, and gave a sad chuckle. "I didn't get the chance to form an opinion of you. I'll tell you what I thought of the way you were coming on, if you like."

"That's what I meant."

"You were demonstrating to the distinguished visitor that you could be an even bigger bleeder than GT's chief executives."

There was a pause. Eventually Elihu dropped his hands to his lap. "Well, I've answered your question, and by your silence you haven't had much benefit from it. Now answer one of mine. What happened to you when you were called down to the disturbance in Shalmaneser's vault?"

Norman swallowed gigantically, his Adam's apple bobbing. "Nothing of much importance," he muttered.

"I don't believe you. When you came back you were on your automatic pilot; there wasn't a spark of genuine personality in anything you did or said throughout the meal, just a set of conditioned reflexes operating well enough to fool anyone except maybe a psychologist—or a diplomat. I've learned to tell the difference, just by walking into a room, between an honest negotiator and a delegate instructed merely to parrot his government's official standpoint. You may be able to lie to the WASPs you work for, but I've grown old in the study of human deceit, and I *know*."

He leaned forward and took Norman's left hand in his. He probed between the tendons with the tips of his fingers. For a moment Norman was too astonished to react; then he snatched himself loose as though he had been stung.

"How did you guess?" he said.

"I didn't. An old man—I suppose you'd call him a witch-doctor—taught me muscle-reading in the back streets of Port-au-Prince while I was ambassador to Haiti. I thought for a moment you must have suffered some sort of major injury to that hand, but I can't feel the effects of one. Whose hand was it, then?"

"My three times great-grandfather."

"Back in slavery days?"

"Yes."

"Cut off?"

"Sawn off. Because he hit his boss and knocked him into a creek."

Elihu nodded. "You must have been very young when you heard about it," he suggested.

"Six, I think."

"A bad thing to tell a child that age."

"How can you say that? It was the kind of important thing kids my age needed to be told! Six wasn't too young for me to have learned that the kid I liked most on our block, the one I thought of as my best friend, was ready at a minute's notice to join with other kids I didn't like and call me a dirty nigger bastard."

"Have you noticed you don't hear that used so much any longer—that particular insult? Probably you wouldn't have. I notice the shifts in usage because I spend years at a time out of the country, and the process has gone quite a long way whenever I return. Nowadays where you used to say 'bastard' you tend to say 'bleeder' instead—to mean 'haemophiliac', I assume."

"What?" Confused, Norman shook his head.

"If the point isn't clear, I'll deal with it in a moment. How did this story about your ancestor affect you?"

"I used to get pains in this arm." Norman held it out. "They called it rheumatism. It wasn't. It was psychosomatic. I used to dream of being held down and having it sawn through. I'd wake up screaming and mother would yell at me from the next room to shut up and let her get her sleep."

"Didn't you tell her you were having nightmares?"

Norman looked at the floor between his feet. He shook his head. "I guess I was afraid she might scold my great-grandfather and forbid him to talk to me about it."

"Why did you want him to? Never mind—you don't have to spell it out. What happened today that connected with this traumatic at age six?"

"A Divine Daughter tried to wreck Shalmaneser with an axe. Chopped the hand off one of our technicians."

"I see. Can they put it back?"

"Oh yes. But the surgeons said he might lose some of the motor functions."

"And you walked in on this, from cold?"

"Prophet's beard—*cold!* I didn't know it was more than one of their sheeting demonstrations, slogan-shouting and waving banners around!"

"Why hadn't your company police taken care of it before you arrived?"

"Worse than useless. Said they didn't dare fire from the gallery for fear of hitting Shalmaneser, and by the time they made it to floor level I'd fixed her."

"So you did fix her. How?"

Norman closed his eyes and palmed them. His voice barely audible between his hands, he said, "I saw a liquid helium leak once, from a pressurised hose. That gave me the idea. I got one of the pipes and—and I sprayed her arm. Froze it solid. *Crystallised* it. The weight of her axe snapped it off."

"They can't put her hand back then, presumably."

"Prophet's beard, no. It must have spoiled instantly—like a frosted apple!"

"Are you facing serious consequences from this? Are you going to be arraigned for maiming her, for example?"

"Of course not." The words were half-contemptuous. "GT looks after its own, and in view of what she was trying to do to Shalmaneser ... We've always cared more about property rights than human rights in this country. You should know that."

"Well, if it's not the consequences it must be the act itself. How has it made you feel about yourself?"

Norman let his hands fall. He said bitterly, "You missed your vocation, didn't you? You should have been a shrinker."

"My neuroses aren't the kind you can project on to other neurotics. I asked you something, and unless I'm much mistaken it's what you came here to talk about, so why not get it over with?"

The forgotten reefer went waveringly to Norman's lips. He got it lit, drew in and held the first puff. After half a minute, he said, "How I feel about myself? I feel I've been conned. I feel ashamed. I finally evened the score. I got a trophy—I got a paleass's hand. And how did I get where I could take that off? By following the rules for living that The Man laid down. And they're no good! Because what use is that hand to my long-ago ancestor? He's *dead!*"

He drew on the reefer again and this time held the smoke for a full minute.

"Yes, I think he probably is," Elihu agreed after a few moments' reflection. "As of today. Think he needs to be mourned?"

Norman gave a quick headshake.

"Right." Elihu resumed his original position, elbows on chair-arms, fingertips together. "A short while ago I remarked on something that apparently struck you as irrelevant—the fact that you don't hear people calling each other 'bastard' so much any more. It's important. To be born out of wedlock doesn't signify, any more than it did in slavery days when our forefathers and mothers didn't marry—they simply bred. What you do hear used as an insult is a word that probably means 'haemophiliac'. It matches the preoccupations of our society; it's become detestable, anti-social, to have children if you're carrying a harmful gene like that one. Are you on my orbit now?"

"Things change," Norman said.

"Exactly. You aren't six years old any longer. A boss can't do to his subordinates what a long-ago white man did to your three times great-grandfather. But is the world a paradise because of those truisms?"

"Paradise?"

"Of course not. Aren't there enough problems to handle in present time, that you should brood over ancient ones?"

"Yes, but—" Norman made a helpless gesture. "You don't know what sort of a dead end I've been lured down! I've been working on the current version of myself for years, for decades! What am I to do?"

"That's for you to work out."

"It's easy enough to say 'work out' the answer! You've been away from this country for years at a time, you said so yourself. You don't know what The Man is like, even nowadays—you don't know how he leans on you all the time, needles you, goads you. You just haven't experienced *my* life."

"I guess that's a fair comment."

"For example . . ." Norman gazed without seeing at the wall behind Elihu's head. "Heard of a woman called Guinevere Steel?"

"I gather she's responsible for the mechanical styles women are affecting here at the moment, as though they were built in a factory and not born of a mother."

"Right. She's planning to hold a party. It'll be a microcosm of what I mean, all there in the one apartment and dripping slime. I should drag you along with me, and then perhaps you'd—"

He stopped in mid-sentence, suddenly appalled at what he was saying and who he was saying it to.

"Mr. Masters, I'm dreadfully sorry! I have no business to talk to you this way!" Rising to his feet, covered in embarrassment. "I ought to be thanking you very sincerely for your tolerance, and here I am insulting you and . . ."

"Sit down," Elihu said.

"What?"

"I said sit down. I haven't finished, even if you have. Do you feel you owe me anything?"

"Of course. If I hadn't been able to talk to somebody tonight, I think I'd have gone insane."

"How well you express my feelings," Elihu said with ponderous irony. "May I take it that right now you aren't excessively concerned with GT's company secrets remaining inviolate?"

"I know too damned well that they aren't."

"I'm sorry?" Elihu blinked.

"A private problem . . . Oh, why try and hide it? The shiggy I've been keeping around lately turned out this evening to be an industrial spy; my roomie discovered an eavesdropping gadget hidden in a polyorgan she brought with her." Norman gave a harsh laugh. "Anything you want to know, just ask—I can always claim she was the one who got away with the secret."

"I'd rather you told me openly if you tell me at all."

"Yes, I shouldn't have said that. Go ahead."

"What do GT's people think is my purpose in approaching them?"

"I don't know. No one has told me."

"Have you figured it out for yourself?"

"Not exactly. I was talking about it with my roomie earlier this evening. But we didn't reach any definite conclusion."

"Well, suppose I were to say my intention is to sell my dearest friend into slavery to The Man, and that I believe it's for his own good—what then?"

Norman's mouth rounded slowly into an O. He snapped his fingers. "President Obomi?" he said.

"You're a very intelligent man, Mr. House. Well—your verdict?"

"But what have they got that GT might want?"

"It isn't GT as such. It's State."

"Not willing to risk another Isola-type crisis?"

"You're beginning to amaze me, and I'm not joking."

Norman looked uncomfortable. "To be frank, it was one of the ideas my roomie and I were tossing around. If I hadn't heard it from yourself, though, I'd never have credited it."

"Why not? GT's annual profit is almost fifty times the gross national product of Beninia; they could buy and sell many of the underdeveloped countries."

"Yes, but even granting their ability to do it, which I can't contest, the question remains: what is there in Beninia that GT might want?"

"A twenty-year rehabilitation project that will create an advanced industrial bridgehead in West Africa, serviced by the best port on the Bight of Benin, able to compete on their own terms and on their own *ground* with the Dahomalians and the RUNGs. State has a computer analysis which suggests that the intervention of a third force is the only factor likely to prevent a war over Beninia when my good friend Zad dies—and that day can't be as far off as I'd like it to be. He's working himself into his grave."

"And this will belong to GT?"

"It'll be—mortgaged to GT, let me put it that way."

"Then don't do it."

"But if the alternative is war—?"

"From the inside, from the status of a junior VP in the corporation, I say that war itself isn't as foul as what GT can do to a man's self-respect. Listen!" Norman leaned forward earnestly. "Do you know what they've duped me into doing? I subscribe to these Genealogical Research outfits, these near-crank businesses which claim to trace your descent on the basis of your genotype. And do you know I haven't commissioned *one* to track my Afram heritage? I don't know where my black ancestors came from to within two thousand miles!"

"And supposing it's a cousin of yours—and mine—who gives the order and the armies march into Beninia! What's going to be left of the country? The loser is going to scorch the earth behind him when he retreats, and there will be nothing left except rubble and corpses!"

Norman's intensity faded. He shrugged and nodded. "I guess you're right. We're all human beings, after all."

"Let me tell you the scheme. GT will float a loan to finance the operation, and State will buy a fifty-one percent interest through front agents—mainly African banks. GT will guarantee five per cent per annum for the twenty-year period of the project, and publish estimates of a yield in excess of eight per cent. That's solidly based, by the way, on State's computations; when they give the data to Shalmaneser they expect it to be confirmed. Then they'll recruit the teaching staff, mainly among people who were colonial administrators and so on in the old days, people who are used to West African conditions. The first three years will go on diet, sanitation and building. The next decade will go on training— a literacy drive first, then a technical education programme designed to make eighty per cent of the population of Beninia into skilled workers. I see you're looking incredulous, but I say I believe this will work. There's no other country in the world where you could bring it off, but in Beninia you can. And the last seven years will go to build the factories, install the machine-tools, string the powerlines, level the roads— everything else, in short, to leave Beninia as the most advanced country on the continent, South Africa not excepted."

"Allah be merciful," Norman said softly. "But where do you get the power to feed into the lines?"

"It's going to be tidal, solar, and deep-sea thermal. Mainly the latter. The temperature gradient between the surface and the sea-bed at those latitudes could apparently run a whole country much larger than Beninia."

Norman hesitated. "In that case," he ventured at length, "the raw materials will presumably be coming from MAMP?"

A new cordiality entered Elihu's manner. "As I said before, Mr. House, you suddenly astonish me. When we met earlier today your—ah—superficial image was so flawless as to conceal from me this sort of perceptivity. Yes, that's going to be the carrot with which we coax the GT donkey into agreement: the promise of a built-in market that will enable them to put the MAMP mineral deposits to work."

"On the basis of what you've told me," Norman said, "I presume they jumped at the idea."

"You're the first person at GT to hear the full details."

"The—? But why?" Norman's question was almost a cry.

"I don't know." Elihu seemed suddenly weary. "I guess because I'd kept it to myself too long, and you were here when it broke loose. Shall I call Miss Buckfast and tell her I want you sent to Port Mey to conduct the initial negotiations?"

"I—wait a moment! What makes you so sure she'll consent when you haven't even explained the project to her?"

"I've met her," Elihu said. "And I only need to meet someone once to know if this is the sort of person who'd like to own nine hundred thousand slaves."

CITIZEN BACILLUS

Si monumentum requiris, circumspice

Take stock, citizen bacillus,
Now that there are so many billions of you,
Bleeding through your opened veins
Into your bathtub, or into the Pacific,
Of that by which they may remember you.

Gravestones, citizen bacillus?
"Here lies in God the beloved husband
Of Mary, father of Jim and Jane"?
But they closed the cemetery at Fifth and Oak
And put up an apartment block on it.

Ideas, citizen bacillus?
They raised you literate and educated,
Equipped to exercise initiative.
But now our technological society
Insists you behave as a statistic.

Products, citizen bacillus?
It's not by any means improbable
You possess advanced crafts and skills.

But there's a tape in the chemical milling machine
Accurate to one molecular diameter.

A son, citizen bacillus?
Apply to the Eugenic Processing Board,
Give them a sample of your genotype.
But be prepared to hear it's disallowed
And don't complain in hearing of your neighbours.

No, no, citizen bacillus!
Here is your monument and it stands high!
The cars which you wore out, the clothes you tore,
The cans you emptied, furniture you broke,
And all the shit with which you clogged the drains.

Si monumentum requiris, circumspice . . .

tracking with closeups (7)

THE TOO MUCH STRAIN

Until very recently Eric Ellerman had thought that this was the worst time of the day, the interval between waking and arriving at his job, spent steeling himself afresh each morning for the ordeal of facing his colleagues. But there seemed to be no "worst time" any longer.

It was purely and simply hell to be alive.

From the breakfast alcove where he was gulping his second cup of synthetic coffee—the three-child tax had taken away his chance of buying the real thing—he could see the morning sun glinting on miles of green-houses, rising from the far side of the valley, climbing up over the hill and vanishing into the next dip. Above them loomed a gigantic orange sign: FOR ME IT'S HITRIP OF CALIFORNIA EVERY TIME, SAYS "THE MAN WHO'S MARRIED TO MARY JANE"!

But how much longer can I live in sight of my work?

Through the flimsy wall separating him from the children's room came the fractious squalling of the twins, neglected while Ariadne dressed Penelope ready for school. She was crying again too. How much longer before the hammering from the next apartment started? He cast a nervous glance at his watch and discovered that he had time to finish his drink.

"Arry! Can't you quiet them?" he called.

117

"I'm doing my best!" came the fierce reply. "If you'd give me a hand with Penny that'd help!"

And, as though the words had been a signal, the banging from next door began.

Ariadne appeared, hair tousled, negligee hanging open to show the way her belly was sagging, shoving Penelope in front of her because the child was rubbing both tear-swollen eyes and refusing to look where she was going.

"All yours," Ariadne snapped. "And I wish you joy of her!"

Abruptly Penny darted forward, throwing out her arms. One small hand struck the cup Eric was holding and the last of its contents shot across the windowsill and dribbled towards the floor.

"You little bleeder!" Eric exploded, and slapped her with his open palm.

"Eric, stop that!" Ariadne cried.

"Look what she's done! It's a miracle she didn't soak my clothes with it!" Eric scrambled to his feet, dodging the dark-brown liquid as it trickled over the edge of the built-in folding table. "And shut up, you!" he added to his eldest daughter.

"You haven't any right to call her dirty names!" Ariadne insisted.

"All right, I'm sorry—does that satisfy you?" Eric seized his lunch-bag. "But go and shut up those twins, will you? Before someone comes to the door to complain and sees you in that state! Don't show yourself outside unless you're wearing your new corset, for God's sake. Maybe that'll quiet some of the lying rumours that are going around."

"I can't do more than I'm doing already! I buy my pills at the block store making sure everyone can hear what I'm getting, I carry the Populimit Bulletin under my arm when I go out, I—"

"Yes, I know, I know! There's no use telling me—try telling some of these sheeting neighbours of ours. But go and shut the twins up, *please!*"

Ill-temperedly, Ariadne went off to make the attempt, and Eric snatched at his eldest daughter's hand. "Come along," he muttered, heading for the front door.

They're as good as telling me openly now that I ought to get a divorce. And maybe they're right. I'm damned certain I should have gotten a raise for the work I put into developing the Too Much strain—heaven knows I need it (mustn't say that, mustn't, they'll be convinced that it implies I really am what they think I am)—and maybe I would have but for what they assume about Arry . . .

He tugged the door open, thrust Penelope out into the corridor, and only then saw what was on the outside under the apartment number. Fixed to the panels with adhesive tape in the form of a rough cross, there was one of the crude plastic Mexican figures of the Virgin Mary which could be had for a dollar in local novelty stores, with a contraceptive pill jammed into its half-open mouth.

Underneath someone had chalked in hasty letters: "What's good enough for her should be good enough for you!"

"A dolly!" Penelope exclaimed, forgetting her determination to go on crying until she was exhausted. "Can I have it?"

"No you can't!" Eric roared. He ripped it down and stamped on it until it was a heap of coloured fragments, then scuffed at the chalked letters with the back of his hand to make them illegible. Penelope began howling all over again.

From the end of the corridor came a loud shrill snigger in the voice of a boy about ten or twelve. Eric whirled, but caught sight only of a foot and leg vanishing.

The Gadsden boy again. The little bleeder!

But it was no use making accusations. Smug in the knowledge he would never have more than his one child, clever enough at petty politics to have been elected blockfather thrice running, Dennis Gadsden would scarcely need even to deny the charge against his son.

Could I help it if our second cub turned out to be twins? Did I plan for all three of the bleeders to be girls? Sex-determination is expensive! It's not illegal anyhow—we have clean genotypes, no diabetes, no haemophilia, nothing!

Not against the law, granted. But a drecky lot of difference that made. There wouldn't have been—couldn't have been—any eugenic legislation at all unless public opinion had already come around to the attitude that having three or more children was unfair to other people. In a country of four hundred million inhabitants raised on a dream of wide-open spaces where a man could do as he liked, it was logical enough.

We can't live here much longer.

But—where else? They teetered on the verge of bankruptcy, thanks to the state tax on families larger than two children. Anywhere else in California the cost of travelling a longer distance to work would be prohibitive—and they'd have to move a good long way before they escaped the legacy of their reputation, even if they were to let one of the twins go for adoption. And although they'd avoid the tax by going over the border into Nevada, precisely because that maverick state had declined to impose child taxes and more than the minimum of eugenic legislation the cost of a home there was double or treble what it was in California.

Although—do I want to keep on at this job?

By a miracle, the elevator to the ground floor was empty apart from him and Penelope. He thought about the idea of quitting his job during the brief descent, and came to the same conclusion as always: unless he moved a long way off, divorced Arry—excessive fertility had been allowed as grounds in a Nevada court, though not yet in California or the other states of the union—and stripped himself of all associations with his family, he wouldn't stand a chance of getting another post comparable to his present one.

In any case, the thing he knew most about was the genetic selection and manipulation of strains of marijuana; it was his most salable skill. And Hitrip of California could easily slap a ten-year injunction on him under the Industrial Secrets Act to prevent him working for anyone else in a competing line of business.

Trapped.

The elevator door slid open, and he led Penlope, protesting as always, along the corridor towards the block school. He quelled his compunction about leaving her to the tender mercies of her peers with the usual glib reflection that she had to learn to sink or swim, and marched off towards the rapitrans terminal.

At least the four yonderboys who'd been haunting him recently hadn't put in an appearance yesterday or the day before. Perhaps they'd grown bored; perhaps it hadn't been him personally they'd been interested in.

He had his ticket checked by the auto gate-control and passed on to the platform to await the humming monorail car.

And there they were, all four of them, lounging against a pillar.

This morning the platform was even more jampacked with people than usual. That meant the trains weren't keeping their schedule—probably there had been sabotage on the track again. The rapitrans system was a prime target for pro-Peking "partisans"; no amount of patrolling was proof against such tactics as dropping a bottle that appeared to contain an innocent soft drink but actually had been spiked with a colony of tailored bacteria capable of reducing steel or concrete to a fragile sponge. Normally this would have made Eric furious, like everyone else, but today the throng of impatient passengers held out the hope of evading the yonderboys' notice.

He moved, sidling, towards the rear of the platform, keeping as many bodies as possible between himself and the four gaudily dressed youths. He thought at first he had made it. Then, as the car finally rolled in, he sensed a shoving behind him and glanced back to discover that they had worked their way over to where he stood and now flanked him in pairs.

With an insincere grin the leader motioned him to enter first, and he did so, quaking.

The car was crowded, of course. It was necessary to stand. Only those lucky people who got on at the first station were able to enjoy a seat for their journey. But the noise made it possible to talk privately if one spoke very close to the listener's ear, and that the yonderboys proceeded to do.

"You're Eric Ellerman," one of them said, and a tiny spray of spittle landed on his cheek with the words.

"You work at Hitrip."

"You live at Apartment 2704 in that block there."

"You're married to a woman called Ariadne."

"And you have too damned many prodgies, right?"

Prodgies? Eric's terror-bemused mind wrestled with the

term, and finally sorted it out. From "progeny". Means "children".

"I'm Stal Lucas."

"A lot of people can tell you about Stal. People who've learned to do as he asks, and been—*safe*."

"And that's my sparewheel Zink. He's a mean codder. He's evil."

"So listen carefully, Eric darling. You're going to get us something."

"If you don't, we'll make sure that everyone knows the facts about you."

"Such as that you have other cubs back where you came from in Pacific Palisades, by another shiggy."

"And what you're up to now is not three, but five—or six."

"They'll love you for that, darling. Just love you!"

"And they'll be pleased to hear you go to Right Catholic services in secret, won't they?"

"And you have a special dispensation from Pope Eglantine in Madrid to buy the Populimit Bulletin—"

"And anyway you don't have a clean genotype like you say but an undercover Right Catholic in the Eugenics office was bribed to alter your charts—"

"And when they grow up your cubs will almost certainly be schizophrenic—"

"Or *their* cubs will be—"

"What do you want?" Eric forced out. "Leave me alone, leave me alone!"

"Sure, sure," Stal said soothingly. "You follow our programme and we'll leave you alone, promise promise. But—ah—you work at Hitrip, and Hitrip's got something we want."

"It's got Too Much," Zink said from the other side.

"One little pack of seeds," Stal said. "Like a dime bag. That's all."

"But—but that's ridiculous!"

"Oh, it can't be *ridiculous*."

"But it doesn't grow direct from seed! And it needs special chemicals all the time, and—and you can't plant it in a window-box, for God's sake!"

"Friend of yours, isn't he—God? You keep Him supplied with new recruits to the heavenly choir. You breed like He wanted us to, Right— Catholic?"

"Fasten it, Zink. What do you grow it from, then—cuttings?"

"Y-yes."

"Cuttings will do. Too Much is too much at three bucks fifty a pack of ten reefers. But it's good pot, I'll grant that. So that's the programme, darling: a dime bag of good fertile cuttings—and you'd better let us have a table of the kind of treatment it needs to grow up. And we'll be generous and keep your secret for you, about those cubs in Pacific Palisades."

The monorail car was slowing for its next station. Eric said frantically, "But it's impossible! The security—the guards they have on it!"

"If they don't let the geneticists who evolved it get a close squinch, who gets one?" Stal said, and the four yonderboys moved towards the door, the other passengers, nervously eying their identifying clothes, making way for them.

"Wait! I can't possibly—!"

But the doors were open and they were gone on the crowded platform.

context (8)

ISOLATION

"At bottom the human species finds idealism an uncomfortable posture. Prime evidence of this can be found in the way neither of the two groups locked in irresoluble conflict around the Pacific has been able to achieve its stated goal—even though, given the lucid, simple, obviously attractive statement of either of their ideals, an impartial observer might wonder why commitment had not ensued like sunrise after night.

" 'Give the wealth back to the people who created it!' Here's an ideal capable of generating crusades among people who interpret it as expropriating greedy landlords, sharing out land so that every family may enjoy reasonable nutrition and repudiating debts to moneylenders at usurious rates of interest. Having hit on this, the Chinese charged ahead—until they overreached themselves. They became unable to distinguish between the evils they were preaching against and those traditional influences which literally constituted the way of life of people they hoped to recruit to their cause. In short order they fell into the same pit as their rivals, who had for decades ignored the plain and simple fact that to a starving man 'freedom' implies a full rice-bowl—or, if he has an exceptional imagination, a healthy ox to pull his plough. It has *nothing* to do with voting for a political delegate.

"Analogously with the way the Tsarist army deserted *en*

masse during the First World War, not because of Bolshevik impact on the soldiers but because they were sick of fighting and wanted to go tend their farms, the eager early recruits to the red flag discovered that while they were dying abroad the things they wanted to guard were being undermined at home. So they quit. China, like Russia before her, found she was surrounded by a gaggle of heirs to the mantle of the late Marshal Tito, not a few of whom were themselves within China's boundary.

"However, by that time, thanks to ineptitude, racial prejudice against them, fighting the right wars with the wrong weapons, and general mismanagement of their affairs, the opposition (or if you prefer, which I don't because I'd rather not identify with such a bunch of incompetents, 'our side') was so far in arrears that the greatest single territorial gain to date in a contest which bids fair to outdo the Hundred Years' War both for duration and for inconclusiveness only restored a rough balance and didn't tip the scales the other way.

"We can't even claim in honesty that it was the result of foresight and planning—only that when the grabbing was good, we grabbed. Don't believe anyone who tries to claim that the existence of Isola is proof of the superiority of the Western system. The Chinese couldn't have taken over. There was no form of discontent they could have exploited. How do you whip up resentment against absentee landlords and pocketers of bribes when the highest ambition of the people concerned is either to become the former or be in a position to receive the latter?

"Life in the Philippines had become intolerable well before the civil war of the 1980s. The state of things obtaining (which some accounts misname anarchy, but which any decent dictionary will tell you was nothing of the sort, but free-enterprise capitalism gone out of its skull) was on the verge of ruining the country permanently. The annual average of unsolved murders was running around 30,000 in a population of under fifty million. In the eyes of the inhabitants of the Sulu Archipelago, where most of them were committed, the offence for which they revolted against and ultimately assassinated President Sayha was that he interfered in their traditional right to slaughter and steal. This was unforgivable.

"Oh, doubtless there were some among the people who gave that celebrated majority of eighty-eight per cent in the plebiscite on secession who hoped that being policed and governed by Big Brother in Washington would ensure them a quieter life, free them from the need to fit bullet-proof shutters and plant man-traps in their gardens. Far more, however, seem to have hoped that the bait on the hook (full States' rights and a billion dollars of aid) would offer another and fatter cake of which they could snatch their slice.

"Which of these parties saw its dream fulfilled? Dear reader, you must be joking. That vaunted billion-dollar aid budget went nowhere near the natives' pockets. It was spent on roads, airfields, port facilities and fortifications. And, while it's true that the smugglers and black-marketeers who had hitherto rampaged unchecked had their hinder ends smartly kicked, to get rid of them the new owners imposed martial law and it hasn't been lifted since 1991!

"Dubbed 'Isola' on the grounds that Montana was a mountainous territory and the new acquisition was an island territory, the Junior State went from the frying-pan into the fire. However, the Americans had been desperately in need of bases closer to the Asian mainland than what they currently had, and they were reasonably well satisfied.

"The Chinese, on the other hand, when they tried a counterstroke by wooing Yatakang, were disappointed. The Yatakangi are descendants of the former dominant people in South-East Asia and firm believers in the traditional military dictum that the first thing you do after contracting an alliance is prepare plans for the day when your ally welshes on you. Just because they're Asiatics it doesn't follow that they're going to invite their yellow fellows into their beds. Nor, because they haven't performed the Peking kotow, should it be assumed (as some blockbottoms I know in Washington have assumed) that they are all set to become the second Isola. Why should they? Things are peachy down in Yatakang; it's among the world's great nations, by Asian standards it's fabulously wealthy, and it can enjoy the game of playing off Washington against Peking until doomsday, on present evidence.

"Until doomsday? Well, perhaps that's a slight exaggeration. There's one bright spot in the generally gloomy picture known as the Pacific Conflict Zone. According to my calculations, by the year 2500 or so we should have killed off every last member of our species who is stupid enough to take part in so futile a pastime as this war between 'ideals', and with luck they won't have left their genes behind because they'll typically have been killed at an age when society thinks they're too young to assume the responsibility of childbearing. And after that we may get some peace and quiet for a change."

—*Better ? than ?* by Chad C. Mulligan

continuity (7)

ARMS AND IDLENESS

Donald felt pitted and pendulumed in the vacant apt. Almost, he could have welcomed the return of Victoria and the need to act as though nothing had happened until Norman programmed the law to pick her up.

He dialled for a meal from the block kitchens, but between ordering it and its arrival his appetite seemed to be eroded by apathy. He put on a recent record he had bought and sat down to watch the play of colour on the screen which matched the music; it had hardly begun before he was on his feet again and tramping restlessly about. None of the TV channels which he checked offered a programme to interest him. A day or two before someone had persuaded him to get a polyforming kit. He opened its box and considered starting a copy of Rodin's *Kiss*, but halted his hand in mid-movement and let the lid fall shut again.

Furious with himself, he stared out the window. The Manhattan-pattern was at its most brilliant at this time of the evening—an Aladdin's Cave of multicoloured lights, gorgeous as the stars at the centre of the galaxy.

Out there: all those millions of people . . . Like looking up at the sky and wondering which of those suns shine on beings like ourselves. Christ: when did I last look up at the night sky?

He was suddenly appalled. These days, a great many

people never left their homes at night except for some specific purpose, when they could call a cab to the door and expose themselves for no longer than it took to cross a sidewalk. It wasn't inevitably dangerous to wander the night streets of the city—the hundreds of thousands who did still do so were proof enough of that. In a country of four hundred millions there were two or three muckers per day, yet some people acted as though they couldn't get past the next corner without being attacked. There were rollings, robberies and rumbles; there were even riots.

But there must still be room, surely, for an ordinary person to go about ordinary business?

The habit had settled on Donald's mind unnoticed, like gradually thickening fog. He had stopped going out after six or seven in the evening for the mere sake of not being at home. Most weekends there was a party; between times, friends of Norman's called or they were invited to join someone for dinner, or a concert, or a freevent. And the cab that came to fetch them was driven by a man or a woman secure behind armoured glass, its doors could only be opened from the dashboard, and affixed to the neat little nozzle of the air-conditioning system was a certificate stating that the sleepy-gas cylinders had been approved by the City Licensing Authority. For all its smoothness and fuel-cell silence, it was like a tank, and encouraged the feeling that one was venturing on to a battlefield.

What do I know any longer about my fellow human beings?

He sensed a recurrence of his panic at lunchtime, and a desperate need to talk to someone to prove that there really were other people in the world, not just puppets on intangible strings. He approached the phone. But that wouldn't do—just conversing with an image on a screen. He wanted to see and hear strangers, to be reassured of their independence from himself.

Breathing hard, he made for the apartment door. At the threshold he checked and returned to his bedroom, to tug open a drawer at the bottom of the built-in closet. Under a pile of disposable paper shirts he found what he was looking for: a Jettigun, the cartridge-charged gas-pistol marketed by

GT under licence from Japanese Industries of Tokyo, and a Karatand.

He debated whether to put it on, turning it over and examining it curiously while reaching his decision because he had never really looked at it since the day he bought it. It was in effect a palmless glove made of impact-sensitive plastic about a quarter-inch thick. Pressed, pinched, drawn on or off the hand, it remained flexible and nearly as soft as good leather. Struck against a resistant surface, its behaviour changed magically, and while the interior stayed soft to act as a cushion against bruising, its outer layer became as rigid as metal.

He thrust his fingers into it and spun around, slamming his fist at the wall. There was a solid thud, and the muscles of his upper arm and shoulder complained, but the Karatand reacted as designed. It was several seconds before he could straighten his fingers against the resistance of the relaxing plastic.

In the box in which he had bought and stored it, there was a leaflet showing with diagrams the various standard ways of employing it: crudely, as he had just done, by balling a fist, or, more delicately, using the side of the palm and the tips of the bunched fingers. He read through the whole text with anxious attention until it suddenly occurred to him that he was behaving precisely as he did not wish to—on the assumption that he was leaving for a mission into enemy territory. He peeled the Karatand off and stuffed it into his pocket along with the Jettigun.

If that phone were to ring, and the Colonel were on the screen activating me, telling me to report for duty at once— this is how I would feel.

And that can't be true. Because if the mere prospect of going out at night caves me in like this, being activated would break me into little pieces.

He shut the door with conscious care and headed for the elevators.

the happening world (6)

"I can't see heaven but I credit hell—
I live in New York so I know it well.
When they shut out heaven with the Fuller Dome
God gave it up and He went home."

ONE WAY NORTHBOUND

"Gotta go dump my passenger—pulled a bolt-gun and I had to doze the bleeder. Dicty, of course. Spotted him right away, but dreck, if I turned down every dicty who wants a ride I'd never get a fare after seven poppa-momma ... So anyhow: I'll be off call until I've sworn out the complaint."

UNDERPASS

Rooms by the hour $3.

"Heard the new one about Teresa?"

ONE WAY WESTBOUND

Licensed panhandler, City of Greater New York. Muldoon Bernard A. No. PH2 428 226.

PEDESTRIANS ONLY

"So I said to him look block I said I've celebrated my twenty-first even if you haven't. I said I didn't treat your daughter like a whore because I never met a freaking whore because they're as obsolete as your idea of a shotgun wedding. I said come to that isn't it better my way than what she's getting up to with that freaking lizzie of a stepmother of hers. He didn't know about that. Took the fuel out of his jets, I do depose!"

ONE WAY SOUTHBOUND

Menu $8.50, $12.50, $17.50.

"Mr. and Mrs. Everywhere hit Times Square yesterday— it'll be crowded."

KEEP TO THE RIGHT

Show nitely—and do we mean SHOW!

ONE WAY EASTBOUND

"Say, I—uh—know my way around the block better than most people. Care I should do you a small favour? Now I have at present just a trifle more Yaginol than I can personally use, and ..."

WAIT

Public lectures daily, demonstrations Wednesday and Friday. Auparishtaka, Sanghataka, Gauyuthika, etc. Coaching by experts. Enrol here any time. Mrs. Grundy Memorial Foundation (may dogs grub up her bones).

"They programmed Shalmaneser with the formula for this stiffener, see, and ..."

WALK

Colossal unbelievable impossible bargains! Store of a million miracles! Cruisers welcome subject to evidence of cash or credit.

DO NOT LOITER

"Attention attention—we have reports of a pseudo cab working the lower East Side, dozing and rolling passengers. Stop and check all cabs vicinity Sixth Street Avenue B."

NO SPITTING

Office space for rent, or would convert to dwelling at client's expense.

"This new homimage attachment is the best I've ever seen."

DOGS FOULING SIDEWALK WILL BE DESTROYED

Psychometrist, clairvoyante, offers guidance to the insecure.

BEWARE OF PICKPOCKETS

"It's like the universe was a hole, catch me? And I'm all spread out thin around the sides, catch me? And then sometimes it's like the room turns inside out and I'm the spots on the six sides of the dice. Or else—ah, why should I bother talking to a block like you?"

RAPID TRANSIT

Municipal ordinance no. 1214/2001. Persons of no fixed abode to register at nearest police station and obtain permits before sleeping rough.

"It trips you further and faster than the Everywheres can manage!"

SANITARY CONVENIENCES

Joe's Joints—N.Y. brands $3 for 10, out-of-state brands $5, $6.

STOMP THAT ROACH! BEWARE OF FIRE!

"Hey codders! Shade and fade—there's a prowlie on the next block!"

DO NOT PLACE NOXIOUS REFUSE IN UNLIDDED RECEPTACLES

> *"What shall we do with our fair city.*
> *Dirty and dangerous, smelly and shitty?*
> *If you're a friend of New York town*
> *You'll find you a hammer and smash it down."*

tracking with closeups (8)

ILL WIND

If I'd guessed it was going to lead to this, Gerry Lindt told himself furiously, *I think I'd have dodged!*

The atmopshere in the apt was like a funeral parlour's, all hushed voices and tiptoeing, as though the stiffly-worded official form propped beside his bed were the symptom of an incurable disease.

It was only a draft notice. Thousands of them must be issued every day, which meant it was a rather ordinary thing. Not, naturally, inevitable—it could be dodged in a great many ways, some legitimate, some dishonest. None of the legitimate ways was open to Gerry: nineteen years old, rather handsome with his fair curly hair and blue eyes, and in perfect physical health. And although he knew all about the alternative methods—one could hardly be nineteen and male and *not* know them—they scared him marginally more than the idea of facing the little red brothers.

Friends of his, whom he had known since he could talk, had cheerfully adopted them: doused themselves in perfume and sat petting with each other in public places to establish homosexuality (though this was a chancy device and might lead to being drafted anyway, with a violent course of aversion therapy as soon as they were under military law); gone out on mugging expeditions and been deliberately clumsy to obtain criminal convictions with the coveted annotation "Anti-social"; left pro-Chinese pamphlets where school or college authorities would be sure to come across them; maimed themselves; or even—and this was what terrified Gerry worst —caught themselves a heavy habit, preferring the risk of being institutionalised to that of being inducted.

So, tomorrow, enter Private Lindt.

He looked around his room. Because it had been his almost all his life, he had grown accustomed to its narrow dimensions; it was half one of the original rooms of the apt, divided when his sister was born. Now he was over six feet tall, though, he could span it on the short axis, and he could foresee that when he came back on furlough he would be dismayed at its tininess.

At the moment it was more cramped than ever, because he had been sorting things from the closet in careful compliance with the instructions on the draft notice: *recruits are required to bring . . .*

But the sorting and packing was all done, and it was still early evening. He listened to the surrounding noises. He could hear the three distinct footfalls of his father, his mother and his sister, moving around, clearing away the supper things, restoring the furniture to its former positions.

I can't stand the idea of spending the whole of this evening in their company. Is that bad? Does it make me an unnatural son? But Sis staring at me with goggling eyes as though measuring me for a coffin because she thinks that block Jamie is God this week and he says only people with suicidal tendencies refuse to dodge the draft—and Mom bravely keeping back the tears so that I feel any moment I'll bust out snivelling too—and Pa . . . Well, if he says to me once more, "Son, I'm proud of you!" I think I'll break his neck.

He took a deep breath and prepared to run the gauntlet.

"Where are you going? Surely you're not going out on your last evening?"

Last evening. The condemned man ate a hearty supper.

"I'm going to wander around the neighbourhood for a bit, say goodbye to a few people. Won't be long."

And made it. Without half as much trouble as I expected.

He was so relieved, it was not until he actually stepped outside the building that he realised he had no clear idea of where he was bound. Stopping in his tracks, he looked about him, savouring the slightly salt freshness of the night breeze which promised to drive away the thin scattering of cloud veiling the sky.

So many things weren't matching the pattern he'd subconsciously expected. Leaving home to be on his own for the first time, so he'd vaguely gathered from hints in novels and TV plays, he should have felt some kind of reinforced attachment to this his childhood home, sensed half-forgotten details stamping themselves on his mind. But a moment ago he'd been thinking that when he next returned he'd be dismayed at the size of his room, and now, out of doors, he was thinking the same as usual: that someone ought to clear all this litter from the roadway, paper, plastic, foil, cans, packs and packages; that it was more than time they repaired the gashed store-front cattycorner across the intersection, where "partisans" had looted a sporting-goods dealer for a supply of weapons; that in general this home of his left a lot to be desired.

Equally misty at the back of his mind had been the idea of a girl to keep him company on this last night before enlistment. He had seldom needed to go to special trouble since he was fifteen to find a shiggy, but his parents were of the older generation—like any parents—and while they had never objected to his staying away all night he had not yet plucked up courage to have a girl in and sleep with him. He had planned to make his declaration of masculinity tonight, when they would feel ashamed to complain. Yet here he was, on his own. All the girls he liked most had sheered off when they learned he was going to let the draft get his balls, and the shock of their unanimous rejection had so thrown him off his gyros he hadn't managed to replace them yet.

Of course, there were places enough where he could be reasonably sure of picking up a shiggy, but that didn't seem appropriate. If what he'd heard was to be relied on, he'd be doing a lot of that during his service, without the option.

No: he needed to call on someone he'd known for a length of time. He thought of his friends one by one, and came to the upsetting conclusion that there was virtually nobody he could trust not to say the same nauseating things as his family.

Except maybe . . .

He clenched his fists. There was one person he could be sure would not utter fulsome and revolting platitudes, whom he had not been to see since deciding he would accept his draft notice because he was unsure of his own ability to resist his persuasive counter-arguments. But now that it was too late to change his mind, it would be interesting, at least, to hear Arthur Golightly's reaction.

Arthur lived, not in a block of apts, but in an early twentieth-century house that had long ago been subdivided to accommodate as many people as it had rooms. It was called "bachelor dwellings" but what it amounted to was a shabby tenement.

Nervously, Gerry pressed the ancient bell and announced himself over the intercom.

"Gerry! Come on up," said a vaguely mechanical voice, and the door swung open.

He encountered Arthur on the first-story landing: a scruffy coloured man in his late thirties, wearing shorts and a pair of loafers. His beard blended without detectable margin into the mat of hair on his chest. Gerry wished the hair continued further down than his solar plexus; he was developing a wobbly pot-belly that could have done with some concealment. However, his display of it was of a piece with his rejection of conformity, and if you objected to that you objected to his total existence.

He was carrying a dish of something white and powdery with a spoon stuck in it, and had to move it from right to left before he could shake Gerry's hand.

"Won't keep you a moment," he apologised. "But Bennie apparently didn't eat anything yet today, and I think I ought to get some sugar down him for energy, if nothing else."

He thrust open one of the doors giving on to the landing, and Gerry had a brief glimpse of a young man, in his middle twenties, stretched out on a chair and wearing even less than Arthur was. He shuddered and walked on to the other end of

the landing, to wait outside Arthur's door and try not to hear
the coaxing words that drifted towards him.

Rotting. Just rotting. What kind of a life is that?

Then the Watch-&-Ward Inc. lock on the downstairs door
clicked open to a key, and he saw a girl coming up the stairs:
her face beautiful, her body shrouded in a street-cloak that
reached below her knees. She was carrying a bag of gro-
ceries. On noticing him she gave him a mechanical smile and
put her hand to Bennie's door-handle.

She stopped while he was still digesting the air of residency
she displayed.

"Does Bennie have someone with him?" she demanded.

"Uh—Arthur went in. Took some sugar." Gerry swallowed
hard.

"That's all right then," the girl said, and twirled off her
cloak. Gerry's breath stopped altogether for a while. Under
the cloak she was wearing a Forlon&Morler housfit of a
type which his sister had once tried to wear around the apt,
only to have her parents put their feet down with shrieks of
horror. It consisted of two long boots of red mesh, supported
with a soft red cord around her waist, and that was that.

Bennie's room opened and Arthur appeared. "Ah—Neek!"
he said with relief. It sounded like "Neek".

"Thanks," the shiggy said. "But not necessary. I'll get him
to eat—he likes my cooking."

"All yours, then," Arthur said with a parodied bow. "You
don't know Gerry, do you? Gerry Lindt—Monique De-
lorne!"

The shiggy gave a preoccupied nod and vanished into
Bennie's room. Arthur dusted his hands and walked past
Gerry to let him into his own.

"That's under control," he said with satisfaction. "Come on
in—come on!"

Gerry complied with a backward glance, but Bennie's door
was shut fast.

Nothing had changed in the cramped space Arthur called
home since his last visit, bar minor details. It was still in
incredible chaos and the smell still suggested decay, as though
the bric-à-brac constituted a domestic garbage pile. That was

part of Arthur too, however; one could scarcely imagine him in any other setting.

For a moment he almost regretted coming. You couldn't expect someone like Arthur to be properly appreciative of anyone else volunteering to defend his chosen way of life. And yet there was something so sickly about the approval expressed by people who *were* appreciative . . .

"The draft got your balls, I hear," Arthur said. "Correct?"

Gerry nodded and swallowed. "I have to report down at Ellay in the morning."

"Goodbye, then," Arthur said briskly. "Well, that's over with. What can I offer you?"

"Ah—what?"

"I said goodbye. Wasn't that why you came around? And having got that out of the way I offered you—well—whatever I can offer you. I believe I have some vodka, and I know I have some pot, and I also have some of this new stuff Triptine that GT's putting out, one of their few justifications for existing. At least, so Bennie tells me. I haven't got around to trying it myself because people of my blood-group are extra susceptible and I'm liable to hitrip for three or four days. So I'll wait for a free weekend. Well?"

"Ah—a drink, maybe."

"Clear yourself a chair, then, and I'll fix it."

Gerry found new places for a box of unlabelled tapes and two used disposable plates and sat down. He looked about him with a sudden urge to fix his surroundings on his memory. The room was a mess because it had so much in it, and Arthur was too impatient to impose a system, but merely shifted whatever was in his way to a new location.

The things that got in his way, however, were endlessly fascinating. Most of them were Asiatic: figurines, ornaments, embroideries, manuscripts in magnificent calligraphy, incense pans, musical instruments, prints of classic paintings. But there were also a wagon-wheel, and an Indian drum, and a silver flute, and uncountable books, and—

"Gerry!"

With a start, he accepted the glass being waved under his nose.

Settling into his own chair, Arthur regarded him contempla-

tively. "Hmmm! I was wrong, wasn't I? We didn't get over
the subject of your departure just by disposing of the good-
byes. It's sunk its teeth right into your veins."

Gerry nodded.

"You surprise me sometimes," Arthur shrugged. "You're
not the adventurous type, yet here you're letting yourself be
ripped out of your cosy regular environment by someone
whose decisions are arbitrary because they're irrational."

"I don't quite catch."

"No? All generals are psychotic. All soldiers are out of
their skulls. Matter of strict psychological fact—they've had
their territoriality stamped on and they can't recover. I hoped
you'd figure this out. Even Bennie did, and you're brighter
than him."

"Would you want me to be *like* Bennie?" Gerry grimaced.
"So he dodged—so what use did he make of the two years he
saved? He'll be dead before he's thirty from the stuff he
keeps pouring down his throat!"

"By his own hand," Arthur said. "You have the right to kill
you. Nobody else does."

"I thought you were in favour of euthanasia."

"Signing the release is the self-directed blow. The rest is
simple mechanics, on a par with waiting for the bath to fill
with blood after you've slashed your wrists."

"But this just isn't adequate," Gerry said doggedly. He felt
the need to justify his decision to someone, and to make
Arthur understand his viewpoint would be a special triumph.
"The fact remains, there are people I owe a debt to, and
there are other people out there willing to take away everything up to and including their lives. The hole! I saw an
example of it just ten minutes ago when I passed the wreck
of Ackleman's—you know, the sporting-goods store across
the way from my home?"

Arthur grinned. "You expect me to display righteous
wrath? I think the guns and ammunition looted from Ackleman's are better off in the hands of people with ideals than
they would have been in the hands of the fat bourgeois slobs
around your district who don't have anything to defend and
would just have let them off nervously at random."

"At random! Christ, wasn't it you who told me about these people who make a hobby of random sabotage?"

"Now don't get confused the way most people do, Gerry. A codder who's taken up sabotage for a hobby isn't on the same footing as someone who loots a gunsmith's for weapons. He strikes out at random because he doesn't know what it is in his environment that's bugging him. Partisans at least have a theory about what's wrong, and a plan to put it right."

"And how long would you last under the kind of government they'd like to impose on us?" Gerry demanded.

"Oh, they'd have me out and shoot me the first day they took charge. Anyone like me is intolerably subversive to an authoritarian régime, because I'm not interested in imposing my ideas by force on other people."

"But a moment ago you were saying no one has a right to take away other people's lives. If they have no right to do it, there can't be anything wrong in trying to stop them."

"Two wrongs," Arthur sighed, suddenly seeming to lose interest in the discussion. "Want to find out what's going to become of you, by the way?"

"What?"

Arthur reached to the floor beside his chair and lifted up a book. He blew the dust off. "Old standby," he said in an affectionate tone. "Haven't used you as much as you deserve lately, have I? You've consulted the Book of Changes before, haven't you?" he added to Gerry.

"Yes. You showed it to me when I first met you." Gerry drained his glass and set it aside. "I told you I thought it was a load of dreck."

"And I told you it works for the same reason there's no such thing as art. I quoted the Balinese who don't have a word for it, but merely try to do everything as well as possible. Life's a continuum. I must have said that to you because I say it to everyone. Did I teach you to use the yarrowstalks?"

"No."

"Then get out three coins, matched if possible. I'd lend you some of mine but I have absolutely no idea where my taels have got to under all this garbage. If my name was

Mary I'd march my lambs through here and they'd bring their taels behind them."

"Arthur, are you orbiting?"

"Descending, descending. This new Too Much strain from Hitrip is—for once and by a miracle—all the advertising claims it to be. Like a pack to take along with you in the morning?"

"I don't believe I'd be allowed to. It says something on the draft notice."

"That figures. One of the standard techniques for breaking a man down into a soldier is to take away the joy that might make him feel life was worth living even for the man on the other end of his gun. Got those coins?"

Choosing three from his pocket, Gerry thought: *I was right to avoid Arthur until it was too late to change my mind. He's so damned certain of his cynical views and I'm not sure about anything—not even about this ancient oracle being a load of dreck.*

The coins tossed, the hexagram drawn, Arthur stared at the result. *"Pi,"* he said, not bothering to consult the book. "With a moving line in the second place. 'What is required is that we unite with others in order that all may complement and aid one another through holding together'—want to read the full version for yourself?"

Gerry laughed and shook his head. "You know what I think of fortunetelling!"

"Yes, I do, and it's a shame you won't take it seriously. Because I don't like what your moving line does to the hexagram. It turns it into *K'an*, doubled—'repetition of danger'. In other words, sparewheel, unless you're very careful you're in trouble."

"I've thought about the risks. I don't need a mystic book to tell me that going into the army can lead to danger."

Arthur ignored the interruption. "Know what I think? I think the moving line goes into effect tomorrow, when you change from uniting with others to exposing yourself to danger."

"But I am 'uniting with others'! Could there be a clearer way of saying 'join the army'—in the context of that book?"

"Oh yes. But no clearer way to say 'stay with your family and friends'."

Gerry rose stiffly to his feet. "I'm sorry, Arthur," he said. "I hoped you'd realise my mind was made up and it was too late to try and argue me out of it."

"Oh, I concede that. I'm only trying to show you what you're doing. Does that make you want to sit down and go on talking?"

"I'm afraid not. I only called to say goodbye. And there are other people I ought to visit before I go to bed."

"As you like. But do me a favour." Arthur began rummaging in a pile of books. "Take this along with you and read it in your spare time—if they allow you any. Don't bother giving it back. I know it more or less by heart."

"Thanks," Gerry took the book he was given and thrust it distractedly into his pocket, not even looking to see what it was called.

"Know something?" Arthur went on. "I have a feeling you need this experience in the army, after all. I only wish the odds against you coming back alive were a bit better."

"The way things are set up now, casualties are very low! Why, they haven't lost more than—"

"There are some people," Arthur interrupted, "more likely than others to do everything, including succeed and fail. You're the type to refuse disillusionment. You're likely to go on looking for the—the glory, whatever—that accounts for men wanting to risk their lives in battle, and you won't have found it so you'll volunteer for some idiotic mission and kick those odds up to a thousand to one against you, and . . ." He turned over his hand as though spilling a pile of sand from the palm.

Gerry stood rock-still for a long moment; then, abruptly, he tugged open the door and went out.

As he passed Bennie Noakes's room, he heard faint noises: a creak, a sigh, a chuckle.

Rotting himself to death with all that dreck he takes! And he's got that shiggy, that beautiful shiggy, and I've got . . .

In that instant he knew he could not disbelieve Arthur's prophecy about his fate.

It couldn't be Boot Camp. It had to be Boat Camp. It was on pontoons isolated from the shore by a mile of water. That hadn't stopped desertions, but it did mean that only the strongest swimmers reached the beach.

There, at long tables, the new recruits had to strip naked and turn out their pockets. A captain accompanied by a top sergeant walked slowly down the far side of each table examining everything, while another sergeant made certain the trembling draftees stood still or *else*. The captain stopped opposite Gerry and turned around the book Arthur had given him so that he could read the title.

"*The Hipcrime Vocab*," the captain said. "Put him under arrest, sergeant—possession of subversive literature."

"But—!" Gerry exploded.

"Fasten it, soldier, or there'll be another charge along with that."

Gerry bit back his fury. "Permission to speak, *sir*," he said formally.

"Granted."

"I've never even opened the book, sir. Somebody gave it to me last night and I just left it in my pocket and—"

"It's been read and re-read until the pages are practically falling out," the captain said. "Add one, sergeant—lying to an officer."

They let him off lightly with twenty-four hours' punishment drill.

As the captain deigned to remark, it was, after all, a first offence.

continuity (8)

THE CAMEL'S BACK

It was almost a shock to Donald to discover how normal the night-time city appeared. It was less crowded than by day because of the phobia he himself had fallen victim to, but that was actively pleasant and made him feel he had gone back in time to the days when he was fresh from college and there had been a million fewer bodies to jostle against on the sidewalk.

Did I not expect the same stores to be in the same places as by day?

He wanted to laugh aloud at his own forebodings. Nonetheless, something was strange. By degrees his mind edged towards recognition of it; it was the kind of problem he was good at, working from hint to clue without having to give the matter his entire attention.

The night was loud. Music came from everywhere, mostly hits from the current popparade in which two or even three disparate rhythms clashed randomly on semitonal discords but sometimes classical—in a hundred yards he identified Beethoven, Berg, Oyaka. That, however, was true of the day as well, especially since the makers of radio-dresslets had begun to fit speakers to their garments instead of phones.

What did strike him as unusual was the sound of talking. Everywhere he heard people gossiping, a luxury for which the day allowed no time.

Hint: these people know each other, say hullo.

Anonymous to him but acquainted among themselves, they grouped in little knots of four or five all over the sidewalks. He had half-assumed they were street-sleepers, until he realised that even by modern standards there were too many of them and began to spot the genuine article: sad-eyed men and women—and children too—clinging to their bags of belongings, waiting for midnight and the legal chance to lie down wherever space presented itself.

"Are you weary, are you heavy-laden? Come to Jesus, come and rest in his bosom!" A woman minister on the steps of a store-front church, addressing the passers-by through a hand shouter.

"No thanks, *madam,* I fly a straight-type orbit!" yelled a passing yonderboy, and his sparewheels screeched laughter and clapped him on the back. The yonderboy was Afram and so was the minister. The proportion of Aframs in view was five or six times higher than by day.

They look at me with curiosity. Is colour a clue?

But that was a false lead. Bit by bit he pinned down the true reason. He was dressed in the conservative, slightly behind-the-style clothes he generally wore. Most of the people he passed either were shabby, like the street-sleepers, who often as not wore disposables meant for one wearing, kept on for ten, or had taken the fall of darkness as a signal to let their imaginations run riot. Not only the yonderboys with their fantastical puffed shirjacks designed to give the impression of enormous muscles, but the older folk too were gaudy as peacocks in scarlet and turquoise, ebony and chrome. They strutted in everything from RUNG-type robes to a coat of paint and a few strategic feathers.

Answer: it feels like a foreign country.

He gave a thoughtful nod. There was a Caribbean mood in these people's casual employment of the street as an extension of their homes. It must have been triggered by the erection of the dome, building on and amplifying the high-summer tradition and extending it throughout the year.

The character of the neighbourhood began to change. He found himself being accosted by shills.

"White noise concert in progress, codder! Only a fin!"

"Excerpts from the Koran in English, live reading, sure to be of interest to an intelligent person such as yourself!"

"Hear the truth which the government screens from you! Recording direct from Peking giving all the facts!"

When he had gone a mile or more the grins and gestures of people he passed led him to discover a small luminescent poster attached unfelt to his back. Annoyed, he removed and read it.

This codder doesn't know where to. On Triptine he'd be there before he had time to worry.

A GT promotion? Hardly. It was notorious that the government discouraged excessive zeal by the Nark Force, because psychedelics drained away so much potential subversion, but there were still—officially—laws in most states. He balled it up and threw it at a trashcan.

A lean, rather scholarly-looking Afram fell in beside him and kept tossing him sidelong glances. When they had gone a score of paces together he cleared his throat.

"Weren't you at—?"

"No," Donald said. "Spit the string and I'll tell you if I'm interested, which'll save your time and mine."

The Afram blinked. After another few strides he shrugged. "No complaints about that, Father?"

"No."

"Want your genotype read? Show me your palms. A fin gets you a strict scientific commentary—I have certificates."

"Thanks, I can afford genalysis."

"But no prodgies, hm?" The Afram looked wise. "Could be the trouble is with the Eugenics Board—no, don't tell me. However bad it is there are ways to fix it. I have certain contacts, and if you can afford genalysis you can probably afford their services."

"I'm clean," Donald said with a sigh.

The Afram stopped dead. Involuntarily Donald did the same and turned so they were facing each other.

"You son of a bleeder," the Afram said. "Here all I'm carrying is sickle-cell anaemia which in the malarial belt is actually advantageous, and they won't let *me* though I've been married three times."

"So why don't you try the malarial countries?" Donald snapped. He slipped his hand into the pocket containing the Jettigun.

"A typical paleass remark!" the Afram sneered. "Why don't you go back to Europe, then?"

Abruptly Donald's annoyance faded. He said, "Look, cousin, you should meet my roomie and learn better. He's Afram too."

"You I don't mind about," the Afram said. "The fewer of you who fly straight orbits the better. But it's a thing to weep about, you having a brown-nose roomie. Another generation, you'll have melanin-high skin on the list of disallowed genes!"

He spat deliberately an inch from Donald's feet and spun on his heel.

Depressed by the encounter, Donald walked on. He was barely aware of the distance he covered. Occasional stimuli made an impact on him—the banshee wail of a prowlie's siren, children fighting over an insult, the ever-present music—but he was preoccupied.

The Afram's reference to the malarial countries had sparked a train of thought, bringing back to mind what Norman had said earlier about Beninia. As ever, his computer-active subconscious had been stirring his information into new patterns.

State would want to know why Elihu Masters was making an approach to GT. Assumption: State does know why. If either the Dahomalians or the RUNGs persuade Beninia to federate, the disappointed party will have to fight or lose face. The only things that can prevent war are (a) President Obomi, who isn't immortal, and (b) the intervention of an outside force they could join in railing against. In which case—!

He had it, all of a sudden. Three hours' reading, five days a week bar vacation for ten years, had stocked his memory with all the information necessary to envisage the plan as it had to be.

But in the very instant it came to him, the knowledge was kicked to the back of his mind. Stopping dead, he wondered where in the name of God he was.

By the street-signs he had reached the lower East Side, an

area presently at the bottom of the cycle of death and renewal that sometimes made the city seem like an organism. At the end of last century there had been a brief moment of glory here; decade by decade the would-be connectors had followed the intellectuals and the pseudos eastwards from the Village into the ruined area close to the river, until by 1990 or so this had been a high-price zone. But the wheel turned further, and the bored and prosperous moved out. Now the grace of the elegant buildings was crumbling again under a bright masking of advertisements: *flagging vigour calls for Potengel, MasQ-Lines take the world in their stride, ask the man who's married to Mary Jane* ... Across the display slanted the unrelated diagonals of fire-escapes, spotted with piles of garbage like forest fungi.

Donald turned slowly around. There were fewer people on the streets here. The very air breathed a sense of decay. Only a few minutes' walk away was the brilliance and activity he had left behind without noticing, so it was small wonder the residents preferred not to spend their time here. The stores were closed except for the few that could afford automated pay-out clerks, and those were almost vacant of customers. There was no silence—there was no silent place in the city—but every sound which came to his ears seemed to be distant: not in that building but the next, not on this street but a block away.

Facing him now was one of the luxuries the architects had included when they worked this district over twenty years ago—an adventure playground elaborated into the gap between two tall buildings, a monkey-puzzle in three dimensions calculated so that a careless child could fall no further than one short level. For a moment his mind refused to accept the connection between the lines and forms he saw, and anything with solidity. Then the perspective separating near from far enabled him to grasp the image and he realised he was looking at a sort of Riemann ladder of concrete and steel silhouetted from behind by the last of the unbroken lamps on the struts.

Something moved among the frightful artificial branches. Donald, uncertain whether it was human, eased his hand into his pocket and began to wriggle his Karatand over his fingers.

The monstrous creature loomed, incredibly flexible, down the lip of a miniaturised precipice, and took on reality—a shadow, cast by a child passing in front of the surviving lamp.

Donald let out a great gasp of relief. The idea occurred to him that he must have been slipped a psychedelic, and then, when he discounted actual ingestion, he found himself wondering if perhaps the air was charged with the fumes of some drug affecting his perceptions.

Mechanically tugging the Karatand towards his wrist, he beat a retreat towards his own manor.

Unexpectedly, because this was not a cab-hiring district, he spotted a cruising taxi within a hundred yards. He called to the driver, who acknowledged him with a wave shadowed on the windshield.

Purring, the vehicle drew level with him. He made to get in as the driver activated the hydraulic door-controls.

Not so fast.

The words were as clear in his mind as if someone had spoken them from inside the passenger compartment. He delayed removing his hand from the door-pillar and looked for anything which might have alarmed him.

Probably imagination. I'm jumpy enough—

But no. Affixed to the air-conditioning nozzles was a device that automatically sent a radio signal to police headquarters if the driver dozed a passenger. It had been tampered with; the plastic seal certifying its annual inspection had discoloured to a warning red. He'd hailed a pseudo, one of the cabs whose drivers dozed their victims illegally and took them to be robbed in a dark side-street.

The door slammed. But not all the way. Even with the force of the hydraulics behind it, it could not crush the impact-sensitive Karatand which Donald had left in its way. There was a clang of hammered metal and a jar that travelled clear to his elbow, but he retained enough presence of mind not to snatch back his hand.

By law, these cabs were designed so that they could not be

driven away unless the doors were closed. But Donald's strength was inadequate to force his way out.

Impasse.

Behind the armour-glass of his cabin, the driver hit the door-controls again and again. The door slammed back and forth, but the Karatand endured. Suddenly very calm, Donald stared at the driver, but the man was too wary to let his face be seen even in the rear-view mirror. It was twisted to the side so that it covered his licence photograph, and its function had been taken over by a miniature TV unit.

What am I going to do now?

"All right, Shalmaneser!"

The voice made him start as it boomed from the speaker set in the roof.

"I'll open up, you hit the sidewalk and we'll say no more about it, how's that?"

"No," Donald said, surprised at his own determination.

"You can't get out unless I let you."

"You can't drive off unless I let you."

"Hoping for a prowlie to come by, hm? Fuzzy-wuzzies don't pass this way if they can help!"

"Somebody's going to notice a cab with the hire sign lit sitting in the middle of the street and not moving."

"Who said it was lit?"

"You can't turn it off without you close the door!"

"Think not? I cut out the police alarm, didn't I?"

"And it shows—you turned the seal red."

"You're the first in two weeks noticed that. Last one I chopped the fingers off."

Donald licked his lips and eyed the adjacent sidewalks. Although this district was comparatively empty, it was not wholly unpopulated. An old Afram woman was this very moment approaching. He leaned to the gap in the door and called out.

"Lady! Fetch the police! This cab's a pseudo!"

The old woman stared at him, crossed herself, and hurried by.

The driver gave a sour laugh. "You don't know what it's like around here, do you, Shalmaneser? Got left out of your programming!"

Donald's heart sank. He was on the point of admitting defeat and offering to hit the sidewalk, when a movement at the corner of the street attracted him.

"You said prowlies don't come this way," he exclaimed.

"Right."

"Then how about that one closing from behind?"

The driver stared at his TV unit, dismayed.

Does he think I'm bluffing? That's no bluff—it's a hundred per cent genuine prowl car!

Armoured, armed with gas and flame, the police car pussy-footed towards the stationary cab. The driver sounded his move-along siren.

"Take your hand off the pillar," the hackie said. "I'll balance the deal for you. What you want? I have contacts—Skulbustium, Yaginol, shiggies, name it and I'll fix it."

"No," Donald said again, this time triumphantly.

He could see the silhouettes of the men in the prowlie now. Also, by this time, half a dozen people had gathered on the sidewalk. A couple of them were teen-age Aframs, who shouted something indistinct at the police and doubled up in laughter.

The door of the prowlie opened, and Donald relaxed. A matter of seconds now—

Except that the moment the fuzzy-wuzzy stood up on the street, a hail of garbage pelted him from nowhere. He yelled a curse, hauled out his bolt-gun and sent a shot high into the darkness towards the adventure playground. Someone screamed. The standers-by dived for cover. The driver piled out of Donald's cab and the policeman loosed another shot at him but missed. A whole can of garbage came slamming down from a higher level now, contents first, then can, squelch, then *crash*. Another policeman leaned out of the car and fired at the approximate source of the attack.

Belatedly aware that the door was no longer pressing on his hand, Donald scrambled out, shouting for the police to stop wasting their shots and go after the hackie. The man peering from the prowlie's window saw him only as a human shape and fired at him. The hiss of the bolt searing past his ear made him gulp and stumble for the sidewalk.

A hand reached up from the protection of a stoop and

caught his ankle. The gesture might have been friendly but Donald could not tell. He tore his Jettigun from his pocket and fired it into the face of the man who had clutched at him.

A scream. A girl's voice: "You do that to my brothah—!" Windows flinging open both sides of the street. Shouting kids, emerging from the senseless shadows of the adventure playground, delighted at the excitement and starting to hurl down whatever came handy—fragments of split concrete, cans and packages, plant-tubs. A dark, pretty face transformed by fury. The erratic brilliance of gun-bolts as the police fired wildly. Someone uttering a resonant Spanish curse: "May that lover of he-goats catch the clap and the pox!"

He struck out at the girl who was trying to claw his face, and remembered his Karatand too late. The metal-rigid glove slammed into her mouth and sent her moaning and bleeding into the middle of the street, into the fierce lights of the prowl car. The red trickling down her chin was brilliant as fire.

"Kill the bleeders!"

Where did they all come from?

Suddenly the street was alive, like an overturned ants' nest, doors and passages vomiting people. Metal bars glinted, throats shrieked animal fury, windows shattered and glass rained slashingly on heads below. The prowlie's siren added to the din and the two policemen who had ventured out climbed back in a second ahead of another salvo of garbage. Between the prowlie and the cab the injured girl rocked on her heels, moaned, dripped blood from her cut lip down her shimmering green dresslet. Donald shrank back into an embrasure decorating the wall of the nearest building, overlooked because the late arrivals had taken it for granted the police were responsible for the girl's crying.

The prowlie tried to back up. Through its still-open window Donald heard its occupants shouting to headquarters for aid. A flame-gun belched at the base of a lamp-post and metal ran like lard in a pan. The post fell across the back of the prowlie and blocked its retreat. Yelling joyfully, scores of people ran to develop the improvised barricade into something more substantial. A can of oil was flung down and the flame-gun ignited it. Capering like dervishes, youths and girls taunted the police by its light. Someone scored a hit on the car's left headlamp with a rock and it shattered. Too late the driver remembered to wind up the wire-mesh screens. Another scream of triumph and another rock, making the car's roof boom like a steel drum. Paint chipped and fragments flew, one of them taking a stander-by in the eye so that he covered his face with both hands and shouted that he was blind.

That settled matters.

"Oh my God," Donald said, and it was more of a prayer than he had uttered since he was a schoolchild. "It's going to be a riot. It's going—to be—a *riot* . . . !"

context (9)

"People who feel the need to foul up their perceptions with hop or Yaginol or Skulbustium simply aren't turned on to the essential truth that the real world can always be identified by its unique characteristic: it, and it only, can take us completely by surprise.

"Take two lumps of greyish metal and bring them together. Result: one wrecked city.

"Could anyone have predicted or envisaged that until they knew enough about the real world to calculate the properties of a substance called Uranium-235?

"People are going around marvelling at the fact that there's a solid scientific basis for palmistry. Anybody with a grain of intelligence could have said, directly the notion of the genetic code was formulated, that there was no *a priori* reason why the pattern of the folds in the palm should not be related to a person's temperament by way of an association of genes sharing the same chromosome. Indeed, there were all kinds of reasons for assuming this actually was so, because we aren't totally stupid—as I've pointed out before—and unless there was in palmistry some element of relevance to real experience we'd have given it up and gone chasing some other will-o'-the-wisp. There's no shortage of them.

"But it took forty years for someone to conduct a properly rigorous study of the subject and demonstrate that the suspicion was well-founded. This I do find remarkable—or disheartening might be a better word.

"All right: what should you be surprised at, these days?

"The fact that, having learned so much about ourselves—the designs on our palms being just one example of the way we've analysed ourselves down to the constituent molecules, so that we can claim to be in sight of the day when we won't merely be able to ensure the sex of our offspring (if we can afford the fee) but also to choose whether we'll have a math genius in the family, or a musician, or a moron (some people might like to breed a moron for a pet, I guess . . .)—having got to this state, then, we know less about our reactions in the mass than we do about the behaviour of non-human things like a lump of U-235.

"Or maybe it's not so amazing. Without being *totally* stupid, we do display a tremendous aptitude for it."

—*You: Beast* by Chad C. Mulligan

(HISTORY   Papa Hegel he say that all we learn from history is that we learn nothing from history. *I* know people who can't even learn from what happened this morning. Hegel must have been taking the long view.

—*The Hipcrime Vocab* by Chad C. Mulligan)

tracking with closeups (9)

POPPYSEED

Was this really a drab corner of the world, or was it only apparently drab because she was back from orbit? To a place like this one had to come walking firm and heavy on one's own two feet, just in case when they did the analyses they thought to check for what was usually there, but according to people who should know the end-products should be flushed out by a thirty-six hour abstinence, which was freefalling.

But it made one so easily bored.

Detail by detail: the plastic walls, of a faded yellow; the windows turned to part-opaque because the sun was shining on the far side of them; various posters displayed in frames, setting forth miscellaneous regulations you were supposed to comply with; benches apparently designed to make the users uncomfortable so that persons of no fixed abode would not care to keep returning on pointless visits for the sake of a seat and a little warmth; and everywhere the smell of staleness, of dust and ancient paper and old shoes.

The only touch in the place which suggested nature was in the floor, covered by tiles with a design of dead leaves embedded under a clear plastic surface. But even that was a failure, for when one looked directly down at the tiles one noticed the way the pattern repeated, and if one looked obliquely, the leaves disappeared behind a mist of scratches and scrapes, the legacy of uncountable feet that had crossed the room, and all one could see was a generally dung-brown expanse.

"Not much longer."

"Better not be."

The other people waiting glanced up, the fact of speech being a distraction and a stimulus. They were all women, from twenty to fifty, and all further advanced than Poppy, some with their bellies protruding far on to their laps, others as yet barely showing a roundness. These latter would presumably have come to hear the result of their karyotypings. Poppy shuddered at the idea of having fluid from her womb drawn off through a needle, and wondered how many of these women would have to be officially emptied of their offspring.

As though to enter the protective aura of her femininity, being the only man present, Roger crowded close and put his arm around her shoulders. She reached up to stroke his hand and smiled sidelong at him.

She was a strikingly lovely girl, even dressed as usual in three-quarter puffed slax that needed laundering and a shapeless bluzette meant to fit a much bigger woman. She had a fine-boned oval face highlighted with big dark eyes and framed with black braids, and just enough tawny admixture to her complexion to make her seem feral. And, as yet, her pregnancy had done nothing except improve the line of her bust.

She giggled at a private thought, and Roger squeezed her with his encircling arm.

"Miss Shelton," said a disembodied voice. "And—ah—Mr. Gawen!"

"That's us," Roger said, and rose to his feet.

Through the door which opened for them on their approach they found a tired-faced man of early middle age seated at a table beneath a picture of the King and Queen and their two—count them, a responsible number, *two*—children. Ranked before him were piles of forms and a number of sterile-sealed containers with spaces on the lids for writing names and numbers.

"Sit down," he said, hardly looking at them. "You're Miss Poppy Shelton?"

Poppy nodded.

"And—ah—how long?"

"What?"

"How long since you became pregnant?"

"My doctor says about six weeks. I went to him when I missed my period and he told me to come along here as soon as I was sure it wasn't irregularity."

"I see." The man behind the table wrote on a form. "And you're the father, are you, Mr. Gawen?"

"If Poppy says so, yes, I am."

The man gave Roger a sharp glare as though suspecting levity. "Hah! Well, it always helps to have the putative father turn up. These days one can't rely on it, of course. And you want it to go to term, Miss Shelton?"

"What?"

"You actually want to bear the child?"

"Of course I do!"

"There's no 'of course' about it. Most of the women who come in here arrive armed with everything they can think of in the hope of being granted an abortion—lists of diseases they caught as children, the story of how grandma became senile after her hundredth birthday, or some specious bit of string tied to a child on the next block who's rumoured to have German measles. Are you getting married?"

"Is that required by law, too?" Poppy snapped.

"No, unfortunately. And I don't like your tone, young woman. The things that are—as you put it—'required by law' are a simple matter of human ecology. With almost a hundred million people in this overcrowded island of ours, it would make very little sense to continue wasting our resources both material and human on such pointless undertakings as training phocomeli or cleaning up after morons. All the advanced countries of the world have come around to this point of view now, and if you want to evade the legal restrictions on child-bearing you'll have to go to a country that can't afford decent medical care for you anyway. Here at least you're assured that your child will on the one hand have no hereditary disabilities and on the other enjoy adequate protection from pre- and post-natal risks. What you make of the child after it's born is up to you."

Poppy giggled again, and Roger clamped his hand on her arm to shut her up.

"If the lecture's over . . . ?" he hinted.

The man shrugged. "All right. Did your doctor tell you what you were to bring with you?"

Roger unloaded containers from the sagging pockets of his shirtjack. "Urine samples—hers and mine. Semen sample in this plastic envelope. Nail parings, hair clippings, saliva and nasal mucus, all here."

"Good." But the man didn't sound pleased. "Stretch out your hand, Miss Shelton."

"Does it hurt?"

"Yes."

He jabbed at the back of her finger with a needle, squeezed out a drop of blood, adsorbed it on a sheet of filter paper and placed it in a labelled envelope.

"And you, Mr. Gawen."

The process repeated, he leaned back in his chair. "That's all for today, then. If there's no immediately apparent hereditary defect you'll be allowed to continue the pregnancy until the thirteenth week when you must present yourself at a hospital for karyotyping. You'll be notified in about three days. Good morning."

Poppy lingered. "What happens if it's disallowed?" she said after a moment.

"Depends. If it's because of something you're carrying, abortion and sterilisation. If it's because of something he's carrying that you contribute a recessive to, abortion and orders not to start another one together."

"And if I don't turn up to have it aborted?"

"You get want-listed, arrested if you're caught, and jailed. In any case, no hospital in the country will accept you in its maternity unit, no midwife will attend you, and if the child is born deformed it will be institutionalised." The man relented a little. "It probably sounds harsh, doesn't it? But I'm afraid it's part of the burden of responsibility towards the next generation that we in the present day have had to accept."

Poppy giggled once more and Roger, flushing with embarrassment, led her out.

On the street, she flung her arms around him and jumped up and down.

"Roger, we're going to make it, we're going to make it!"

"I hope so," he said with less enthusiasm.

"Oh, you're an old pessimist. Must be because you're down on the surface. Got anything with you?"

"I have some Skulbustium gum. But isn't that one of the things you're supposed to avoid?"

"No, the doc said it was only Yaginol that was likely to harm the kid."

"You sure?"

"Absolutely. I asked him specially and that's what he told me."

"Okay, then."

He extracted the pack from his pocket and together they chomped on the vaguely aniseed-flavoured chicle lumps, waiting for the lift to catch them. They stared at their surroundings in search of clues. At the far end of the grimy London street barriers had been erected with big signs on them stating that the road was closed for development; as at many places in the metropolis the plan was to build over the original roadway and leave only pedestrian passages.

Bit by bit the red and white poles of the barriers began to seem like the stems of exotic plants, the red in particular glowing hot as fire. The memory of the drab official waiting-room, of the unpleasant bureaucrat who had interviewed them, receded into a dream-like distant past. Poppy, one hand on her belly to bless the miracle taking place there with a willed contact, grew round-eyed in awe.

"He's going to see this world, isn't he?" she whispered. "Not that one—not that shit-floored dingy horrible kind of world, but a beautiful place that never stops being exciting. Roger, which of the lifters comes out in the milk? I've got to make sure he never sees the ugly world at all!"

"We'll have to ask the doc," Roger said. His face had

settled into an expression of tranquil certainty. "The doc's helped lots of others besides us and he's bound to know."

He took her hand and they walked, the only two real people in the universe, down a street paved with jewels toward a land of love.

context (10)

THE BABY AND THE BATHWATER

"All right, I'll grant you that it's ridiculous to spend years training highly-qualified medical personnel and psychologists and so on and then set them to a job that's going to show no tangible results because the material they're working with is hopeless from the beginning, like imbeciles. I'll even concede the bit about such people having a nasty power complex and liking to lord it over helpless human vegetables, though that's something I really need to be convinced about before I'll swallow it entirely. And I certainly won't contest the fact that there *are* too many of us—the news is evidence enough for me, what with all these famines they're having in Asia and plague still cropping up in Latin America and the development of this seasonal nomadism in Africa because half the year the land won't support the people who are on it. All this I'm giving you without argument.

"But are we adopting the *right* measures to cope? Look at haemophilia, for example; it didn't stop victims of it being the crowned heads of Europe, and most of them showed up pretty well compared to some of the right bleeders who'd kept their thrones warm before the gene put in an appearance. You're not going to tell me that Henry VIII of England or Ivan the Terrible was a descendant of Queen Victoria. Or take the way some of the states have banned people with web-fingers and web-toes; you'll find plenty of doctors to argue that's no more than an adaptation that got started in the days when men were beach-creatures inhabiting swamps and shallows and living mostly off weed and shell-fish.

"And how about schizophrenia? They're still trying to settle it for sure whether the chemical symptoms are due to a stress reaction or whether they're innate and some people are merely more prone to it but can be kept safe in the correct environment. *I* don't believe there's a genuine hereditary effect at all—I think it's just that we tend to copy the behaviour-patterns of our family, and it's one of these in-group extended responses like infanticide being higher among the children and grandchildren of bad, affectionless families regardless of their genotype. You have schizoid-prone parents, you learn the action pattern, and that's that.

"And how about diabetes? It's crippling, admittedly, and you have to lean on a chemical crutch. But—well, my own name's Drinkwater, which almost certainly means that some of my ancestors, like French people named Boileau and Germans named Trinkwasser, must have been hereditary diabetic polydipsomaniacs.

"And if there'd been eugenic legislation back in the days when people were adopting surnames, they'd have been forbidden to have children and I wouldn't be here now.

"Don't you understand? *I wouldn't be here!*"

continuity (9)

DIVIDED AGAINST ITSELF

Like the monstrous shaped negative-plate of an explosive forming press the environment clamped itself on the personality of Donald Hogan, as a hand clenched around a lump of putty will leave the ridges between fingers, the imprint of the cuticular pattern. He felt his individuality squirt away from him into the darkness, carrying off in solution his power to conceive and act on decisions, reducing him to a reactive husk at the mercy of external events.

Some social theorists had argued that urban man was now at the point of unstable equilibrium; the camel's back of his rationality was vulnerable to a straw. Gadarene swine rooting and grunting at the top of a hill overlooking the sea, people sensed this, said the theorists, and therefore when there was an option to do otherwise they did not venture to crowd themselves still further into the already crammed cities. In countries such as India there was no alternative; starvation was slower in an urban community because people were closer to the distribution points for subsistence rations, and mere lethargy induced by hunger reduced friction and outbursts of violence to a sporadic level. But comparatively well-nourished American and European populations might be tipped over the precipice with no more warning than the sort of aura of irritability for which one carried a pack of tranks.

The last coherent thought Donald was capable of formulating declared that it was one thing to have read of this risk, another altogether to watch it being proved real.

Then the world took over and he was lost.

FOCUS: the prowlie. White-painted, trapezoidal vehicle thirteen feet long by seven wide, its wheels out of sight underneath for protection against shots, dispersed around the flat slab tank of the fuel-cell powering it, its forward cabin for four men windowed with armour-glass and additionally screened with retractable wire grilles, its rear section designed for carrying off arrestees and if necessary the injured having a solid metal drop-down tailgate with stretcher rails and a sleepy-gas air-circulation system. On the nose, two brilliant white lights with a field of 150°, one extinguished because the driver had waited too long to roll up the wire screen and protect it; on each corner of the roof other lights with adjustable beam-spread; revolving in a small turret on the roof, a gas-gun shooting fragmenting glass grenades to a distance of sixty yards; under the skirt, for ultimate emergency use only, oil-jets that could flood the adjacent street with a small sea of fire to keep back attackers while the occupants waited out the period till help arrived, breathing through masks from a stored-air system. It was vulnerable to mines, to three successive hand-gun bolts striking within about two inches of each other on the shell, or to the collapse of a building, but to nothing else encountered during an average urban riot. However, its fuel-cell was inadequate to push out of the way either the stationary cab ahead, whose brakes were automatically set because its door was open, or the lamp-post dropped across its stern, which had now been wedged in position with much sweating and swearing against its own stump on the one side, and a well-anchored mailbox on the other.

FOREGROUND: materialised as though from air, crowding the sidewalk, scores—hundreds—of people, mostly Afram, some Puerto Rican, some WASP. One girl with an electronic accordion, fantastically loud at maximum volume, making windows rattle and eardrums hum, shrieking a song through a shouter which others took up and stamped to the rhythm of: *"What shall we do with our fair city, dirty and danger-ous, smelly and shitty?"* Clang on the body of the prowlie whatever they could find to throw—lumps of concrete, gar-bage, bottles, cans. How long before the gas-gun and the flaming oil?

SETTING: the uniform twelve-storey faces of the buildings, each occupying a block or half a block, hardly punctuated by the canyon streets because the abandonment of cars within the city meant that a one-way lane for the use of official vehicles or cabs was enough. Buses ran only to the next corner left, two corners away right. The sidewalks were defined by four-inch concrete barriers, small enough to step over, high enough to prevent any legally passing vehicle from running into a pedestrian. On the face of almost every building, some sort of advertising display, so that spectators in upper rooms looked out of shabby oceans, the middle of a letter O, or the crotch of a receptive girl. A single exception to the cliff-wall nature of the street was formed by the adventure playground, like the intrusion of Einstein into the ordered world of Euclid.

DETAIL: the face of the building against which he cow-ered, opposite the playground, was ornamented more than the average of its neighbours, possessing both a broad stoop above street-level for access to the interior and a number of integral buttresses, flat-faced, arranged in pairs with a gap of about two feet between each, tapering from a thickness of two feet at the bottom to nothing at the level of the fourth floor. One of these embrasures sufficed to shield him from light, the passing and re-passing rioters, and the hurling of improvised missiles. Clanging of metal above made him look up. Someone was trying to get the retractable fire-escapes to angle outwards from the wall instead of straight down, so that from their vantage point things could be dropped on the roof of the trapped prowlie.

Fsst-crack. Fsst-crack. Whir-fsst-crack.
Gas-gun.
Grenades smashing against the walls of the buildings, each releasing a quart of sluggish vapour that oozed down into the narrow culvert of the street. The first victims coughed, howled

and keeled over, having sucked in a full concentrated
dose, and those lucky enough to be out of range of the first
salvo ducked to the ground and hustled away crouching.

Fsst-crack. Whir-fsst-crack.

The girl whose mouth he had cut was staggering away
from the middle of the street, coming towards him. Possessed
of some vague impulse to help, Donald emerged from the
shelter of the embrasure between the buttresses and called to
her. She came because she heard a friendly voice, not seeing
who spoke, and a clubbed arm slammed at the back of his
left shoulder. From the corner of his eye he saw the hand
was Afram. He ducked, dodged. The gas-gun crashed grenades on this side of the street now, and the first whiffs made
breathing hateful. Those who had evaded gassing so far were
taking to the skeletal branches of the playground like archetypal proto-man eluding a pack of wolves. The girl saw
her brother, who had hit Donald, and together they hurried
to the corner of the street, forgetting him. He followed
because everyone was going away in one direction or another.

At the corner: late arrivals following a group of yonderboys who had equipped themselves with sticks and big empty
cans to make drums of, and howling with joy on seeing the
stuck prowlie.

"Gas!"

The shouting faltered. There was a store across the road
which had been open under automated supervision; the owner or manager had turned up and was hastily slamming the
wire grilles over the display windows and the entrance, trap-
ping three customers who seemed relieved rather than annoyed. An anonymous hand flung a rock through the last
exposed window, which happened to have a liquor stand
behind it. Cans and bottles thundered down, a heap of the
former jammed the grille before it could rise and lock in
place, and several of the crowd decided that was a better
target than the prowlie.

Overhead a roaring noise. One of the tiny one-man copters
capable of being manoeuvred between the tops of the high
buildings and the Fuller Dome whose blushing underside
formed Manhattan's sky was scouting the scene to notify

police headquarters of the extent of the disturbance. From a skylight somewhere away to the right there came a bang—an old-fashioned sporting gun. The copter wobbled and came down into the middle of the street, vanes screaming as the pilot fought for altitude. Mad with delight at having a fuzzy-wuzzy delivered into their hands the crowd went forward to greet him with clubs.

Donald fled.

On the next corner he found riot containment procedure already under way. Two water-trucks with hoses going were methodically washing people off the sidewalks into doorways. He turned at hazard in the opposite direction and shortly encountered sweep-trucks, paddywagons adapted with big snowplough-like arms on either side, serving the same purpose as the hoses but much less gentle. Keeping the crowd on the move was supposed to take away the chance of their organising into coherent resistance. Also another one-man copter droned down and started shedding gas-grenades into the street.

He was one of about fifty people being hustled and driven ahead of the official vehicles because they were off their own manor and had no place to go. He worked his way towards the wall of the building because some people, he saw, were dodging into hallways and vanishing, but at the first door he came close enough to to stand a fair chance of entering there were two Aframs armed with clubs who said, "You don't live here, WASP—blast off before you get stung."

At an intersection two hose-trucks and the sweep-truck he was running from coincided. A mass of people from all three streets was shoved into the fourth, taking them back towards the focus of the trouble. Now they were body to body, stumbling on each other's heels and shrieking.

The prowlie was still stuck where it had been. Its driver sounded a blast of welcome to his colleagues in the sweep-truck. The gas had mostly dispersed, leaving victims choking and vomiting, but there was no end in sight to the riot. On the concrete arms of the playground men and women were still bellowing the song that the girl with the electronic accordion thundered out for them: *"Find you a hammer and SMASH IT DOWN!"* Virtually every window had been broken and glass crunched underfoot. The human beings were being shovelled together with the garbage into one vast rubbish pile, not only in the direction from which Donald was coming but from the other end of the street as well. The stock plan had been applied: close the area, keep 'em moving, jam 'em together and pack 'em off.

Adventurous mind-present youths jumped up on the arms of the sweep-truck as it passed the adventure playground and from there leapt to the security of the random concrete branches. Donald was too late to copy them; by the time he thought of it he had been forced on by.

Mindlessly he pushed and thrust and shouted like everyone else, hardly noticing whether it was a man or a woman he jostled, an Afram or a WASP. The gas-gun on the sweep-truck discharged grenades over his head and the booming music died in mid-chord. A whiff of the gas reached Donald's nose and wiped away the last trace of rationality. Both arms flailing, careless of who hit him so long as he could hit back, he struggled towards the people from the opposite direction now impacting on the group he was enmeshed with.

Settling on the roofs with a howl of turbines: paddycopters to net and carry off the rioters, like some obscene cross between a spider and a vulture. He sobbed and gasped and punched and kicked and did not feel the answering blows. A dark face rose before his eyes and seemed familiar and all he could think of was the boy he had fired his Jettigun at, the one whose sister had attacked him in retaliation so that he struck her in the mouth and made her bleed. Terrified, he began to batter at the man confronting him.

"Donald! Stop it, Donald—*stop it!*"

More gas rained down from crunching grenades. He lost the energy needed to drive his fists and a modicum of sanity returned to him before he blacked out. He said, "Norman. Oh my God. Norman. I'm so—"

The apology, the recipient, the speaker, whirled together into nothing.

THE STATE OF THE ART

I saw scrawled on the corner of a wall scrawawawled on a wawawall caterwauled cattycorner on the wawall what did I see scrawled on the wawl I forget so it can't be that important KNOW IN YOUR OWN HANDS WITH A POLY-FORMING KIT THE SENSATIONS OF MICHELAN-GELO AND MOORE OF RODIN AND ROUAULT *let us analyse your metabolism and compound for you a mixture that's yours and yours alone guaranteed to trip you higher further longer* by cross-breeding the kaleidoscope with the computer we created the Colliderscope that turns your drab daily environment into a marvellous mystery HE THAT HATH EARS TO HEAR LET HIM HEAR ALL THERE IS IN THE RANDOM SOUNDS OF A WHYTE NOYSE ® GENERATOR tomorrow's architecture will be a thing of space volume introversion and compaction BEETHOVEN VIOLIN CONCERTO SOLOIST ERICH MUNK-GREEN *when you're redecorating don't forget to consult us for orig-inal computer-created artworks to complement your colour-scheme* rare exotic taste sensations from the most ordinary food if you dredge it with a little "Ass-salt" before cooking THE LATEST PLANETARY COLLISION SIZE SMASH OF THE EM THIRTY-ONES IS ON SPOOL EG92745 *if you haven't read it you haven't celebrated your twenty-first "gives a totally new meaning to the term 'novel'!"* NETSUKE

WAS NEVER LIKE THIS BEFORE THE TEXTURES THE FORMS ARE ENDLESSLY ABSORBING THOUGH NOT HABIT-FORMING (G'TEED) one of the great creative artists of our generation is responsible for clothes by "Gondola" MACBETH OF MOONBASE ZERO BY WILLIAM SHAKESPEARE AND HANK SODLEY *freevent tonite pyrotechnics and ample opportunity for self-expression bring your own hatreds* you mean you haven't yet bought one of Ed Ferlingham's time-boxettes? *make your home a frame for your individuality* WE THE MARIONETTES A NEW BALLET BY SHAUN *the most fascinating pursuit of this century is to study the stochastic potential of English "verbal Karezza because it always seems almost to be there and never makes it"* THE GREATEST ART IS THE MOST NEGLECTED WHEN DID YOU LAST EXPERIENCE ECSTASY IN BED? *at the 22nd Century Gallery now wear your oldest clothes or buy our unique disposables or come buff to "shit-shower" by Alan Zelgin* at last perfume achieves the status of true art in the delicate flagons of Twenty-first Scentury by Arpège TONIGHT ON CHANNEL FIFTY IN THE PERFECTION OF HOLOGRAPHIC SOLIDARITY *polychrome enigmata by The Triple at Shoplace Shoplace Shoplace* LOVE YOUR DISINTEGRATIVE TENDENCIES AND GET US TO HELP THEM ALONG antiques you've never seen before because we invented them and there are lots and lots how about a Balinese hubcap or a non-genuine art nouveau hi-fi set? *learn the zock with that true accustomed-to-free-fall touch at our studios* THEATRE IN THE HOLE PRESENTS WAGNER'S LOW END GRIN the autoshout for intellectuals fitted free of charge to your set EXPERIENCE "STENCH" BY QUATROMANE FULL DIRECTIONS AVAILABLE *never be bored by the popparade Tonvaria makes them over in the style you love from Bach to Beiderbecke to Bronstein to whoever* WHEN WE SAY SENSATIONAL WE MEAN IT HEIGHTEN ALL YOUR PERCEPTIONS WITH MILD NON-ADDICTIVE sick and tired of it all send for us example $1000 for invasion of apt by 3 with paint and buckets of dreck $1500 for armed hold-up and theft of all movables with dialogue and max. damage to fixtures special quotations up to $3000 *at last gastronomy*

acquires the status of true art at the hands of Noël Noël
OUR CANS ARE INDIVIDUALLY DESIGNED BY
SOME OF TODAY'S GREAT CREATIVE ARTISTS you
too can exploit your artistic potential with one of our personalised courses BE THE ONLY PERSON ON YOUR
BLOCK TO READ THESE STORIES ON HAND-
TOOLED VELLUM WITH BEAUTIFUL CALLIGRAPHY
*at last that neglected sense of touch can enjoy the fruits of a
great artist's creativity get "Stingle"* ® HAVE YOU PAINT-
ED "CHRIST STOPPED AT EMMAUS" YET? throw that
old camera on the dreck-pile and get with the holographic
trend LIMITED EDITION OF ONE MILLION NUM-
BERED COPIES *we can re-programme your life to make an
artistically rounded whole* WHEN THEY SAY BOTTICEL-
LI DO YOU THINK IT'S A CHEESE WELL AS OF
TODAY IT IS AND GASTRONOMES ACKNOWLEDGE
OUR ACHIEVEMENT *School of Free Television presents*
a black blind journey into wherever is theme of freevent to-
moro *Museum of Last Week exhibition changes daily* THE
ART OF THE BLUE MOVIE LECTURE WITH REAL
FILM NOT TAPED REPRODUCTIONS at last television's
potential is realised in the hands of a great creative artist
*how have your dreams been lately and it's not your shrinker
asking but the people who've taken the sleep-inducer the next
logical step* at last dress assumes its rightful status among the
creative arts at the hands of A TRUE CREATIVE ARTIST
IN THE FIELD OF COSMETIC SURGERY IS DR. don't
waste the chance to make your family a work of ART OF
SUCCESS CALL AND INQUIRE *you'll appreciate not hate
what the world offers when you* VOLUNTEER DICTY FOR
FREEVENT WITH 24-HOUR SENSORY INTERFER-
ENCE decorative shells rocks relics LIVING NOVEL
COME AND INTERACT WITH THE AUTHOR OF
breaking apart is another aspect of the whole not art not
life but experience *match your pets to your personality geno-
type-moulded animals of all descriptions* AT LAST THE
STATUS OF TRUE CREATIVE ART IS CONFERRED
ON rearrangement of your experience into a symmetrical
pattern YOUR END TOO CAN BE A WORK OF ART
CONCEIVED BY YOURSELF ALL TRADITIONAL

FORMS OF EXECUTION AVAILABLE IN RIGOROUS-LY ACCURATE HISTORICAL DETAIL EXPLOSION DROWNING PRECIPITATION FROM HEIGHT ALL WEAPONS SELF- OR OTHER-DIRECTED REASONABLE TERMS FROM TERMINATION INC. THE COMPANY THAT MAKES AN ART OF YOUR END FOR YOU (not legal in following states . . .)

(ART   A Friend of mine in Tulsa, Okla., when I was about eleven years old. I'd be interested to hear from him. There are so many pseudos around taking his name in vain.
                    —*The Hipcrime Vocab* by Chad C. Mulligan)

tracking with closeups (10)

SMOTHERLOVE

Stretched out on the couch naked, hair dyed the fashionable bronze shade that everyone said suited her so well, a screen protecting the majority of her body from the scan of the camera on the phone but bathing her in the blue-white of the sunshine lamps, Sasha Peterson did not look her forty-four years. Rounded enough for her skin to be full and firm everywhere, on the shoulders, on the breasts tipped with carnelian nipples, on the belly underlined with hair dyed to match her head (never overlook anything, never give away anything, never never never miss a trick), she weighed a little more than she should have done but not enough to matter.

"Not exactly *suitable*," she said. "Of course, Philip was disappointed when I said so, but I don't believe in secrets between mother and son, which is of course the most intimate of all human relationships, isn't it? If I feel strongly about something I speak my mind on the subject and of course I expect Philip to do the same. Excuse me just a moment, Alice. Darling!"

Fully dressed in slightly conservative clothing of a cut that had been popular among young men ten years before, Philip looked up from his chair the other side of the room. He was a husky youth of twenty with pimples that even the most modern dermal treatments had not totally conquered.

176

"Bring me another whistler, will you?"

A hand tipped immaculately with chrome polish held out an empty Jacobean glass whose cut-crystal facets caught and shattered the light of the sunshine lamps into diamond brilliance.

"Do you mind if I fix myself another, too?"

"I think not, darling. You've had one already, and you're not—ah—*case-hardened* like your old mum, are you?" As he took the glass: "So I don't expect we'll be seeing any more of Lucy. It's a shame because in some ways she's quite a nice girl, and no one could say she's not intelligent. But she's—not to be too mealy-mouthed—a bit common, don't you think? And she's almost three years older than Philip, and I feel it makes such a disproportionate amount of difference at that age, don't you? I mean, considering it percentage-wise, with Philip being only twenty as he is. Ah, thanks a trillion, lovey!" With one hand she reached up and ruffled her son's hair as he bent over her before accepting the glass and setting it beside her.

"And while you're up, sugar-loaf, light me another of those Bay Golds, will you? Be sure not to inhale it, though, won't you?"

Philip crossed the room, opened the reefer-box, applied a flame to the tip and wasted the first eighth of an inch dutifully on the unappreciative air.

"I'm going to be on my own tonight anyway, though—he's going to see that nice boy Aaron he was in the same class with when he was doing ... Goodness, it's about time you left, isn't it, plum-pudding?"

"If you don't mind."

"No, gracious! Of course I don't mind! But you'll be back as soon as you can, won't you?" She accepted the reefer with those same metal-gleaming claws. "Kiss your old mum goodbye, then, and give Aaron my regards."

Peck-peck.

"Ah, you're mother's boy, aren't you, Philip? See you later, then. Oh, by the way, Alice, the reason I called: I seem to remember you saying you knew somebody in the department who sorted matters out when a draft notice came in for the Wilkins boy. Well, we've had the inevitable trouble at last, and though it's a lot of nonsense of course I was wondering whether ..."

"Yes, Sasha," Philip said in answer to the question she had long forgotten.

continuity (10)

DUE PROCESS

A vast expanded hollow human void, arms belly legs like tunnels thrumming to the disgusting pulse of nausea. Bit by bit and painfully drawn together by spider's-web frail links and assembled into . . .

Person. Vomit-prone, bruised, aching, Donald Hogan. He would rather have stayed in the nowhere of unconsciousness but there was a sharp cut-off with the sleepy-gas the police department used; the side-effects were carefully restricted to nausea and weakness, the most undermining sensations.

He rolled on one side and discovered that support ended. Terror of falling blind jolted his full awareness back. He looked and grabbed simultaneously, hand reaching a metal bar, eyes receiving a crazy insoluble mystery of shapes and lines.

He had almost rolled off something that was more of a shelf than a bunk, but if he had done so he would have fallen mere inches to the floor; he was on the lowest level. He saw through a steel grille a stacked layer of horizontal compartments, each containing a human body, and foggily deduced that on this side of the grille there must be other similar compartments, one holding himself. A man and a woman in police uniform activated the roller to retract a grille separating one bank of prisoners from the next and the metal shrieked as it cleared their way. They walked, holding a

179

recorder for notes that they exchanged according to whether the next subject was male or female, to a point level with his vision and began to search one of the unconscious captives The one on the corresponding shelf to his own, he saw, was a girl lying in a pool of her own vomit.

"Jet along," the policewoman said. "Some of this lot only got a whiff and they may be shaking out of it any minute."

"All right. This one's ID says he's—"

Donald tried stupidly to sit up and discovered he had only nine inches clearance, but banging his head on the underside of the next shelf made a noise and attracted their attention.

"See what I mean?" said the woman, and turned with a sigh to speak through the partition of mesh. "Lie down— your turn will come!"

Donald forced his feet and one arm to the floor and then his whole incredible weight into a standing position, his hand clutching the side of the fourth shelf up to steady him. He said, "What's going on? Where is this place?"

In both directions, as far as he could see by poor shielded lamps, human bodies laid out as if in a mortuary.

"Ah, fasten it," said the woman, and turned her back.

"Listen! You picked up all these rioters but it was the driver of the pseudo cab—"

"Ah, dreck!" The policeman stamped his foot, an incongruously camp gesture because he was over six feet tall, brawny and broken-nosed, but nowadays ... "All right, messy-mouth, what is it?"

"The way the riot got started! Did you find the driver of the cab?"

"What cab?"

"I was trapped in a pseudo cab, and I managed to stop him closing the door because I was wearing a Karatand and jammed it, and—"

"Anything about a cab on this?" the man said to the woman, who shrugged.

"Do I have time to find out why they got brought in?"

"So shut up and wait, messy-mouth," the man told Donald "Or I'll gas you again. Now this one," he resumed, the woman raising the mike of the recorder to collect his words, "is—"

Donald, astonished, saw and recognised the man whose pockets the policeman was searching.

"A vice-president of General Technics, and you'll hear a lot more about *this!*"

"What?"

"That's Norman House of GT!" Stretched out like a wax dummy, eyes tiredly closed, hands tossed at random on his chest by whoever brought him in.

"Right," the man said slowly, inspecting the ID he had discovered. "How do you know?"

"He's my roomie."

The man and woman exchanged glances. "Prove it," the man said, holding out his hand.

Donald searched his own pockets, finding that the Karatand and the Jettigun had gone—of course—and ultimately locating his own ID. He thrust it awkwardly through the intervening grille.

"The address checks," the policeman admitted reluctantly. "Better get them out of here, Syl—can't afford to buck GT."

The woman gave Donald a look of pure butch loathing and switched off the recorder. "The drecky bleeder," she said. "As if we weren't on a tight enough schedule. But okay."

"Wait there," the man said. "We can't get to you without we go right around the end and come back."

"What about this one?" asked the woman, pointing to Norman.

"Get a stretcher party. If there's time before any more of them wake up and start causing trouble."

Grilles whined and groaned as they retracted and slammed back, making a crazy metallic counterpoint to the footsteps of the pair while they retraced their path to the end of the line of cells. That was what he was in, Donald now realised, though the original layout had been overlaid with several alterations until now at last the limit had been reached and there was no more space unless you simply closed the prisoners into drawers like coffins and extracted them like solving a glass-puzzle.

They reached him eventually and he stumbled out ahead of them towards a tiled corridor where another woman took him in charge and showed him to an office without occupants.

"Wait here," she said. "Someone will come to see you in a moment."

The moment stretched. Donald sat on a hard chair and put his head in his hands, wondering if he was now going to throw up.

Behind his closed eyelids he saw a pattern of human bodies laid out under a mesh of wire.

"Your name Hogan?"

Donald started. A man with captain's shoulder-badges had entered the room and was going around the corner of the central table to sit at its far side. He held a file of papers.

"Y-yes."

"Apparently you know something about how the trouble got started tonight." The captain opened a drawer of the table, pulled out the mike of a recorder and clicked over a switch. "Let's have it."

"I got in a psuedo cab and . . ." Wearily, recital of the details.

The captain nodded. "Yeah. We had a report there was one of those bleeders working the area—Christ knows why, you'd think they'd work an uptown district where people use cabs more, where they carry more cash or credit cards than they do down your manor."

"It's not my manor."

"Then whatinole were you doing there?"

"I—uh—I'd been for a walk."

"You what?" The captain looked at him unbelievingly. "Do you do this kind of thing often?"

"N-no. I just suddenly realised I'd got out of the habit of going out in the evenings unless I was going somewhere particular, like to call on people. So I—"

"Christ. Don't make a habit of it, will you? We have enough trouble to handle without you adding to the pile."

"Now look!" Donald was beginning to recover; indignation made his back straighten. "It's not my fault if a pseudo—"

"No? Look at yourself, then!"

Confused, Donald glanced down at clothes smeared with the garbage that had been hurled into the street around the prowlie, and the sight made his nausea return in full force. He said weakly, "I'm a mess, but—"

"Mess has nothing to do with it. How many people did you see on that manor who were dressed like you? You were marked as an intruder at once. It didn't have to be a pseudo cab that made you the spark for an explosion—it could have been an Afram yonderboy and his spareweels making mock, or a mugger estimating you as prosperous, or anything. You did a damn-fool thing, and as a result my department has better than two hundred extra people in this building, which wasn't meant to cope with half its present occupants!"

"I don't see what right you have to talk to me like that!" Donald flared. "Have you caught the driver of the cab along with the couple of hundred innocent people you've swept up off the street?"

"You're free with your figures, aren't you?" the captain said in a soft voice. "A couple of hundred *innocent* people? I doubt it. The cabdriver may well be among them if he was slow in running, and that cuts it by one, you must admit that if no more. Also we have, I expect"—and he raised his hand to count finger by finger the groups he was listing—"the vandals and looters who smashed the window of a store and made off with most of its stock of liquor and reefers, plus the people who chopped down a street-light, plus the people who damaged one of my prowl cars, plus any number of people who flooded a street with decaying garbage and created a health hazard, and certainly several dozens who were excessively ready with assorted weapons, like a gun used to bring down one of my patrol copters and—the clubs with which the pilot was beaten to death. You were saying . . .?"

"They killed him?" Donald said slowly.

"You can't do much to revive a man whose skull has been smashed open and his brains spilled on the street. Can you?"

"Oh my God," Donald said.

"I don't believe in God," said the captain. "I wouldn't care to believe in anyone who could make such a stinking lousy species as the one you belong to. Get the hole out of here before I charge you with incitement to riot."

He turned off the recorder and dropped the mike back in its drawer, which he slammed shut. "And if I had time," he concluded, "I believe I very well might do that!"

Donald forced himself to his feet, trembling. He said, "You mean a man can be forbidden to walk the streets of his own home town nowadays just because something might happen to him like happened to me?"

"You calculate the odds," the captain said. "So far, we have evidence of one hundred per cent certainty that it does happen. Get out before I change my mind—and take your brown-nosed roomie along with you, *please*. He's still in no state to get home by himself, but I'd appreciate the extra space to move around."

context (11)

COME OUTSIDE AND SAY THAT

"To my mind the most frightening book ever published is Lewis F. Richardson's *Statistics of Deadly Quarrels.* You've probably never heard of it even though its relevance to the mess you're in is at least as great as that of Darwin's *On the Origin of Species,* which you learned about in fourth grade. And that's because it's so completely terrifying only those 'experts' who are adequately armoured with preconceived contrary ideas which will enable them to disregard Richardson's work completely ever get to study it.

"The subject, of course, is one which you think you're an expert on, too—just as was the case when Darwin started stirring things up. People *knew* they were conscious, intelligent beings and apparently if they conceded the resemblance between themselves and the animals they were well acquainted with they attributed it to a lack of imagination on the part of the Creator—or perhaps even lauded a proper Puritan parsimony in His unwillingness to waste a good working design after it had been field-tested by the apes.

"So you believe that it's in the interests of your family, friends and compatriots when you doll yourself up in uniform, take the gun you're issued and go off to a messy death in the swamps of some place you wouldn't visit on vacation even if you were a centenarian who'd been every place else bar Mars.

"What Richardson demonstrated in essence (and what has been reinforced by the small handful of people who've followed up his work over the past half-century) was that war follows a stochastic distribution: that's to say, it's neither absolutely random, nor yet is it definable in a systematic pattern, but something between the two. The pattern is there, but we cannot attribute one-for-one a causal relationship that would account for every specific case.

"In other words, the incidence of war is independent of the volitional element. It makes no odds whatever whether a rational decision has been taken—war, like the weather, just happens.

"Much earlier than Richardson, before World War I, in fact, Norman Angell had shown that the idea of fighting a war for profit was obsolete. The victors would pay a heavier cost than the losers. He was right, and that First World War proved the fact. The second one hammered it home with everything up to and including nuclear weapons. In an individual one would regard it as evidence of insanity to see someone repeatedly undertaking enterprises that resulted in his losing precisely what he claimed he was trying to achieve; it is not less lunatic to do it on the international scale, but if you've been catching the news lately you'll have noticed it's being done more than ever. The Chinese go on bleating about the withering away of the state and never stop conducting a series of harassing skirmishes on their neighbours' territory that compels them with true Marxist inevitability to regiment and regulate their population. The Americans and their allies—what few we have left—boast of their unprecedented degree of personal freedom and submit their sovereignty to a computer in Washington, known as the draft selector, which every day condemns several hundreds of them to a death as pointless as that of the Roman gladiators. Put it this way: suppose there were a mindless idiot on your block (and until GT produces proof that Shalmaneser really can develop intelligence I shall go on regarding computers of whatever breed as *idiots savants*), and once a week his mental condition cycled into a state where he needed to tear someone else apart with his nails and teeth—and the consensus among your neighbours was that every family in turn should detail one of its members to stroll along to where this idiot lived and lie down for him to slaughter . . .

"There: I told you you were an expert on this subject. This is exactly what the draft does except that it doesn't take the sort of member your family might spare— grandma aged 107 who's been senile for years, for example or that baby who somehow crept through the filter of eugenic legislation and wound up with phenylketonuria It takes the handsomest, healthiest, most vigorous, and nobody else.

"Remind you of something? It should do; the folk imagination has occasional curious insights and one of them has been repeated for uncountable millennia. From Andromeda chained on her rock to the maidens offered up to the dragon St. George slew, the theme of destroying the most precious, the most valuable, the least replaceable of our kinfolk recurs and recurs in legend. It tells us with a wisdom that we do not possess as individuals but certainly possess collectively that when we go to war we are ruining ourselves.

"But you're an expert on this, aren't you? You know very well that it's thanks to the Confederate dead, or the victims of the Long March, or the heroic pilots of the Battle of Britain, or self-incinerated *kamikazes,* that you're here, to-day, enjoying your wonderful daily life so full of pleasure, reward, love, joy and excitement.

"Actually I'll wager that it's rather more full of anxiety, problems, economic difficulties quarrels and disappoint-ments, but if you're so attached to them I shan't be able to shake you loose. Love and joy are incredibly habit-forming; often a single exposure is enough to cause permanent addic-tion. But I have no doubt you steer clear as much as you can of anything so masterful."

—*You're an Ignorant Idiot* by Chad C. Mulligan

tracking with closeups (11)

"Close now," said the navigator. He was also the pilot, insofar as there was a human pilot. The course-setting and control were mostly done by computers, but if their delicate machinery were to be disabled by—say—a near-miss with a depth-charge, a man could continue to function after sustaining injuries that would put computers out of action.

The intelligence officer shivered a little, wondering whether this man he shared the fore-compartment of the sub with would be as reliable in emergency as he claimed. However, there had been no contact with the enemy so far.

Overhead, under a clear sky and very little wind, the surface of the Shongao Strait must be almost like a mirror, rippled only by tides and currents. The sub itself, creeping along the deepest part of the channel, would not visibly disturb the water.

"That's it to within a few yards," the navigator said. "I'll put up the listeners now. Better go warn the cargo."

The intelligence officer looked back along the spinal tunnel of the vessel. Just big enough for a man to ease himself through, it framed Jogajong's head in a circle of light.

Sealed train . . . Lenin . . .

But it was hard to think in those terms. The agelessly youthful Asian, who was in fact over forty but could have passed for ten years less, with his neatly combed black hair and sallow skin, had none of the charismatic quality of a man like Lenin.

Perhaps revolutionaries on your own side never do seem so impressive? How about our own Founding Fathers?

Annoyed for no definable reason, the intelligence officer said, "I don't care for the way you keep calling him 'the cargo'. He's a man. An important man, what's more."

"On the one hand," said the navigator in a slightly bored tone, "I prefer not to think of the people I deliver out here as if they *were* people. It's a lot better to think of them as expendable objects. And on the other, he's a yellowbelly same as the rest of them out here. It's your business to tell them apart, I guess, but for me they all look like monkeys."

As he spoke he had been operating the controls which released the listeners, allowing them to bob gently to the surface. Now he activated them, and the hull was suddenly alive with the night noises of the world above: the murmur of waves, the screeching of parakeets disturbed at their roosts, and the immense plop-plopping of something very close at hand.

"Turtle," the navigator said, amused at the way his companion started. "Friendly. At least I hope so. You'd be the one to know if the slit-eyes had started to enlist them on their side, hm?"

The intelligence officer felt himself flushing, and concealed the fact by turning to climb along the spinal tunnel. The navigator, behind him, chuckled just loudly enough.

The bleeder. I hope he doesn't return from his next mission.

The sounds from the listeners had already alerted Jogajong. By the time the intelligence officer completed his crawl down the tunnel, he was ready except for his helmet. He was clad in a flotation-suit of pressure-sensitive plastic which would resist the water rigidly until he surfaced, then relax to allow him to swim ashore. Empty, it could be infected with a small vial of tailored bacteria and reduced to an amorphous mess on the beach.

They must have rehearsed him very well ... No, of course: he's done it before, and for real. He's going back the way they got him out. Him, and lord knows how many others.

"Any time you like now," the navigator called. "Don't stretch our luck, will you?"

The intelligence officer swallowed hard. He checked over the security of the suit as Jogajong silently turned around for inspection. Everything was in order. He picked up the final item, the helmet, and set it in place on the neck-seal, wondering what was going on behind that so-calm face.

If they wanted me to do what he's going to do—pop out in midocean, risk the coastal patrols on my way to the shore—could I? . . . I don't know. But he seems so relaxed.

He thrust out his hand to grasp Jogajong's in a final good-luck gesture, and realised too late that the pressure-sensitisation of the plastic instantly turned the gauntlet into an inflexible, chilly lump. He saw Jogajong's lips form a smile at his discomfiture, and was all of a sudden angry with him too.

Doesn't the bleeder realise—?

No, probably not. The computers gave this man better than a forty per cent chance of being the next Leader of Yatakang, provided the intelligence assessments of his contacts and influence were to be relied on. The intelligence officer could cope with that kind of power only as an abstract; he could not feel in his bones what it would be like to give orders to two hundred million people.

"Move it along there!" the navigator shouted. "Blast off, for pity's sake!"

Jogajong drew back to await the flooding of his compartment. The intelligence officer scrambled feet-first into the tunnel again, dogged the door shut and listened to the noise of water beyond it.

You have to envy a man like that. What makes you jealous is the confidence he feels. Forty per cent chance of making out . . . I wouldn't have come on this free-falling stroll, as the navigator terms it, if I'd been told the odds against my return. Wonder if I should ask when I get back? Better not, I guess. I prefer to think of success as a foregone conclusion.

The whole sub shook gently with the discharge of Jogajong from the flooding compartment. "Hah!" the navigator said.

"Not before time. I have a slit-eye patrol-boat at the extreme edge of the detectors."

"You mean they'll notice him swimming ashore?"

"Him? No—his suit won't give a blip at this range, not on their equipment. But we might. We'll have to sit here and wait them out."

The intelligence officer nodded and rubbed his sweating palms on his thighs, mechanically continuing the motion until long after the fabric of his pants had absorbed the moisture.

How did Lenin feel about the driver of his sealed train after he'd become unchallenged boss of the Russians? Did he even remember there had been a driver?

When he grew desperate to relieve the tension, he essayed a joke. He said, "How does it feel to have just changed the course of history?"

"I don't know what you mean," said the navigator. "To my way of thinking, by the time history happens I'm going to be dead."

continuity (11)

THE SOUND OF FALLING ROCK

Donald had not thought to wonder what the time was. Out on the street, under the Fuller Dome, the cycle of night and day seemed suspended. It was somewhere around dawn by now, apparently; there had been too many other demands on their time for the police to process the rioters as soon as they were brought in. The city was dead and drained, its roads like veins bled dry, garbage and cleansing vehicles inching along them like a few stranded leucocytes struggling against hopeless odds to defeat an invading disease.

Norman slumped beside him in the rear of the cab, eyes opening every now and then, but for the most part too preoccupied with the sickness and lethargy bequeathed to him by the gas to be able to pay attention to his surroundings. When they reached their apartment block, Donald had to half-carry him first to the elevators, then into the living-room.

In the middle of the carpet he trod on something hard and went back to look at it when he had deposited Norman in his favourite old Hille chair. It was a Watch-&-Ward Inc. key. He compared it with his own and found it apparently identical. Then a change in his surroundings registered. The poly-organ was missing. The door to Norman's bedroom, which had been closed when he went out, was now standing ajar, and a glance through it showed that Victoria's section of the closet was empty.

Gone. Coincidence? Or tipped off? That was a problem he had no energy left to wrestle with. He helped himself to one of Norman's Bay Golds from the humidor. Though he almost never smoked pot, he needed some kind of a lift very badly, and to take alcohol on top of the police's sleepy-gas would entail renewed nausea.

"Want one?" he said to Norman, seeing the Afram had stirred. Norman shook his head.

"What the hole happened? What were you doing out there?"

Donald waited till he ran out of stored breath before answering through a thin mist of smoke. He said, "I—owe you a big apology. I was out of my mind. We all were. Maybe the gas had something to do with it."

Overlaying the familiar environment, remembered visions of the street, the churning bodies, Norman's face appearing unrecognised before him. He shuddered.

"What were *you* doing there?" he added.

"Sentimental journey," Norman said. "I saw Elihu Masters at the UN Hostel, and when I left him I thought, well, here I am further east on the island than I've been in months, I'll walk down to where my parents used to live."

"Are they still alive?" Donald said.

"I don't know."

"What?"

"I don't know." Norman passed a limp hand over his forehead and briefly closed his eyes. "They separated when I was a kid. I've been on my own since I was eighteen. I think my mother's in the Bahamas, but I don't know. I thought I didn't care. Oh, the hole!"

He paused long enough to lick his lips.

"Then suddenly having this riot burst out all around me— it was a nightmare. One moment I was walking along looking for the places I remembered and the next all the people were moving and forcing me along with them and the sweep-truck came around the corner and we were all jammed together like trapped rats. I wasn't really frightened, though, until I recognised you and tried to make towards you and when I got close you started swinging both fists and you wouldn't stop even though I kept shouting your name."

Is he talking about me? It feels like a different person. Donald drew and drew on the reefer, overloading the automatic dilution effect of the tip so that the smoke was hot and harsh in his throat, like a punishment. He said when he had finished storing the latest lungful, "I was frightened. I was scared out of my mind. You see, I started it."

"You must be crazy."

"No—no, literally I did start it. And this is what's so terrifying." Donald clenched his empty hand so that the nails bit deep into his palm. Another shudder tremoloed down his spine and set up a resonance that became whole-body shivering within seconds. He felt the unreal chilliness of shock reaction now, his hands and feet growing numb.

"What sort of a person am I? I don't know what sort of a person I am. I didn't think I was the sort of person who could fail to recognise one of his closest friends and try to hit him with both fists. I didn't think I wasn't safe to be allowed out on the streets."

Norman had apparently forgotten his own physical condition and was sitting up staring with an expression of disbelief.

"Did you see them bring down the police helicopter?"

"No."

"They did. Somebody shot it down with a sporting gun. And when it crashed they beat the pilot to death with clubs. Honest to God, Norman"—his voice cracked—"I don't remember clearly enough to be sure I wasn't in there with them!"

I'm going to cave in. Some part of his mind retained enough detachment to realise, sensing an aura like that of a gathering storm. *I mustn't drop the roach on the carpet.* He aimed it at an ashtray and the controlled gesture blended smashingly into something that must be done this instant, this very quantum of time, so that his hand began to move normally and ended up making a blind jab and letting the roach go and jerking back up with its mate to cover his face as he leaned forward and broke down sobbing.

Norman, uncertain, got up, took half a pace forward,

changed his mind, changed it again and came near. He said, "Donald, some of this is from pot and some of it's from the police gas and some of it's tiredness . . ."

The facile excuses faded away. He stood gazing down at Donald.

Started it? Did he? What did he—what could he—do? He's a colourless sort of codder, inoffensive, never blew up even when I snapped at him about bringing home nothing but Afram girls. Mild. Underneath: temper?

The admission came as a dismaying shock: *I don't know. For years we've shared a home, traded shiggies, talked small talk for politeness's sake—and I literally don't know.*

And Elihu Masters seems to think I'm fit to take charge of a helpless little country and make it over like Guinevere making over one of her clients, slicking it into the latest modern style.

One of us is genuinely crazy. Me?

He tapped Donald's shoulder awkwardly. "Here!" he said. "Let me help you to bed. There's time for a couple of hours' rest before I leave for work. And I don't have to disturb you."

Passive, Donald allowed himself to be led to his bedroom. He threw himself down across the coverlet.

"Want I should put your inducer on?" Norman asked, stretching out one hand towards the cable of the little Russian device concealed in the pillow, which guaranteed rest to the worst insomniac by induction of sleep-rhythms in the medulla.

"No, thanks," Donald muttered; then, as Norman was about to leave, he called, "By the way! When did I say Guinevere was having her party?"

"Ah—tonight, I guess."

"Thought so. But I'm so confused . . . They picked up Victoria pretty quickly, didn't they?"

"What?"

"I said they picked her up pretty quickly." Detecting a note of puzzlement in Norman's voice, Donald raised himself on one elbow. "Didn't you shop her? When I saw her things were gone, I—"

He broke off. Norman had turned in the doorway to look

across the living-room. Without further movement he could see, through the open door of his own bedroom, the closet door standing ajar to reveal vacancy where the current shiggy was allowed to hang her clothes.

"No, I didn't shop her," he said at length without a trace of emotion. "She must have decided to shade and fade while her news was still warm. Much good may it do her. But frankly I don't care. As you saw, I hadn't even noticed that her gear was gone until you mentioned it." He hesitated. "I guess I should tell you right away, come to think of it, in case I don't see you in the morning before I go out. I—ah—I may not be in New York much longer."

With shocking suddenness Donald remembered the inspiration which had come to him earlier in the evening, and then had been driven instantly to the back of his mind by the irruption of the pseudo cab. Yet weariness overlay even his pride at the insight he had displayed in figuring out the truth. He had to let his head fall back on the soft engulfing mound of the pillows.

"I didn't imagine you would be," he said.

"What? Why not?"

"I thought they'd send you to Beninia sooner or later. Sooner, huh?"

"Howinole did you know that?" Norman closed his hand violently on the jamb of the door.

"Worked it out," Donald said in a muffled voice. "That's what I'm good at. That's why they picked me for my job."

"What job? You don't have a . . ." Norman let the word die, listened to silence for a while, and eventually said, "I see. Like Victoria, hm?" The question shook with fury.

"No, not like Victoria. Christ, I shouldn't have said it but I just couldn't help it." Donald forced himself into a sitting position. "No, please, not like Victoria. Nothing to do with you."

"What, then?"

"Please, I'm not supposed to talk about it. But—oh, Jesus God, it's been ten mortal years and . . ." He swallowed convulsively. "State," he said at last in a tired voice. "Dilettante Dept. If they find out that you know I'll be activated in my army rank and court-martialled in secret. They warned me. It sort of puts me at your mercy, doesn't it?" he ended with a wan smile.

"So why did you tell me?" Norman asked after a pause.

"I don't know. Maybe because if you want a chance to get even with me for what I did tonight I think you deserve one. So go ahead. The way I feel right now, I wouldn't care if an avalanche fell on me." He slumped back on the bed and shut his eyes again.

In Norman's mind there came the grinding sound of rock breaking loose down a mountainside. A pang as sharp as an axe-blow struck across his left wrist from bone-tip to bone-tip; wincing, he caught at the hand to make sure it was still whole.

"I've got even with enough people to last me for life," he said. "And it's done me no good. No damned good at all. Go to sleep, Donald. You'll feel better by this evening, I'm sure."

He closed the door gently, using his left hand and ignoring the pain that was still as violent as if it had been real.

context (12)

THE SOCIOLOGICAL COUNTERPART
OF CHEYNE-STOKES RESPIRATION

"If you want to know what's shortly due for the guillotine look for the most obvious of all symptoms: extremism. It is an almost infallible sign—a kind of death-rattle—when a human institution is forced by its members into stressing those and *only* those factors which are identificatory, at the expense of others which it necessarily shares with competing institutions because human beings belong to all of them. A sound biological comparison would be the development of the fangs of the sabre-tooth tiger to the point where the beasts can't close their mouths any more, or the growth of armour that's indisputably impregnable but which weighs so much the owner can't support his bulk.

"On this basis, it's fairly certain that Christianity won't last out the twenty-first century. To take but a couple of prime instances: the hiving off from Rome of the so-called Right Catholics, and the appearance of the Divine Daughters as an influential pressure-group. The former exhibits a remarkable deviation from the traditional attitude of the Catholic Church as an institution that above all concerned itself with the family, Western style; the Right Catholics have become so obsessed with the simple act of fucking that they appear to have no time left for other aspects of human relationships, although they issue pronunciamenti galore on them. None of these bears even the slight relevance to contemporary reality which a sympathetic eye (not mine) can detect in similar statements originating from the Vatican. And the latter, who professedly model themselves on the mediaeval orders of nuns but who actually have borrowed the majority of their tenets—antimechanisation, distrust of bodily pleasure and so on—from respectable, well-integrated groups like the Amish and then soured them by a judicious admixture of the vinegar of hatred, are capitalising on about *the* most self-defeating of modern trends, our reluctance to further overburden our resources by having large families. They exploit our vicarious appreciation of people, especially women, who decline to have any progeny whatever, thus relieving us of a sense of personal responsibility for the whole damned mess.

"They won't last.

"I can't say I see much better times ahead for Muslims, either; though Islam has become a sizeable minority religion in the Western West in the past half-century, the spearhead of its advance has been the descendant of a schism, like the Right Catholics. I mean, naturally, the Children of X, who have constructed nothing more than an analogue of Christianity using their murdered patron as their Osiris-Attis-Jesus figure. They'll go the way of the mystery religions of ancient times, and for the same reason: they're exclusionist, and you aren't allowed in unless you fulfil certain conditions of birth, primarily that you should be recognisably coloured. (I feel a lot less strongly, by the way, about racial discrimination in organisations I don't want to join. It's an indication that they'll die out eventually.)

"Regrettably, however, this leper-mark of extremism isn't confined to such expendable traits as religion. Look at sex, for example. More and more people are spending more time at it, and resorting to ever more devious ways of keeping up their enthusiasm, like commercially available aphrodisiacs and parties that are considered to be failures unless they evolve into orgies. A hundred different shiggies a year, which is something a young man can achieve without doing more than taking off his clothes, fulfils neither of the essential biological requirements of the sexual urge: it doesn't lead to a stable environment for the cubs of the next generation, nor does it establish the kind of *rapport* between couples (or multiples—marriage works on all kinds of bases, not invariably monogamous) which serves to avert crisis over the possession of other members of the species. On the contrary, it leads rather to a kind of frenzy, because instead of the partners enjoying a continual and reciprocal reassurance about their respective masculinity/femininity they are driven to seek that reassurance anew every few days.

"In effect, applying the yardstick of extremism leads one to conclude that the human species itself is unlikely to last very long."

—*You're an Ignorant Idiot* by Chad C. Mulligan

continuity (12)

IT'S SUPPOSED TO BE AUTOMATIC BUT ACTUALLY YOU HAVE TO PRESS THIS BUTTON

A shrill ringing gaffed Donald through the ears and dragged him struggling out of the deep water of sleep. Cursing, he managed to focus his eyes on the wall-clock and saw it was only nine-thirty anti-matter. He tried for a while to convince himself that what had disturbed him was nothing more than Norman leaving for work a quarter-hour later than usual. But the ringing repeated.

He almost fell off the edge of the bed and forced his arms into the sleeves of a robe. A good few people didn't own such garments any longer; if they had callers before they were dressed they went to the door as they were and if the callers were shocked that was their problem. At least half the shiggies off the circuit who had briefly stayed in this apartment owned nothing but street-clothes, and those exiguous enough to pack in a single bag. But he was a little old-fashioned.

He made it to the door still less than normally alert, and when he checked through the spy-port to see who was outside all that registered on his mind apart from the number—four of them—was that his callers were from out of town. This was demonstrated by their carrying coats slung over their arms.

Stifling a yawn, he opened the door.

All the visitors were youthful in appearance, though at closer sight the one standing closest to the entrance might have been older than Donald. All wore rather formal clothing: sweaterettes and slax in shades of grey, green, dark blue and beige. The effect was that they were wearing uniforms, one apiece. All seemed to have natural hair, neither dyed nor coiffed. It struck Donald, much too late, that if a group of yonderboys wanted to gain access to someone's home this was exactly how they would have disguised themselves, discarding their gaudy shirjacks with the built-in fake musculature and their skin-tight codpieced slax.

The one who headed the rest said, "Morning, Mr. Hogan. You don't have any shiggies here at the moment, do you?"

"I—uh—what's it got to do with you? Who are you?"

"One moment please." The man gestured to his companions and advanced with them at his heels; Donald, even yet incompletely awake, fell back, feeling very vulnerable with nothing on except his flimsy thigh-length robe.

"Didn't expect to be back here so soon," the spokesman said affably, closing the door. "All right, check it out fast!"

The three sparewheels tossed their coats on handy pieces of furniture. Each proved to have been concealing something in his covered hand. Two of them had small instruments which they proceeded to point at the walls, ceiling and floor, watching them intently. The third had a bolt-gun, and he strode rapidly from room to room of the apartment peering around suspiciously.

Donald's heart began to feel very heavy inside his chest, as though it were pressing on his intestines and threatening to squeeze up vomit from him like toothpaste from a tube. He said weakly, "Back so soon . . . ? But I've never seen you before!"

"I get only our own stuff," one of the sparewheels said, lowering his incomprehensible instrument. The second nodded. The third returned from his tour of inspection putting his gun away in a concealed pocket beneath his left arm.

"Thank you," the spokesman said mildly. "Ah—shagreen, Mr. Hogan. I think that should explain our visit adequately . . . ?"

There was no menace in the gentle questioning note on which he uttered the words, but abruptly the heaviness of Donald's heart became so great it seemed to have stopped altogether, and he could imagine the ponderous burden dragging him down to the floor.

Shagreen. Oh my God. No!

He hadn't heard the word, to his knowledge, since a day ten years before when the colonel, in that office in Washington, warned him how he would be activated if the need arose. And the reference to "coming back", and to "our own stuff"—!

I told Norman. Last night I was sick and stupefied and couldn't control myself. I told him the truth. I'm a traitor. Not just a spy, not just a fool who can start a riot without trying. I'm a traitor too!

He licked his lips, absolutely unable to react even to reveal his dismay. The spokesman was going on, and certainly he did not have the air of an official sent to arrest a traitor.

But all the things he could do would be equally bad.

"I'm Major Delahanty. We haven't met before, but I feel I know you better than most of your friends do. I took you over from Colonel Braddock when he retired last year. These are my assistants, by the way—Sergeant French, Sergeant Awden, Sergeant Schritt." The sparewheels nodded but Donald was much too confused to think anything except that he now, finally, knew the name of the colonel who had administered his oath was Braddock.

He said, "You've come to activate me, hm?"

Delahanty looked quite sympathetic. "Didn't pick the best time, did we? What with that shiggy turning out to be an indesper and then you getting fouled up in the riot last night . . . Schritty, why don't you fix some coffee for the lieutenant here and maybe for all of us?"

That fixed it firmly in Donald's mind: "the lieutenant here". Probably the choice of phrase was calculated. It bit home on his brain like a steel claw.

"I—I have to go to the bathroom," he whispered. "Sit down and make yourselves at home."

When he had emptied his bladder he tugged open the

medicine cabinet and stared first at his own reflection, bleary-eyed, unshaven, then at the bottles, packets and phials ranged on the shelves. He stretched out his hand for some Wakup tablets, and his fingers brushed a neighbouring jar. Out of habit he read the label. It said: POISON. NOT TO BE TAKEN.

All of a sudden he was as frightened in reality as he had imagined in his long-ago nightmares. He clung to the side of the washbasin to stop himself keeling over, teeth chattering, vision tunnelled down to a single bright white patch, which was the label bearing the burning words.

Faust felt like this. The stars move still, time runs, the clock will strike, the devil will come and Faustus must be damned ... How long did he buy with the currency of his soul—ten years?

What are they going to make me do? At least I have one hope denied to Faust ... Might not be quick, but provided they assume I'm favouring my bowels not my bladder they'll give me five or ten minutes. The lot at one go should be enough.

He snatched up the jar and flipped off the lid. At the bottom of the opaque container a dusting of whitish powder lay, mocking him.

He was abruptly very cold, but the shaking from terror was at least driven away by the honest shivers that now racked him. He dropped the jar, and the lid after, in the disposall, and gulped down the Wakup pills he had at first intended to take.

After another couple of minutes he turned and left the bathroom with careful, unhurried strides.

It was a fresh shock to discover that, instead of dialling for coffee from the block kitchen as a stranger might be expected to do, Sergeant Schritt had used Donald's own maker, kept in his bedroom along with a can of his favourite blend.

Christ, how much do these people know about me? Earlier, when I talked so dangerously to Norman ...

His voice, though, remained reasonably steady when he

said, "I didn't realise you'd been watching me so thoroughly."

"Routine, I'm afraid." Delahanty shrugged. "We much prefer our operatives to live alone, as you know, but that in itself, these days, is pretty much of a suspicious circumstance, what with there not being enough accommodation to go around. Mr. House is as clean as they come, of course, a good respectable mosque-goer and holding down a very responsible position, but the fact that you were both working the shiggy circuit has given us some uncomfortable moments, I must confess. Especially last night when we detected that ingenious gadget in the polyorgan. I haven't run across that one before, and it's the next best thing to foolproof, blast it."

Holding his cup of coffee very carefully so as not to spill a drop over the rim, Donald sat down. He said, "Ah—how did you find out about that?"

"We had the activation notice yesterday afternoon, but one doesn't simply rush in to turn the operative on. One does a preliminary sweep to make sure nothing has changed since the last time we investigated, and—well, something most definitely had changed. We chimed in on the very moment when the shiggy was doing her eavesdropping."

"You have the place bugged."

"There are more bugs in here than a slum apartment has roaches," Delahanty said with a faint smile. "Not all of them ours, of course. Schritty?"

Sergeant Schritt bent down to the side of Norman's Hille chair and did something with one finger that Donald could not follow. When he removed his hand it held, between finger and thumb, a little glittering spike.

"I think that one is a Frigidaire plant," Delahanty said. "Or rather, the body of it is. The tip *is* ours. Like they say, little bugs have smaller bugs. Nothing went out of here that wasn't edited; we didn't want Mr. House fouled up by successful acts of indesping. Someone might have turned his attention to you and put two and two together. We came within an ace of falling down yesterday evening, though—it was sheer luck we caught up with the girl."

"It was you who took her away?"

"Oh yes. By the skin of our teeth. I had to pull everybody off watch and go hunt for her, but we did track her down before she'd sold the goods."

"Are you telling me that someone's been monitoring everything I did and said for ten solid years?" Donald demanded.

"Oh no. We have to rely on random sampling with inactive agents. Everything gets recorded, half of it gets computer-scanned for certain key words—a vocabulary of about a thousand are listed for you, I think—and we follow up the appearance of any of them in conversation. But actually we haven't paid serious attention to more than twenty or twenty-five hours of your activities in the past year." He hesitated. "You seem disturbed," he added. "Very natural—in this overcrowded world of ours privacy is our most precious defence. Be assured, please, we've intruded to the least possible degree."

"You've been watching me continuously since you had the—the activation notice, though?"

Delahanty's eyebrows rose. "No, I just told you. I had to pull everyone off your back to go look for the shiggy."

Don't push it. With luck they won't bother to examine the tape from the small hours of this morning; I may get away with it. And the worst of all the horrible things I'm faced with is the risk of being court-martialled for breach of my cover. They may only want me for something very minor; they may need me to help analyse intelligence reports, say

. . .

"I hope I'm not seeming too inquisitive," Donald ventured. "But—well, over the past ten years the whole thing has become more and more unreal to me, until just lately I've had trouble convincing myself that activation was still a possibility."

"That's an honest comment," Delahanty approved. "I keep telling Washington myself that they should risk breaches of cover and make random activations to keep operatives alert, even if it's no more than giving them token assignments during their official vacations. More coffee?"

"I haven't finished my first cup yet, thanks."

"Mind if I do? Anyone else . . . ? Right! Let's get to the nub of it, shall we?" Delahanty leaned back and crossed his legs. "Boat camp, Ellay, six poppa-momma tomorrow. We have travel documents for you, free passage warrant and so forth—Sergeant French will give them to you in a minute. Between now and then, what have you by way of appointments?"

"*Tomorrow?*"

"I know—the suspense will make it difficult. But that's the way the planet spins, I'm afraid. Appointments?"

Donald put one hand to his forehead. "I guess nothing—Oh. A party tonight. Guinevere Steel's."

"Go to it by all means, but don't let anyone slip you anything, of course. Did you hear about the case the other day when someone smeared the stuff they call 'Truth or Consequences' on the pulpit rail of a cathedral and a respected bishop said some highly unclerical things to his congregation?"

"I don't think so."

"The regular news channels didn't carry it—caved in by pressure-groups, I imagine. But it happened, and by all accounts it must have been spectacular. Don't let it happen to you, that's all. The rest of your instructions are in the packet French will give you. You'll receive a call in the morning notifying you of some financial trouble in a company you're supposed to have a lot of stock in, and that'll be the reason for your departure; the reason for your staying away will be a rather charming shiggy whom I regret to say you aren't actually scheduled to enjoy, but who'll serve as a highly convincing alibi to anyone flying a reasonably straight orbit."

Sergeant Awden grinned to himself.

"You mean I'm going to be away a long time?" Donald demanded.

"I don't know." Delahanty swallowed the last of his coffee and rose. "However, that's the programme and I didn't draft it. There's a full computer evaluation in Washington, presumably."

"Can't you at least tell me"—the half-forgotten phrase rose to his lips like a bubble from decaying weed on the bottom of a stagnant pool—"whether it's a field job?"

"Oh yes!" Delahanty seemed surprised. "I thought that was implicit in your linguistic speciality. Yatakangi, I believe."

"They're going to *send* me to Yatakang?" Donald was on his feet without realising, hands clenched to stop them shaking. "But that's absurd! I mean, all I did was take a high-pressure lang-lab course the best part of ten years ago, and—"

"*Lieutenant,*" Delahanty said with dangerous emphasis, "you don't have to worry about your ability to do the job. You'll be made able to do it."

"I—what?"

"Made able. You've run across commercial advertisements for a process called eptification, I imagine?"

"Y-yes."

"And thought it was another misleading come-on?"

"I guess so. What's that got to do with—?"

"*We* eptify people. And it works. If there's nobody available who's equipped for a particular job, we make someone over until he is equipped. Don't worry; you'll manage—assuming the job to be done is humanly feasible. Reflect on that and relax. But I guess you should go suck a trank as well."

Delahanty gestured to his sparewheels. French handed a sealed official packet to Donald, who accepted it in numb fingers, and they all muttered a good morning as they filed out, leaving him feeling small and scared and regretting that he hadn't managed to die.

After a while, he was sufficiently recovered to consider arranging for someone at the party to slip him some of the drug Delahanty had warned him against.

tracking with closeups (12)

IF YOU CAN'T BEAT THEM BEAUT THEM

BEAUTIQUE said letters suspended in empty air, and underneath ever so discreetly the name of Guinevere Steel. Beyond the lettering, indicative of the lavish personal attention one might be sure of getting, a blonde, a brunette and a redhead waiting with expectant expressions for *you*, madame, each one an immaculate product of the Beautique's art, finished to molecular tolerances, gleaming, shimmering, polished not like diamonds but like the parts that went into Shalmaneser where nothing could be allowed to go wrong. Their clothing concealed only those sections of their bodies where the raw material the cosmeticians had had to work with left something to be desired.

Also in plain sight was a sleek young man garbed in the traditional style of an artist from the *Quartier Latin* about 1890—floppy beret over his left ear, smock with a huge bright bow at the neck, and tapered check trousers ending in high-sided boots. In deference to the original image he was affecting there were three or four stripes of random colour on the hem of the smock supposed to represent smears of paint, but they were entirely symbolic. He was as sterile and designed as the girls beside him.

One could see no further into the premises from the street than the partition against which the girls were ranged, a changeochrome surface flowing with impermanent colours weighted to favour the girls' costumes.

He marched in, wondering with casual amusement how long it would take those eager, alert, welcoming expressions to dissolve.

Guinevere sensed that something was wrong before anyone had a chance to tell her. There was normally a particular kind of quiet buzz from the body of the shop, a variable but never-ceasing susurrus accompanying the gentle relaxing music that oozed on to the air from dozens of hidden speakers. A false note entered it, and she looked up, head cocked on one side, from the list of final preparations she was making against tonight's party.

Half-convinced she had been misled, she activated the internal scanners and looked over the main salon. Screened by floor-to-ceiling curtains of imperviflex, the clients sat or lay enjoying the luxy atmosphere while their imperfections were soaked, or filed, or painted away. Mrs. Djabalah in Post 38 was requiring slightly more than the conventional services from her masseuse again, Guinevere noticed with resignation, and scribbled herself a memo to surcharge the bill by a hundred per cent. So long as the girl herself didn't complain —and there was something rather magnificent about the Djabalah woman's six feet two of statuesque ebony . . .

She took a long shot down the central passageway separating the posts and caught a glimpse of a commotion near the entrance. Abruptly alarmed—if that could be seen from the street it had to be stopped *now*—she switched to the storefront viewers.

At the same moment a nervous voice whispered from the intercom, "Gwinnie, there's the most awful man down here shouting at us. I think he's drunk. And he niffs like a whole barrel of whaledreck. Can you blast off and cope with him?"

Guinevere told him crisply. "I'm on my way."

But she spared time for one rapid survey of her appearance in the mirror.

She found the intruder confronting Danny-boy, her chief usher—him of the Parisian artist's smock—and growling belligerently. Fortunately, to call it "shouting" was an exaggertion, so the customers in even the nearest posts were unlikely to have noticed anything wrong. Moreover the blonde member of the come-hither team had shown enough presence of mind to move the changeochrome partition so it screened the disgusting stranger from outside.

He was a hulking man, well over six feet, and probably strong in spite of his revolting condition. His hair hung in lank strands all over his collar and merged into a beard and moustache that might as well never have been trimmed, but served as a soup-filter and catch-all for scraps of food. There was a singed indentation in the right lower edge of the moustache as though from smoking hand-rolled joints to the last fraction of a roach. His sweaterette had once been red but was now patched, smeared and streaked with other colours, and if his slax had ever fitted him that must have been years ago; now the waistband had given up struggling against the encroachment of his belly. His feet were planted four-square on her lovely hand-inlaid floor in things that might have been loafers but now were incrustations of garbage totally concealing any fabric that might separate dirt from skin.

He broke off his tirade at Guinevere's approach. "Ah!" he exclaimed. "You must be Steely Gwin from Port of Sin—I've heard such a lot about you! I even wrote a poem about you once. Just a second . . . Ah yes—'Girls made up by Guinevere Steel Look a treat but are lousy to feel. She turns meat that was cute Into plasticised fruit With the juices locked under the peel.' One of those shiggies called you Danny-boy, didn't she?" he added to the quaking usher. "That should make you feel right at home, then. Limericks are Irish too." He hee-hawed with laughter and rocked on his heels.

"Want to hear another? 'If you fancy a shiggy and seize her, And find she's as cold as Teresa, She isn't a freak, It's because the Beautique—' "

Guinevere said with all the dignity she could command, "What do you want in here?"

"Whatinole do you think I want? One of your window-display dummies?" He gestured with black-tipped fingers at the cowering come-hither girls. "Thanks, if I need an inflatable masturbator I'll build my own. Ah, whatinole do you *think* somebody wants who comes into a place like this?"

"You must be drunk or orbiting," Guinevere snapped. "I don't believe you know where you are." She cast a nervous glance at the wall-clock. The current hour's appointments were nearly up, and if the clients were to emerge and see this revolting specimen blocking their exit . . . "Danny-boy, you'll have to call the police. I don't see anything else for it."

"What for?" the stranger demanded in an aggrieved tone. "What do I do? All I want is to be beautified."

"To be what?" Guinevere said. Her breath ran out on the third word. "You must be insane! We don't accept male clients anyway, let alone—let alone *objects* like you!"

"No?" The intruder took a threatening pace closer to her. "New York State Code provisions on discrimination, any commercial establishment offering a service to the general public and declining to accept a prospective client on racial, linguistic, religious or *sexual* grounds shall forthwith have its licence revoked!"

Belatedly Guinevere realised that the man neither spoke nor acted as she felt would match his appearance.

"In any case I know perfectly well you don't discriminate. Apart from Danny-boy—and you're not going to tell me *he* doesn't get you to help him with that impeccable surface sheen!—my old beddy Doll Clark has been coming here for years and he still has his balls. What do you want I should do? Come back in a kilt wagging my hips?"

Guinevere said, with a faint sensation of unreality as though someone had slipped her a cap of Yaginol, "I can ask for proof of ability to pay, at least. And if you could meet my rates you wouldn't be walking around stinking like"—she borrowed Danny-boy's simile because it was definitive—"a whole barrel of whaledreck!"

"Oh, if credit is all that's eating on you—!" The stranger made a face. "Here!"

He reached inside his sweaterette and produced a thick wad of documents. Flipping through them like a dealer riffling a new deck of cards, he extracted one and held it out.

"That do?"

"Hold it so I can read it," Guinevere snapped. "I don't want to touch it, or you."

She looked. It was a bank credit authorisation good for a thousand dollars at sight of bearer. But that wasn't what shook her to the core. It was the name neatly printed across the bottom, under the picture of a much younger man with his moustache and beard trimmed into Louis-Napoleon elegance.

"But he's dead!" she said faintly. "Danny-boy! Surely Chad C. Mulligan is dead!"

"Who?" Danny-boy looked blank for a moment. Then: "Did you say *Chad* Mulligan?"

"Dead?" said the filthy stranger. "Christ, no. And if you make me stand around much longer I'll prove it conclusively. Come on, come on!"

The clock crept towards the final five minutes of the current session. Any second now the first of the clients being attended to would leave the shelter of the curtains. Guinevere swallowed hard. Which of her assistants could be persuaded to handle this job for a hundred-dollar bonus?

"Danny-boy," she whispered, "take Mr. Mulligan in charge and do whatever he wants."

"But, Gwinnie—!"

"Do as I tell you!" She stamped her foot.

After all, he is a considerable celebrity . . .

Forcing herself to overcome her nausea, she said, "Forgive me, won't you, Mr. Mulligan? But—well, this is rather an incongruous guise to find you in!"

"Incongruous my insalubrious hole," Chad Mulligan grunted. "It's the same way I've been looking for the past two years or more. What I'm going to find incongruous is what I'll be like after your mechanics have overhauled me. But I'm giving up. I'm quitting. The sheer God-blasted inertia of this asinine species has defeated me. I can't make people pay me attention whether I argue, or bellow, or daub myself with shit. I propose to pretty myself up and join the rest of you Gadarene swine in debauching myself magnificently to death. All right, where do you want to put me so your other customers won't see the state I'm in?"

And he added over his shoulder as Danny-boy led him away: "Send someone out for a quart of liquor, will you? I need something to nerve me for this."

BE KIND TO YOUR FORFEITED FRIENDS

LOCALE: since it was illegal by city ordinance to occupy that much space by herself what Guinevere had done was to make a settlement on her husband whom she was divorcing largely because his name was Dwiggins and get him to buy with it the vacant apartment below her penthouse and then lease it to her for an indefinite period at a peppercorn rent which was not illegal and the chief method by which the ostentatiously wealthy in the modern super-crowded city secured for themselves that ultimate in contemporary status symbols a home many times larger than one person could reasonably require—to wit two rooms one above the other forty-eight feet by thirty-two, two (ditto) thirty by eighteen, two (ditto) twenty-one by eighteen, four bathrooms *en suite* and two not, four additional toilets, two kitchen-eateries, and a roof-garden which Guinevere had had as it were hollowed out by an ingenious architect so that it became a bower with its main level corresponding to the lower apartment and the upper containing the automatic watering and fertilising sprays together with the artificial sunlight lamps required to keep the plants and flowers healthy.

CONTENTS (PERMANENT): the largest unit-based suite of polyform furniture ever manufactured for a private customer including large tables convertible into desks or screens and small tables convertible into book-racks or trolleys and chairs upright convertible into chairs relaxing and chairs relaxing convertible into lounges and lounges convertible into sofas and sofas convertible into beds and beds convertible for single or double or multiple occupation and so on—in theory capable of adapting the apartment for everything from a well-attended political meeting with everyone sitting around paying serious attention to the subject in hand to a party like the present one with everyone paying serious attention to the subject hoped to be in hand eventually.

CONTENTS (TRANSIENT IMMOBILE NON-PERISHABLE): the latest decorations and pictures and ornaments and models of phone and TV and polyformer and holographic record reproducer and cosmoramic projector and even books—though the latter were hanging in the balance as potentially nonfashionable.

CONTENTS (TRANSIENT IMMOBILE PERISHABLE): an assortment of seven dozen different kinds of foodstuffs guaranteed by the catering company to be accurately twentieth-century in substance and appearance but not necessarily in flavour—certain essential compounds in such items as free-ranged chicken and slow-smoked bacon being no longer reproducible under modern manufacturing conditions—plus bottles and cases and barrels and boxes and jars and cans and packs of liquor and incense and wine and marijuana and beer and even tobacco to give the guests a decadent life-in-my-hands thrill that would also be properly in period.

CONTENTS (TRANSIENT MOBILE BUT IN A SENSE EQUALLY PERISHABLE): a hundred fifty people including the hostess and her guests and many human staff from the catering company which had a good reputation among the new poor of the happening world for concealing payments to waiters and cleaners by inflating their charges for purchase of goodies and thus enabling them to escape the moonlighting tax supposed to wipe out the profit a fully-supported recipient of welfare might derive from odd jobs like these.

EXCUSE AND REASON: making the guests pay forfeits which if she chose she could make so hideously embarrassing the victims would never want to see her again.

COST: about three thousand dollars.

VALUE RECEIVED: that would have to wait until the end of the party to be assessed.

Click and cram the elevators cycling, splash and crash the guzzling well begun.

AUDIO: the most bearable re-made recordings from the latter part of last century, not the most recent (stuff from the nineties was intolerably *vieux-jeu*). No, it had to be from the seventies, endowed now with a certain quaint charm, and on top of that it had to be the kind of music which led most directly to what was currently acceptable in the real world outside—*chants sans paroles* in the rather bland monotonous rhythms of five against four and seven against eight. The quality of the recordings was lousy and the divisible-by-two rhythms seemed banal and boring after subtleties like five against eleven. But each of the records allegedly had sold a million.

If someone comes in wearing Arpège Twenty-first Scentury or anything else like that what shall I make her—or him—do?

COSMORAMIC: mostly the fashionable colours of the nineties because they were currently bearable—apple-green, sour lemon-yellow, and the inevitable pale blues—but changeochrome was newer than the century and there wasn't a moiré setting on the projector which would have been marginally allowable, so it was all stark flat colours and rather drab.

Come to think of it, that stuff of Mel Ladbroke's is new, so what if someone drecky claims forfeit off him for bringing it? The hole; it's my party and I say what's allowed.

GUSTATORY: likely to be the biggest success of the party, no whistlers or moonjuice or any other this-very-instant drinks, but that weird cocktail chart dug up from about 1928 and programmed specially into the consoles—things called "Old-Fashioned" and "Bosom-Caresser" ought to appeal if only for their amusing silly names. Also the food exotic. Out of period, but absolutely unavoidable, generous supplies of antalc, disgorgeant and counter-agents to the most popular lifters, Yaginol, Skulbustium and Triptine. Not permitted at the party, all too new, all post-turn-of-century, but people would certainly turn up orbiting on one or two or maybe all of them.

Snff . . . ? That's Dior Catafalque, I swear it is! Where-inole did she dredge it up? It's been off the market for twenty years! Make a point of asking her what it is; recognising it would date me . . .

SARTORIAL: the most incredible, the most phenomenal mish-mash assembled under one roof this generation except maybe in the General Assembly of the UN.

That girl's wearing Nipicaps. I can tell—who better? Bit early to start imposing forfeits but that will be a lovely lovely start. Something mild—after all, they're one of my own products—but something forceful enough to make people realize I mean business. One moment: girl? That's no shiggy! Well, that forfeit defines itself, doesn't it? Yum!

1969: the hostess in an outfit of PVC which was about as near as they were coming in those days to the stark sleek mechanical styles of the current trend, regrettably needing to be underpinned with the badly engineered and somewhat uncomfortable brassière and girdle appropriate to it—a discovery she had made too late, not having obtained and tried on the costume until it was too close to the start of the party to change her mind. But at least the slick surface was a kind of foreshadowing of 2010; she hated the idea of fur or velvet or one of those other crudely textured fabrics women used to stuff themselves into.

"My dear, haven't seen you in lightyears! That's a most marvellous rig you're sailing under—did it belong to your grandmother?"

19??: Norman House in a full set of jet-black evening dress with a genuine stiff shirt and white bow-tie and even shoes of that revolting stuff called "patent leather"—a hundred per cent genuine to judge from the cracks in them. Guinevere gave him a venomous smile for not allowing her an instant opening for attack and wished that he didn't look so inarguably magnificent in the sombre garb.

"You mean this is really tobacco? Cigarettes of that stuff that was supposed to cause so much cancer? My dear, I must try some—my parents didn't smoke it ever and I hardly believe I saw the stuff before!"

1924: Sasha Peterson in a softly draped tea-gown of semi-translucent chiffon hanging almost to her ankles but slashed behind to the waist, invoking an old-fashioned air called "elegance". Guinevere thought of what the mode-masters were saying about a swing back to a more natural look in shiggies and wished she had never dreamed up this sheeting party.

"Well, if I can't have a whistler whatinole can I have? Oh, give me some bourbon on the rocks, then—I take it that's allowed? I mean, if they had cold drinks at the court of Emperor Nero they had them in the last century?"

1975: a very young shiggy with a beautiful bosom wearing a niltop over a minisarong. Can't legislate for that—any girl who's recently discovered that her body attracts men will go the available limit to display it to them.

"Are we not even supposed to talk about the real scene? I mean, I don't know whatinole people did talk about at parties in the last century—I wasn't old enough to go to them.

1999 and only scraping under the limit by a chronological accident: Donald Hogan in a curiously antique-seeming brown and green totalsuit with a spiral zipper going from right ankle twice around to the left shoulder, face flushed and apparently worried about something but ascribing it for official purposes to the fact that if Norman hadn't remembered to book him whatever was available from the rental agency he'd have had to turn up in the only univer-sally acceptable costume—his skin.

"I shouldn't hope for too much, darling. All tobacco ever did to me was make me throw up. I don't know whatinole people used it for. No, darling, you can't take it in like the smoke from a joint, you have to sort of puff it in straight and then accustom yourself to inhaling it without dilution."

1982 or thereabouts: a positive travesty in the literal sense, in one of these ghastly outfits with five or six layers of mesh in contrasting colours hanging from the hips and shoul-ders, and shoes of enormous size sticking out below.

"One of the reasons I come to Gwinnie's parties is she doesn't feel obligated to ask all these sheeting brown-noses you keep treading on everywhere else, but there are too many of them here for my liking tonight!"

Right. Find out who they are and why.

"Of course the whole thing is sheeting crazy. That was the wildest roller-coaster of a century the human race has ever lived through, if you can call it living—hey, notice that good in-period catchphrase I used?"

Any time: Elihu Masters in a regal suit of Beninian robes, a loose red-and-white top over baggy pants and open sandals his round balding head framed in a kind of crown of upright feathers varnished into brown rigidity around a velvet skull-cap.

"Yes, but what kind of a twentieth-century party? One of those stiff soirées you read about in old magazines dating back to 1901, or something right up close to our own day like a Sexual Freedom League meeting? I don't know what-inole I'm supposed to be doing and Gwinnie has that forfeit light in her eye. Maybe it's safest to tag along after her and be in the support group when she picks on someone."

1960: Chad Mulligan perspiring in a hound's-tooth check tweed suit which was all the costume rental agency had left in his size when he shrugged and let Guinevere persuade him to attend.

"Yes, of course I'm nervous. I hate to miss these parties of Gwinnie's because normally I make out fine and she's never picked on me yet, but this time I'm violating the conditions so flagrantly—I mean, this isn't a last-century costume, it's all I could dig out from my father's wardrobe and it says right on the label 'Summer collection 2000' but there wasn't anything older."

1899: an incredible multi-caped garment vainly hauled in around a large waist and a skirt dangling to the ground and a silly bonnet on top of it all and the excuse prepared that there was no reason in *those* days why a dress shouldn't have been worn for two years or even longer.

"When Gwinnie gets really nasty I'm going to blast off. I know another party which ought to be humming by then."

Any time: Gennice, Donald's one-time shiggy, in a minor

stroke of genius, an undatable Japanese happi-coat and traditional slippers to match.

"Must have been funny living in those days. I know someone who rebuilds and runs cars for a hobby, for instance, but for all he can do to the—what's it called? Exhaust?—they stink worse than a barrel of whaledreck. Makes my eyes water just to go near one when he's got it running!"

1978: Horace, a friend of Norman's, in a ventilated parka with contrasting hood over jodhpurs, a perfect memorial to the way men's fashions were going over the edge into pure schizophrenia in that hysterical epoch.

SITUATION: a lot of people drifting about and looking each other over covertly or sometimes overtly, knotting gradually into groups of former acquaintances separated by strands of people who never met before and who haven't yet softened their self-consciousness to the point of blending in. In short, as was probably the case in Pharaonic Egypt where they first established the tradition of giving parties, a party that hasn't jelled.

"That's a very curious perfume you're wearing, darling."

Nervous laugh. "Of course, you're an expert on that, aren't you? Do you like it? It's a bit musty, isn't it? It's something called Dior Catafalque that my mother gave me when she heard I was coming to your party."

"Catafalque? Really? Isn't that the thing they lay out corpses on when they're lying in state?"

"Yes—I think that's the idea. It's supposed to be sort of musty and decaying." Shudder. "Actually it's pretty horrible, but it is in period, isn't it?"

"Goodness, I wouldn't know for certain. I'll take your word for it, though."

SITUATION: same.

"Don! Don!"

"Oh—hullo, Gennice. Nice to see you again."

"Don, this is Walter that I'm living with now—Don Hogan

that I was with before, Walter. Don, you don't look as if you're enjoying yourself at all."

It shows that much? But they said keep on with your ordinary life until you leave, so ... Wish I had the guts to back down. I'm frightened!

"I need a lift, I think. Don't suppose Guinevere would approve, though."

"There's plenty of pot. And someone did say that that codder there—I think the name's Ladbroke—was from Bellevue. He may have something."

SITUATION: same.

"You're *Chad Mulligan?* Prophet's beard, I thought you were dead!"

"Might as well be. Intend to be. Just think I might as well take a lazy man's way out. Get me another drink."

"Elihu, here's a man you ought to meet! I saw one of his books in your room when I called the other night!"

SITUATION: same.

"I say, someone told me you were from Bellevue and ... Oh. Excuse me. I just saw somebody I know."

"Yes, that's right. My name's Schritt—*Mister*—Helmut Schritt." A quick glance around and an insincere smile. "Routine precaution. There's a vanishing chance that someone might try to foul up your—uh—business along the lines I recall being mentioned last time we met. Act as normally as you can and avoid any entanglements that would prevent you leaving a bit earlier than the mass, okay?"

"Act normally!"

"That's what I said. Like keep your voice down when you talk about the—uh—subject of importance, hm?" Another of the insincere smiles.

SITUATION: same.

"Darling, that's a wild rig you're sailing under!"

"Gwinnie, I'm so glad you like it!"

"But aren't those Nipicaps a trifle out of period . . . ?"

Sudden tension. A personal silence for all the screaming of the records in the background. A shifting of several of Guinevere's closest sparewheels to encircle the victim and savour the inaugural forfeit of the evening.

"I—uh—I . . ."

"Well, I mean, I should know, darling, since I have them made specially for the Beautique and sell them by the literally *thousands!* And they only made their splash two years ago."

"Forfeit!" someone said decisively, and there were grins.

"Ye-es, I think so. And it sort of writes itself, doesn't it? Take it off, darling, from *there*"—shoulder—"to *there*"—waist.

Sickly embarrassed but complying: result, the strange hermaphrodite. Scalp to neck, elaborate coiffure, immaculately painted face with eyebrows arched and lashes lengthened and lips clear red and earrings jangling; waist to floor, skirt and hose and jewelled 1988-style boots; between them, that incongruous bare male chest with good solid muscle and hair in concentric curves swirling out from the nipples.

"I think that'll do nicely," Guinevere said with satisfaction, and those around chortled and clapped her and each other on the back and those as yet out of range of her decisions relaxed and began to chatter loudly again.

SITUATION: same but with an admixture of high nervous laughter.

"Darling, of course I'm only really well grounded in feminine fashions, but I do seem to detect something a teeny bit incongruous in that outfit you're wearing . . . ?"

"Well"—swallow hard—"ah . . . as a matter of fact—"

"Darling, don't prevaricate. You know how much I detest prevarication."

"Forfeit! Forfeit!"

"Well, Gwinnie dear, it's as old as I could lay hands on, honestly it is."

"No doubt, darling, but you've been to lots of my parties

and I'm sure you've had as much fun out of seeing other people pay forfeits as they're going to get out of you. Now let's see. What would be appropriate? Bearing in mind that it's early yet, so because of that and because we like you a whole great slobbering lot we'll want to keep it a mild one, won't we?"

SITUATION: less laughter, more tension.

"Sadistic bitch, isn't she?"

"You should see her when she gets on to an Afram, Mr. Mulligan."

"If you call me 'Mr. Mulligan' one more time I'll throw this liquor all over your smart period-piece." Gulp. "Cancel that—I'll break the glass on your ought-to-be-nappy skull. Anyway, she's wrong."

"What?"

"She's wrong. But that's irrelevant, I guess. If that's the way her guests like her to run her parties I'll just sit quietly here and give thanks to any deity who may exist that I ran into intelligent company. Elihu, I'd like to know something more about this place Beninia. There are some highly anomalous factors in what you've been telling me—"

"Excuse me, Chad, *please*. How did you mean, 'she's wrong'?"

"Norman, you do have eyes, hm? And you're blessed with a reliable memory, hm? The hole, then! What were *you* wearing in the summer of 2000? Something like that, I'll wager."

"The summer of—? Prophet's beard, of course! I'm an idiot."

"You belong to an idiotic species. I even wrote a book to draw attention to the fact. I was idiotic myself to think it would do any good."

He turned back to Elihu and waved his empty glass without looking away to his right, hoping that a passing waiter would take it in exchange for a full one.

Norman shouldered his way through the people crowding close around Guinevere and her intended victim. He heard suggestions: "Take it off and put it back to front! Take off everything that's newer than the century! Make it look a bit older—like by tearing a few holes in it at the right places!"

"Just a second, Gwinnie," he said boredly, triumphantly.

"What do you want to do, Norman—arbitrate?"

"As a matter of fact, yes. That looks like a year 2000 garment to me. How about it, friend?"

"Why, it says right here on the label that it is, but—"

"Twentieth century, then."

"What? Norman, you're spouting dreck. Go away. Now I think what we ought to do is—"

"The twenty-first century didn't begin until a minute past midnight January first 2001."

Awkward pause. Someone: "Sheeting hole, I think he's right."

"Dreck. I recall distinctly on New Year's 2000 we all—"

"And the commentators did say that wasn't right, it comes back to me now."

"The hole, let's make him do it anyway."

"No, got to fly by the course we set in the first place."

Silence in the immediate vicinity.

"Gwinnie, I'm dreadfully afraid he's right. He is, you know."

Nods.

"Well, how funny! Lucky for him you came along, isn't it, Norman? Never mind, sparewheels, there's bound to be someone else. Break it up and let it fall free, hm?"

And, as she contrived to brush against Norman on her way to match orbits with a circulating waiter: "Fix you later, you clever brown-nose!"

"You're welcome to try, darling," Norman said. "You're welcome to try."

SITUATION: suddenly and to Guinevere's enormous chagrin, a real party flying high and free in a genuine party-type orbit.

"Chad Mulligan? Never in a million lightyears!"

"I so testify."

"Not the fat Afram?"

"No, the one with the beard."

"The lean Afram?"

"Sheeting hole! *No!* The WASP talking to both of them."

"Christ, everybody's been saying he was dead!"

"Mel, I think some time later on we might break out a few caps of that stuff I asked you to bring. There's a too-clever bleeder here I'd like to fetch down from orbit."

"Hi, Don. Elihu, this is my roomie Donald Hogan—Chad Mulligan, Don."

"Hi. Now, as I was saying, what McLuhan didn't foresee although he came sheeting close to it was—"

"I'm delighted to meet you, Mr. Masters, but this is about the last place I'd have expected to run into you."

"When Norman called on me the other night he mentioned this party and said I should come if I wanted to see the kind of problems Aframs still have to cope with in this country, so I thought it over and decided he was probably right, I ought to."

"You won't get the full measure of Guinevere's ingenuity just standing by and watching, sir. You need to *be* someone like Norman, who's about on her own level, not someone with cachet like yours."

"Why?"

"If you'd turned up wearing your ordinary street-clothes she'd only have made you pay some kind of nominal forfeit— standing on your head for ten seconds, or singing a song, or taking off your shoes. Something that wouldn't have interfered with your enjoyment of the rest of the party, I mean."

"That's what one generally expects at a forfeits party, isn't it?"

"There's been a change since you went abroad, sir." *Why all this "sirring"? Must be a subconscious response to the fact that as of this morning I'm officially Lieutenant Hogan!* "A few years ago that was true. Not any more."

"I see. I think. Give me examples."

"Oh . . . Well, I've seen her compel guests to daub themselves all over with ketchup—and shave their heads bald— and crawl around the floor on hands and knees for an hour, until she got tired of enforcing that—and, if you'll forgive me going into such details, to piss themselves. That comes later and is used to get rid of people she doesn't want to stay around when the orgy starts."

"That goes without saying, does it?"

"Oh yes."

"Is that why people stand for such treatment?"

Chad Mulligan broke in; for the past few moments, unnoticed, he had abandoned the conversation he was having with Norman and had been listening to Donald and Elihu."

"Sheeting hole, no! At least I'll wager it's not why Norman keeps coming, unless you've got a well-concealed masochistic streak—hey, Norman?"

"Some people come out of masochism, definitely," Norman shrugged. "They like to be publicly humiliated. You can generally spot them; they're blatantly infringing whatever the rule of the evening is, but steering clear of Guinevere's direct attention until fairly late when they've drunk enough or smoked or ingested whatever they need to give them sufficient offyourass for the show-down. Then they go in for cringing and begging to be let off and being jeered at for spoilsports—the whole shtick—and generally they come while they're getting the treatment. Which of course makes everything free-falling for them and that's why they accepted the invitation anyway. Harmless, mostly."

"I was asking about you, not them," Chad said impatiently.

"Me? I keep coming here because—okay, I'll open up wide. It's a constant challenge. She's a mean bitch, but she's never yet caved me in on one single forfeit, and there have been times when there were thirty or forty of her pet sparewheels yelling for me to pay one. That's why I keep on accepting. And frankly it seems to me like a damned stupid reason. This one is going to be my last, and if you weren't here, Chad, and if I hadn't conned Elihu into coming, I'd have left already."

Donald looked at Chad Mulligan. He still only half-believed that this was the genuine article, but the resemblance to the pictures on the jackets of Mulligan's books was unmistakable—the keen eyes peering out from under heavy brows, the hair combed diagonally back, the neatly trimmed moustache and beard setting off the cynical line of the mouth. There was a more dissipated look to the face in reality than there had been in the publicity shots, but maybe that was due to age rather than actual surrender.

He hoped so.

"Darling, you do the zock marvellously! You have the genuine free-fall touch!"

"Why, Gwinnie, that's sweet of you."

"There's just one trouble, darling. The zock is strictly a this-minute dance, isn't it?"

"Forfeit! Forfeit!"

"I'm afraid they're right, darling, much as it pains me to insist. Don't you know any of the *old* dances? How about the shaitan? That goes to this kind of rhythm, I think."

"Of course it does, Gwinnie. I'm terribly sorry, I should have thought. You want me to do the shaitan for my forfeit?"

"That's right. But—somebody hand me that dish of honey from the table there? *Thank* you, lover-girl. Hold this in between your elbows while you're demonstrating it."

"But—*Gwinnie!* It'll get all over everything!"

"That's the idea, darling. Come on now, and make with the whole bit. I want to see you touch the floor with the back of your head."

"Well, yes, I am a bit out of sorts, I guess. You see, I'm taking this metabolic-rebalancing course that the Orbital Clinic provides for people who don't respond to Triptine— you've heard about that? Uh-huh. And there's one drecky drawback, which is it makes you much more susceptible to colds, so I'm full to *here* with counteragents and what with one thing and another my hormones and enzymes are going over Niagara in a barrel. I say, is that twentieth-century or nineteenth?"

"Of course, it's public knowledge that if the Nark Force was given the funds and support it needs to enforce the legislation it's supposed to the government would be out on its ear tomorrow. But the discontent needed for a genuine revolution is being drained off into orbit somewhere and that suits Washington fine."

"So they got these two volunteers, you see, this codder and this shiggy who didn't give a pint of dreck about doing it in public, and they laid on this exhibition of human reproductive processes for Shalmaneser."

"No matter what they say I can't tolerate adherents to a cult which doesn't respect the human rights of non-members. That's bigotry irrespective of what verbal haze you generate around it. And these Right Catholics with their insistence on unrestricted breeding are trespassing on the human rights of everyone else's children. They sheeting well ought to be banned."

"Right across the block from where my brother-in-law lives. And such a mild-mannered old codder too, he said. Just picked up this butcher's cleaver and chopped the heads off the kids he was looking after, then went up on the roof with this crate of empty bottles, and started hurling them down on the people below. Killed one, blinded another, had to be fused by a police copter. Could be *anybody*, you see—and without universal personality-profiling how can one be sure who's going to turn mucker?"

"Well, we're pretty lucky, you see. We managed to get into a club—about fifteen couples, all celebrated their twenty-first, very nice people—and there's a sitting rota so we get to look after the prodgies of members who have clean genotypes. There are nearly a dozen altogether and one of the shiggies is supposed to be preg with twins. Marvellous. We can reckon on having prodgies around the place at least one night a week. It's not like having one's own, but—well, there's no help for it. We have schizophrenia on both sides of the marriage and the risk is far too great."

"Oh no. Philip is much too young to come along to a party like this. Time enough later on to become sophisticated and cynical and debauched like us oldsters, that's what I keep telling him. Of course he doesn't like it—goes on all the time about what other parents allow their prodgies to do at his age—but one doesn't want to see the bloom of innocence rubbed off too soon, does one? You're only young once, after all."

"Frank and Sheena? Oh, they went to Puerto Rico. Didn't have any choice—they'd sold the apt, bought the tickets, got jobs out there . . . But they were *furious!* Said they were going to get out of the States altogether as soon as possible so they could after all have their own prodgies. But lord knows where they can go. Can't see them roughing it in some benighted backwater country for long, myself, and of course they'd never be allowed back if they did start a family after being forbidden to do so here."

"You heard what happened? Thought they were being clever. Found someone in the Eugenics office who was open to—ah—persuasion and got themselves a forged genalysis. Went to a private clinic, and the karyotype said they were going to have a mongoloid idiot. Twenty-five thousand buckadingdongs it cost them to get that gene certificate, and they had to have the kid aborted after all!"

"We got ours through the Olive Almeiro Agency. Very big operation. Naturally it can't be passed off as our own—my wife is even fairer than I am and the kid is dark, hair, skin, eyes, the whole shtick—but we could have waited five, six years for a baby to match our own genotype and then not been able to afford the cost."

"So when these two had finished Shalmaneser said where's the baby? And they said oh, you have to wait nine months for that."

"Look, I don't mind panhandlers as such—in fact I think it's a damned good idea to license them because at least that gives you the option of choosing whether you're going to support a given individual case instead of simply taxing you and passing the money on in welfare allotments to wastrels and vagabonds. But the way the union has got whole districts of the city sewn up now and insists on kickbacks and drives non-members out of the area—that's more than I can swallow!"

"Oh, are those the new Too Much joints? May I try one? I heard very good things about the strain. Thanks. I hope Gwinnie doesn't recognise them or she'll make us pay forfeit on them and I don't like the look in her eye. She's building up to something really nasty, I suspect."

"The draft got his balls. They're cracking down very hard

at the moment. Did everything he could—turned up for the board with mother in tow, wearing one of her dresses, orbiting like crazy, and they took him anyway. He's in that horrible army hospital St. Faith's right this minute undergoing aversion therapy for ambivalence *and* tripping both at once. It's absolutely inhuman, and of course if it works when he comes back he won't want to know any of his old friends, he'll be one of their automatic push-button people, a good solid respectable citizen. Doesn't it make you want to weep?"

"One thing about this crazy party, I do depose—I never expected to see so many shiggies at Guinevere's place looking like shiggies instead of like sterile-wrapped machines. Do you suppose she's testing the temperature to see if she should move the Beautiques over to the natural trend?"

"Happened all in a moment. One second, just a bunch of people walking down a street, not going any place in particular, and the next, these brown-noses clanging on big empty cans with sticks like drummers leading an army and all sorts of dreck flying through the air and windows being smashed if they weren't out already and screaming and hysteria and the stink of panic. Did you know you can actually smell terror when people start rioting?"

"Louisiana isn't going to last much longer, you know. There's a bill up for next session in the state legislature which will ban child-bearing by anyone who can't prove three generations of residence. And what's worse they're only offering five to two against it being passed. The governor has his two prodgies now, you see."

"I was in Detroit last week and that's the most eerie place I ever did set foot. Like a ghost town. All those abandoned factories for cars. And crawling with squatters, of course. Matter of fact I went to a block party in one of them. You should hear a zock group playing full blast under a steel roof five hundred feet long! Didn't need lifting—just stand and let the noise wipe you out."

"It's more than a hobby, it's a basic necessity for modern man. It fulfils a fundamental psychological urge. Unless you know that if you have to you can kill someone who gets in your way, preferably with your bare hands, the pressure from all these people is going to cave you in."

"I graduated with a master's rating on throwing knives and a grade one rating on hand-to-hand. I already have a marksman certificate on bolt-guns, and next I'm intending to collect one for projectile weapons—rifles, pistols and crossbows."

"Sure you can come around, but don't hope for too much. I'm living in a group, you see, and there are eight of us, so I don't feel much need for variety. Also we have two kids and our shrinker says they have positively Polynesian emotional stability so the last thing I want is to interfere with a setup that's paying such fine dividends. It's the extended family bit, of course."

"Nevada's mavericking again, did you hear? There's a bill up for next session to recognise polygamy and institute proper marriage and divorce laws to cover it. Up to groups of ten, I think it says in the draft."

"Don't lie to me, *darling.* I saw that codder's blip go up on your screens the moment he asked you to dance. I've told you before and I'm telling you again, I don't mind you bivving it privately but I won't stand for it in public. So I'm an old-fashioned block, so I'm still your wife and if you want me to stay that way you behave when you're in company—catch me?"

"So Shalmaneser said well, if it takes nine months, why were you in such a sheeting hurry at the end? Haw-haw-haw!"

"I've been hoping to have a word with Chad Mulligan, but I can't pry him away from those Aframs he's talking to. I want to ask him whyinole when all our dreams are about wide-open spaces and room to move and breathe we like to cram ourselves together at parties till we can't hardly cross the floor of a room without shoving aside twenty other people."

"Look, lover, you carry it off very well but I fly a perfectly straight orbit and what's more I'm married so why don't you find someone who likes to biv and stop harassing me?"

"I got one of these super disposalls, too, because the garbage clearance down our block is five weeks—catch me, *five!*—overdue. And the first day I try to use it comes in this sheeting little pest and says I'm violating the clean-air laws.

Great balls of dreck, clean air! There hasn't been any clean air in our neighbourhood for sheeting weeks because of rotting dreck all over the streets and now it's beginning to block the passages!"

"Yes, but what's the use of arguing about politics these days? Isn't such a thing as politics. There's just a choice between the ways you're going to cave in through force of circumstances. Look at Common Europe, look at Russia, look at China, look at Africa. The sheeting pattern's the same except in some places it's gone further than others."

"Look, Schritt—all *right!* Look, *Helmut!* If you don't get off my orbit and let me fall free for a bit I'm going to stand right up where everyone can hear me and pull rank, do you hear me? I don't give a pint of whaledreck if Chad Mulligan does sound subversive to you—he happens to be talking to our ambassador to Beninia and I'm interested in what they're saying. I was told to carry on with my ordinary activities and if you've read my original brief you sheeting well ought to know that it includes being interested in everything relevant or not relevant to my assignment. Now go dig a hole and lie down in it!"

"Things are getting tough again in India, apparently. It's the protein that was lost when the slit-eyes poisoned the Indian Ocean. And by the way, I hear the containment programme is running behind—a current spilled over past one of the barrages and they've been hauling out contaminated fish as far north as Angola."

"I have this new autoshout of GT's that programmes itself on a signal from the satellite. Haven't missed a show in three weeks through rescheduling. Should get one."

"I use nothing but Kodak Wholopan R myself. The rating is 2400, to start with, which means there's practically nothing you can't catch, and there's ninety-five per cent recovery on a division factor of twenty, which means you never need more than one print and a pair of scissors."

"No, that's what's so extraordinary. Freefly-suiting is *terrific* exercise, a sort of dynamic tension method because all your muscles are working against each other. Of course, you have to watch your calcium balance like a spy, but there are treatments which actually improve it over normal Earthside levels now."

"The acceleratube makes commuting perfectly possible. I can get to work quicker from Buffalo than I used to when I lived in Elizabeth."

"I think I'll have to take copter lessons."

"You know that magnificent new block in Delaware that we spotted from the plane as we were coming in and thought what a great place it could be to live? Well, I just met someone who told me what it's meant for, and unless you feel like going out and shooting a fuzzy-wuzzy we can kiss the dream goodbye. It's a sheeting jail, that's what it is—a new maxecurity jail!"

"We're going to have to do as they've done in London and Frankfurt. We're going to have to make better use of the space already enclosed by the cities we have. In London they've more or less given up the idea of streets except for arterial throughways. They're building over them and leaving nothing but tubeways for passenger transit."

"It just sort of folded like a leaky accordion, all thirty storeys of it. Girders bulged outwards, floors lay down on top of each other, and *squelch*, all the people who were living in it—I think they said nine hundred—were flattened out like sardines in a sandwich. Apparently when they programmed the computer which designed it they forgot to instruct it to allow for the weight of the occupants."

"Exceptionally good freevent the other night. It was literally indescribable because it was so abstract. I still haven't got over it."

"What it does is sort of *invert* the responses—for example I never found anything in my life quite so funny as the B Minor Mass. And let's face it, you know, in the ultimate analysis that's a *proper* response in contemporary terms."

"Yes, I knew somebody who applied to them. Wanted to go out being gored by a bull in front of a big cheering audience, believe it or not. So they fixed it, got the setup from Mexico, wrung the buckadingdongs out of him and the cost ran to plenty, of course, and he had a heart attack from overexcitement before they turned the bull loose, so back he went to hospital to be revived and he ran out of funds while he was getting better and in the end he just signed an ordinary release and they withdrew his prosthetics. A débâcle on a grand scale, but still a débâcle!"

"He and his sister joined the Mrs. Grundy Memorial Foundation and some sheeting little prig turned up some forgotten ordinance and the case comes up next week. Going to be a major point of principle at stake."

"Skiing in Patagonia, I think. We were going to spend it under the Caribbean, but Mr. and Mrs. Everywhere go there such a lot we're afraid it'll be dreadfully crowded."

"She's quite marvellous. All I did was give her that lock of my mother's hair and she told me the most fantastic things— I mean, I never knew mother had all those affairs, one after the other, and most of them with brown-noses! I knew I was right not to trust her with what father left!"

"The Vedantas, of course, say something quite contrary."

"One of these Antarctic treks, probably. I hate the snow but whereinole else is there that Mr. and Mrs. Everywhere haven't been recently? I can't stand all these interchangeable people!"

"The future is inherently perfectly knowable. All the faculty takes to develop is the proper kind of exercise and meditation."

"You sound as though you fell in love with Beninia right from the start. Was it just because you knew and admired Zadkiel Obomi or was there something else to it?"

"There's this tour to Khajuraho which sounds like fun, with all those parties planned around the erotic sculptures on the old temples, but apparently the tourists have to go there under armed guard because of danger from native robbers and frankly I don't see how I could enjoy it to the full with a circle of gunmen standing all around me."

"This marvellous recording of the Ninth which puts you right in the middle of the choir—when the Ode to Joy lets loose it's like an earthquake!"

"I've been painting some Jackson Pollocks with my polyformer this week and it's left my arms stiff as fenceposts."

"Moonbase Zero is more like a submarine than anything else. I really admire the people who stay there for a whole tour—some of them stick it for over six months, you realise?"

"Our shrinker recommended sending Shirley to this new school at Great Bend and I think that's a marvellous idea but Olaf has these dreadfully antique views about juvenile eroticism and says they lay too much emphasis on sensuality, so I'm going to file for divorce and get custody and then Wendy and I will take her out there ourselves."

"Makes you wonder how our ancestors ever managed to breed such a sheeting horde of human beings when every time you felt like it you had to take off all these layers and layers of cloth."

"I think I'm going to sue them even though they didn't give me a guarantee. I mean, eight thousand isn't to be dropped like an empty pack of reefers, is it? And all the pup did when we got it home was sit around snivelling and pee on the floor every half-hour. The prodgies were heart-broken, of course, because they did so much want a green dog and they just wept and wept so I'm sure it was traumatic for them. Edna says I should have gone to some other company who've cut down the side-effects, but believe me I'm not going to risk another gene-moulded pet. They can make do with a regular cat next time."

"Well, if your genotype is okay, why don't you just get yourself preg by someone else who's also clean? Me, for example? I have my genalysis with me, as it happens."

"Charlie, got any stiffener with you? I just had this shiggy in the roof-garden and I promised Louise as well and I don't want to be left dangling when the big scene takes over later."

"This mutated cactus with the huge orange flowers that last for weeks after they're cut, but you have to keep them under a glass bell because they do stink rather, a bit like rotting meat."

"I never took to polyforming. Rather stay with my old hobby of vicarious music. Blocky it may be, but I don't have the talent to go through a Cage score on my own jets, and I do love the feeling of actually creating the sounds with my fingers."

"The bleeder slipped her a cap of Yaginol while she was

preg and of course they had to abort the phocomelus. She's suing him."

"Thinking of cutting out to join one of these communities in Arizona."

"Dead set on going into the space service but I guess he'll grow out of it when he discovers shiggies."

"Sold my shares in Hitrip like a sheeting idiot and then two months later they announced the Too Much strain and I guess I lost fifty thousand buckadingdongs on the deal."

"So they programmed Shalmaneser with the formula for Triptine, you see, and then these jokers fed in the question How Hi is a Chinaman."

"I think instead of increasing it to four months' vacation they should operate two shifts on monthly rotation. Of course it would cost but the degree to which it would increase the self-respect of the employees would more than make up for it."

"Most of them seem to be at it in the roof-garden. Want to go and watch, get some pressure up for later?"

"I think these cigarettes are horrible. Made my throat so sore. And my guts are all sour and nasty. Did people really use twenty in a day?"

"They call it streamlining, of course, but what it comes down to is they're undermining my responsibility in the firm and I'm going to fight tooth and claw to hang on to what I've got. If I have to play it dirty that'll be their fault, not mine."

"It makes genuine three-dimensional poetry possible for the first time in history. Right now he's experimenting with motion added, and some of the things he's turned out are hair-raising."

"You hold the knife this way, see?"

"Refuse to teach their children to read and write, say it handicaps them for the post-Gutenberg era."

"Not many people have spotted it but there's a loophole in the Maryland eugenics law."

"A polyformer for water-sculpture, quite new."

"Of course I don't love Henry the way I love you but the shrinker did tell me I ought to occasionally."

"I'm just cutting jets for a prayer or two but I'll be back—don't get involved with anyone else."

"That makes seventeen different mixtures I've tried, and I'd better have some antalc, right away."

"I think it was bitchy not to tell Miriam it was pig-meat."

"They're trying to ranch the orange ones in Kenya but apparently so far only the pale-blue ones will breed true in the wild state."

"I think I'm going to shake off my holding in MAMP. It's been years after all and by this time I'm wondering if the rumours about the big strike were just propaganda."

"Had a chance to talk to Chad Mulligan? Nor have I. I was wondering whether to be really twentieth-century and go ask for his autograph."

"Campaign to get whales back by breeding up from smaller aquatic mammals but the cost is astronomical!"

"Blew up three bridges before the fuzzy-wuzzies fused them and one of them turned out to be in the same class as my son Hugh."

"I'm sorry to snivel like this but it's damned unfair having him killed in a stupid sheeting accident like that and now being married to someone who's not allowed to father prodgies. And he was only six, he couldn't even read yet!"

"Watch out for Guinevere—I think she's building up to the big staged ones. I'm going up to the other floor for a bit. Some of the things she does when she's in that mood don't strike me as funny."

"I got on fine with Don and to be quite honest I half-hoped he'd ask me to make it permanent. But I couldn't stand his roomie."

"Of course it can't be the Chinese who supply them with sabotage equipment. Explosives and thermite maybe, but not the tailored bacteria they used to bring down that apartment building in Santa Monica."

"So Shalmaneser said how high is a Chinaman? I don't know, but if he's any higher than I am we might as well quit because they have us beat."

"Accused of reviving thuggee—you know, Kali-worship?— and the crowd stormed the court and set them free."

"Spend my vacation taking that induced-schizophrenia

course they offer at the Leary Clinic—think it'll broaden my horizons."

"Wanted to be burned alive in protest against the draft but the directors of the company apparently decided it was interfering in politics and not in accordance with their corporation charter so he tried to do it by himself and they put him out before he'd done more than sustain third-degree burns. Going to jail for ten years, I gather. Evasion."

"A *totally* corrupt police-force is the next best to a perfectly honest one. Ours is quite livable with. Mark you, it takes a bit of time occasionally finding out who's bidding against you, but there are only a few possibilities in a small community like ours."

"So when he said he had a clean genotype but he was going to be sterilised anyway I lost my temper—can you blame me?"

"It's twentieth-century for me to be jealous, isn't it? You keep away from my wife or I'll get Gwinnie to make you pay forfeit for behaving in a twenty-first century manner!"

"I'm going to have to find out more about Beninia, Elihu. I can't really believe what you say is true."

"I got two glasses of the '98 Château Lafite before it ran out and believe me it was quite an experience."

"Have you tried it intravenously? You can get diadermic guns for about forty or fifty bucks, and it makes a galaxy of difference to the lift."

"Talking about clearing the old Renault factory but it'll be like civil war—there are sixty thousand squatters on the ground and apparently some of them have bolt-guns and the place is crawling with old projectile weapons of course because they went over to sporting guns when they closed."

"Told me about this public execution he went to in Algeria and it got me so excited I just couldn't help myself. Why don't you ask him about it? He did say he bivs occasionally."

"So she told her to smear her belly with apple-butter and let the sparewheel lick it off. She's getting nasty, darling. Next time it won't be licking, it'll be biting. Want to blast off for home?"

"Look out, he's got a knife!"

"But the whole aesthetic of holographic television is being called in question by Eldred's work."

"I've taken over the selection programme for the Museum of Last Week, did you hear? How about letting me have some of your stuff?"

"Tripping."	"By the way, Norman, I did men-
"Work."	tion, didn't I, that I'm being
"Religion."	thrown out of my place and I'm
"Psychology."	looking for a spare tatami?"
"Eugenics."	"How are we doing for liquor?"
"Society."	"Mel Ladbroke, right? Look,
"War and peace."	you don't by any chance——? Oh,
"Sex."	*sheeting hole!* Forget it."
"Food and drink."	"Are you by yourself, lover?"
"Politics."	"It would make a difference if
"Hobbies."	they could afford to buy gene-
"Art."	moulded maize stocks, for exam-
"Entertainment."	ple. But they can't."
"Housing."	"Gwinnie's saving you up, you know!"
"Travel."	"People are stupid, including me."

"Guinevere got anybody's balls yet?"

GRAPH GUINEVERE: an early peak followed by a flat low line marked at its inception by Norman's correction of her judgment regarding the man in the year 2000 suit. Since then, a state of suppressed anger, punctuated by only enough minor forfeits to keep that hard core of her sparewheels contented. Saving up the remainder—all noted with sharp eyes and double-checked mentally to avoid a second similar gaffe—for an unusually extensive series of set-piece forfeits at the end of the evening. Included with question-marks, people like the ambassador who has completely wasted his cachet and Chad Mulligan's into the bargain by talking together non-stop throughout the evening despite several attempts to make them circulate. Trust a brown-nose to foul things up, ambassador or no.

GRAPH DONALD HOGAN: a jagged line varying between sick dismay masked with polite and occasionally quite interesting chat to Elihu, Chad, Gennice and other acquaintances, and raw fury at being dogged by Sergeant Schritt. Four separate attempts to corner the man from Bellevue privately and perform that quasi-suicidal act of obtaining from him some sort of lifter or whatever that would enable him to break his cover under the pretence of being slipped a cap by someone unknown. Shortly, the line due to snap up into the unknowable hyperbolic future course of the activated spy.

GRAPH GENNICE: a high-level curve with a lot of peaks of amusement and enjoyment because she's very fond of her new man, but with occasional wistful dips caused by wondering whether it's her departure that made that nice Don Hogan feel so low tonight.

GRAPH CHAD AND ELIHU: an early plateau low on the scale, then a simultaneous rise and a long, long parallel run not across the regular chart of the party but away from it at an angle of their own, pacing each other and still rising.

GRAPH NORMAN: an early peak caused by so successfully scoring off Guinevere, followed by a slow decline with occasional bumps tending towards determination to see her look equally foolish if she tries to involve him in a set-piece forfeit or towards self-disgust because he prizes such a petty achievement.

GRAPH THE PARTY: a planar representation hillocking over the roof-garden where those interested mostly in sex congregated early and heavily indented in the vicinity of Donald, Norman, Guinevere herself and one or two more, otherwise generally on an acceptably high level although a good many people have had the edge taken off their enjoyment by the aura radiating from Guinevere by now consulting in whispers with certain chosen sparewheels and who can be sure what infelicity, what incongruity, as minor as having referred to a post-turn-of-century artwork has given her the opening for another arrowed forfeit?

"If Gwinnie picks on me I'm going to give her a present. From this firm that sends people around to invade your apt and wreck the furniture!"

Now I can get the two shiggies, the fat and the thin ones, to change clothes, which ought to be good for five minutes and a few giggles, and during that time slip Norman a cap of

. . .

"What was that?"

"That girl with the hideous caped outfit, I think—I saw Gwinnie consulting a history of costume in the other room just now."

"Excuse me, do you mind saying that again?"

Like a cool breeze soughing through the room: a wave of interest and curiosity.

"No, that weird codder Lazarus hasn't been through the mill yet and I never knew him to miss. He loves being humiliated, gives him the strangest kind of lift, apparently."

"Are you sure? Who told you?"

"I made a wager with myself that she'd pick on Renée—you know, the fat shiggy with the glandular thing they can't cure, like a big sagging jelly? She always gets hit hard."

And what I'm going to do to Norman will make history. Not this time the cunning brown-nose doesn't get off lightly! That codder with the Black Belt in case he tries to duck out, to be safe. Where is he? Not involved with another *shiggy!*

"But it must be pure propaganda! I mean, so far not even the dogs and cats and bushbabies they've made over for pets are . . ."

"Is something going on over there?"

"Let's find out, shall we?"

"Darlings, how convenient for me to have caught you talking to each other! You see, I'm terribly afraid that—"

"If SCANALYZER carried it the news must have been processed by Shalmaneser so it's at least possible. Unless they carried it in the rumour slot, was that it?"

It began to dawn on Guinevere by slow degrees that for the first time ever since she took to throwing forfeits parties the arrival of her well-briefed gang of sparewheels in the neighbourhood of the victims chosen for the first of the grand forfeits, the set-pieces that would include dialogue and climax in acts of maximum humiliation to get rid of people she was tired of knowing, had not signalled silence and giggling and craning of necks and climbing on furniture for a better view. Instead, on the far side of the room, a large number of the guests were talking to each other with serious faces, apparently sceptical but not scoffing. She waited a moment. A few people drifted away from the unidentified focus of attention and others joined; somebody hurried out of the room and came back with half a dozen friends also to be told—whatever the news might be.

"Hullo!" Norman said softly. "What's going on? Guinevere isn't getting the rapt audience she counts on."

"Think war's broken out?" Chad muttered and grabbed a fresh drink from a passing tray.

Alarm transfixed Donald like a lightning strike. The randomness of his activating this morning, unaccountable in terms of what the news channels were carrying, made him think for a moment that it could all too easily be war.

"Chad, what did you say about crying wolf in *The Hipcrime Vocab?*"

"Howinole do you expect me to remember? I'm drunk!"

"Wasn't it something about—?"

"Ah, sheeting hole! I said it was an ad-hoc form of Pavlovian conditioning adopted by those with a lust for power to prevent the people due to be slaughtered in the next war from taking them out and humanely drowning them. Okay?"

"Why do you hate Miss Steel so much?" Elihu asked Norman under his breath.

"I don't hate her personally, though if she were enough of a person to be worth such a strong emotion I think I easily could. What I hate is what she represents: the willingness of human beings to be reduced to a slick visual package, like a new television set—up-to-the-minute casing, same old works."

"I hope I can believe that," Elihu said unhappily.

"Why?"

"People who hate in concrete terms are dangerous. People who manage to hate only in abstracts are the only ones worth having for your friends."

"Plagiarist!" Chad threw at him.

"Did you say that?"

"Christ yes. Put it in a book."

"Someone quoted it to me once." A look of wonder

crossed Elihu's face. "As a matter of fact it was Zad Obomi."

"Profit but no honour in my own country," Chad grunted.

"What's she going to do now?" Norman said, watching Guinevere intently. They all turned to look; they were in a good spot from which to see what happened, able to view it along a sort of alley between the clump of people who had congregated to witness the humiliation of the fat girl and the thin one, and the other group worriedly muttering to each other about the as yet mysterious news.

"Shelley-lover," Guinevere said to the man at the centre of the latter assembly, "if the news you're spreading is so millennially important don't you think you should share it with everybody rather than letting it wander around on its own, suffering the folk-process? What is it—have the Chinese towed California out to sea, possibly, or has the Second Coming been announced?"

"Second!" someone unidentifiable said within earshot of Don. "Prophet's beard, you should try that new stiffener Ralph's been feeding me!"

Guinevere looked for him with a glare of murderous ferocity and failed to locate him.

"Well, it's something that was on SCANALYZER earlier this evening, Gwinnie," the man she had addressed as Shelley explained in an apologetic manner. "Apparently the government of Yatakang has announced a two-generation programme based on a new breakthrough in tectogenetics. First off they're going to optimise their population by making sure that only children of first-class heredity get born, and later, when they've done that, they're going to start improving the genalysis and—well, I guess the only way you can put it is to say they propose to breed supermen."

There was a stunned pause. The woman whose six-year-old son had been killed in an accident and who had by then re-married a husband forbidden to father children shattered the silence with a moan, and instantly everyone was talking, forfeits forgotten, except Guinevere, who stood in the middle of a clear patch of floor with her face whiter than chalk and her long sharp chromed nails digging deep, deep into the

palms of her hands. Watching her, Norman saw how the
tendons stood out on the backs of them like thick knotty
cables feeding power into a machine.

"You!" Chad said. "You there—what's your name! Don
Hogan! This is your line, isn't it? Is it dreck or not?"

At first Donald couldn't answer. This must be why they'd
activated him. Somewhere, ten years in the past, someone—or far more likely, something, since it would have been
a computer analysis they trusted to make forecasts on such
an important subject—had suspected the possibility of a development along these lines. Against that vanishingly small
risk they had taken precautions; they had chosen, and nur-
tured, a man who—

"Are you going deaf, codder?"

"What? Oh—sorry, Chad, my mind was wandering. What
did you say?"

Listening to the repetition of Chad's question, already
aware of what it was, Donald cast his eyes around nervously
for Sergeant Schritt, and there he was, a few places distant in
the throng. But his cocksure manner of earlier had faded in
an instant; he looked, in fact, as though he was going to
cry.

His lips moved. He didn't see Donald before him although
he raised his face and his gaze swept across where the other
was standing. Off the writhing mouth Donald read what he
was saying too quietly for it to carry through the mounting
chatter. It was approximately, "Sheeting hole, sheeting hole,
and they wouldn't let me and where is she now who's got her
who's making her preg—?"

It went on. Donald, embarrassed, turned his eyes away. He
felt he had just looked into another man's personal hell.

But in a state like that Schritt wasn't going to worry about
his charge delivering classified information to a potential
subversive like Chad Mulligan. In any case, everything Donald knew about the subject was thanks to his college courses
and the New York Public Library. Only the all-
encompassing patterns he had been able to formulate out of
what he read were in any sense less than public knowledge.

He said tiredly, "It doesn't have to be dreck.
SCANALYZER carries both gossip and hard computer-

evaluated fact, and the guy didn't say it had been in the rumour slot."

"Who've they got over there who could handle such a programme?" Chad was leaning forward now, elbows on knees, eyes sharp and alert, his drunkenness magically forgotten. Also, Elihu and Norman were listening intently to what Donald and he were saying.

"Well, the first part—the simple optimising of your embryos—has been theoretically possible since the 1960s," Donald sighed. "Reimplantation of externally fertilised ova is offered in this country as a commercial service, though it's never been popular enough to become cheap. Governmental decree, though, might—"

He stopped short and snapped his fingers. "Of course!" he exploded. "Chad, you impress the hole out of me, know that? You did ask, didn't you, 'who've they got over there?' "

Chad nodded.

"It was the right question. For the second stage—the bit about going beyond the mere purification of your gene-pool to actual improvement of the stock—you do need the genius of someone with high-level breakthrough capacity. And they have a man like that, somebody who hasn't been heard of for almost ten years except as a professor at Dedication University."

"Sugaiguntung," Chad said.

"That's right."

Elihu looked, puzzled, at Chad first, then Donald, asking a question with lifted eyebrows.

"Sugaiguntung was the man who put Yatakang into the tailored bacteria market when he was in his twenties," Donald said. "Brilliant, original, supposed to be one of the world's greatest tectogeneticists. Then he—"

"Something about rubber," Chad interrupted. "It's coming back to me now."

"Right. He developed a new strain of rubber-tree which replaced the natural strains in all the Yatakangi plantations and as a result it's the last country anywhere on Earth where synthetics can't compete with tree-grown latex. I didn't know he'd been working on animal stocks, but—"

"Has he any? What would you need, anthropoid apes?"

"Ideally, but I imagine quite a lot could be done on pigs."

"Pigs?" Norman echoed in a disbelieving tone.

"That's right. Pig-embryos are often used for teaching purposes—the resemblances are astonishing until very shortly before birth."

"Yes, but we're not talking about the embryonic scale," Chad pointed out. "This is deep-down stuff, right inside the germ-plasm. Orang-outangs?"

"Oh my God," Donald said.

"What?"

"I never made the connection before. The Yatakangi government has been diligently preserving and breeding orang-outangs for the past five or six years. Right out of the blue they imposed a death penalty for killing one and offered a reward equal to about fifty thousand dollars for capturing them and bringing them in alive."

"Let's get out of here," Chad said with decision, dumping his glass on the nearest table and jumping to his feet.

"Yes, let's," Norman agreed. "But—"

"I don't mean stop talking about it," Chad snapped. "You live together, don't you? We'll go to your place. Elihu, will you come along too? When we've sorted this out there are still more questions I want to ask you about Beninia. Okay? Right, let's blast off out of this freaking awful party and go find some peace and quiet!"

They were not the only ones who had had the same idea. Glancing back as they waited for a chance to filter through the exit door, the last thing Donald saw was Sergeant Schritt leaning on the wall with one hand, with the other holding a large glass of vodka or gin from which he tossed gulp after gulp down his throat to put out the fire of sorrow in his heart.

And by tomorrow, how many more like Sergeant Schritt?

context (13)

THE OLD NEWSPAPER

"BOY SHOOTS FIVE DEAD IN BEAUTY SCHOOL

"Mesa, Arizona, 12 November

"FIVE PEOPLE, including a mother and her three-year-old daughter, were shot dead today by a boy who forced them to lie down on the floor of a beauty school here.

"Two other victims—including the three-month-old baby of the dead mother—are in hospital.

"It was the third mass murder in the United States in four months. In August a sniper shot dead 15 people in Austin, Texas, and in July eight student nurses were strangled or knifed in Chicago."

"THE LONGEST RISK YET IN SPACE

"by our Science Correspondent

"ASTRONAUT Edwin 'Buzz' Aldrin opened the hatch of his Gemini-12 spacecraft yesterday and stood up in space. Two hours and 28 minutes later he withdrew, having set a record for direct exposure to the hazards of space."

"NEW EINSTEINS FROM 'CUTTINGS'

"by JOHN DAVY, our Science Correspondent

"IT MAY soon be possible to propagate people in much the same way as we now propagate roses—by taking the equivalent of cuttings.

"According to the Nobel prize-winning geneticist, Professor Joshua Lederberg, writing in the *Bulletin of the Atomic*

Scientists, we should consider the implications of this now, since it would offer the possibility of making dozens or hundreds of genetically identical individuals like multiplied identical twins . . .

"The techniques are likely to be tried 'even without an adequate basis of understanding of human values, not to mention vast gaps in human genetics.' This makes it essential to think out the implications beforehand, since otherwise policies are likely to be based on 'the accidents of the first advertised samples.' Public opinion might be determined by the nationality or public esteem of the cloned person, or 'the handsomeness of para-human progeny.'

"The prediction and modification of human nature, the professor urges, badly need the planning and 'informed foresight' which we apply to other aspects of life."

—Three adjacent news-stories from the front page
of the London *Observer,* 13th November 1966

continuity (13)

MULTIPLY BY A MILLION

Riding home from Guinevere's, Donald felt the Yatakangi claim oppressing his mind, a monstrous mattress of news. He hardly spoke to the others in the cab. He was half-dead from fatigue, having contrived only a couple of hours' sleep before Delahanty broke in on his rest. Tiredness and the tranks he had taken had combined to mute his feelings all day long. He had not even been able to convert his fury at Schritt dogging him into decisive action.

Yet knowing he had let himself slide through his last day as a free agent before the maw of government engulfed him did not seem to disturb him unduly, and the reason why gradually emerged into awareness.

Yesterday, when he had left the Public Library after his stint of duty, the illusion had overtaken him that all the masses of New York were animate dolls, less than human, and he among them. Determined to prove he was not really inhabiting a hostile world, he had wandered from illusion into the harsh reality of a riot. A small one, granted—not like some that had taken place in Detroit, for example, with a death-toll in the hundreds—but final enough for the copter pilot who had been killed with clubs.

Suddenly, today, this was not the familiar world he had lived in for the past decade, but another plane of reality: a fearful one, like a jungle on an alien planet. The police captain had said that on present evidence it was a hundred per cent certain he would start a riot if he went for a harmless evening stroll. So not only the world, but he himself, was different from what he had imagined.

Caught like this, suspended between the wreck of former convictions and the solidification of new ones, he could no more have rebelled against the decision of the computer in Washington to activate him than he could have brought the dead pilot back to life.

Apathetically, not assigning meanings to the words, he heard Norman address Elihu.

"Did you put the scheme to GT today as you intended?"

"Yes."

"And—?"

"Shalmaneser had already given them four possible reasons for my approaching them. This was the one he—I mean *it*—rated highest." Elihu shuddered. "They had contingency plans prepared, trial budgets, even a tentative advertising programme. And they loved every moment while they were explaining how they'd pre-guessed me."

"Their security must have been better than usual," Norman said. "Not a word of it filtered through to me."

"You referred to Shalmaneser as 'he'," Chad said. "Why?"

"The people at GT do it all the time," Elihu muttered.

"Sounds as though he's becoming one of the family. Norman, *is* there any truth in this propaganda about making Shalmaneser genuinely intelligent?"

Norman made a palm-up gesture to pantomime ignorance. "There's a non-stop argument over whether his reactions are simple reflex any longer. But it's out of my range, I'm afraid."

"I think," Chad grunted, "that if he really is intelligent nobody will recognise the fact. Because we aren't."

"When are they going to make the news public?" Norman inquired of Elihu.

"Not yet awhile. I insisted. I'm going back for further discussions tomorrow, and someone from State is supposed to join us—probably Raphael Corning, the synthesist. And you too, naturally, because I think you should make the first contact with Zadkiel on the company's behalf."

He concluded bitterly, "In view of what I'm wishing on them, though, I can't help wondering if the Beninians will ever forgive me."

It'll be a relief to get away from here, Donald realised with amazement. *Christ, I think I'd have been glad if they'd put me in jail this morning. I'd take a job on the moon, or at MAMP—anything, even in Yatakang—for the sake of being in a place that I expect to take me by surprise instead of my home city where things I thought were comfortable and ordinary got up and kicked me in the face.*

When they entered the apt, Chad set off on a survey of the premises without asking permission, peering into each room in turn and shaking his head as though in wonderment. Over his shoulder he said, "Like coming back to a dream, know that? Like waking, and going back to sleep next night, and finding the dream's been going on without you and here you are entering it at a later stage."

"Do you think the kind of life you've been living the past few years is—is more real, then?" Elihu inquired. No one had invited him to sit down; because it was closest he took Norman's favourite Hille chair and settled his bulk in it with much adjustment of his Beninian robe. He set aside his velvet-and-feathers headdress, rubbing the line it had indented across his forehead.

"More real? Sheeting hole, what a question! But the whole of modern so-called civilised existence is an attempt to deny reality insofar as it exists. When did Don last look at the stars, when did Norman last get soaked in a rainstorm? The stars as far as these people are concerned are the Manhattan-pattern!" He jerked his thumb at a window beyond which the city's treasure-house of coloured light glimmered gaudily. "To quote myself—the habit that persuaded me I ought to quit trying to influence people because I'd run out of new ways to express my ideas—where was I? Oh yes. The real world can take you by surprise, can't it? We just saw it happen at Gwinnie's party. The real world got up in the middle of the apt and did it ever shake the foundations of those people!"

Sober, Norman said, "What's the effect going to be, do you think?"

"Christ, why do you have to treat me as a Shalmaneser-surrogate? That's the trouble with you corporation zecks—you trade your faculty of independent judgment against a bag of cachet and a fat salary. Mind if I help myself to a drink?"

Norman started. He pointed mutely at the liquor console, but Chad was already there scanning the dials.

"I saw some of the effect right there at the party," Donald said. He wanted to shiver, but the muscles of his back refused to respond to the urge. "There was a man—doesn't matter who. I read his lips. He was saying something about a girl he'd lost because he wasn't allowed to be a father."

"You can multiply him by a million as a start," Chad said, raising a whistler from the console's outlet. "Maybe a lot more. Though that party was hardly a fair sample. The sort of people who go to such romps are on average too selfish to make parents."

He poured the whistler down his throat in a single gulp, nodded approval at the impact it made, and dialled another.

"Just a second," Elihu put in. "Mostly, people talk as though it's the parents who are the selfish ones. And this alarms me. I mean, I can see how having three, four or more children could be regarded as selfish. But two, which only maintains a balance—"

"It's classic economic jealousy," Chad said with a shrug. "Any society which gives lip-service to the idea of equal opportunity is going to generate jealousy of others who are better off than you are, even if the thing that's in short supply can't be carved up and shared without destroying it. When I was a cub the basis for this resentment was relative intelligence. I recall some people back in Tulsa who spread slanderous gossip about my parents for no better reason than that my sister and I were way ahead of all the other pupils in our school. Now the scarcity item is prodgies themselves. So two things happen: people who've been barred by a eugenics board, feeling they've been unjustly deprived, hide their sour-grapes pose behind a mask of self-righteousness—and a lot of people who can't face the responsibility of raising prodgies seize on this as an excuse to copy them."

"I have a grown son," Elihu said after a moment. "I

expect to be a grandfather in a year or two. I haven't felt this effect you're talking about."

"Nor have I, on the personal level, but that's mainly because I don't like to choose my friends among the kind of people who react that way. Mark you, I'm not much of a father except in the biological sense—my marriage caved in. Also my books act as a splendid surrogate for the basic function children perform for their parents."

"Which is?" Norman demanded in a faintly hostile tone.

"Temporal extension of personal influence over the environment. Children are a pipeline into the posthumous future. So are books, works of art, notoriety and sundry other alternatives. But you can't have a score of millions of frustrated parents using authorship to sublimate their problems. Who'd be their audience?"

"As far as I'm aware I have no desire for children," Norman said challengingly. "Despite my religion! A lot of Aframs feel the way I do because our prodgies would be raised in what remains a foreign and intolerant setting!"

"Oh, someone like you acts as his own child-surrogate," Chad grunted. "You're too sheeting busy making yourself over in a preconceived image to want to spend time licking a cub into shape as well."

Norman rose half out of his chair, an indignant retort on his lips. With it still unuttered he contrived to turn the movement into reaching for a reefer from the box on the nearest table.

He said, more to himself than the others, "Prophet's beard, I hardly know who I am any more, so . . ."

Donald repressed an exclamation at hearing his own predicament so patly echoed. But before he could speak, Elihu had put another question to Chad.

"Granting you're right, what's going to happen if this breakthrough in Yatakang takes away the excuse for forbidding parenthood on eugenic grounds? I mean, if you can have a healthy, normal child even if genetically it isn't yours, it's one step closer to the natural process than adoption, and I know dozens of people who've adopted and been apparently quite satisfied."

"Why don't you ask Shalmaneser? Sorry, Elihu—didn't

mean to snap. It's just that I really have decided to give up trying to keep track of the human race. Some of our behaviour is so unbelievably irrational . . ." Chad rubbed tired eyes with his knuckles. "Sorry," he said again. "I can make a guess. There's going to be trouble. Come to think of it, that's a safe catch-all prophecy. *Whatever* happens in present circumstances there's going to be trouble. But if you want to know what an expert thinks, why don't you ask Don, not me? You have a degree in biology or something, don't you?" he concluded, addressing Donald directly.

"Yes, that's right." Donald licked his lips, resenting having been drawn into the conversation when all he wanted to do was sit and be miserable on his own. For the sake of politeness he tried to order his thoughts.

"Well . . . Well, there's nothing radically new about the first half of the Yatakangi programme, if what the man at the party said was correct. The techniques for optimising your population by ensuring only children of good heredity get born have existed for decades—you could even say for centuries, because if all you want to do is select, you can do it by conventional breeding methods. But I assume they're talking about something more ambitious. Even so, you can donate semen, you can reimplant an externally fertilised ovum if it's the mother's heredity that's at fault rather than the father's—the hole, that's available as a commercial service right here in this country! It's expensive, and sometimes it takes three or four attempts because the ovum is very fragile, but it's been being done for years. And if you're prepared to stand the cost of missing a dozen launch windows before the tectogeneticists achieve a viable nucleus, you can even have a parthenogenetic embryo—a clone, as they call it. There isn't anything so new in this claim from Yatakang."

There was a pause. Norman said at length, "But the second stage, the bit about deliberately modifying the children into supermen . . . ?"

"Wait a minute," Chad cut in. "Donald, you're wrong. It seems to me there are two very new factors involved even before you get on to the point Norman just raised. First off, a scarcity product is suddenly not going to be scarce any more.

You can't carve up and distribute fair shares of the available healthy prodgies, though people have been trying to do exactly that, by forming these clubs you keep running into which give non-parents a night or two a week to look after other members' prodgies. What's the population of Yatakang, though—something over two hundred million isn't it? There's no *question* of scarcity if the government intends to carry out its promise on that scale.

"And the second new factor, which is even more important, is this: *somebody else has got it first.*"

He let the words lie heavy in the air like a haze of smoke for long seconds before he gulped the last of his drink and gave a sigh.

"Well, I'd better go find a hotel, I guess. If I'm coming back from the gutter to join the merrymaking on the eve of Ragnarök I might as well go the whole hog. Find myself an apt tomorrow, load it with all the goodies people go for nowadays . . . Anyone know a good interior decorator I could call up and tell to get on with the job without bothering me?"

"Where have you been living, then?" Norman demanded. "Oh—the hole. I didn't mean to be inquisitive."

"I haven't been living anywhere. I've been sleeping on the street. Want to see my permit?" Chad reached inside his fancy-dress suit and produced his greasy billfold. "There!" he added, extracting a card. "This is to certify—etcetera. And the hole with it."

He stuffed the billfold back in his pocket and tore the permit into four pieces.

The others exchanged glances. Elihu said, "I didn't realise you'd carried your policy of opting out quite that far."

"Opting out? There's only one way to do that, the same as throughout history: you kill yourself. *I* thought I could resign from society. The hole I could! Man's a gregarious animal—not very social, but damnably gregarious—and the mass simply won't let the individual cut loose, even if the bonds are no more than police permits for sleeping rough. So I came back, and here I am in this idiotic outfit of grandfather's clothes, and . . ."

He scowled and threw the scraps of card at a disposall.

One of them missed and fluttered to rest on the carpet like a dying moth.

"I could fix you a room at the UN Hostel," Elihu suggested. "The accommodation is basic, but it's convenient and cheap."

"Cheap doesn't bother me. I'm a multimillionaire."

"*What?*" Norman exclaimed.

"Sure—thanks to the bleeders who bought my books and refused to act on what I said in them. They're set in college courses, they're translated into forty-four languages ... I'm going to spend some of this credit for a change!"

"Well, in that case ..." Norman let the words die away.

"What were you going to say?"

"I was going to say you were welcome to spread your tatami here," Norman explained. "Assuming Donald doesn't mind. I don't know how soon they'll be sending me to Beninia, but I'm bound to be away a fairly long time. And—ah—I'd count it a privilege to have you as a guest." He sounded uncomfortable.

"Chad can have my room as of tomorrow night," Donald said, and thought too late of the shiny spike he had been shown, hidden under the Hille chair.

But the hole with that.

Norman turned to him incredulously. "What happened? What decided you to leave?"

"I've been told to," Donald said.

What will they do to me for this? I don't know. I don't care.

He leaned his head back and sleep came while his eyelids were still sliding down.

tracking with closeups (13)

THE GOOSEBERRY BUSH

Fat, black-haired, slightly sallow, with a big red mouth and bright dark eyes, Olive Almeiro looked the very model of a peasant materfamilias, except that her arms were weighed down by bracelets of emeralds and diamonds. The image of motherhood was part of her stock-in-trade. In fact she had never even married, let alone borne children.

Nonetheless, she insisted on her staff calling her "señora" rather than "señorita", and in a sense she was entitled to the aura of maternity. She had stood proxy-mother, so to speak, to more than two thousand adoptees.

They had provided her with her floating home, the yacht *Santa Virgen* (a name from which she derived wry amusement); with the office-building she owned and operated from; with an international reputation; with all the comfort she could buy and a second fortune in reserve to purchase more.

It was just as well they had done all this before today.

Her office, windowed on all four sides, was decorated with dolls from every period of history: ancient Egyptian clay animals, Amerind toys of knotted and coloured straw, carved wooden manikins from the Black Forest, velvet teddy-bears, Chinese figurines made from scraps of priceless silk . . .

Imprisoned behind glass, too precious to be touched by the fingers of a child.

She said to the phone, staring out across the blue morning waters of the ocean, "What's it going to do to us?"

A distant voice said it was too soon to tell.

"Well, work it out and do it fast! As if the trouble we're having with the dichromatism bit wasn't enough, these bleeders in Yatakang have to—ah, never mind. I guess we could always move to Brazil!"

She cut the connection with a furious gesture and leaned back in her polychair, swivelling it so that instead of the calm blue sea she faced the teeming city on the landward side.

After a while she pressed an intercom switch. She said, "I've made up my mind. Unship the Lucayo twins and the Rosso boy that they sent from Port-au-Prince. Before we dispose of them they'll eat as much as we can make in profits."

"What do you want us to do with them then, señora?" asked the voice from the intercom.

"Leave 'em on the steps of the cathedral—put 'em out to sea in a basket—why should I have to tell you what to do, so long as you unship them?"

"But, señora—"

"Do as I say or you'll be out to sea in a basket yourself."

"Very well, señora. It's only that there's this Yanqui couple who want to see you, and I thought perhaps . . ."

"Oh yes. Tell me about them."

She listened, and within the minute had summed them up. Doubtless having given up everything at home—their jobs, their apt, their friends—for the sake of a legal conception in Puerto Rico, they had been cornered by the J-but-O State's unexpected ratification of the dichromatism law and were now driven back to considering adoption, which they could have arranged without leaving the mainland.

I'm sick of them. The brown-noses are the worst, lording it over us spics when our ancestors came here as conquerors and theirs came as slaves, but just about any Yanqui gives me morning-sickness.

The silent joke lightened her mood enough to permit her to say, "All right, send them in. And what did you say was the name?"

"Potter," said the intercom.

They came in holding hands, and stared at her covertly while settling in the chairs she waved them to. One could almost hear the mental comment: "so this is the famous Olive Almeiro!" After a while, the wife's attention wandered to the display of dolls, and the husband cleared his throat.

"Señora Almeiro, we—"

"You got caught with your pants down," Olive cut in.

Frank Potter blinked. "I don't quite—"

"You don't imagine you're unique, do you? What's your trouble—colour-blindness?"

"That's right. And my wife is sure to pass it on, so—"

"So you decided to migrate and because Nevada is expensive and Louisiana doesn't like being used as a conception refuge you chose Puerto Rico and the legislature shot your ship out from under. What do you want me to do about it?"

Taken aback by the baby-farmer's curtness, Frank exchanged glances with his wife, who was very pale.

"It was on the spur of the moment," he admitted. "We thought you might be in a position to help us."

"To adopt? I doubt it. If you are willing to consider adoption you need have moved no further from New York than New Jersey." Olive fingered her jowl. "You probably want me to disguise a child of your own as an adoptee. It's already on the way, isn't it?"

Frank flushed to the roots of his hair. He said, "How could you possibly—?"

"I told you you're not unique. Was it intentional?"

"I guess so." He stared at the floor, miserably. "We decided to celebrate our decision to move, you see. But we didn't realise it had happened so quickly. We didn't find out until we'd arrived here."

"They didn't spot it at Immigration? No, come to think of it, they only check women arriving from abroad and from the maverick states. In that case you're already in a cleft stick. Either the prodgy was conceived in New York State where you'd been specifically forbidden to start one, or it was conceived here where transmission of your genes is now illegal, or between the two which makes it a prohibited immigrant the moment it leaves the womb. So . . . ?"

"We thought maybe if we went out of the country altogether," Sheena whispered.

"And got me to adopt it back in, and reunite you with it?" Olive gave a humourless chuckle. "Yes, I do that sort of thing. For a flat fee of a hundred thousand."

Frank started. "But that's far more than——!"

"Than the cost of a regular adoption? Certainly. Adoption is legal, subject to certain conditions. What you're proposing is not."

There was silence. Eventually Olive said, having savoured their discomfort, "Well, Mr. Potter, I'd suggest the only solution for you is to start over. I can recommend GT's line of abortifacients, and I know a doctor who won't insist on the kind of pregnancy check he's supposed to carry out before prescribing them. Then I could put you on my regular waiting list. Beyond that I can't be any help."

"There *must* be something else we can do!" Frank almost jumped out of his chair. "We want our own prodigies, not someone else's second-hand! Over in Yatakang they've just announced they can——"

Olive's face went as hard as marble. She said, "You will oblige me by leaving, Mr. Potter."

"What?"

"You heard me." A podgy hand stabbed a button on her desk.

Sheena plucked at her husband's arm. "She's an expert, Frank," she said in a dead voice. "You've got to take her word for it."

"No, this is too much! We came in to make a civil inquiry and——"

"The door behind you is open," Olive said. "Good morning."

Sheena turned and headed for the exit. After a moment in which he looked ready to scream with fury, Frank let his shoulders droop and followed her.

When they had gone, Olive found herself panting from the effort of self-control. She pronounced a curse on the government of Yatakang and felt a little better.

But her hatred was new and raw; like a dressed burn it hurt despite salving.

Over the years she had built up a huge network of necessary contacts, expended a million dollars in bribes, risked prosecution a score of times, secure in the belief that products of contemporary tectogenetic skill such as cloned embryos could never compete with traditional "unskilled labour". She had begun when only two states, California and New York, had eugenic legislation, and Puerto Rico was full of overburdened mothers with passable genotypes prepared to let a fifth or sixth baby go for adoption to some rich Yanqui. As the eugenics laws spread and grew teeth, as voluntary sterilisation after the third child became commonplace, she developed alternatives. A clean genotype, while still desirable, posed less of a problem than proving the adoptee was an American citizen when for brown-nose parents-to-be it hailed from Haiti, for gringos from Chile or Bolivia.

With much trouble and care she had mothered an enterprise that coped with all the difficulties. Now, suddenly, the sheeting Yatakangis had laid a long black shadow of disaster half around the world. They were not merely offering for free a chance hitherto denied to all but the richest families—they were intending to insist on it. The child born of any womb could be a genius, a Venus, an Adonis . . .

And if their further claim was true, who would want a run-of-the-mill child when there were going to be improved versions with unguessable new talents?

From her desk she picked up its only ornament, a conch-shell of exceptionally vivid colouring, and threw it at the window overlooking the busy city. It fell in pieces to the floor. The glass was unmarked, and the universe outside was still there.

continuity (14)

THE RIGHT MAN FOR THE JOB

There was no longer a real world. It receded from him like the half-grasped images of a dream: epitome of the uncertainty principle, torn asunder by the effort of clutching them. It was already hazy when he committed himself to the East River acceleratube, and the last shreds dissipated behind the plane which arced him across the continent on the fringe of empty space, where the stars might be like white-hot needles if they could be seen.

They were, of course, not seen. Through radiation shielding and crash protection and layers of heat insulation that at re-entry glowed (by report) dull red, the stars could not penetrate to the eyes of Donald Hogan.

He thought of Chad Mulligan asking when last he saw the stars—asking when Norman last got wet in the rain—fading, illusory, spawn of a drug. A woman in the next seat spent the journey chuckling to herself, making a wholly personal trip, and he sometimes caught a sweetish whiff of something she had in a smelling-bottle with a foam wad closing the neck. He thought at one point she was going to offer it to him, but she changed her mind.

Why kill a man you've never seen before? The pilot of the shot-down copter, whose skull the crowd had smashed, seemed more real to him than Norman, than Chad, than anyone. The abstract truth of that death grew solid in his mind, making him think of Haldane's argument that an intelligent bee would conceive ideas like "duty" to be concrete.

If they wished to, legally they could put a weapon in his hand and tell him to go across the Pacific Conflict Zone to kill strangers. They did it daily to hundreds of young men picked by an anonymous computer. The New York rioters had been armed, too, and that was called crime. Between that act and this ran only the tenuous dividing line called an order.

From whom? In these days, from a man? Probably not. His illusion on Fifth Avenue outside the library, therefore, was not illusion. *First you use machines, then you wear machines, and then . . . ?*

Then you serve machines. It was obvious. It followed so logically it was almost comforting. And Guinevere was right after all to make the clients of her Beautiques into glossy factory products.

It was even clear why people, including Donald Hogan, were willing to accept the instructions of a machine. Many others besides himself must have discovered that serving human beings felt like treachery—like selling out to the enemy. Every man and woman *was* the enemy. Biding their time, perhaps, masking their intentions with fine polite words, but in the end clubbing to death you a stranger on their own home street.

They opened the can-container of the plane and spilled the passengers like pilchards into the warm hesitant sun of early Californian summer. The expressport was featureless, like an aircraft carrier, its passenger terminal and service depots sheltered by a thickness of earth from the risk of a crash and an explosion. Accordingly what he saw of the sunlight was through armour-glass, and he did not smell the salt air off the ocean but the perfumed exhaust of the conditioning system. The burrow-like passages divided him from the last vestiges of the world he had left on the other coast, seeming to force his thinking into an analogue of their uncompromising square section with sharp right angles where they joined. Everything seemed new and improbable, as though he were under a drug that destroyed perceptual sets. The spectacle of so many men and women in uniform was a source of wonder: the olive-drab of Army, the dark blue of Navy, the light blue of Air, the black and white of Space. The PA system uttered cryptic orders full of numerical and lettered codes until in addition to visual confusion he began to lose control over his auditory faculties, imagining that he was in a country he had never heard of where they spoke the staccato language of machines: *01101000101* . . .

A clock told him what time it was and his watch assured him the clock was a liar. Posters warned him about danger from spies and he began to be afraid of himself because he was a spy. A rope fence hung on coloured metal poles isolating a branch corridor down which char-marks and bright scratches suggested an explosion. An unknown hand had chalked on the wall DREKY REDS. A man went by holding his head consciously high: eyes aslant, complexion marginally yellow, a Nisei badge pinned to his shirjack seeming like the flimsiest of armour. More uniforms, this time the blue and black of police, scrutinising everyone. On galleries there were zoom TV cameras and a team of four men were collecting all the fingerprints that accumulated on the escalator handrails and taking them to a computer readin to be checked against headquarters files. ASK THE MAN WHO'S MARRIED TO MARY JANE.

But STOMP THAT ROACH.

"Lieutenant Hogan?" a voice said. TUNE IN AND TURN ON TO THE WORLD IN A RADIO-DRESSLET.

But KEEP THE WORLD AT BAY THROUGH SAFE-T-GARD INC.

"Lieutenant Hogan!" HERE TODAY AND GONE TODAY IS THE PIDGIN WE PLUCK.

But SEE IT THROUGH THE EVERYWHERES' EYES
. . .

He wondered if Sergeant Schritt was supposed to have been on his plane; he wondered if the man had managed to get as drunk as he wanted; he wondered if oblivion had brought surcease. That was the last and final courtesy he paid to the dead alien world of the past decade. It was out of reach now, receding along the fourth dimension at the speed of light. It had been his, private, like the illusions of a hitripper, and as Chad had promised the real world had reserved its unique power to take him by surprise.

He said, listening with interest to the disbelief in his voice, "Yes, I'm Hogan. Were you sent to meet me and take me to Boat Camp?"

Among the dead-whale hulls of military craft soiling the once-fine beaches, the incongruously small, incongruously bright and incongruously noisy cockleshell of a cushioncraft ferried him and his anonymous companion over the rolling inshore surf towards the Devil's Island bulk of Boat Camp on the skyline. Clambering among the struts supporting the vast main platform as though preparing to return to the simpler and less dangerous universe of the race's monkey ancestors, recruits in full combat gear struggled to evade their sergeant's wrath.

"I sent to Washington to have you re-evaluated," said the colonel he was brought to see. "It's something I'd have thought they'd make sure you appreciated before recruiting you, let alone activating you—that no individual has the whole picture, or even enough of it to make trustworthy judgments on his own initiative. However, I see your special aptitude is pattiducking, so you have a marginal chance of being right more often than most people. Don't do it again, is all."

"My special aptitude is what—sir?"

"Pattiducking! Pattern generation by deductive and inductive reasoning!" The colonel pushed his fingers through his hair in a combing movement.

Another barrier went up between Donald and the man he had believed himself to be. It made no real difference—the past was already out of reach. But he had always cherished that talent as something particularly his own, and in a ghostly fashion he was hurt to find it was well enough known to have a nickname.

"What is it I'm not supposed to do again, sir?" he demanded.

"Jump to conclusions, of course!" the colonel rapped. "I

guess you decided it was a foregone conclusion that your mission was connected with this new genetics programme, but you sheeting well shouldn't have pre-guessed an official decision to shed the cover Delahanty gave you."

Shed? . . . Oh. He means tell Norman and the others that I'd been instructed to leave New York.

Donald shrugged and remained silent.

"You have your sealed orders with you?" the colonel asked.

"Yes, sir."

"Give them here."

Donald handed over the package. The colonel scanned the documents it contained and placed them in a chute alongside his desk labelled *Destruct Secret Material.* Pressing a button, he sighed.

"I don't yet have the full details of your revised cover," he said. "As I understand it, though, the official announcement from Yatakang means that more foreign visitors than usual can be fed into the country convincingly by the regular channels. You'll find them a sight easier than the irregular ones." His eyes wandered to the office's single window, which overlooked a parade-floor where a group of raw draftees were doubling to and fro.

"Broadly, at all events, you're to be sent in openly as a freelance scientific reporter accredited to SCANALYZER and Engrelay Satelserv. It's perfectly authentic, and before you raise the point I'll say that your lack of experience is of no consequence. You need only ask the kind of questions legitimate journalists will be asking about the eugenics programme. You'll be given a certain amount of additional information, however. Most importantly, you will be the only foreign reporter in Yatakang with facilities for contacting Jogajong."

Donald stiffened and his scalp began to crawl.

I didn't know he was back there! If he's what they claim him to be I'm liable to walk into a civil war!

Mistaking Donald's dismay for incomprehension, the colonel rasped, "Don't you know who I mean?"

"Yes, sir," Donald muttered. Nobody who had had to learn contemporary idiomatic Yatakangi could have avoided mention of Jogajong. Jailed four times by the Solukarta government, banned titular head of the Yatakangi Freedom Party, leader of an abortive revolt after which he had had to flee the country, author of books and pamphlets which still circulated despite police seizures and public burnings . . .

"Any questions?" the colonel said suddenly, sounding bored.

"Yes, sir. Several."

"Hah! Very well, let's hear them. But I warn you, I've told you as much as you're supposed to know at this stage."

That disposed of about four questions immediately. Donald hesitated.

"Sir, if I'm going to be sent openly to Yatakang, why was I told to come to Boat Camp? Won't they be suspicious if they find out I've been at a military establishment?"

The colonel thought that over. He said at length, "I believe that's answerable on current terms of reference. It's a question of security. Boat Camp *is* secure. Land-based installations often aren't. Come to think of it, I'll tell you an educational story which may drive home what you're up against.

"A certain base on shore was overlooked from a hillside which was good for flying kites. One boy about fourteen or fifteen used to go up there to fly a specially fine box-kite he'd built himself, about five feet high. And he'd been doing this daily for two mortal months before one of the base officers wondered how come he never spent his vacation from school doing anything *but* play with a kite. He went up and on the end of that kite's cord he found a recorder, and on the kite itself a miniature TV camera. And this kid—no more than fifteen, mind—threw a knife, took him in the thigh, and tried to strangle him. Point made?"

Donald agreed with a slight shudder.

"And there's a further reason, of course. It's the best place to eptify you for your mission."

"Major Delahanty told me about that," Donald said slowly. "It's still not quite clear to me."

"Eptification is derived from an acronym—EPT stands for 'education for particular tasks'. Most softasses don't take the idea seriously. To them it's just one more among a horde of commercial panaceas which conmen are using to part the marks from their money. And that's partly true, of course, because to use the technique properly you more or less have to have had it done to you, and we don't turn many people we've done it to back into civilian life."

"You mean that afterwards I'm not going to—?"

"I'm not talking about you specifically," the colonel cut in. "I'm saying that in principle there's not much application for it outside the service!"

"But if I'm going to be required to pose as a reporter—"

"What's that got to do with it? You only need to feed back facts. They'll be monitored and edited in this country. Engrelay Satelserv has a staff of experts to look after that end of the problem."

Confused, Donald said, "I seem to have missed the point somewhere. When you said lack of experience as a reporter didn't matter, I naturally assumed . . ."

He broke off. The colonel was regarding him with mingled amusement and contempt.

"Yes, you do make a lot of assumptions, don't you? We're not in business to provide the beam agencies with star talent, though—as you'd have figured out if you'd stopped to think! Anyhow, that's not what you need eptification in."

"What, then?"

"In four short days," the colonel said, "you're going to be eptified to kill."

tracking with closeups (14)

LIGHT THE TOUCHPAPER AND RETIRE

There were still a few openings left for one-man businesses even in this age of automation, computers and the grand cartel. Jeff Young had found one.

Whistling, he limped down the narrow alley between two rows of tape-controlled machine-tools, a lean man in his early forties with receding dark hair and heavy rings under his eyes suggesting a slight, not socially reprehensible habit— possibly a stimulant like Procrozol with a strong insomniac side-effect. He did in fact get less sleep than most people; furthermore he acted as though he was always a trifle pepped. But it wasn't due to any kind of drug.

He carried a small plastic sack. At one of the whining lathes he halted and set the neck of the sack against the swarf-hopper. From it he spilled half a pound of fine magnesium chips and curls.

Then he crossed to a sander which was buffing the grey surface of a piece of cast iron into mirror smoothness and added a dredging of iron filings.

Still whistling, he hobbled out of the machine-shop and closed the doors. The lighting went off automatically—tape-controls didn't need to see what they were doing.

The only other member of his staff, a shiggy who some-times struck customers as too stupid even to act as mouth-piece for a gang of lathes and mills, had already left the front office for home. Nonetheless he called her name and listened for a reply before approaching a row of shallow aquaria ranged along the room's rear wall. Small bright fish gazed uncomprehendingly as he dipped a hook into the water of each in turn and withdrew from concealment in the fine white sand at the bottom a series of plastic globes half-full of something cloudy and brown.

Satisfied, he replaced the globes, set the burglar alarms, and turned on the lumino sign identifying this as the home of *Jeff Young Custom Metalwork—Functional and Artistic Designs Executed.*

The sack dangling from his fingers, he locked up and headed for the rapitrans.

Having eaten a leisurely meal watching his new but not ostentatiously expensive holographic TV, he left home again at eleven-ten poppa-momma, carrying the sack in a small black satchel. He took the rapitrans to a station where very few people stopped after sunset, a beach stop favoured by sunners and surfers, isolated between the sprawling tentacles of the city because here the ground was too weak to bear the weight of buildings of economic height. He had established the habit of a nightly constitutional along the beach over several years. It was one of the things that kept his sleeping-time down.

He wandered at a leisurely pace until he was out of sight of the rapitrans. Then, with sudden swift purpose, he dodged into the total shadow of some ornamental bushes and opened the satchel. From it he withdrew a mesh mask and put it on. Then he sprayed the plastic sack with an aerosol which would destroy both the greasy trace of fingerprints and the give-away epidermal cells which might have rubbed off on it.

Finally he took out a bolt-gun—legitimately owned, licensed by the fuzzy-wuzzies as suitable for a man owning a valuable machine-shop—and moved on along the beach.

He came to the prearranged rendezvous and stopped, checking his watch. He was two minutes early. Shrugging, he stood in silence, and waited.

Shortly a voice addressed him out of the darkness. It said, "Over here—this way."

He turned towards the sound. The voice had been male, but beyond that he could tell nothing about the owner. Dealing with partisans, that was the way he preferred things to be. Almost certainly he was in the field of a black-light projector, so he acted as though the invisible speaker could watch every movement he made.

With his gun he indicated a point on the sand near his feet. A small package arced through the air and landed with a thud. Dropping on one knee, putting down the satchel but not the gun, he felt its contents and gave a nod. He exchanged the package for the plastic sack, rose, and took a couple of paces backward. By now his vision had adjusted fully to the dimness, and he could see that the person who emerged from shadow to collect the sack was not the one who had spoken, but a shiggy, probably young, certainly with a good figure.

Bending—slowly, so as not to alarm the man waiting in the background—he selected a stick and with it wrote upside-down words on the sand.

WHAT FOR?

A muted chuckle. The man said, "It'll be in the news tomorrow."

THINK I'D SELL YOU OUT?

"I've stayed free for eighteen months," the man said. "It wasn't by advertising my movements."

ME—8 YEARS.

By now the shiggy had withdrawn to the company of her man. He scuffed over what he had written with his bad foot, and substituted GT ALUMINOPHAGE.

"You've got that?" the partisan said, startled.

BREEDING NOW.

"How much?"

CHEAP. TELL ME WHAT THERMITE FOR.

Then he crossed that through, and wrote EXPENSIVE.

"I catch. Name some figures."

Once more he scuffed over the letters.

$150 PER 1000. BREED 1,000,000—6 DAYS.

"Are they as good as GT claims?"

12 HR BROKE INCH MONOFILAMENT ROPE.

"Christ! That's the stuff they hang suspension bridges on!"
RIGHT.

Scuffed over again. Expectant waiting.

"We could use that," the man said finally. "Okay, I'll gamble. We're going to put out the Bay Bridge rapitrans."

TRACK WELL GUARDED.

"We're not going to put it on the track. There's a stretch where the vacuum parcels tube parallels the monorail. If we time it right it should melt through and short the power cables."

PHOS-ACID IGNITER?

"No, we have a timer with an HT arc."

NOT MINE.

Another chuckle, this one with a wry inflection. "Thanks, when I can afford your standards I'll send to Switzerland. Okay, I'll let you know when we need the aluminophage."

NIGHT.

"Good night."

From the direction of the voice there came soft scuffling sounds. He waited till they were over, then found a bit of flotsam and stirred up the sand where he had written his part of the conversation.

He turned for home with as brisk a step as his short leg allowed, leaving the last of his footprints to be wiped out by the night's tide.

Instead of going to bed in his apt, he did as he often did on fine nights and carried an inflatable mattress up to the roof of the block. He also took a pair of binocs, but these were well concealed inside the mattress-roll.

A boy and a shiggy were enjoying themselves up there when he arrived, but that was a customary hazard. He would have plenty of privacy where he wanted to be, on the far side of the ventilator stacks. Contentedly he spread the mattress, calculating in his head how long to wait before beginning his watch. He estimated an hour, and that was close. It was sixty-six minutes before a brilliant glow bulged and dripped through the Bay Bridge parcels tube and sagged sections of it into contact with the monorail power leads.

He gave a nod of professional approval. That little lot

would take all night to sort out. Not bad for amateurs, not bad at all. Though when he expanded his services to handle the requirements of partisans as well as ordinary hobby-type saboteurs, he had hoped they'd target on something more ambitious. Nuisance-value was all right in its place, but . . .

It wasn't that he shared the partisans' political convictions. He was neither a nihilist nor a little red brother, which were the two polar-opposed factions that kept them as busy quarrelling among themselves as attacking the established society around them. There was simply no other outlet for his greatest talent. The army had eptified him as a saboteur, and after the incident which bequeathed him his bad leg they had refused to re-enlist him.

What else can a hungry man do but eat the food he finds in front of him?

They hadn't yet had the presence of mind to cut the power feeding the shorted cables on the bridge, and the display of sparks was making the struts and girders glow like the pillars of hell. Jeff Young felt the heat of the thermite bomb seem to penetrate his belly and move downwards, and with the hand not holding his binocs he began rhythmically to afford himself relief from it.

continuity (15)

DO NOT PASS GO, DO NOT COLLECT

Some corporations still maintained the traditional table for meetings of the board. Not GT, a modern product. The boardroom on the presidential floor of the tower was a place of soft pearly lights under an arched ceiling, punctuated by thrones consisting in a comfortable padded seat surrounded with electronic equipment. Every place had a holographic projection screen, a sound-recorder, a computer readout, and phones giving direct access to any of GT's forty-eight subsidiary plants and better than nine hundred local offices in fifteen countries, some of them by satellite relay.

The thrones for the officers were upholstered in genuine leather, those for senior VP's in woven fabric, and those for junior VP's and specialist staffers called in to give advice in resilient plastic. Two extra thrones in leather had been installed today, one for Elihu Masters—one could hardly accord less to an ambassador—the other for the scarecrow-gaunt synthesist from State whom Norman had met during their preliminary discussions, Dr. Raphael Corning. It was the first time Norman had had to work in direct co-operation with a synthesist, and the man's range of immediately available knowledge had depressed him, making him feel he had wasted the whole of his earlier life.

But that was not the only thing which was bringing him down. He felt hollow, as though he was about to crumple under intolerable strain. On all previous occasions since he was promoted to board status he had relished the fact that he was the only Afram who attended these meetings and looked forward to the day when he would inherit first a fabric-, then a leather-covered throne. Accident had kicked him ahead of his plans. The whole Beninian venture would turn on him as a pivot, regardless of what rank they officially allotted him.

He looked at the pale palms of his hands and wondered how heavy the future of an entire country might weigh.

At intervals he uttered a mechanical hullo.

Sharp on time Old GT herself came in, attended as usual by a secretary who was human but so strung about with portable equipment as to make him effectively an extension of the corporation's massive information-processing resources up to and including Shalmaneser. Behind there followed Hamilcar Waterford, the treasurer, and just after him E. Prosper Rankin, the company secretary. As they took their seats a taut silence filled the room.

"This extraordinary meeting of the board," Old GT began without ado, "has been called to receive and vote on a special report from the vice-president in charge of projects and planning. Two non-members of the board are also present: Mr. Elihu Masters, U. S. Ambassador to Beninia, and Dr. Raphael Corning of the State Department. Those in favour of their continuing presence—?"

Norman fumbled for the "aye" button on his throne. On the front panel of Old GT's a pattern of lights, all green, displayed the result of the vote.

"Thank you. Rex, will you introduce the report?"

Old GT sat back and crossed her arms on her bosom. For the first time he could recall, Norman decided that her manner was smug. And then he wondered whether he could have avoided acting the same way if he had had the vision and persistence to achieve such tremendous personal power.

There are odds against Aframs, but there are odds against women too, and they're a bigger minority group than we are!

Rex Foster-Stern cleared his throat. "Background," he

said. "Beninia faces a crisis on the impending retirement of President Zadkiel Obomi. On his demise or vacation of his post two consequences are possible. A civil conflict over the succession is the less likely in view of the exceptionally peaceful course of events there since independence. The probabilities are weighted in favour of its powerful African neighbours attempting to annex its territory. Intervention by a third party may prevent this by providing them with a common target for recriminations, and State wishes to try this.

"A parallel situation arose when the Sulu Archipelago seceded from the Philippine Republic. As you know, the solution of integrating those islands into our country as the State of Isola did not lead to the desired result, pacification of the area. Moreover in the case of Isola the conflicting parties included an enemy acceptable to public opinion, the Chinese. As neither the Dahomalians nor the RUNGs are a military threat to us intervention on the Isolan pattern would be resented as an unnecessary waste of our resources.

"However, Ambassador Masters has hit on a feasible alternative: to integrate Beninia not into our national but into our commercial orbit, and this is the proposal we are going to ask you to approve today.

"Beninia offers a source of inexpensive and potentially skilled labour admirably sited for expansion into the hinterland. What is more, it's equally well located to process raw materials derived from the so-far unexploited mineral deposits discovered by MAMP.

"You will have seen from our briefing summary that the predicted turnover of this operation is comparable to that of a national budget and the scheme will not be completed until 2060. Despite the scale of it, however, evaluation of even the most minor details has proved to be possible and all information in your briefing has been thoroughly explored by Shalmaneser as a hypothetical case. Without his favourable verdict we'd not have presented the report."

"Thank you, Rex," Old GT said. "I see question lights going on in several places—kindly wait until we've heard from Dr. Corning and Mr. Masters. Dr. Corning?"

The gaunt tall man leaned forward.

"I need only add minor glosses to the admirable document Mr. Foster-Stern has circulated," he said. "First, as to State's involvement. Although we don't possess the unique Shalmaneser we're not ill-equipped with computers and we analysed Mr. Masters's suggestion very fully before okaying his approach to you. State's prepared to buy a fifty-one per cent share in the loan floated to finance the project, but to minimise political repercussions we'll have to do so through front agents. These should keep down complaints about neo-colonialism so that by the ten-year mark we can hope for active co-operation from Beninia's neighbours in digesting the fruits of the plan. And, second, I'd like to emphasise that Mr. Masters conceived his idea after very wide experience in the country and you should give great weight to his personal recommendation."

"Mr. Masters?" Old GT invited.

"All right, I'll make it personal, then," Elihu said after a barely noticeable hesitation. "The reason I put this project to State has nothing to do with the profit your corporation can expect. If you're at all acquainted with the recent history of Africa you'll have noticed that the withdrawal of the colonial powers left the map in a terrible muddle. Arbitrary lines separated potential economic units—they weren't even tribally based, but dictated by nineteenth-century European power-struggles. As a result, many countries have been in chaos. There have been civil wars, hordes of refugees, poverty, famine and pestilence.

"Since the idea of federation took hold, things have improved. Countries like Dahomalia, for instance, or the Republican Union of Nigeria with Ghana, have become reasonable places to live, with an adequate GNP and stable public services. But they didn't settle down in Dahomalia until they'd killed about twenty thousand members of a dissident tribe, and as for what went on in South Africa— ah, never mind. Everyone knows what a living hell *that* was.

"In the middle of all this, my good friend Zad Obomi has performed the miracle of creating the equivalent of an African Switzerland, free from alliances that might drag it into wars it didn't care about, as happened to Sierra Leone and Gambia; not being milked of irreplaceable resources by a richer foreign ally, as happened to the Congo—and so forth.

"Beninia's a poverty-stricken country, but it's a wonderful place to live. About five per cent of its people fled there from tribal clashes on adjacent territory, but there's been no tribal violence in Beninia. There are four language-groups, but there's been no conflict such as we've seen right close to home in Canada, or in Belgium prior to partition. It's a peaceful country, and it seems to me it's got something too valuable to be swallowed up by greedy neighbours merely because President Obomi can't live forever."

He fell silent. Glancing around at his colleagues, Norman detected expressions of puzzlement, and his heart sank.

Old GT coughed politely. She said, "I hardly need point out the relevance of what Mr. Masters has told us. An access point to the developing African market which is free of civil commotion and the other hazards of an African beach-head is quite remarkable, isn't it?"

Norman saw the puzzled looks disappear, and felt a stir of honest admiration at Old GT's ingenuity in manipulating her staffers.

"Next," GT continued, "I call on Norman House, whom Mr. Masters personally recommends to initiate our negotiations with the Beninian government. Norman?"

The big moment was here. For a terrible pulsebeat-long span of time he felt panic, as though amnesia had wiped away everything he had carefully rehearsed to say. The sensation, however, passed so rapidly that he was already speaking before he realised he had recovered.

He said, "Thank you, GT," and noticed the rustle of reaction. Traditionally, junior VP's said "Miss Buckfast" or—by analogy with the form of address to the British Queen—"ma'am". Several eyebrows were raised to signal recognition of impending promotion. Norman was too preoccupied to care. He had expended infinite pains on sounding out his colleagues, trying to judge the approach that would most impress them, and Rex had put a computer at his disposal to evaluate the various possibilities in terms of their personality-profiles; an instant of inattention could waste all that trouble.

"Mr. Masters has drawn our attention to a remarkable aspect of the history of Beninia, which I'd like to amplify. The legacy of colonialism there was seemingly a pleasant one. Beninia never underwent—even in the crisis years of the 1980s—agitation to expel foreigners, let alone massacres of them. Beninians seem self-confident enough to treat with anyone on terms they find acceptable. They know they need aid. They won't reject an offer because it comes from—say—Britain, the former colonial power, or from ourselves just because this is primarily a white-skinned country. And so on.

"A feature common in the rest of Africa—greed for what richer countries can afford to give them combined with resentment of foreigners—this is absent in Beninia. This implies the solution to a major subsidiary problem posed by the project we're considering.

"No doubt some of you are saying, 'What experience do we have to draw on? As a country whose very formation was predicated on rejection of overseas interference, how are we going to cope with running the internal affairs of another country on another continent?'

"A very fair question—with a ready-made answer. A fund of experience exists for us to draw on, mainly in Britain but also in France. In both places there are a large number of talented executives who used to work in colonial administration and who are now marking time in other fields. Our investigations have proved that many of them would be willing to go back as advisors—I stress that, not as zecks or officials, merely as expert advisors.

"Additionally, you'll all remember the much-lamented Peace Corps which was discontinued in 1989 as a result of the wave of xenophobia then engulfing Africa and Asia. Disillusioned, Congress abolished it as not justifying its by then colossal cost. If any of you come much into contact with young people, though, you'll be aware that its legend survives. Working for the OAS in Chile or Bolivia is a serviceable substitute, but it doesn't provide an adequate outlet for the available volunteers. We can pick and choose among tens of thousands of adventurous young people to staff—especially—our educational programme in Beninia.

"Financing of the project is assured. Raw materials for it are assured. As I think I've just shown, staffing for it is assured. I strongly urge adoption of the report."

When he ceased he was astonished to find his heart hammering, his skin moist with perspiration.

Why, he realised with vague dismay, *I'm really desperate to get this through. If they turn it down, what then?*

Quit. Go to Yatakang with Donald Hogan. Anything except continue in GT. The idea was unthinkable.

He barely heard the expositions that followed his: the treasurer's report from Hamilcar Waterford, a market preview, a psychological analysis of the major stock-holders suggesting a probable sixty-five per cent majority at a general meeting. He tuned in again on the questions, for these would foreshadow the decision of the board.

"I'd like to ask Dr. Corning why State approved Mr. Master's approach to us, instead of setting up a consortium themselves." That was Paula Phipps, the rather masculine senior VP in charge of commercial organics.

"The plan stands or falls on the question of raw materials," Corning said shortly. "And no one but GT has MAMP."

"Did the psychological analysis of our stock-holders take into account the fact that four-fifths of them are white and may object to spending so much in a black country when return on the investment will be deferred for several years?" That was Macy O'Toole, junior VP in charge of procurement, with a half-scowl at Norman.

"Return on the investment will not be deferred," said Hamilcar Waterford. "Macy, you haven't been listening!" A fierce snub; Norman started, because it implied that Waterford was firmly on the side of the ayes. "The anticipated proceeds from proper dredging of Port Mey, which will attract cargo that currently goes to other less favourably situated ports, are ear-marked for immediate dividends. Take another look at your briefing document, hm?"

There was a pause, no one else being eager to risk the officers' displeasure. Old GT said, "Anyone got another question?"

Nora Reuben, senior VP in charge of electronics and communications, spoke up. "Why isn't there a representative of the Beninian government here? I feel I'm operating in a vacuum."

Good question. In fact, Norman decided, the only good one so far. GT was inviting Dr. Corning to handle it.

"Mr. Masters is the right person to answer this," Corning countered, and all eyes turned to Elihu.

"Once more," the latter said, "I have to speak more personally than you would perhaps expect. Some of you may recall the speculation that ensued when I was posted to Port Mey instead of the places that were being canvassed for me, which included Manila and Delhi. The reason I went to Beninia is simple, though. I wanted the post. Zad Obomi is a long-time friend of mine; we first met at the UN when I was attached to the American delegation as special counsellor on ex-colonial territories. When my predecessor at Port Mey retired, Zad asked for me and I accepted. He has only ever asked me one other favour, and that was very recently.

"Zad is now seventy-four years old. He's an exhausted man. As you know, he was half-blinded in an assassination attempt, and the consequences have been psychological as well as physical.

"And a few weeks ago, he called me to his office and said this to me—I'll try and quote him word for word." Elihu shut his eyes and drew his brows together. "He said, 'Forgive me for putting this burden on you, but I know of nobody else I can ask. My doctors promise me only another few years of life even if I retire. I want to leave my people a better legacy than chaos, famine and poverty. Can you tell me how?'

"Madam, there's no need for a representative of the Beninian government. To Zadkiel Obomi the people of Beninia are his friends, practically his family, and he's been their sole support and breadwinner ever since 1971. He's not asking for help in the name of a government. He's asking for a way to provide for his dependants when he dies."

There was silence. During it, Norman found himself trying to signal telepathically to Old GT: *don't call the vote now, they didn't understand what Elihu was saying, you'll risk catching them while they're unconvinced . . .*

But GT was saying, "Unless there are further questions

. . . ? We'll proceed to the vote. Those in favour of accepting the report from projects and planning—?"

Finger almost numb from the pressure he was applying to his own affirmative button, Norman stared at the pattern of lights on GT's throne. Green nine-eleven-fifteen . . .

Made it!

He glanced at Elihu, wanting to share by an expression of jubilation the delight the verdict had provoked, and discovered that the older man was gazing at him with a wholly different look. There was a sort of fierceness in his face, as though to say: *I trusted you, you'd better prove me right.*

And all the implications of what had just happened came crashing down on Norman's undefended mind.

context (14)

Yatakang (YAT'-a-KANG), *Guided Socialist Democracy of:* country, SE Asia. Over 100 islands, lgst. Shongao 1790 sq. mi. Est. pop. 230,000,000. *Gongilung (4,400,000). Aluminium, bauxitte, petroleum, tea, coffee, rubber, textiles.

Medieval seat of Takangi Empire (c. 1250—1475). Indep. kingdom to c. 1683. Partitioned 18th-19th cent. Dut. col. 1899—1954. Indep. repub. 1954—date.

Mixed Khmon, Nger. 70% Buddh. w. pagan admx., 20% Muslim, 10% Xian (Prot.)

"... and shows the way forward free of foreign contamination to all the peoples of Asia. History is being made in Yatakang. Never before has any country been promised liberation from the caprices of fate; never before has any government been able to look forward to a citizenry perfectly equipped both to contribute to the forward progress of the state and to enjoy to the maximum their lives as individuals. Under the direction of internationally renowned scientist Professor Dr. Sugaiguntung, and following the leadership of our beloved Marshal Solukarta, to whom in every city of Yatakang masses of people have gathered spontaneously and paid tribute ..."

(LEADERSHIP   A form of self-preservation exhibited by

283

people with autodestructive imaginations in order to ensure that when it comes to the crunch it'll be someone else's bones which go crack and not their own.

—*The Hipcrime Vocab* by Chad C. Mulligan)

"Sheeting hole, what I want to know is, why can't we have what people in some muddy rice-paddy plodding behind their buffaloes or whatever are going to get for free?"

SHAMBLES

"*Arms thru the Ages*" Hobbikit. Ideal gift b'day or Xmas. Suitable ages 7–12. Caveman (flint axe, knife), Roman Legionary (spear, sword), Crusader (lance, mace), Archer (longbow, crossbow), Musketeer (musket, horse-pistol), Commando (rifle, grenade), Marine (bolt-gun, kazow). Durable precision-made plastic. Only $112.50!

"In the fiercest engagement so far this year, units of the 23rd Pacific Combat Group inflicted severe losses of men and material on Chinese aqua-bandits in mid-ocean this morning. Our own casualties are reported light."

FLAMMABLE

His hot breath launched a spray of spittle across her face. His wild hands clawed at her tender breasts. She remembered what Dad had told her an infinity of time ago and pretended to relax, let him do as he wished. Then, the moment his guard was down, she groped across his cheeks with stiff fingers and located his eyes. They popped from their sockets like wet gooseberries and he screamed. She had never heard a more wonderful sound in all her thirteen years. *NOW READ ON.*

RADIATION

"Chairman Yung today sent a personal message of congratulations to the daring sailors of the Blood-Red Banner flotilla who yesterday inflicted great damage in men and material on the imperialist aggressor. Our own casualties were very light."

LOADED

Lonely on the edge of space, Patrol Pilot Eugene Flood keeps watch and ward over the security of your homes and families. Thanks to General Technics, weapons capable of taking out—clear from orbit—anything from a single boat-load of saboteurs to an entire megalopolis lie under his hand.

SHELTER ENTRANCE

"A note was today sent to Cairo protesting the infringement of Israeli air-space by a photographic spy-plane. The aircraft was brought down and the pilot failed to escape."

SHARP

Again and again he hammered at the bleeding face beneath him until he heard the satisfying sound of crunching bone. The man's teeth were rammed down his throat and he was choking to death on his own blood.

INFECTIOUS

"A strong protest was lodged in Tel-Aviv today against the unwarranted attack by Israeli army units on an innocent Egyptian aircraft that had been blown off its course. Compensation for the dead pilot's dependants was demanded."

PROCEED AT YOUR OWN RISK

Centuries of expert craftsmanship culminate in the new range of Purdy sporting guns. Our unique side and long arms call forth the greatest skill from you, their proud owner.

PLAGUE AREA

"Fanatical Italian youths crying 'Death to all heretics' this morning attempted to storm the palace of Right Catholic Pope Eglantine in Madrid. When under fire from Spanish police they refused to run for cover but tore off their shirjacks to reveal large red crosses tattooed on their chests. The survivors will be interrogated in hospital when they are well enough to answer questions."

PUT ON BREATHING MASK

He lay without moving except for the gentle up-and-down rhythm of his chest that barely disturbed the blanket. She crept towards him, trying not to notice that in sleep his face had the smooth handsomeness of a teenage boy, trying to remember only how much she hated him. Convulsively she raised the broken bottle and ground it down over his nose and mouth.

IT'S A MAN'S LIFE IN THE ARMY

"Right Catholic saboteurs today exploded a time-bomb aboard a ship carrying desperately-needed contraceptive pills to Bombay, India. Divers will attempt to raise the sealed packing-cases at next low tide, but all hope of saving the crew has been abandoned."

Protect yourself, your home, your family, with Japind's unparalleled range of personal defences. Jettiguns, Kara-tands, electric fences, mines, boobytraps of all descriptions at reasonable prices, fully g'teed.

POISON

"A mob protesting against recent language reforms designed to bring Brazilian-Portuguese into closer conformity with the Spanish spoken over the remainder of Latin America today set fire to a number of buildings on the outskirts of Brasilia."

He seized her ankles and before she could react even with surprise raised them and tipped her bodily forward over the sill of the open window. Far below there was a sound half-way between a splash and a thud. When he looked out she lay spreadeagled on the ground. He gave a nod of grim satisfaction. She had cheated on him for the last time.

HIGH TENSION.

A kazow fires a stream of miniature rockets, no larger than reefers, each with a seeking device that homes on the body-heat of a human being. Learn to use one at your local Militia Readiness Centre. It's part of your responsibility as a citizen to defend yourself from tyranny.

"Election agents of the ruling Shangaan Party are reported to have demanded police protection when venturing into predominantly Zulu constituencies to canvass for the forthcoming South African elections. This follows the stoning of Eurasian Harry Patel, the Minister for Home Affairs and Education, on a visit to Johannesburg last week."

RESTRICTED ZONE.

"Police arrested self-styled 'generals' and 'colonels' of the French Canadian Republican Army in Montreal last night, alleging discovery of a plot to dynamite the parliament buildings in Ottawa when the members reconvene on Monday."

His lip curled as he watched the missile's trail home on the crude shacks of the slit-eye village. The world was a better place without those dirty bleeders.

FIRE WHEN READY

He glared at the cowering figure before him. "You've always wanted to be more of a daughter than a son!" he snarled. "See this razor? It's going to give you exactly what you want! Now do you take off that dress or do I cut it off?"

The Missile and Weaponry division of General Technics offers graduates an exciting career with the continual challenge of work on the very frontiers of human achievement.

NO QUARTER

"Frenzied mobs in Tokyo last night burned the effigy of the Emperor in protest against his intention to abdicate to facilitate Japan's adoption of a republican system of government. Spokesmen declared that if he does resign his throne they will recognize Mr. Oyoshita, head of one of the country's oldest noble families, as his successor and will refuse to co-operate with the new government. Victims of the rioting are already being described as 'martyrs'."

Her eyes lingered on the bright new disc of metal pinned to the breast of his uniform. "Son, I'm proud of you," she whispered, and embraced him because she did not want him to see her tears.

MINEFIELD

"The Ellay expressport is tonight out of service for quote an indefinite period unquote following an explosion that fired forty-three thousand gallons of stored rocket-fuel. Casualties are expected to number over two hundred. The authorities state that the explosion followed sparking of a static charge on the tanks of an express newly arrived from Manila. Accident has been ruled out, and in a statement just networked the Paul Revere Society calls for a total ban on the landing of all foreign-owned aircraft in the United States to prevent a repetition of this disaster."

Among the securest investments open to anyone are shares in the ever-booming defence industries. Currently offering above-average returns are Specialised Air Conditioning Inc. (war and police gases), Public Health Research Inc. (mutated bacteria and viruses), and the Rapid Expansion Corporation (explosives of all types).

CHARGE

I am directed by the General Officer Commanding to perform the sad duty of notifying you of the demise of your son Peter. He was today buried with full military honours at censored. During an attack on censored he displayed the highest possible courage and was personally responsible for killing censored of the enemy by planting a censored on one of their censored vehicles. He has been posthumously recommended for a decoration for gallantry.

"Which means there's no need for you to knuckle under to anybody from now on. With your bare hands, with a knife, with an axe or broadsword, with a narrow sword, with a projectile side-arm, long arm or spray-gun, with a bolt-gun, kazow or rocket-launcher, with pocket and non-pocket nukes, with chemical explosives, with instant or delayed time-bombs, with gas, with infectious bacteria, with hot iron or razors or poison or a club or a rock, with a lance or a mace or a box of matches, with an H-T cable or thermite or acid, with your teeth or your nails or a hypodermic or a diadermic, with a flame-thrower or a kitchen carver or a length of rope or a hammer or a belt or a chisel or a boot or a bath of water or a Karatand or a Jettigun or a modified domestic laser or a quarterstaff or a broken bottle or a bucket of cement or an ordinary door or window or a staircase or a pillow or a piece of adhesive tape or a cooking-pan or an article of clothing or wet mud or long hair or a sewing-needle or a brand out of the fire or a splinter or a bottle of medicine you can give those freaking Chinks their own back."

WAR GRAVES COMMISSION

Briefly, Bennie Noakes remembered someone had had his balls caught in the draft. He wondered whether he had imagined it or whether it was real, and decided it was real because he didn't imagine things as unpleasant as that.

But he took a little more Triptine to prevent a recurrence.

"It is the sentence of this court that you shall be taken hence to the place from which you came, and thence to a place of execution, there to be hanged by the neck until you are dead. And may God have mercy on your soul."

SHAMBLES (sham'-blz) *n. pl. constr. as sing.* [Ang-Sax. *scamel* or *sceamol*, Lat. *scamellum*] Abattoir, slaughterhouse; *metaph.* scene of death and destruction. (Not cogn. w. SHAMBLE. *v.i.* above.)

context (15)

BRED AND BORN

" 'We're all Marxists now' is a common cry among the world's intellectuals, and it is true insofar that it remains the mark of a progressive man to feel that social forces, rather than genetic ones, mould our behaviour. But today's commonplace is often tomorrow's fallacy, and arguments from biology are increasing both in scope and precision.

"J. Merritt Emlen of the University of Washington, writing in the current issue of the *Journal of Theoretical Biology* (vol. 12, p. 410), puts forward the view that modern genetic theory can provide more subtle interpretations of human behaviour than is generally realised. Of course it is difficult to unravel the tangle of culture and biology which shapes man. Genetic influences on behaviour are always masked by social processes like teaching and parental care; but equally, these social processes are themselves reflections of man's biological possibilities and limitations ... Complete explanation or not, this genetic apppoach is worth exploring ..."

—*New Scientist*, London, no. 531, p. 191, 26th January 1967

continuity (16)

THE REVISED VERSION

If anyone had asked him, Donald could have said why the discontinuation of Donald Hogan Mark I was so quick and so efficient. It was because the process had begun before he arrived at Boat Camp, triggered off by the discovery that the assumed-familiar world was only biding its time before springing a trap and making him its prey.

But nobody did ask. The people he encountered treated him as though he were a faulty bread-board mock-up for a novel device, to be tested and made over into a version suitable for the production-line. Were he to meet any of them again in other surroundings, he would fail to recognise them. They had no identity apart from the frame they occupied. He categorised them not by name but by what they did to him.

Some administered drugs, chiefly to destroy perceptual sets. When new knowledge was laid across his plastic mind it sank in deep with neither preconceptions nor independent judgment to hinder its passage. It was as though one were to remove a man's skeleton and replace it with another of stainless steel—and nowadays, in fact, bones could be changed.

In Donald's case, of course, nothing so immediately detectable could be risked. Whatever was done to him had to be confined to that citadel of private thought no one had yet penetrated except with weapons as clumsy as blunderbusses.

But they did make him allergic to "Truth or Consequences". Administration of a usable dose for interrogation purposes would drive him into fever and delirium.

Certain other drugs stimulated his auditory and tactile memory, atrophied by long years of studying the printed page and the replay screens of recorders. Another heightened his kinesthetic faculty, giving him an almost painful awareness of the relative positions of his limbs. There were more, which he didn't bother to ask about. He was not co-operating in what was done to him, so much as passively accepting it as a possible cure for the impending death of his old self.

After that, they moulded him. In a drugged trance designed to ensure that something told to him once would reverberate in his circulating memory until it had grooved as deeply into his brain as something rehearsed a thousand times in real life, they taught him what he might need to know during the task ahead.

Engrelay Satelserv equipped all their reporters with a communikit in a nine-inch case, specially designed and built for them by GT's electronics section. It combined an instreplay recorder with a polytelly, a miniature TV adaptable to the line standards and sound frequencies used anywhere in the world. Army experts modified one of these and gave it to him. Now, it incorporated a transceiver hidden under a changeochrome coating, the circuit elements reduced to molecular monofilaments. He was supposed to book routine calls to headquarters via whichever of Engrelay Satelserv's satellites was overheard at the time, precisely as a legitimate correspondent would. But if he had something to say which he didn't want overheard, he could record it in advance and the communikit would impose it as a parasite modulation on the phone signal, automatically scrambled and compressed into half-second blips.

Additional frills were dealt with by sleep-teaching; he was taught an acrostic verbal code, an association-code, and a cipher.

They did not, however, allow him to sleep while teaching

him the serious aspects of his subject. As one of the interchangeable instructors told him, the last service a secret
agent could perform after his cover had been broken was
to tie up a disproportionate number of the opposition while
they were trying to capture him, and in pursuit of that end
they were going to make him capable of taking on a bat-
talion.

That promise stirred the first emotion in Donald Hogan
Mark II.

There was something impressive about it.

To begin with: bare hands.

"Now on this dummy of a yellowbelly I've marked the
most vulnerable points: blue for temporary disablement, like
the groin, the solar plexus and the eyes; red for the places at
which a blow can kill, like the vocal cords. A blow with the
closed fist works best here, here and here. If you can get a
shod foot to any of these points, so much the better, of
course. Here, the bunched fingers are the optimum choice.
Here, stabbing with a single stiff finger. And at these places
you grip and press, at these you apply leverage and at these
you twist. Now we'll move on to attacks from the rear,
which are always to be preferred."

Next: with a blade.

"There are two main classes of blade, the close and the extended. The former and latter classes each divide into the
same two types, the stabbing type and the slashing type.
The former are typified by the stiletto and the cut-throat
razor respectively, while the later are typified by the rapier
and the axe."

Next: with a cord.

"This group of weapons exhibits the common characteristic
of thinness and flexibility. They include the whip and trip-
wire, which are disabling weapons, and the noose and the
garrotte, which are killing weapons. The lasso and bolas fall
into either category according to the user's purpose."

Next: with traditional guns.

"Projectile weapons fall into three classes: side-arms,
calling for extreme skill especially in the smaller calibres,
long arms, calling for almost as much skill, and spray-guns

firing large numbers of slugs, which are the best for unskilled operators at medium and close range."

Next: with power-weapons.

"Bolt-guns exist as side-arms, firing about twelve to fifteen bolts between rechargings, and as long arms firing up to forty. Advantages include the fact that a direct hit anywhere in the body is fatal and a near-miss may be so if the target is for example touching a metal hand-rail or standing on wet ground in uninsulated footwear. Also, they can be re-charged from domestic current of one hundred volts and up, or from cross-country power-lines. However, they require a lot of down-time and are normally reserved for situations where at least three weapons are available per user, two on charge and one in the field."

Next: with modern military weapons.

"This is a kazow, standard equipment for marines going in for such tasks as raid on an enemy supply-dump. The magazines each contain twenty miniature rockets, discharged in five seconds, and the heads can be set—in darkness, by counting the clicks as you turn the fuze-knob—to seek a human being, a refrigerated tank, and metal against a background of vegetation. Or, naturally, to fly a straight course to wherever the kazow is pointing."

Next: with portable nukes.

"These have the drawback that their half-life is rather short, a matter of a few months, so they become poisoned with their own decay-products during long-term storage. Also the radiation level is high enough to show on police scanners, which incidentally makes them dangerous to anyone who carries them for more than a few hours at a time. However, nothing else, of course, matches them for destructive power combined with portability. Current types can be time-fuzed and placed by hand, or launched by a special attachment from a Mark IX kazow."

Next: with chemical explosives.

"Two main types are in use: grenade or bomb packages, and disguised packages. The former are chiefly for military purposes, so we'll concentrate on the latter. Modern explosives have the great advantage that they can be moulded to look like almost anything and won't go off without the proper catalyst. For example, the casing of your communikit is made of about half a pound of PDQ. It would completely wreck a room of two thousand cubic feet. But it won't explode, even if it's dropped in a hot fire, unless you combine it with phosphorus. The regular way to detonate it is by laying a full match-book face down inside the lid and turning the volume knob to the unmarked setting. This gives you eighteen seconds to get clear before the full charge of the battery is shorted across the uppermost face and triggers the bang."

Next: with gas-guns and grenades.

"You've used a Jettigun, I gather. You'll be equipped with its military counterpart, which is about as large as a regular pen and cartridge-filled on the same principle. There's a choice of fatal nerve-gases including the old standby, potassium cyanide, which is a thirty-second killer provided you get it into the target's nose or mouth and not to be disregarded merely because it's been around for a while. Then there are disabling gases—emetics, vesicants, strangulants and so forth—which have the drawback that they don't dilute so fast and may all too easily affect the user as well as the target."

And finally: with ad-hoc weapons.

"Anything which was said about attacks with the unaided human body applies to the use of improvised weapons. Some are obvious, like the use of a pillow for suffocation, which is quick and if properly managed is also silent. Some, like smashing a bottle or a window to obtain a sharp cutting-edge, are reasonably self-evident. But some require a good deal of insight. In the vicinity of a machine-shop, for example, magnesium swarf may be available, and that becomes thermite. On a building-site, a man can be suffocated very efficiently with quicklime or undamped cement-dust. Cracking a man's hand or foot in a door as you slam it; pushing his face at a window; smearing a regular domestic needle with a compound from a home medicine-cabinet and putting it where he'll scratch himself on it; strangling a long-haired codder or shiggy with his or her own hair; placing pressure-sensitive tape over the mouth or nose; biting through the windpipe; tripping at the head of a steep flight of steps; throwing a pan of scalding water off a stove—the possibilities are endless."

Donald Hogan Mark II, born into a strange hostile world where any innocent thing in the home or on the street could become an implement of death, where any other person no matter how apparently polite and civilised might turn and rend him, nodded intently and absorbed the information as gospel.

When Delahanty flew in to give him his final briefing before departure, four short days after his arrival at Boat Camp, Donald sat opposite him in the office of the colonel who had welcomed him originally and waited while he checked through the various reports that had been compiled to show his progress. There was one other man present, a sergeant who had discreetly accompanied Donald wherever he went for the past twenty-four hours, unquestioned and nameless, his individuality fined down to his gun and his constantly worn Karatand.

Sitting stiffly on the edge of his chair, wearing the anonymous fatigues of a draftee but with incongruous lieutenant's bars on the shoulders, Donald paid the sergeant no more attention than hitherto.

He was much too puzzled by Delahanty. He had a curious feeling that the man was not real. He came out of the life of Donald Hogan Mark I, a dead man. There was a bridge where there ought to have been at most a ford with a few stepping-stones. Since leaving home he had moved into another zone of time, which nowhere connected with the customary world. He had existed for ten years on the assumption that he was linked to exterior events through his study of reports of them, through talking with people he knew, through surveying the streets he walked along and checking the news daily on TV. All that, suddenly, had been switched off.

Delahanty finished his perusal of the reports. Without looking up, he said, "That'll be all, sergeant."

"Yes, sir," the man said—the first words Donald had heard him utter—and went out of the room, his feet making the inevitable soft clanging because all the floors everywhere in Boat Camp were of resonant metal.

"You figured out who he was, presumably," Delahanty said

almost affably, raising his head at last to look at Donald. Donald shrugged. It was obvious the man must be a bodyguard.

"Fast eptification of the kind you've undergone can be risky," Delahanty amplified. "The killer instinct exists in all of us, but it has to be overlaid with certain social inhibitions. Taking them all off at once occasionally leads to random outbreaks of violence in the subject. You seem to have responded very well, though. All that remains for me is to issue you with your travelling kit and documents, and then we'd better get you along to the emergency expressport."

"Emergency?" Donald repeated.

Delahanty betrayed faint surprise. "Of course. You don't imagine they could already have— Ah, you wouldn't have heard, possibly. The yellowbellies put another one over on us. An express from Manila went to the refuelling bay and proved to be carrying a static charge on its tanks. When they coupled up the hoses it blew the entire fuel-store."

Donald nodded with new-found professional appreciation of an ingenious trick.

"However, it's perhaps a blessing in disguise for our purposes," Delahanty continued. "There's forty-eight hours' worth of accumulated traffic being pressure-hosed out of the emergency port, and with luck they'll also be bottlenecked at the arrival end, so you won't rate too intense a scrutiny. You can't exactly call it turning the tables, but when the advantage presents itself one grabs it—as no doubt you've been taught. Now, as to your equipment!"

He pointed at a pile of baggage stacked in the corner. "Some of that is gear reclaimed from your own apt. Some of it's new. All the new stuff is trigger-rigid, like a Karatand. Make sure you're wearing some of the new clothing all the time over your vital organs. It's almost bullet-proof and an excellent insulator.

"Your communikit, as you've been shown, is a bomb. But that's for dire emergency only. For minor emergencies— which had sheeting well better *be* emergencies, nonetheless— you'll have a well-disguised gas-gun. We daren't give you anything more in the way of weaponry. You must have gathered from your study of Yatakangi that no slit-eye government these days gives a pint of whaledreck whether a round-eye gets lynched or mugged or chased through the streets with a halter round his neck. That's why we decided we'd have to eptify you. Otherwise you'd be defenceless. Okay?"

Donald nodded.

"Good. As to your professional cover, then! You've been taught the use of the standard communikit. I'm going to give you a press authorisation and a Satelserv credit card, and a correspondent's manual which you must study at the first opportunity. It's been convincingly well-thumbed, with facsimiles of your own prints, but there's nothing like the genuine article.

"Your main contact in Gongilung is Engrelay Satelserv's regular stringer, an English-speaking woman called Deirdre Kwa-Loop. She's a black South African, which is why her name and picture aren't much used over internal American services, but they think very highly of her indeed—so highly, they've been satisfied to rely on her dispatches throughout this big sensational series of stories from Yatakang. If we hadn't asked for their co-operation, they wouldn't have planned on sending anybody to give special coverage. As it is, you may find her a little touchy—she's apt to feel that your assignment is an expression of lack of confidence in what she's been doing. Watch that, won't you? Be tactful.

"And remember, too, that as far as she's concerned you're exactly what you claim to be. She has *no* inside data. The man who has—the man who acts as our link to Jogajong—is a freelance, a Pakistani immigrant called Zulfikar Halal. While it's wholly convincing that he will want to sell exclusive information to someone like yourself, representing one of the world's biggest beam agencies, this piece of the cover must be reserved until you're in sight of the successful completion of the assignment.

"Which is, in the full official version: to investigate the claim made by the Yatakangi government regarding the optimisation of future births; to file normal press dispatches on it, some of which will actually be used by programmes up to and including SCANALYZER, by the way; and to seek out—with all due diligence, as the phrase goes—proof that the claim can't be substantiated.

"When you have it, you're to rendezvous with Jogajong and give it to him in full. The disappointment resulting from refutation of the claim, so our computers tell us, may well spark the wave of indignation that sweeps him to power in place of Solukarta."

"And supposing I don't find such proof?"

Delahanty looked bewildered. "You're to keep at it until you do, or until you're recalled. I thought that went without saying."

"You miss my point. I read all the scientific papers Sugaiguntung ever published, while I was on standby." The jargon phrase tripped lightly off Donald's tongue; what did feel uncomfortable was saying "I"—it seemed like laying false claim to someone else's work. "And if there's anyone alive in the world today who can make the promise come true, it's Sugaiguntung."

"Our computer evaluations show the project is uneconomic," Delahanty answered stiffly. "You've just been through eptification, so you know what techniques exist already to make optimised individuals. But we can't even afford to eptify our adult population *en masse,* let alone apply pre-natal techniques that call for vast numbers of skilled tecto-geneticists."

"But what if he's made a breakthrough to something quick and easy? Suppose he's envisaging a modified Gershenson technique—say by immersing the ovum in a solution of a template organic?"

"In that case, obviously, we've got to have the details. And very, very fast."

Donald hesitated. He said eventually, "I saw Sergeant Schritt at Guinevere Steel's party."

"I wager you did," Delahanty sighed. "So did everyone else. I can't really blame the poor bleeder, I guess—but he'll be no more use to me."

His tone made it clear that he didn't intend to pursue the subject, but he went on regarding Donald thoughtfully. "I should have made more allowance for your not being able to follow the news," he continued at length. "You must put that right at once, because a lot has happened since the claim was made public. To give you a rough idea, multiply Schritty's reaction by a thousand."

Chad Mulligan, Donald recalled—and the recollection was like the echo of a dream—made it a mllion.

"You get the picture? Very well, then. I'll wish you luck and send you on your way. Unless you have any more questions?"

Donald shook his head. The one thing Delahanty had not said straight out was perfectly clear; whether the process could be made to work or not, it must not be allowed to work in Yatakang.

tracking with closeups (15)

OUR PARENTS' FEET WERE BLACK

After the greetings, the sisterly and the sister-in-lawly kisses, the invitations to sit down and the how have you been since we saw you lasts: an absolute dead pause, as though neither Pierre Clodard, nor his sister Jeannine, nor his wife Rosalie, had anything to say to one another.

The house, in a sought-after district of Paris within easy walk of the Bois de Boulogne, was the one which Etienne Clodard *père* had bought on coming home unwillingly from Africa following Algeria's independence. The whole of it, but this *salon* in particular, retained the flavour of another continent and another century. The layout, betrayed North African influences in the long low couches against the walls, the use of a carpet not to walk on but as a wall-hanging, the small tables on one of which rested a set of tiny copper cups for Algerian coffee, each nestling in its own hollow in a tray of beaten brass with formalised Arabic script enamelled around the rim. In absolute contrast the room also memorialised what Etienne Clodard the ex-colonial administrator had thought of as proper Parisian elegance when he was out there in the heat and barbarity of Africa: the florid wall-paper, the heavy glazed chintz of the curtains, the two intrusive overstuffed armchairs.

Some of Pierre's friends said it was impossible to tell

whether the house reflected the way his mind worked or whether his mind had been conditioned by the house.

He was a person of some elegance and presence: a nervous, lean man whose avocation of playing the piano might have been guessed even without seeing the handsome instrument occupying the best-lit corner of the room. Further, one might have predicted his actual preference for Debussy and Satie without exploring the rack of recordings flanking the narrow screen of his early-model holographic reproducer. His black hair was beginning to recede a little. For a while when he was younger he had conformed to the current tendency of beardedness, but a few years ago he had shaved his chin and cheeks, leaving only a neat moustache to stress the sensitivity of his mouth.

What in him emerged as handsomeness of a refined, rather intellectual and potentially weak kind, was recognisable in his sister Jeannine as something marginally less than beauty. Like him—and both their parents—she was thin and dark, but with paler complexion, lighter bones and larger eyes. At forty-one the only clue to her actual age lay in the lined skin around her eyes and at the base of her throat; otherwise she might have passed for thirty.

Rosalie, on the other hand, was a total contrast: buxom, plump-cheeked, with bright china-blue eyes and fair brown hair. Normally she was a cheerful person, but—for some reason she wished she could discover, because she hated it as an intolerable failing—the presence of her husband and her sister-in-law in the same room at the same time made her vacant and gloomy.

With a desperate effort to restore gaiety, she said, "Jeannine! May I make you some coffee, or would you rather have liquor?"

"Coffee would be excellent," Jeannine said.

"And some kief?" Pierre suggested. He took up a chased silver box from the nearest of the many low coffee-tables, releasing as he lifted the lid the curious fragrance of the best Moroccan hashish.

Bustling, Rosalie left the room, unable to disguise her eagerness to be gone. When the door had closed Jeannine looked at its old-fashioned moulded panels, barely inclining towards the light Pierre was offering.

She said, "I hope you're not finding life as difficult as I am."

Pierre shrugged. "We get along, Rosalie and I."

"There must be more to be had than simply 'getting along'," Jeannine said with a kind of obstinacy.

"You've had a quarrel with Raoul," Pierre said, naming the latest of his sister's many lovers.

"Quarrel? Hardly. One doesn't quarrel any longer. One lacks the energy. But—it's not going to last, Pierre. I can feel the disillusionment gathering."

Pierre leaned back on his couch. He preferred couches to the big armchairs, though the latter were better scaled to his length of leg. He said, "I can almost measure the progress of your *affaires du coeur* by the number of times you come to call on us."

"You think I treat you as a wailing wall?" Jeannine gave a bitter little chuckle. "Perhaps so—but can I help it if you are the only person I can talk to openly? There's something between us which outsiders can never enter. It's a precious thing; I'm sparing with it."

She hesitated. "Rosalie senses it," she added finally. "You can see the effect on her when I arrive. That's another reason why I come only when I need to very much."

"Do you mean she makes you feel unwelcome?"

"That? No! She's the soul of courtesy. It's only that she like the rest of the world cannot understand what she has never experienced." Jeannine straightened, stabbing her kief cigarette through the air as though it were a teacher's pointer indicating words on a blackboard. "Consider, *chéri*, that we are not unique, being expatriates! Since they cut down the barriers between the countries of this tired old continent there must be fifty nationalities in Paris alone, and not a few of them—such as the Greeks—are better off than they would have been at home. As we are."

"At home?" Pierre echoed. "Our home is nowhere. It never existed except in father's and mother's minds."

Jeannine shook her head. "I don't believe they could have been discontented in a fine city like Paris unless they had been truly happy in a real country."

"But they grew more and more to talk only of good things. They forgot about the bad. The Algeria they imagined has gone forever under a wave of disorder, assassinations and civil war."

"Yet it made them happy. You can't deny that."

Pierre gave a sigh and a shrug.

"In short, we're not expatriates, you and I. We're extemporates, exiled from a country that vanished even before we were born, of which our parents made us citizens without intending to." She paused, searching her brother's face with sharp dark eyes. "I see you understand. I never knew you not to understand."

She reached over and gave his hand a squeeze.

"You're not discussing Algeria again, are you?" Rosalie said, entering with the handsome coffee-jug that matched the tray of cups on permanent display. She sounded as though she was trying to make a joke of the question. "I keep telling Pierre, Jeannine—it may have been fine to live there in the old days, but I wouldn't care to live there now."

"Of course not," Jeannine said with a forced smile. "Life in Paris is bad enough—why should anyone wish to go and live under the even grosser mismanagement of a native government?"

"Is life in Paris so bad, these days?"

"Perhaps you're lucky and don't notice it so much as I do, having this fine quiet home and nothing to do except look after it while Pierre reaps his fat salary from the bank! But I work, and in fashion advertising life isn't so secure as in banking. There are more *salauds* to the square metre and they wield far more power!"

Pierre gave his sister a look of alarm. When she was in a particular mood kief sometimes loosened her tongue more than politeness would permit, and more than once—not with Rosalie but with his first wife—he had to smooth over serious rows based on something she let slip while she was high.

"But even *salauds* have their uses," she continued. "That was what I came to tell you, Pierre. You're aware that Raoul works for the Common Europe prediction department?"

Pierre nodded. The prediction department was a building at Fontainebleau that had once housed a NATO detachment; now it was filled with computers to which intelligence reports, commercial as well as military, were daily fed for trend analysis.

"Something rather interesting . . ." Jeannine went on. "You know, too, that the prediction department processes not only European material but also what our former colonies send, giving a discount rate for old times' sake? And you've heard of the underwater mining project sponsored by the American corporation General Technics?"

"Naturally."

"The Americans have been sending agents to price the cost of transporting bulk raw materials from Port Mey, in Beninia. Also the same company is conducting inquiries among former colonial administrators in London. Raoul tells me that the computers foresee a great new company being launched in Port Mey to handle all these minerals."

There was a pause. Handing coffee to Jeannine, Rosalie looked in bewilderment from her to her husband and back, wondering at the look of wistful speculation that had appeared on both their faces.

"You've met Hélène, who used to work in Mali?" Pierre said at length, ignoring his wife.

"Yes. And you've met Henri, from Upper Volta?"

"Yes."

"You seem to understand as much as the computers."

"It follows very logically."

"I don't understand," Rosalie said.

Pierre glanced at her with a sort of pity. "Why should a big American corporation be sounding out former colonial officials in London unless they were well aware of the ignorance Americans display regarding the African mentality?"

Before Rosalie could admit that the question had done nothing to enlighten her, Jeannine said, "Wouldn't it be wonderful? Americans are a little better than barbarians, one must concede."

"But a country on the Bight of Benin, which has not benefited from French culture—"

"Part of it was settled by Berbers, and they for all their faults are cousins to the people of Algeria and Morocco."

Rosalie said with sudden uncharacteristic mistress-in-her-own-house determination, "Will you two tell me what you are talking about?"

Brother and sister exchanged glances. One of Jeannine's eyebrows rose, as though to say, "With a wife like her what do you expect?" Rosalie detected the action and flushed, hoping Pierre would disregard it for loyalty's sake.

Instead, he copied it.

"I'm talking about going back to Africa," Jeannine said. "Why not? I'm sick of France and the French who aren't French any longer, but some sort of horrible averaged-out Common European mongrels."

"What makes you so sure you'll get the chance to go?" Pierre countered.

"Raoul says they're intending to recruit advisors with African experience. There can't be so many people to suit their requirements. After all, *chéri*, neither you nor I is a chick fresh from the shell!"

"*I* don't want to go to Africa," Rosalie said, and set her chin mutinously. "Jeannine, drink your coffee—it'll be cold."

She leaned forward to push the copper cup closer to her sister-in-law. Over her bowed back the eyes of brother and sister met, and each recognised in the other the matching half of a dream, that had been broken a long time ago like a coin divided between sweethearts faced with years of separation.

MR. & MRS. EVERYWHERE: CALYPSO

"Like the good Lord God in the Valley of Bones
Engrelay Satelserv made some people called Jones.
They were not alive and they were not dead—
They were ee-magi-nary but always ahead.
What was remarkably and uniquely new—
A gadget on the set made them look like you!

"Watching their sets in a kind of a trance
Were people in Mexico, people in France.
They don't chase Jones but the dreams are the same—
Mr. and Mrs. Everywhere, that's the right name!
Herr und Frau Uberall or *les Partout*,
A gadget on the set makes them look like you.

"You can't see all the places of interest,
Go to the Moon and climb Mount Everest,
So you stay at home in a comfortable chair
And rely on Mr. and Mrs. Everywhere!
Doing all the various things you would like to do,
A gadget on the set makes them look like you.

"Wearing parkas and boots made by Gondola
You see them on an expedition polar.
They're sunning on the beach at Martinique

Using lotion from Guinevere Steel's Beautique.
Whether you're red, white, black or blue
A gadget on the set makes them look like you!

"When the Everywhere couple crack a joke
It's laughed at by all right-thinking folk.
When the Everywhere couple adopt a pose
It's the with-it view as everyone knows.
It may be a rumour or it may be true
But a gadget on the set has it said by you!

"English Language Relay Satellite Service
Didn't do this without any purpose.
They know very well what they would like—
A thousand million people all thinking alike.
When someone says something you don't ask who—
A gadget on the set has it said by you!

" 'What do you think about Yatakang?'
'I think the same as the Everywhere gang.'
'What do you think of Beninia then?'
'The Everywheres will tell me but I don't know when.'
Whatever my country and whatever my name
A gadget on the set makes me think the same."

"Which is the real time—his or ours?"

Norman had not intended the question to emerge in audible form. It was sparked by the sight of the enormous pile of printouts from Shalmaneser that had been delivered overnight to his office, and by recollection of the way they would have been produced. No conceivable printing device—not even the light-writers which had no moving parts except the fine beam from a miniature laser that inscribed words on photo-sensitive paper—could keep up with Shalmaneser's nanosecond mental processes; the entire problem posed to him would have been solved, or at any rate evaluated, then shunted to a temporary storage bank while he got on with the next task his masters imposed, and the conversion of it into comprehensible language would have taken fifty or a hundred times as long.

Elihu glanced at him. His eyes were a little red from lack of sleep, as were Norman's; one could not afford to sleep if one wanted to keep up with modern information-handling techniques. He said, "Whose?"

Norman gave a sour laugh, ushering the older man past him and closing the office door. "Sorry. I'm thinking of Shalmaneser as a 'he' again."

Elihu nodded. "Like Chad said, he's becoming one of the GT family ... How is Chad, by the way? I expected him to

311

take more of an interest in this project—after all, when I first met him at Miss Steel's, he spent practically the entire evening interrogating me about Beninia."

"I've hardly seen anything of him," Norman said, moving around his electronic desk and shoving at the swivel chair with his knee to turn it so he could sit down. "He's been using Don's room, I know that, and I think much of the time he's been going through Don's books—he has about three thousand of them. But apart from a hello, we haven't talked much."

"I see what you mean about the real time," Elihu said.

Norman blinked at him, puzzled.

"This!" Elihu amplified, tapping one of the three foot-deep stacks of printouts awaiting their attention. "Both you and I want to talk about the Beninian project. But we can't. Anything we say without reference to computers is already out of date before it's uttered, isn't it? The information to correct and shape our opinions exists, and we know it exists, so we decline to communicate until we've briefed ourselves, and because Shalmaneser works thousands of times faster than we do, we can never catch up so we never genuinely manage to communicate."

Norman hesitated. After the pause, he said, "Speaking of information to shape and change our opinions . . ."

"Yes?"

"Could you get me some data from State, do you think?"

"It depends." Elihu settled into a chair facing him. "I can get anything that touches directly on my own interests, but even ambassadorial rank, these days, doesn't carry infinite cachet."

"It's about Don," Norman said. His mouth twisted into a wry grin. "What you said about failing to communicate made me think of it. I lived with that codder for years, you know, and I never really got to be close friends with him. And now he's not around my place any longer, I miss him. I feel sort of guilty. I'd like to know if it's possible for me to keep in touch."

"I can inquire, I guess," Elihu agreed. "What happened to him, by the way?"

"I thought you knew. Oh! If you don't, maybe I shouldn't

... The hole with that, though. If a U.S. ambassador can't be trusted, who can?"

"They don't trust anybody, literally," Elihu shrugged. "Except computers."

"I do," Norman said. He glanced down at his hands and wrung them together absently. "As of a few days ago, and on principle. Don's gone to Yatakang on State business."

Elihu mulled that over for a while. He said, "That places him for me. I'd wondered where to pigeon-hole him. You mean he's one of these standby operatives State keeps on tap as insurance against the eventuation of low-probability trends."

"I believe that's correct, yes."

"And the only thing that's happened in Yatakang lately is this fantastic genetic programme they're boosting. Is that connected with his visit?"

"I assume it must be. At any rate, Don took his degree in biology, and his doctorate thesis was on the survival of archetypal genes in living fossils like coelacanths and king crabs and ginkgos."

"State wants the alleged techniques, presumably."

"I've been wondering about that," Norman said. "I wonder if we *do* want them."

"How do you mean?"

"It's a bit difficult to explain ... Look, have you been following television at all since you came home?"

"Occasionally, but since the Yatakang news broke I've been much too busy to catch more than an occasional news bulletin."

"So have I, but—well, I guess I'm more familiar with the way trends get started here nowadays, so I can extrapolate from the couple or three programmes I have had time for." Norman's gaze moved over Elihu's head to the far corner of the room.

"Engrelay Satelserv blankets most of Africa, doesn't it?"

"The whole continent, I'd say. There are English-speaking people in every country on Earth nowadays, except possibly for China."

"So you're acquainted with Mr. and Mrs. Everywhere?"

"Yes, of course—these two who always appear in station identification slots, doing exotic and romantic things."

"Did you have a personalised set at any time, with your own identity matted into the Everywhere image?"

"Lord, no! It costs—what? About five thousand bucks, isn't it?"

"About that. I haven't got one either; the basic fee is for couple service, and being a bachelor I've never bothered. I just have the standard brown-nose identity on my set." He hesitated. "And—to be absolutely frank—a Scandahoovian one for the shiggy half of the pair. But I've watched friends' sets plenty of times where they had the full service, and I tell you it's eerie. There's something absolutely unique and indescribable about seeing your own face and hearing your own voice, matted into the basic signal. There you are wearing clothes you've never owned, doing things you've never done in places you've never been, and it has the immediacy of real life because nowadays television *is* the real world. You catch? We're aware of the scale of the planet, so we don't accept that our own circumscribed horizons constitute reality. Much more real is what's relayed to us by the TV."

"I can well understand that," Elihu nodded. "And of course I've seen this on other people's sets too. Also I agree entirely about what we regard as real. But I thought we were talking about the Yatakangi claim?"

"I still am," Norman said. "Do you have a homimage attachment on your set? No, obviously not. I do. This does the same thing except with your environment; when they— let's see ... Ah yes! When they put up something like the splitscreen cuts they use to introduce SCANALYZER, one of the cuts is always what they call the 'digging' cut, and shows Mr. and Mrs. Everywhere sitting in *your* home wearing *your* faces watching the same programme you're about to watch. You know this one?"

"I don't think they have this service in Africa yet," Elihu said. "I know the bit you mean, but it always shows a sort of idealised dream-home full of luxy gadgetry."

"That used to be what they did here," Norman said. "Only nowadays practically every American home *is* full of luxy gadgetry. You know Chad's definition of the New Poor? People who are too far behind with time-payments on next year's model to make the down-payment on the one for the year after?"

Elihu chuckled, then grew grave. "That's too nearly literal to be funny," he said.

"Prophet's beard, it certainly is! I found time to look over some of Chad's books after Guinevere's party, and ... Well, having met him I was inclined to think he was a conceited blowhard, but now I think he's entitled to every scrap of vanity he likes to put on."

"I thought of asking State to invite him to come in on this project as a special advisor, but when I broached the matter to Raphael Corning I was told State doesn't approve of him."

"Why should they? He's successfully mocked everything authority stands for."

"He doesn't think he's been successful."

"He's certainly coloured public opinion. He may not have changed it radically, but what social theorist since Mao *has* managed to turn it over? The mere fact that his books are prescribed for college courses means his views are widely disseminated."

"Yes, but so are Thoreau's and— Never mind, we're digressing. You said something about our not wanting the Yatakangi genetic technique and then you started off about Mr. and Mrs. Everywhere."

"Right. I've almost forgotten to make my main point. I've watched this happen a couple of times, over eugenic legislation and over the question of partisans. After they've been using a personalised TV set for a while, especially if it includes a homimage unit, people begin to lose touch with actuality. For instance, you're supposed to have a fresh base-recording of your appearance put in about once a year. But I know people who've merely had a fresh track made of the first one, for four and even five years successively, so they can go on looking at their younger selves on the screen. They deny the passage of time. They live in an extended instant. Do you see what I'm steering towards?"

"People who can't even reconcile themselves to growing

older won't submit to someone else's good fortune when it comes to children?"

"Right. In other words: either our own government, and everyone else's, has got to match the Yatakangi claim forthwith, or else it's got to be shown up for an empty boast. The latter possibility would obviously suit State far better, because applying tectogenetic improvements to millions of pregnancies would cause a fantastic social upheaval—even worse than what followed the establishment of the Eugenic Processing Boards. But there's no middle way. Success in Yatakang, denied to people in other countries, and even success in a limited area of our society denied to people in other groups, will lead to such widespread resentment . . . Am I stretching my argument too far?"

"I don't believe you are." Elihu tried and failed to control a visible shudder. "I haven't been watching TV, as I told you—but since I'm rooming in the UN Hostel, I've been getting first-hand opinions from people of a hundred different nationalities, and take my word, Yatakang is the most cordially hated country on the face of the globe right now, not excluding China."

"And here's the crunch," Norman said, leaning forward to emphasise his words. "There hasn't been a *new* crisis since Mr. and Mrs. Everywhere took over. They emerged full-blown into the existing contemporary world, with its generation-long antipathies and hatreds. Even so, I've seen what they've done to public opinion. Tens—scores—of millions of people are becoming identified with that imaginary couple. The next presidential campaign will pivot on what they think, not on the validity of the rival policies. But the Yatakang question is going to hit first, and what's worse it'll hit people in the balls. Below the waist you don't think, you react. Let Mr. and Mrs. Everywhere only say that this isn't fair, and you'll have a party in favour of war against Yatakang within a week."

There was a short silence.

A kind of anguish was written on Norman's face. Studying it, Elihu said finally, "It's remarkable how much you've altered in the few days since I met you."

"What? How do you mean?"

"Laying away your ancestor to his long-time rest has improved you out of recognition. A couple of weeks ago I can imagine you chortling over the discomfiture of the paleasses in face of this breakthrough by yellowbellies. Now what seems to worry you most is the fact that people won't get the chance to judge the idea dispassionately for themselves, but may get stampeded into stupid emotional reactions."

"My whole life has been one long emotional reaction," Norman said, not looking at the older man. "Shall we leave the subject and get back to the business in hand?"

He picked up the first clipped-together section of printouts and riffled the pale green pages. Pale green signified that Shalmaneser had processed the information there contained as a hypothesis; when they keyed in the real-world assumptions the printouts would be on light pink sheets.

"What does the summary say?" Elihu inquired.

"It'll work," Norman muttered. He set the item aside and glanced at the top page of each of the following documents. "And that, and that, and that . . . 'Given the assumptions in the programme, the evaluation is favourable.' "

"It's nice to know something is on our side," Elihu commented caustically, and, reaching for a pen, began to make a neat tabulation of the various areas of the proposed Beninian venture where Shalmaneser said the idea was feasible.

He—one had to use the personal—had even revised the drafts of the advertisements for ex-colonial personnel.

the happening world (10)

SOUR GRAPES

"Already surgeons, doctors and nurses from all of the hundred islands are pouring into Gongilung to join the tremendous new venture directed by Professor Dr. Sugaiguntung. Parties of them have been standing in Liberty Square sometimes for hours on end in the hope of seeing Marshal Solukarta appear at the windows of the palace so that they may express directly to him their appreciation of the wonderful new era he has opened up. As the Leader explained in a television message last evening, fulfilment of this unique and magnificent programme will take time, but it is expected to be under way early next year. Meanwhile, thousands of husbands are applying to clinics all over Yatakang for vasectomy operations, explaining that they do not want to father inferior progeny now that the chance of optimising the country's population has been offered to them."

Delhi, India: a crowd estimated at forty thousand led by members of the League of Parents of Crippled and Handicapped Children besieged the Yatakangi Embassy for six hours today and police had to use tear-gas and sleepy-gas to disperse them.

"Chairman Yung sends congratulations to Marshal Solukarta and expresses the hope that the remarkable advance in medical science recently announced by Professor Dr. Sugaiguntung will shortly be made available to all Asians. While, of course, the great strides forward made in China, in the fields of nutrition, sanitation and genotyping, have already made the country's population the healthiest and most able in the world, the people of Yatakang's great ally are eager to hail and adopt this impressive Asian achievement."

Stockholm, Sweden: the streets of every city in this, the country with the world's oldest and most stringent eugenic legislation, were alive last night with crowds of helpless drunks bemoaning their childlessness. Ancients of seventy and eighty mingled with recently-sterilised youths and girls and drank the entire available supplies of akvavit in Stockholm, Malmö and Göteborg, according to a statement by the national liquor corporation. No fatalities were reported during subsequent disturbances.

"Secretest scramble and pass by hand of secure messenger Jogajong reports sitn unfavourablest propaganda impact of announcemt kuote fantsatic unquote."

London, England: the Minister of Health is expected to make a statement in the Commons on Tuesday.

Johannesburg, South Africa: Nathan Mdlele, a self-styled "doctor" practising here, has been arrested on charges of fraud following publication of handbills in which he claimed to be able to apply the Sugaiguntung technique to pregnant women.

"I don't care what they say, the fact remains Larry isn't as bright as the rest of the prodgies in his class. I know I promised that we'd have our second when I got my raise in pay, but I don't want another dullard in the family—not now geniuses can be had to order!"

Port Moresby, New Guinea: several hundred men and women banned from parenthood under local eugenic legislation set out from the harbour here today *en route* for

Gongilung where they hope to be able to apply for the Sugaiguntung treatment. Observers recalled the last-century spread of the cargo cults when describing the wave of hysteria that has swept the country.

Athens, Greece: in a bold stroke of publicity agents for popular TV idol Hector Yannakis today announced his willingness to help optimise the population himself, provided the shiggies calling on his services were quote reasonably attractive unquote. A storm of protest at his alleged bad taste has been overshadowed by the clamorous response from his fans.

"A hundred thousand buckadingdongs and no guarantee that it'll work? You must be crazy! Over in Yatakang they're doing it on the Health Service!"

Alice Springs, Australia: hospitals here are overwhelmed with disconsolate abos who had been misled by fanatical preacher Napoleon Boggs into believing that they could obtain white-skinned babies on request, according to a claim he made at a recent corroboree. Some had trekked a hundred miles on this vain errand. In a statement circulated earlier today Boggs declared it was his way of dramatising the still-inferior status of the aborigines in modern Australia.

"Look at you, you great *oaf!* It's no use saying you're sorry—that was an expensive present and when I tell Aunt Mary you broke it on the first day you had it she'll be furious! Why did I have to start a family before I could be sure my prodgies would be fit to look after themselves?"

Tokyo, Japan: despite police activity the clock around, the wave of public suicides by men denied fatherhood owing to genetic shortcomings continues at all major Shinto shrines in the city. At one shrine which was closed to the public after five such incidents, a man succeeded in climbing to the roof sixty feet above the floor and hurling himself head-first from a ledge.

Portland, Oregon: partisans armed with thermite, napalm and explosive this morning attacked the local Eugenic Processing Board offices in broad daylight. When police swooped, cheering crowds assisted the partisans' escape by swarming across roadways and blocking the path for the prowl cars.

"Well, one of the techniques the experts say they're going to use in Yatakang is what they call 'cloning', where they take a nucleus from one of your own body-cells and put it into an ovum to grow. If they can do that, why can't I have a child of yours? No freaking male need have anything to do with it!"

Moscow, Russia: students at the university here, members of the class due to graduate this summer who will be offered the standard alternatives of sterilisation or removal to one of the Siberian New Towns, staged an all-day sit-in at the main biological research laboratory in protest against Russia's lagging behind a comparatively backward country like Yatakang in the crucial field of tectogenetics.

Munich, Germany: at a mass rally Gerhard Speck, leader of the influential Aryan Purity Brigade, claimed that but for the unification of German into Common Europe the country could long ago have been re-populated with pure Nordic stock, quote without mongrelisation and barbaric contamination unquote.

"I've had it aborted. The Americans think genes like yours are serious enough to make their transmission illegal. I'm not going to start another with you or anyone else. My second is going to be optimised, like they're doing in Yatakang."

Washington, D.C.: at his press conference this morning the President stated that his advisors regard the Yatakangi optimisation programme as a mere propaganda gesture, quote a boast which even a far richer country like ours could not dream of carrying out this century unquote.

Paris, France: the incumbent chairman of the Board for Common Europe, Dr. Wladislaw Koniecki of Poland, declared that the Yatakangi claim was unfounded in reality, being quote a programme not even the combined wealth of all our countries could make possible unquote.

"That sheeting little bureaucrat in the Eugenics Office! I bet he's got a genotype so dirty you could use it for a mud-pack! *And* I wager he has prodgies—someone in his position could fix things, couldn't he?"

Caracas, Venezuela: in a spectacular departure from previous policy, representatives of the Olive Almeiro Agency, Puerto Rico's world-famous adoption service, announced the availability of pure Castilian ova from Spanish sources, to be shipped trans-Atlantic by express while in deep freeze and implanted in the quote mother unquote. This confirms authoritative predictions that Puerto Rican legislation will be a death-blow to the operations of baby-farmers in the entire U.S.A.

Madrid, Spain: Pope Eglantine denounced the Yatakangi programme as another blasphemous interference with God's handiwork and promised eternal damnation to any Catholic in Yatakang who complied with government policy. An emergency decree by the Royalist party will impose the death penalty for the donation of ova for export, if approved by the Cortes tomorrow.

"Darling, you're talking nonsense! So we don't have Shalmaneser, so we do have some of the world's finest computing equipment, and they ran a programme through this morning and it turned out the Yatakangis can't possibly keep their promise. The whole thing's a bluff . . . You aren't listening, are you? What's the good of talking?"

Cairo, Egypt: addressing a rally of pilgrims bound Mecca-ward for the *hajj*, a government spokesman denounced the

Yatakangi optimisation programme as quote a barefaced lie unquote.

Havana, Cuba: at a meeting to mark the anniversary of the death of Fidel Castro, the Cuban Minister of Welfare and Parenthood accused the Yatakangi government of quote deliberately misleading the world's under-privileged peoples unquote and was booed off the stand by his audience.

"Sheeting hole, Frank, I'll never forgive those bleeders! Here we are stuck in this Godforsaken town and we could have stayed home among our friends and even if we couldn't have used a nucleus from one of your cells we could have used one from mine and at least had a daughter, couldn't we?"

Port Mey, Beninia: in an Independence Day broadcast to the public, during which he announced that his doctors had given him only a short time to live, childless President Obomi declared that with or without the Yatakangi treatment he could not have wished for a better family than the people he has ruled for so long.

Berkeley, California: Bennie Noakes sits in front of a set tuned to SCANALYZER repeating over and over, "Christ, what an imagination I've got!"

(The fathers have eaten sour grapes, and the children's teeth are set on edge.

—Ezekiel XVIII, 2.)

THE MESSENGER OF THE GOSPEL
OF UNIVERSAL LOVE

"Which was the lady who lost her baby so unfortunately?"
Henry Butcher inquired of the ward sister.

The sister, her face weary, glanced up at the plump jolly
man in front of her. Drawn lines of tiredness changed to
those of a smile.

"Hullo, Henry," she said. "Go along in—I'm sure she'll be
glad to have a few words of sympathy from someone. The
blonde in the third bed on the right."

"It's the first for a long time, isn't it?" Henry asked.

"Lord, yes. First since I came to work here, and that's
nearly eleven years. The path lab is checking up now to see
what went wrong."

"Should it have been a normal case?"

The sister leaned back in her chair, tapping one white
tooth with the tip of a well-shaped nail. "I guess so," she said
thoughtfully. "That is, there was a rhesus problem, but that
kind of thing used to be routine—a whole-body blood-
transfusion prior to the birth, and plain sailing from then
on."

"A rhesus problem?" Henry repeated.

"Yes—you know, or at least you should, working in the
blood-bank."

"Oh, I *know* about it," Henry agreed. His jolly face wore

its solemn look rather awkwardly. "But I didn't think rhesus-incompatibles were allowed to start children any longer."

"Not in this country. But the girl's been working in Africa somewhere. Her husband sent her home specially to have the prodgy in a proper hospital. And one can't refuse to accept a maternity case just because it wasn't conceived under our laws."

"Of course not . . . Well, well, it's all very sad. I'll pop in the ward and see what I can do to cheer the lady up a bit."

Still smiling, the sister watched him leave the office, his sterile white plastic coverall glistening wetly under the lamps and making shush-slap noises as his legs brushed together at each step. It was very kind of him to take the trouble for a perfect stranger, she thought. But just the sort of thing you'd expect from him.

Everyone in the hospital liked Henry Butcher.

When he had spent a few minutes with the mother of the dead child, he gave her one of his little inspirational pamphlets, which she promised to read—it was divided into sections with such titles as *Love Thy Neighbour* and *The Truth Shall Make You Free*. By then it was the end of his lunch-break, so he headed back to the blood-bank where he worked, exchanging cheery greetings with everyone he met on the way.

A requisition had come down during his absence, ordering the preparation of a hundred donor-flasks with labels for a routine session at a nearby block. He sorted out the appropriate file of names, ages and blood-groups from the records cabinet, selected the right number of labels plus ten per cent for spoilage to match the numbers in each group, broke off for a moment to issue two flasks of O blood to an orderly from the maternity ward, and then mixed and measured the correct quantity of citric-saline solution into each flask, to prevent the blood clotting in storage.

Finally, making a careful check to be sure he was unobserved, he inserted a hypodermic through the rubber penetration-seal on each flask and squirted in a hundred milligrams of Triptine in solution, beaming.

The idea had escaped him for a long, long time. He had achieved a number of successful public demonstrations of his treasured credo—in particular, the Sunday morning when he had managed to smear the front of the cathedral pulpit with "Truth or Consequences" and thus ensured that the bishop told the honest truth for once instead of his usual prevaricating falsehoods—but it was only recently that he had discovered this far more effective means of exposing people to the actual effects of the panacea he believed in.

He could not imagine himself hating anyone; all hate had been leached out of his personality by the warm glow due to psychedelics. Yet there were people, among them staff-members of this hospital, who denied that universal love could take on chemical form. Why in the cosmos not? After all, it was a commonplace of Christian tradition that Love could take on the substance of bread and wine . . .

Of course, the death of that baby was a terrible shame; the poor thing must have had an overdose. A shadow clouded his round, smiling countenance, but lasted only an instant. The sister had said it was the first such case in the eleven years she had worked here. There wouldn't be another in the foreseeable future, or perhaps ever again, now that people were forbidden to start rhesus-problem prodgies.

He completed his task, meticulously rinsed and dried the hypodermic as he had seen the doctors do all around the hospital, and returned it to its case. Then he locked away the phial of Triptine from which he had drawn the necessary amount, and began to rack up the flasks for outward shipment. He whistled as he worked.

Who wouldn't whistle, knowing that every patient who required a blood-transfusion in this hospital would from now on experience the wonderful, mind-opening enlightenment that Triptine could bestow?

About half an hour later the young pathologist who was investigating the reason for the baby's inexplicable death came in and asked for a flask of O blood, which Henry issued to him. He was genuinely surprised when the pathologist returned and hit him under the jaw so hard that he crashed backwards into a stack of crated flasks and brought the whole lot tumbling.

As for the policeman who charged him formally with murder, Henry could not credit that such a person might be real.

continuity (18)

THE WALLS OF TROY

The hostility Donald felt when he returned to the everyday world was not illusion. It came from the other intending passengers crammed into the emergency expressport now serving the Ellay region. This was in fact a military base, hastily cleared of equipment the public was not allowed to see and patrolled continually by armed guards. Diverted, delayed, their schedules thrown out, hungry and thirsty because the Air Force canteens could not cope like the facilities at the regular port, and to top the lot uncertain whether their flights would materialise because expresses re-routed to the base were firing their sonic booms on to populated areas and there was talking of the residents taking out an injunction, they were looking around for someone to vent their resentment on, and the appearance of Donald armed with clearances that scissored through the red tape entangling everyone else offered a ready target.

He didn't give a pint of whaledreck about their feelings. His head ached slightly. One of the many successive processors at Boat Camp between whom he had been shuttled like a machine on an assembly-line had warned him that this might happen at intervals for a week or two. But the pain wasn't severe enough to cancel out his basic state of mind.

He felt proud. The Donald Hogan of the previous thirty-four years had ceased to exist, but he was no loss. He had been passive, a recipient or rather a receptacle, open for the shovelling-in of external data but making no contribution of his own to the course of events, reserved, self-contained, so neutral that even Norman House sharing the same apt could call him in a fit of rage a bloodless, featureless zombie.

Not that he cared about Norman's opinion now, either. He knew what latent capabilities resided in himself, and was possessed by savage eagerness for the moment when he could let them go.

At one of a range of folding tables spanning the hangar they were using as a transit hall, a weary official checked his documents. "Going to Yatakang, hm?" he said. "Off to get yourself optimised, I suppose!"

"Me? No, I function pretty well in all areas. You look like you're saving up for a ticket, though."

For a second he thought the man was going to hit him. His face burned dark red with the effort of self-control. He could say nothing more to Donald, but slapped the documents wordlessly under the cameras and stamping-machines before him, then waved him through.

"There was no call to say that," the official from the next table said as Donald passed close enough to hear a whisper.

"What?"

The second official made sure his colleague was engaged again and not listening. "There was no call to say that," he repeated. "He got married without having their genes matched and their first kid just had to be aborted. Pink spot."

The sign of hereditary schizophrenia. Donald shrugged.

"I think I'd have hit you," the official said.

"If he'd hit me, he'd have given up hitting people permanently," Donald said, and grinned. It was wonderful to know it was more than a boast—it was a promise. He added after a moment. "You don't have work to do?"

The official scowled and turned back to deal with his next passenger.

"Yatakang?" said the purser of the express, an elegant young biv-type sporting ambisextrous shoulder-long bangs. "You must be Mr. Hogan, then—I believe you're the only person scheduled this flight . . ." He checked a list he was carrying. "Yes, that's right. Here's your seat-number, sir, and a pleasant flight. I'll be round to see you before we take off." He handed over a little plastic tag.

Donald took it and walked on into the cheerless coffin of the express. Settling into his seat among anonymous accidental companions, he recalled Delahanty's injunction to make good his ignorance of the last few days' news. When the purser toured the ship to perform the airline's vaunted "personal touch service", he answered affirmatively to the inquiry about wanting anything.

"You said I was the only person going to Yatakang, didn't you?"

A flutter of long eyelashes and a mechanical smile. "Why, yes, sir."

"Does this often happen?"

"Frankly, sir, as I understand it, if the terms of our charter under international agreement didn't require us to make at least one stop a day in Gongilung, we wouldn't bother. But there's something about granting overflight facilities—I could get the details from the captain if you like . . . ?"

"Don't bother. But have you not had any other passengers for Yatakang lately? I'd have thought, what with the big news that broke out there the other day—"

"You mean reporters like yourself, sir? I'm afraid I haven't noticed particularly," the purser said in a frigid tone.

Donald sighed. It was all very well when professional ethics and respect for privacy were confined to a few expert groups like doctors and priests; now it was being adopted by the world and his uncle, the attitude was frustrating.

"I have a polytelly. Is it okay for me to use it during the flight?"

"I'm afraid not, sir. But I can pipe in a condensed-news channel to your seat-screen."

"Do that, then. And if you have any recent papers on board I'd appreciate a sight of them."

"I'll see what I can find for you, sir. Will that be all?"

Flushed, the purser returned just as the tugs started to track the express across the field to its launch-ramp. "I could only find one of today's and one of yesterday's, I'm afraid," he apologised.

That was more than Donald had expected, even so. He accepted them with a mutter of thanks and spread them out. The older of the two papers was beginning to fragment in accordance with the Federal anti-litter law which forbade ephemeral publications to be printed on permanent stock for other than historical purposes. Handling it carefully, he searched it for stories with a Yatakang dateline.

He found only one, and its credit was to a beam agency, one of Engrelay Satelserv's major rivals, Video-Asia Reuters. That, of course, wasn't surprising; these days, newspapers were ninety per cent trivia and features, unable to compete with TV news—indeed most of them, including the respective *Times* of New York and London, had switched their major cachet to television slots. And all he learned from his reading was something he could have deduced anyway: the people of Yatakang wanted to believe their government's claim, whether or not it was exaggerated.

As he turned the next page it disintegrated, showering him with flakes of yellowing paper. He cursed it and thrust it into his seat's disposall tube.

The take-off warning followed immediately, and he had to wait to tackle the second paper until the upward leg of their ballistic orbit had been entered.

This time, there was an entire page devoted to material on the subject of optimisation: one beam agency story from Gongilung reporting that voluntary funds were being raised in outlying islands so that doctors and nurses could go to the capital for training under Sugaiguntung, and about a dozen reporting reaction in other countries. There were several hints that public opinion was ranged against the verdict of the experts. When it came to a Minister of the Cuban government being booed at a Castro Day rally . . .

Donald frowned. Somehow these news items suggested a

deeper pattern, but his head was aching again and he could not concentrate. The Mark I version of himself would have turned the problem out to graze in his subconscious, but now he did not have the patience. Instead of mulling the question over, he stuffed the paper down the disposall and switched on the condensed-news programme the purser had provided.

On the miniature screen set into the back of the seat ahead he saw a series of short visual clips with earphone commentary. He studied them with what attention he could manage. He happened to have struck into the cycle at a point just before the sports news, and had to wait out four minutes' worth before the bulletin cycled back to the station identification and began to repeat. And then he discovered he was watching a programme compiled by the staff of the same paper he had just thrown away, containing almost exclusively the same stories.

Annoyed, he reached out to switch off. At the same moment the picture quality deteriorated, and a sign appeared to say that because of increasing distance from Ellay there would be a change to a satellite-based service. Hoping that the airline might use one of the field leaders like Engrelay Satelserv, he stayed his hand.

Correct. The familiar figures of Mr. & Mrs. Everywhere took shape almost at once. Obviously this was a special signal for passengers in transit; it used only back views and the environment was the interior of an express identical to this. It had never occurred to him before, but it was logical that having secured maximum viewer-identification by selling so many personalised sets with homimage attachment the company would not wish to remind people actually going to some of the exotic places where Mr. & Mrs. Everywhere kept dropping in that in fact the couple were only models.

The purser had set his screen for a Caucasian version of the signal, and that was momentarily unfamiliar. On moving in with Norman he had accepted the latter's offer of a TV just about to be discarded in favour of a newer model, and never bothered to alter the Afram standard to which it was set, so he was accustomed to seeing Mr. Everywhere as an Afram and his wife as one of Norman's typical Scandahoovian shiggies. Here now he was getting the "white stocky young mature" version of the man, and it jarred.

He was annoyed with himself for feeling so concerned about something which was, after all, a commercial figment more appropriate to his former life. From now on Donald Hogan was going to make news, not watch it.

As though the programmers had read his mind, his own face appeared on the screen.

He thought it was an illusion until the commentry corrected the impression. "Donald Hogan!" said the small voice directly into his ears. "Engrelay Satelserv's newest man on the spot!"

Whereinole did they dredge up these clips? There was a younger Donald Hogan on a New York street, then gazing up at distant mountains—that was a Sun Valley vacation five years ago—and then, more familiar, boarding the express he had taken a few days ago from New York to California.

"Specially retained by Engrelay Satelserv, life-time expert in genetics and heredity Donald Hogan is bound on your behalf to Yatakang!"

Clips of a Gongilung street-scene, a fishing-prau chugging between islands on a noisy reaction-pump, a crowd massing in a handsome square.

"Yatakang, focus of planet-wide interest! Programme your autoshout for the name of Donald Hogan, whose dispatches from Gongilung will be featured in our bulletins from tomorrow on!"

Donald was stunned. They must be making a sensaysh out of it, to sacrifice so much time from even their ten-minute condensed-news cycle! His Mark II confidence evaporated. Euphoric from his recent eptification, he had thought he was a new person, immeasurably better equipped to affect the world. But the implications of that expensive plug stabbed deep into his mind. If State were willing to go to these lengths to maintain his cover identity, that meant he was only the visible tip of a scheme involving perhaps thousands of people. State just didn't issue fiats to a powerful corporation like English Language Relay Satellite Service without good reason.

Meaningless phrases drifted up, dissociated, and presented themselves to his awareness, all seeming to have relevance to his situation and yet not cohering.

My name is Legion.

I fear the Greeks, even bearing gifts.

The sins of the fathers shall be visited on the children.

Say can you look into the seeds of time?

Was this the face that launch'd a thousand ships, And burnt the topless towers of Ilium?

Struggling to make sense of these fragments, he finally arrived at what his subconscious might be trying to convey.

The prize, these days, is not in finding a beautiful mistress. It's in having presentable prodgies. Helen the unattainable is in the womb, and every mother dreams of bearing her. Now her whereabouts is known. She lives in Yatakang and I've been sent in search of her, ordered to bring her back or say her beauty is a lie—if necessary to make it a lie, with vitriol. Odysseus the cunning lurked inside the belly of the horse and the Trojans breached the wall and took it in while Laocoön and his sons were killed by snakes. A snake is cramped around my forehead and if it squeezes any tighter it will crack my skull.

When the purser next passed, he said, "Get me something for a headache, will you?"

He knew that was the right medicine to ask for, yet it also seemed he should have asked for a cure for bellyache, because everything was confused: the men in the belly of the wooden horse waiting to be born and wreak destruction, and the pain of parturition, and Athena was born of the head of Zeus, and Time ate his children, as though he were not only in the wooden horse of the express but *was* it about to deliver the city to its enemy and its enemy to the city, a spiralling wild-rose branch of pain with every thorn a spiky image pricking him into other times and other places.

Ahead, the walls. Approaching them, the helpless stupid Odysseus of the twenty-first century, who must also be Odin blind in one eye so as not to let his right hand know what his left was doing. Odinzeus, wielder of thunderbolts, how could he aim correctly without parallax? "No individual has the whole picture, or even enough of it to make trustworthy judgments on his own initiative." *Shalmaneser, master of infinite knowledge, lead me through the valley of the shadow of death and I shall fear no evil . . .*

The purser brought a white capsule and he gulped it down. But the headache was only a symptom, and could be fixed.

tracking with closeups (17)

BRIGHTER THAN A THOUSAND MEN

"Shalmaneser, pizzle-teaser,
Had a wife and couldn't please her.
Go and tell the big computer
(*Mary's*) lover doesn't suit her."

> —*Children's singing game reported from*
> *Syracuse, N.Y., November 2009*

"A randy young wench named Teresa
Tried her charms out upon Shalmaneser.
    For the first time quite frigid
    She, not he, grew rigid,
And the scientists couldn't unfreeze her."

> —*Graffito from University Hall of Residence,*
> *Auckland, New Zealand; variants common*
> *throughout English-speaking world*

"They surely are condemned to Hell
    Who rule their lives by greed and lust
And Satan waits for those as well
    Who in machines repose their trust."

> —*Hymn composed for Tenth International*
> *Rally of the Family of Divine Daughters*

i wish codders i had cool detachment
                    like
chilledchild*chilled*

                    how are you feelium
                    in the liquid helium
HERE WE GO ROUND THE HUNGARY FLUSH
Meg

                    a brain computer
SHALL MAN EASE HER OR WOULD YOU ADVISE
AGAINST IT

                    don't
                    —*From GRAUNCH::prosoversepix*

"It is dismaying—one may even say disheartening—to see
the degree to which blind faith in the manufactured objects
that we dignify by the name of 'computer' has replaced trust
in prayer and the guidance of God. You will never find
anyone to admit that he or she has substituted a machine for
the living divine presence, yet that is exactly what has happened to the bulk of our population. They speak of the
evaluations which computers print out for them in the
hushed, reverent tones which our ancestors reserved for Holy
Writ, and now that General Technics has made its arrogant
claim about this new piece of hardware, nicknamed 'Shalmaneser', we can foresee the day when everyone will have
surrendered his responsibility as a thinking being to a machine which he has been deluded into respecting as more
intelligent than himself. That is, unless we with God's help
manage to reverse the trend."
                    —*From an earlier sermon by the luckless
                    bishop whom Henry Butcher sabotaged*

"Okay, Shalmaneser—*you* tell me what I ought to do!"
                    —*Colloquial usage throughout N. America*

(SHALMANESER That real cool piece of hardware up at
the GT tower. They say he's apt to evolve to true consciousness one day. Also they say he's as intelligent as a thousand

of us put together, which isn't really saying much, because when you put a thousand of us together look how stupidly we behave.

—*The Hipcrime Vocab* by Chad C. Mulligan)

Never in human history did any manufactured object enter so rapidly into the common awareness of mankind as Shalmaneser did when they took the security wraps off. Adaptation of him as a "public image" for prose and verse followed literally within days; a few months saw him apotheosised as a byword, a key figure in dirty jokes, a court of final appeal, and a sort of mechanical Messias. Some of these cross-referred; in particular, there was the story about the same Teresa who cropped up in the New Zealand limerick, which told how they sent for a Jewish telepath to ask what happened, when they discovered that thanks to the liquid helium she was in a state of suspended animation, and he explained with a puzzled look that he could only detect one thought in her head—"Messias has not yet come."

Also, until GT published a rota and scale of hire-charges, consultant computing firms in twenty countries trembled on the verge of bankruptcy as their clients decided to switch their custom to Shalmaneser.

Mr. & Mrs. Everywhere had been shown visiting Shalmaneser one hundred and thirty-seven times, more than was accorded to any other activity except freefly-suiting.

Orbiting on Triptine, Bennie Noakes was prouder of the fact that his imagination had produced Shalmaneser than he was of any other event he had dreamd up.

Factually: he was a Micryogenic ® device of the family collectively referred to as the Thecapex group (THEoretical CAPacity EXceeds—human brain, understood) and of that family's fourth generation, his predecessors having been the pilot model Jeroboam, the commercially available Rehoboam of which over a thousand were in operation, and the breadboard layout Nebuchadnezzar which turned out to have so many bugs in it they discontinued the project and cannibalised the parts.

The number of technical problems which had had to be

solved before he could be put into operation beggared description; the final programme for the schematics required fourteen hours' continuous operation of six Rehoboams linked in series, a capacity which the publicity department calculated would be adequate to provide a thousand-year solution for the orbits of the Solar System correct to twenty decimal places. And at that, using so much capacity for so long on a single task brought the chance of a sixfold simultaneous error to the thirty per cent level, so there was one chance in three that when they built the final version and switched it on something would have gone irremediably wrong.

Indeed, some of the original design team had recently been heard to express the heretical view that something *had* gone wrong with the schematics. By this time, they claimed, it should have been established beyond doubt that Shalmaneser was conscious in the human sense, possessed of an ego, a personality and a will.

Others, more sanguine, declared that proof of such awareness already existed, and evidenced certain quite unforeseen reactions the machine had displayed in solving complex tasks.

The psychologists, called in to settle the argument, left again with headshakes, divided into two equally opposed camps. Some said the problem was insoluble, and referred back to the ancient puzzle: given a room divided in two by an opaque curtain, and a voice coming from the other side, how do you discover whether the voice belongs to a cleverly programmed computer or a human being? Their rivals maintained that in their eagerness to see mechanical consciousness the designers had set up a self-fulfilling prophecy—had, in effect, programmed the schematics so as to give the impression of consciousness when information was processed in the system.

The public at large was quite unconcerned about the debate between the experts. For them, Shalmaneser was a legend, a myth, a folk hero, and a celebrity; with all that, he didn't need to be conscious as well.

A few days after they rigged up the direct-verbal inputs—

Shalmaneser was the first computer ever with sufficient spare capacity to handle normal spoken English regardless of the speaker's tone of voice—one of the technicians asked him on the spur of the moment, "Shal, what's your view? Are you or aren't you a conscious entity?"

The problem took so long to analyse—a record three-quarters of a minute—that the inquirer was growing alarmed when the response emerged.

"It appears impossible for you to determine whether the answer I give to that question is true or false. If I reply affirmatively there does not seem to be any method whereby you can ascertain the accuracy of the statement by referring it to external events."

Relieved to have had even such a disappointing answer after the worrying delay, the questioner said fliply, "So who do we ask if you can't tell us—God?"

"If you can contact Him," Shalmaneser said, "of course."

> "The case of Teresa's instructive—
> It shows how extremely seductive
>   A shiggy can be
>   If her an-atom-ee
> Is first rendered super-conductive."
>
> —*Quoted in the General Technics house organ, January 2010*

continuity (19)

SEMPER ALIQUID NOVI

The leisurely niche he had carved out for himself, Norman recognised with dismay, had unfitted him to cope with a storm of information like the one now swamping him. He forced himself to keep going, red-eyed, sometimes hoarse, often suffering violent indigestion, until he was almost ready to welcome his physical discomfort as growing-pains.

If the Beninia project was to become reality, it had to negotiate three major obstacles. First, the early glamour of MAMP was wearing thin and shareholders were beginning to shake off their entitlements—which, while it allowed GT personnel in the know to buy at cut rates, created an unfavourable climate in the market. Second, a two-thirds majority at a general meeting had to be secured. And, third, President Obomi had taken the climactic step of informing his country about his illness, which meant that time was running out. Elihu claimed that he would like the scheme provided it was vouched for by his long-time personal friend, but there was no way of predicting what his successor would agree to.

Urgency drove them to exploit Shalmaneser's incredible speed to the utmost. Not content with erecting and demolishing half a hundred hypothetical courses a day, they began to clear down on external contract work and make time for direct-voice questioning on aspects not fully clarified in the written programmes.

It was the first occasion Norman had ever worked directly with Shalmaneser. The night before he first spoke to the computer he dreamed of being imprisoned by walls of the pale green "hypothetical" printouts he had grown familiar with; the night after, his dream was of hearing it address him from his phone, his TV set, and the empty air.

There was little opportunity for dreaming, though. At the cost of near-exhaustion he kept abreast of the demands made on him. Half a dozen times a day Old GT called him for information which could have been had more readily from an encyclopedia bank, but he managed to convey acceptable answers. At endless conferences people applied to him for views and guidance and he responded as mechanically as if he were himself a computing engine, reeling off statistics, dates, local customs, snippets of history, even undisguised personal opinions which his listeners took in as uncritically as the rest.

He began to feel a little more pleased with himself. Under the slick professional mask he had adopted in order to make his way to the top in a paleass world, there was some kind of substance after all. He had been half-afraid there was only a hollow, like the candle-lit void of a turnip-ghost.

Even more than his desire to prove himself to himself, two other motives drove him on. One was admiration for Elihu Masters, who had detected that substance when the mask was still in place and gambled on it the outcome of a successful career. Norman had always cultivated the company grapevine; now it informed him that provided the Beninia project worked out Elihu could almost certainly be the next Ambassador to the UN, thus recouping the cachet lost when he opted for Port Mey instead of Delhi.

If it failed, on the other hand, he was finished.

And the second reason was simple puzzlement. By the end of the first week's intensive planning, he knew rather more about Beninia than about most of the places he had lived in, without ever setting foot on its soil. Early on, the data he absorbed were simply shovelled in, making a heap in his mind through which he had to rummage to find out what he knew.

Gradually they grew more organised, developed relationships, and ultimately took on the pattern of a baffling question.

How in the name of Allah the Merciful did Beninia come to be this way?

But for the mass of historical evidence, he could have suspected a gigantic public-relations confidence trick. "Everyone knew"—this was what it boiled down to—that when the European colonial powers moved in the tribes of equatorial and southern Africa had been in a state of barbarism instanced by a thousand recorded facts from Chaka Zulu's murderous raiding to the readiness of tribes to sell their own children to the Arab slavers. "Everyone knew" that after the European withdrawal things went back to where they had been, aggravated by bitterness at the long period of foreign rule.

Not in Beninia. As Elihu put it, Zadkiel Obomi had performed the miracle of creating an African counterpart of Switzerland, walking a tightrope of dogged neutrality over a hell of intermittent violence.

But what had he got to—to *power* this achievement? That was where Norman ran into a blank wall. Switzerland's neutrality was founded on clear advantages: a key location which only Napoleon had had the gall to trespass over among all the would-be modern Attilas—even the Nazis had found it profitable to leave Switzerland alone; a jealously guarded reputation for honesty in commerce that made her an international financial centre; skill in precision manufactures that converted the country's lack of mineral resources into a positive blessing.

Contrast Beninia: located between powerful rivals either of which would cheerfully have sacrificed an army or two of burdensome unskilled labourers for the sake of annexing its fine main port and its river-routes through the Mondo Hills; economically non-viable, kept going only by constant foreign aid; and far from being industrialised, backward to a degree exceptional even in Africa.

Thinking of the anomalies gave Norman a headache, but he ploughed on, extending the area of his inquiries until the research department sent back a furious memo demanding whatinole connection events in the first year of the Muslim calendar could have with a twenty-first-century business venture.

Norman felt obscurely that if he could answer that he wouldn't be so baffled by this hole-in-corner country.

However, the Research Dept was quite right—it was pointless to dig that far back because the records didn't exist. There were hardly even any archaeological remains. Digging up the past was an expensive luxury in Beninian terms.

Norman sighed, and went back for yet another review of what he had learned.

"Happy is the country that has no history"—and for a long time the area later called Beninia qualified. Its first impact on the world scene occurred during the heyday of internal African slave-trading, when Arab pressure from the north drove the Holaini—a sub-branch of the Berbers, of Muslim faith and Hamitic race—past Timbuktu toward the Bight of Benin. There they came across an enclave of Shinka, hemmed in on one side by Mandingo and on the other by Yoruba.

These neighbours were accustomed to leaving the Shinka strictly alone, claiming that they were powerful magicians and could steal the heart out of a valiant fighting man. The Holaini scoffed; as good Muslims they discounted the idea of witchcraft, and certainly the unaggressive, welcoming Shinka —whom even the idea of slavery did not seem to arouse to anger—offered no obvious threat.

With the full intention of ranching the Shinka, cattle-fashion, as a constant source of slaves, the Holaini installed themselves as the new masters of the area. But, as though by the magic neighbouring tribes had described, the venture crumbled. After twenty years, no more slave-caravans were formed. The Holaini gradually became absorbed into the base population, leading a quiet rural existence, until by the twentieth century only their dialect and such physical traces as the "northern nose" and breadth of forehead remained to testify to their independent identity.

Superstition—perhaps—accounted for the subsequent unwillingness of the dealers who supplied the European slave-ship captains to tangle with the Shinka. They excused themselves on the specious ground that Shinkas made bad slaves, or that they were sickly, or that they were under the special protection of Shaitan. One or two European-led raids apart, they remained largely unmolested until the age of colonial exploitation.

When the carving was well under way, the British kicked out the Spanish, who had been maintaining a trading-station near the site of the modern Port Mey as an adjunct to their larger settlement on the nearby island of Fernando Po, and let the French in neighbouring Togo understand that Beninia was henceforth shadowed by the Union Jack.

And that, by and large, was that, apart from the legalistic regularisation of the situation into one analogous with Nigeria, the setting up of a "British Crown Colony and Protectorate".

Until 1971, when the Colonial Office in London was seeking ways of disposing of its last few embarrassing overseas charges. Some, like the smallest Pacific islands, were pretty well hopeless cases, and the best that could be managed was to shuffle them off into someone else's lap—the Australians', for example. Beninia did not look at first as though it would pose the least difficulty, however. After all, Gambia, which was about the same size, had been independent for a few years already.

The trouble arose when they tried to find someone to hand over the government to.

There were a good few competent officials in Beninia, but owing to the fact that the Muslim pattern of paternalism conformed to the masculinist prejudices of nineteenth-century English public-school boys, most of them had been recruited among the northern minority, the Holaini. Exactly the same thing had happened in Nigeria. There, following independence, the majority group had revolted against this legacy of Victorian prejudice. The Colonial Office had no wish to repeat that mistake, even though the Shinka seemed to be peculiarly unpolitical. In fact, if they'd had the kindness to organise a proper political party to agitate for independence, the problem would never have arisen.

Casting around, the London bureaucrats hit on a young Beninian who, if he didn't have a popular following, at least enjoyed popular esteem. Zadkiel Frederick Obomi had been educated in Britain and the United States. He came from a respectable, moderately well-to-do family. His ambition was to become an educational broadcaster, and he was doing jack-of-all-trades work at the only TV station serving the Bight area—lecturing, reading news bulletins, and commenting on current affairs in Shinka and Holaini. He had been seconded to supervise the news coverage of the last meeting of the Organisation for African Unity, and the delegates from Ethiopia and South Africa had both singled him out for praise, so there was no question of his acceptability outside Beninia.

Inside the country it was a different matter, chiefly because he himself had never thought of being president. Eventually, however, he was persuaded that no one else was qualified, and when his name was put to a plebiscite both Shinka and Holaini voters approved him by a thumping majority over a candidate backed largely by Egyptian funds.

Thankfully the British re-named Governor's House, calling it the Presidential Palace, and went home.

At first, owing to inexperience, the new president seemed to be bumbling along. His first cabinet, chosen in ratio to the population of Holaini versus Shinka with a slight bias towards the former because of their administrative background, accomplished practically nothing. Bit by bit, however, he replaced the British-trained ministers with people of his own choosing, some of whom volunteered to come home from comfortable foreign posts, like the incumbent minister of finance, Ram Ibusa, who had been teaching economics in Accra.

To everyone's surprise, he coped well with a crisis that threatened him at the very end of his first term.

In former British and French colonies adjacent to Beninia, a commonplace feature of late twentieth-century Africa broke out—tribal quarrels flared up into rioting and sometimes a week or two of actual civil war. Large movements of Inoko and Kpala took place. Since Beninia was handy, and since it wasn't in turmoil, both tribes' refugees headed for there.

The people who had kicked them out weren't interested in what had become of them. It was only later, after the

economic facts of life had forced several ex-colonial countries to federate into groups sharing a common European
language—such as Mali, Dahomey and Upper Volta into
Dahomalia, and Ghana and Nigeria into RUNG—that they
became aware of a curious phenomenon.

The Shinka were even poorer than the Inoko and the
Kpala, and might have been expected to resent the extra
burden the refugees placed on the country's strained resources. But they had demonstrated no hostility. On the contrary,
a generation of foreigners had been raised in Beninia who
seemed perfectly contented and immune to all suggestions
about insisting that their lands be incorporated with their
original home nations.

Almost as though they regarded Obomi with the traditional awe accorded to his "magician" ancestors, the neighbouring giants seesawed back and forth between placation and
aggression. The latter usually set in when some internal
disorder made the invocation of an outside enemy desirable;
the former was rarer, and only followed the intrusion of a
common rival from elsewhere. Allegedly the German soldier
of fortune whose bungled assassination attempt cost Obomi
his eye had been hired and paid in Cairo. The resultant
hostility among the Holaini against the notion of Pan-Islam
decided the Arab world to return to its accustomed railing
about Israel.

But now the long-time calm of Beninia seemed likely to
be shattered for good. If a succession dispute followed Obomi's retirement, the jealous neighbours would certainly
pounce. The intervention of GT might prevent the war.
Shalmaneser had reviewed the various hypothetical outcomes
and given his quasi-divine opinion.

Yet Norman kept being nagged by doubt. After all, Shalmaneser could only judge on the basis of the data he was
fed; suppose Elihu had allowed his love for Beninia to
colour his views with optimism, and this had affected the
computer's calculations?

It seemed absurdly sanguine to suggest turning a poverty-
stricken, famine- and sickness-ridden ex-colony into a bridgehead of prosperity within twenty years. Why, there wasn't
even a university, not even a major technical school—noth-

ing better than a privately financed business school in Port Mey from which the government already skimmed the cream of the graduates.

Of course, they did claim that all the country's male children acquired a minimum of literacy and numeracy, and a grounding in English as well as one other of their country's tongues. And there was no disrespect for education in Beninia—they were even shorter of truants than of teachers. Eagerness to learn might make up for a good few deficiencies in other areas.

Might . . .

Sighing, Norman gave up worrying. The exclamation-mark shape of Beninia might twist on the map into an imagined question-posing curl, but that was in his mind. The facts were in the real world, and he was acutely aware how he had systematically isolated himself from reality.

He said as much to Chad Mulligan, on one of the increasingly rare occasions when he was at home long enough to spend a few minutes in talking. The sociologist's heart had not proved to be in his intention to debauch himself to his grave; habit unweakened by three years in the gutter had dragged him back into familiar patterns of study and argument.

His response to Norman's remark began with a grimace of disgust. "What you're up against, codder, is the intractability of the outside world! Okay, I sympathise—I have the same trouble. I can't keep enough liquor in my guts to rot them the way I planned. Before I pass out, I throw up! So what's making you so angry with Beninia, hm?"

"Not the country itself," Norman sighed. "The fact that nobody seems to have noticed this weird anomaly of a whole nation sitting on the edge of a political volcano and hardly getting singed."

"With a volcanic eruption in progress, whoinole is going to take time out and wonder about folk who are getting on with their ordinary business?" Chad grunted. "Why don't you save the guesswork until you've been there and seen for yourself? When are they sending you over, by the way?"

"Directly the project is finalised," Norman said. "Elihu and

I are going to present it to President Obomi together. Another three or four days, I guess." He hesitated. "You know something?" he continued. "I'm scared of what I'm going to find when I actually get there."

"Why?"

"Because . . ." Norman tugged at his beard with awkward fingers. "Because of Donald."

"Whatinole does he have to do with it? He's off the other side of the world."

"Because I shared this apt with him for years, and always thought of him as a neutral kind of guy, leading a rather dull easy-going life. Not the sort of person you'd form strong opinions about. And then all of a sudden he told me he'd been responsible for the riot I found myself caught up in— down the lower East Side. I told you about that, didn't I?"

"You talked about it at Guinevere's party. So did a lot of other people." Chad shrugged. "Of course, to claim responsibility for starting a riot is arrogant, but I see what you're setting course for. You mean you're wondering whether the Beninians are set up the same way he was, capable of starting something disastrous when they blunder out into the big scene."

"No," said Norman. "I'm wondering whether I'm the one who's ignorant and apt to trigger a disaster."

context (17)

FEELING THE OVERDRAFT

"Yes, my name's Chad Mulligan. I'm not dead, if that was going to be the subject of your next silly question. And I don't give a pint of whaledreck about what you called up to say to me, even if you are from SCANALYZER. If you want me to talk I'll talk about what *I* want to, not what you want me to. If that's acceptable plug in your recorders. Otherwise I'm cutting the circuit.

"All right. I'm going to tell you about the poor. You know where to look for a poor man? Don't go out on the street like a sheeting fool and pick on a street-sleeper in filthy clothes. Up to a few days ago the man you picked on might have been me, and I'm worth a few million bucks.

"And you don't have to go to India or Bolivia or Beninia to find a poor man, either. You have to go exactly as far as the nearest mirror.

"A this point you'll probably decide to switch off in disgust—I don't mean you, codder, taking this down off the phone, I mean whoever gets to hear it if you have the guts to replay it over SCANALYZER. You out there! You're on the verge of going bankrupt and you aren't paying attention. I don't suppose that telling you will convince you, but I'm offering the evidence, in hopes.

"A codder who lives the way I've been living for the past three years, without a home or even a suitcase, isn't necessarily poor, like I said. But free of the things which get in the way of noticing the truth, he has a chance to look the situation over and appraise it. One of the things he can see is what's changed and what hasn't in this brave new century of ours.

"What do you give a panhandler? Nothing, maybe—but if you do cave in, you make it at least a fin. After all, his monthly licence costs him double that. So he's not really poor. Costs have gone up approximately sixfold in the past fifty years, but fifty years ago you were liable to give a panhandler a quarter or a half. Relatively, panhandlers have moved up on the income ladder.

"You haven't.

"The things which have gone up the standard, average, six times include your typical income, the cost of food and clothing, the cost of the gewgaws without which you don't feel you are anybody—a holographic TV, for instance—and rents and housing costs generally, like heating charges.

"The things which have come down a little include intra-urban transportation—that's to say, a New York token, which I cite because I'm a New Yorker by adoption now, costs only eighty cents instead of the dollar twenty or so it would cost if it had kept pace with everything else—and, to most people's surprise, taxes, which finance things we're not going to carp about such as medicare and education. These aren't bad at present, by the way.

"But what's gone up, way *way* up? Things like water. Did you know you're paying *eleven* times as much for water as people did fifty years back, and you're not managing to use any more than they did then because there isn't any more?

"And recreation space! Did you know that having a decent-sized open space within easy walking distance adds thirty per cent to your assessment for urban taxes?

"And health itself! I'm not talking about hospital care—that's okay these days. I'm talking about natural, normal, everyday health with its resistance to infection and abundant energy.

"You can probably recognise the New Poor, as the phrase calls them. You may not know how; you may indeed be puzzled about how you can tell when they're wearing clear clothes and carrying all kinds of lovely doodads which may not be the year after next's model but are serviceable and numerous. You can tell them, though—can't you?

"Well, what you recognise them by is the fact that they don't spend—they *can't* spend—on the things you add to keep yourself going. They eat mass-produced force-grown meat. So do you, but you add protein capsules and B12. They drink pasteurised unperishable milk. So do you, but you take calciferol tablets. They eat battery eggs. So do you, but you take Vitamin A. And even with all this, you probably also take Wakup pills, energisers, tranks, niacin, riboflavin, ascorbic acid—I've been going through a friend's medicine cabinet, and they're all there.

"Even so, you're losing out. You're falling further and further behind.

"I used a fifty-year baseline a moment ago. Let's use one again. What have you got that's new, around the place? The fifty years from 1910 to 1960 saw the arrival in the average Western home, and a good few mon-Western ones, of the telephone, the radio, the television, the car of unlamented memory, plastics, the washing-machine, the electric stove, iron, toaster and mixer, not to mention the freezer, the hi-fi set, and the tape-recorder.

"I've been around the place where I'm staying, which belongs to a highly paid executive with one of our biggest corporations. I cannot find one single object which is as revolutionary as the things I just listed. True, the TV is holographic—but the holographic principle was discovered in the 1930s, catch that? They were ready to apply it to TV by 1983 or 1984, but it didn't come in for another decade after that. Why not?

"Because you couldn't afford it.

"Same with the screen on your phone. They had videophone service operating in Russia in the 1960s. You couldn't afford it until the eighties. And that's supposed to be new, anyway—thirty years old already?

"Why do you think you get such a generous trade-in allowance when you switch from next year's model of some gadget to the year after next's? Because some of the parts are going to be put right back into the new sets, and what can't be cannibalised will be sold as precious—I repeat, *precious*—scrap.

"The biggest single building project in this country right now is costing a hundred million buckadingdongs. What do you think it is? You're wrong. It's a jail.

"Friends, you don't have to go to India or Africa to find people existing on the borderline of poverty. *You* are. Our resources are stretched to the point where reclaiming a gallon of water so someone can drink it a second time costs eleven times more than it did in 1960. TV you can live without, a phone you can live without, but water? Uh-*huh!* We don't starve to death, but if you want a diet that's fit to match your unprecedented tallness and muscularity you pay not six times as much as your grandfather did but more like nine to ten times, depending on how you take in your vitamins and other supplements.

"I'm just going to tell you about a few odds and ends you don't have because you can't afford them, and I'll quit. You could have in your home a domesticated computer of approximately Rehoboam standard, that would give you access to as much knowledge as most provincial libraries as well as handling your budget problems, diagnosing and prescribing for illness and teaching you how to cook a *cordon bleu* meal. You could have *real* polyform furniture that changed not only its shape but its texture, like Karatands do, over a range from fur to stainless-steel slickness. You could have a garbage disposal system that paid for itself by reclaiming the constituent elements of everything fed into it and returning them as ingots of metal and barrels of crude organics. You could have individual power-units for every single powered device you own, which would save the purchase price within months and render you immune from overload blackouts in winter.

"Shut up just a moment—I've nearly finished.

"When I say *you* could have them, I don't mean all of you. I mean that if you did, your next-door neighbour wouldn't, or in the case of big things on an urban scale, that if your city did the next city along the line wouldn't. Is that clear? The knowledge exists to make all these things possible, but because we are so damned nearly broke on a planet-wide basis your home contains virtually nothing that your grandfather wouldn't immediately recognise and know how to use without being told, and what's more he'd probably complain about the stink of uncleared garbage from the street and he might even complain about *your* stink because water was cheaper in his day and he could take as many showers and even tub-baths as he felt like.

"All right, codder, I know perfectly well you've been trying to interrupt me and say you can't possible use all that on SCANALYZER. But how about showing Mr. and Mrs. Everywhere sleeping on the street in Calcutta some time?"

continuity (20)

THE SHADOW OF GRANDFATHER LOA

The tight adjustable harness passengers were not supposed to unfasten throughout the flight, because at this height emergencies arose so quickly, constricted Donald and made him think of straitjackets and padded cells. The whole passenger compartment could become exactly that—a padded cell—in the event of accident. An express had once collided with the tumbling third stage of a satellite launcher, its orbit decaying back to atmosphere, but all the sixty-seven occupants had lived.

That's right. That's wise. We need padded-cell protection from our own mad cleverness.

Also, of course, it was a womb, carrying its litter to a destination they could not see. For all the passengers knew, they might be borne to Accra instead of Gongilung, emerge blinking among tall black strangers instead of short yellow ones.

Donald rather hoped for that.

But when the can was cracked—for his exclusive benefit—he was spilled on to the Gongilung expressport just as promised. Mechanically, watched by the curious eyes of his companions, he made his way to the exit and stepped on to the travolator that would deliver him package-fashion into the arrivals hall. Glancing sidelong through its windows, he realised with jarring astonishment that he was looking at two things he had never seen before in his life.

Only fifty yards away, a Chinese express nursed at the refuelling bay, its long sides marked with the symbol of the red star and white sun. And beyond, veiled but not screened by a drizzle of light rain, was the first active volcano he had ever set eyes on.

Why—that must be Grandfather Loa!

What he had previously seen on maps acquired actuality. Nine thousand feet high, the mountain brooded over the Shongao Strait, smoking ruminatively, sometimes stirring like a drowsy old man dreaming of his youth and shaking a few rocks down the far side of the cone. There had been a strait on that side too, until 1941, but now there was a narrow land bridge made of lava and ash. Grandfather Loa had taken about two thousand lives on that occasion, mostly fishermen killed by the *tsunami*. He was not in the monster class with Krakatoa, boasting thirty-six thousand victims, but he was a powerful and dangerous neighbour.

On this side, then, the long narrow island of Shongao, bearing Gongilung the capital city and several others of considerable importance. Beyond the volcano, the smaller and rounder island of Angilam. To the left, or east as he was standing, the long catena of the archipelago swung in an arc that if extended would encounter Isola; to the right, the islands diffused more and were scattered into a rough hexagon. It was a popular image among Yatakangi writers to compare their country to a scimitar, the westernmost islands forming the pommel. And here, at the hilt, was the centre of control.

He was staring with such fascination that he stumbled off the end of the travolator when the moving belt brought him to the fixed floor of the arrivals hall. Confused, struggling to retain his balance, he almost bumped into a girl in the traditional costume of shareng and slippers who was regarding him with an expression of cool contempt.

He had chiefly written and read, not spoken, Yatakangi since completing his original high-pressure course in the subject; his grip on the subtle Asiatic sounds had lessened. Attempting to undo the bad impression he had just created

he essayed a formal Yatakangi apology anyway, but she ignored it so completely he wondered if he had garbled it.

Consulting a radiofaxed copy of the express's passenger
manifest, she said, almost without the trace of an accent.
"You will be Donald Hogan, is that correct?"

He nodded.

"Go to Post Five. Your baggage will be delivered."

At his muttered thanks she at least inclined her head, but
that was all the attention he received before she moved on to
greet passengers descending from an adjacent travolator. His
face hot with embarrassment, Donald walked across the hall
towards a row of long counters such as one might see at any
expressport, divided into posts each manned by an immigration officer and a customs man, uniformed in off-white
with black skullcaps.

He was very conscious of being stared at. He was the only
Caucasian in sight. Almost everyone else was of Asian
extraction: local-born, or Chinese, or Burmese. There were
some Sikhs at Post One, and scattered about there were a
few Arabs and a solitary African negro. But no concessions
were made to non-Asians; the only signs he could see were in
Yatakangi, Chinese Cyrillic and Indonesian.

Reaching the line before Post Five, he fell in behind a
family of prosperous expatriate Chinese—expatriate, clearly,
because Yatakangi was the language they discussed him in.
Their small daughter, aged about eight, marvelled loudly at
how pale and ugly he was.

Wondering whether to embarrass them in revenge for his
own discomfiture a moment earlier, by letting them know he
understood what they were saying, he tried to distract himself
by enumerating the ways in which this place differed from an
expressport hall at home. The list was shorter than he had
expected. The décor, of fierce greens and reds, matched the
wet tropical climate of sea-level Shongao—up in the hills that
spined the island, it was a trifle cooler but not much drier.
There were about as many advertising displays as at home,
though fewer of the items were commercial because more
public services were under state control. Among them, too,
were several political ones, including a couple that praised
Marshal Solukarta for his promise to optimise the popula-

tion. Many airlines had big displays on the walls: Chinese, Russian, Arab, Japanese, even Afghan and Greek. There were the inevitable cases showing local curios and souvenirs, and visible—though not audible—there was a thirty-three-inch holographic TV playing to people in the departures lounge separated from this hall by a pane of tinted glass.

As though to spite him, the line he had been assigned to was moving more slowly than its neighbours. Eventually he could foresee himself envying the people around him who were accustomed to sitting on the floor, and who did not mind looking absurd if they frog-hopped forward when the line moved.

The delay seemed to be due to a Japanese in front of the Chinese family, apparently a salesman for Japind, because his open bags contained scores of samples of goods Donald recognised, including Jettiguns. The official behind the counter was checking each one off in a bulky manual. Donald added one more to the list of differences; at home, they would have a computer reading at each customs point to cost the duty.

Fretting at the delay, he noticed that the line at Post Six had reduced to one person, a very attractive Indian girl in a microsari that swathed her slender body only to mid-thigh—a fashion, so he'd heard, which the Indian government encouraged because it reduced the demand for textiles. Her slim legs tapered to tiny gold sandals, her long dark hair was piled on her head to emphasise her patrician profile, and she wore the ancient style of nose-jewel in her left nostril—a curious atavism when the rest of her was so modern.

Were Yatakangi officials so hidebound that they would refuse to transfer his bags to the next position when the shiggy had gone?

He was still wondering whether to ask, when he realised that the girl was having trouble. The customs officer dealing with her was leaning forward aggressively, and the immigration man next to him was gesticulating with her passport.

Judging by the behaviour of the Chinese family, it wasn't bad manners to be openly inquisitive here. Donald strained his ears. At first he couldn't make out what was being said; then he realised the customs man was skinning his language down to a kind of baby-talk, and the girl wasn't getting his meaning even so.

Nobody else had yet joined his line. He debated whether to ask the Chinese family to keep his place, decided he'd better not risk addressing them in Yatakangi, and strode over to the girl's side.

"You probably speak English," he said.

She turned to him with frank relief, while the men behind the counter scowled. "Yes, I do!" she said, with the strong north-western lilt the British had nicknamed Bombay Welsh. "But I don't speak a word of Yatakangi!"

Then she placed his own accent, and started to frown. "But—aren't you an American?"

"That's right."

"Then—"

"I do speak the language. Not many of us do, but a few. Have you any idea what the trouble is?"

She shook her head, eyes wide under the small red caste-mark decorating her high forehead.

The customs man said sharply to Donald, "What do you want?"

Fishing deep in memory for the inflections to correspond with words habit made him see, rather than hear, Donald said, "The lady doesn't understand you. I will explain to her if you tell me—slowly, please."

The two officials exchanged glances. At length the immigration man said, "We do not allow prostitutes to enter our country."

For an instant Donald was baffled. Then he saw what they meant, and almost laughed. He turned to the shiggy.

"They think you're a prostitute," he said, and grinned.

Surprise, horror, and finally matching amusement showed in her expression.

"But why?"

Donald risked the guess he had arrived at. "Are you a widow, by any chance?"

"Yes—how could you . . . ? Oh, of course: I had someone write it on my passport in Yatakangi before I left home."

"No, I didn't read it off your passport. What's happened is that you've run foul of a couple of local conventions. First off, the clothes you're wearing."

The girl glanced down at her body, self-consciously.

"Yatakangi national dress is the shareng, which is like one of your old-time saris except that it's gathered between the legs into a sort of Turkish trouser arrangement. The only women who wear a skirt as short as yours are high-powered businesswomen and—ah—good-time girls. And second, most Yatakangi prostitutes describe themselves as widows for official purposes; it's not considered a disgrace for a woman who's lost her husband to get other men to support her."

"Oh my goodness!" the girl said, eyes wider than ever.

"And to cap the lot, the written word for 'widow' can actually become the slang term for 'tart' if the writer isn't very careful. I'll see if I can sort it out."

He turned back to the impatient officials and explained with a maximum of flowery phrasing. Their faces relaxed a trifle, and after some discussion they proposed a compromise.

"They say," Donald translated, "that if you'll change into something more becoming to a respectable woman they'll let you go through. You may take a change of costume out of your bags and go to the ladies' powder-room over there." He pointed. "But they advise you to get some Yatakangi clothes as quickly as possible, or there may be some more awkward consequences."

"I can imagine," the girl said with a twinkle. "Thank you very much. Now let's see if I have anything that won't offend them."

She rummaged in her bags. Donald, seeing that the Japanese salesman was still having trouble, stood by and watched. Finally she produced a full-length sari in green and gold and held it up for him.

"This is really for formal evening wear, but it's all I brought with me. Will it do?"

Donald confirmed with the officials that it was passable, and she thanked him again and vanished into the ladies' room.

And the salesman was still arguing. Donald hesitated; then

he suggested to the officials, who were leaning back for a breather, that they might perhaps just this once move his bags from the adjacent post ... ?

With a bad grace they conceded that they might. Their surliness puzzled Donald. He wondered whether they suspected him of misleading them about the girl's profession, or whether they expected a bribe. But he dared not offer anything; the Solukarta régime had one achievement to its credit, the elimination of venality among public employees. It was not until the bags had been fetched—to the annoyance of the Chinese family—that he suddenly realised the true reason.

I'm a round-eye. If it weren't for my speaking a little of the language, they'd happily keep me waiting till Doomsday.

He stared at the immigration man as he flipped through the green American passport he held, and read the correctness of his guess in the downward turn of the other's mouth. He swallowed hard. This was a new experience for him, and it was going to take getting used to.

"So now!" the official said. "You are a reporter, I see. What brings you to Yatakang?"

I'm going to have to be very polite. Donald said, "The genetic optimisation programme. It has excited great interest."

"That is true," the customs man said with a smirk, glancing up from his scrutiny of Donald's belongings. "We have had reporters from all over the world coming to Yatakang since it was announced."

"Except America," the immigration official countered. "In fact, as I have heard, the Americans and other"—he used a word for European which corresponded approximately to the Afram term "paleass"—"are denying the honesty of the claim." He scowled at Donald.

"You say it has excited great interest?"

"Because of it I have been sent here."

"And took a week on the journey?" the immigration man said, curling his lip. He looked at the passport again, very thoroughly, page by page. Meantime his colleague turned over the contents of Donald's bags, not so much searching them as stirring them about. Pride smarting, Donald stood in silence and waited for them to get bored.

Finally the immigration man slapped the passport shut and held out his other hand. He said something Donald did not understand, and he asked for a repetition.

"Show me your proof of unfatherliness!"

"I have no children," Donald ventured.

The immigration man raised an eyebrow to his colleague. "Listen!" he said, as though addressing an idiot. "While you are in Yatakang you must not make a child. It will interfere with the optimisation programme. Show me the paper which certifies"—this time he used easier turns of phrase than the verbal shorthand of the first request—"that you cannot make children."

They want a certificate of sterilisation. That's something that bleeder Delahanty missed!

"I'm not sterile," he said, using a term which included impotence and unmanliness in its referents and trying to sound as though he had been insulted.

The immigration man pressed a stud on the counter and swivelled his chair around. A door in the far wall opened to reveal a man in a medical coverall carrying a medikit, a docustat and a fat reference book. Seeing Donald he stopped dead.

"That one?" he called. On receiving a gesture of confirmation he stepped back and exchanged his medikit for another, similar one. Returning, he gave Donald a searching look.

"You speak English?" he demanded.

"And Yatakangi!" Donald snapped.

"You understand what is necessary?"

"No."

"It is the law for foreigners to be sterile while they are in our country. We do not wish to have our genetic pool contaminated. You have not sterility certificate?"

"No, I haven't."

What are they going to do—send me home?

The man in the coverall flipped through his book and found a table of dosages. Having run his finger down and across it, he clicked open his medikit.

"Chew this," he said, proffering a white pill.

"What is it?"

"It confers forty-eight hours' sterility in a man of your race and build. Otherwise you have three alternatives: you must consent to immediate vasectomy, you may accept exposure to sufficient radiation to incapacitate your gonads, or you may get on the next plane leaving. This you understand?"

Slowly Donald reached for the pill, wishing he could break the arrogant yellowbelly's neck instead.

"Give me the passport," the man in the coverall continued, switching to Yatakangi. From his docustat he extracted a self-adhesive label, which he placed over the centre front panel of the passport.

"You can read this, yes?" he said, reverting to English and showing the label to Donald.

The label said that if he did not report to a hospital within twenty-four hours for a reversible sterility operation he would be jailed for one year and deported after confiscation of his goods.

The pill tasted of dust and ashes, but he had to swallow it, and along with it his nearly uncontrollable fury at the glee with which these slit-eyed runts were witnessing the discomfiture of a white man.

tracking with closeups (18)

IN MY YOUNG DAYS

Victor Whatmough waited to hear his wife Mary close the door of the bathroom, and still a little longer until he distinguished the noise of splashing which meant she was actually in the tub. Then he went to the phone and punched the number with shaking fingers.

Waiting, he listened to the quiet sough of the breeze in the trees outside the house. His imagination transmuted the tap-tap of one branch against another into a sort of drumming, as though to mark the march of the houses advancing over the far crest of the valley which his home overlooked. They had occupied the summit of the hill like an army taking station for an assault on an untenable position. In another few years, this gracious villa set among rolling fields to which he had unwillingly retired would be surrounded. He had bought as much as he could of the nearby land, but now the developers were actually in sight, none of his neighbours would forego the chance of immense profit and sell their ground for what he could afford to pay. And who would buy this empty ground off him, except those same developers he hated?

His mind clouded briefly with visions of wild youths in gangs, roaming the district at night and breaking windows, of small boys clambering over his fences in search of fruit, trampling down his beautifully kept flowerbeds and making off with the jewel-bright stones from the rockery he had assembled from half a dozen different countries.

He thought of a black child who had come into the compound at home, when he was about eighteen, to steal eggs. That one hadn't come back—had hardly been able to leave. But take a stick to some dirty urchin in this strange new Britain, and the next caller would be a policeman with an assault charge to be answered in court.

The phone's screen lit, and there was Karen glowing with all the freshness of her nineteen years. He came back to the present with a start, worrying about how his own image would show on the screen at her end. It shouldn't be too bad, he assured himself; for all his sixty years he was presentable still, being of a durable wiry build, and the grey at his temples and on the tips of his beard only added distinction to his appearance.

"Oh—hullo, Vic," Karen said without noticeable enthusiasm.

He had made a rather astonishing discovery a week ago, that had undermined his previous dogmatic distaste for modern Britain. In the person—to be precise, in the *body*—of Karen, he had discovered that there could be contact across the gulf of the generations. He had met her in a quiet hotel in Cheltenham, where he had dropped in for a drink after some business with his lawyers, got talking with her, and without any fuss whatever had been invited upstairs to her room.

She wasn't local, of course. She was studying at Bristol University, and to check on some ancient records connected with a historical research programme she had come to spend a couple of days in the neighbourhood.

She had been a revelation to him: on the one hand interested in what he had to tell her about his early life, spent partly at school hereabouts and partly in Nigeria, where his family had hung on and hung on until finally the xenophobia of the eighties had made their position untenable; on the other, delightfully matter-of-fact about sex, so that he had not even felt embarrassed about his own impaired capacity for orgasm. He was a thrice-married man, but none of his wives—least of all Mary—had given him so much unalloyed pleasure.

Maybe there *was* something to justify the changes in his world, after all.

He cleared his throat and smiled. "Hello there, Karen!" he said in a bluff manner. "Keeping well?"

"Oh yes, thanks. A bit busy—it's getting towards exam time now and life is hectic—but otherwise I'm fine. You?"

"Better than I've been for ages. And I don't have to tell you who deserves the credit for that, do I?" He tried to make his words arch and conspiratorial.

Something—no: *someone* moved in the ill-focused background of the room where Karen's phone was located. A blurred human figure. Victor felt a spasm of alarm. He had thought in terms of being discreet as regards Mary, but not—for some unaccountable reason—as regards Karen.

He said, "Well—ah ... Why I called you up: I'm thinking of coming over to Bristol some time in the next few days. I have a bit of business to attend to. I thought I could take the chance of dropping in on you."

A voice—a male voice—said something which the phone did not pick up clearly, and Karen told the interrupter to fasten it for a moment. Conscientiously, Victor added that to the stock of current phrases he had decided to compile so as not to seem intolerably antique. One said "antique", not old-fashioned or even square; one said "fasten it" instead of telling someone to shut up; one jocularly insulted a person by calling him a "bleeder", because terms like bastard and bugger had ceased to be pejorative and become simply descriptive. Victor had had some difficulty reconciling himself to the last-mentioned. A preference for one's own sex had been something literally unspeakable when he was Karen's age, and to hear her include it in characterising someone she knew as casually as if she were talking about his having red hair was highly disturbing.

On the other hand, she had managed to convey the impression that it might be rather a good thing to have "celebrated one's twenty-first"—to have shed the irrelevant preconceptions of the last century and decided to enjoy the world as it was, faults and all.

"Well, I don't think it would be terribly convenient," Karen said. "I told you, I have exams hanging over me—"

"Ah, but surely it's bad, isn't it, to work at full pressure all the time before exams? You'd benefit from the chance to relax for an evening." Victor flavoured his voice with all the coaxing he could.

"Fasten it, Brian!" she snapped sideways at the half-seen person in her room. "If you and Tom can't keep quiet I throw you out, catch? Sorry, Vic," she added, facing the camera again. "But—no, I don't think so, thanks all the same."

There was a frozen instant in which the only sound was from the bathroom overhead: Mary stepping out of her tub.

Eventually Victor said, and knew he sounded both idiotic and peeved, but couldn't help it, "Why *not?*"

"Look, Vic, I really am very very sorry. I shouldn't have done it because I realised afterwards you'd probably make a big scene of it and I can't. I don't want to, candidly, but even if I did I couldn't. I just happened to be on my own in Cheltenham and you really were very sweet to me when I was feeling a bit lonely and it was a very interesting evening hearing you talk about the old days especially what you said about Africa because I was able to come back and tell Tom some things he didn't know and he comes from there—"

"But if you mean that why wouldn't you like—?"

"Vic, I'm *terribly* sorry, honestly I am. I should have told you straight out, I guess, but I didn't know how you'd react and I didn't want to upset you because lots of people do get a bit upset." Her pretty face wore an unhappy look which he couldn't for the life of him believe was pretence.

"You see, I'm spoken for here. I'm in a triple with Brian and Tom and we've got a good thing going for us and I just don't go outside unless—you know—it's an accidental thing, like my being away looking up those old parish records. So all I can say is it would be very nice to have you drop in and say hullo when you come to Bristol but don't hope for any more. Is that horribly blunt?"

The past reached out and closed a dead hand on Victor's brain. He looked past Karen's worried face and made sense of two shapes immobilised at her insistence in the background of the small square picture. Like badly unfocused photos, they still conveyed their essential identity: one pale and one dark male figure, both bare to the waist, with some sort of blurred pale bar over the shoulder of the dark one. In exact painful words, Karen's two boy-friends sitting on something low, probably a divan-bed, one with his arm around the other.

And that "other"—she had just said so—an African.

The bathroom door overhead opened. He switched off the phone and moved away from it, mechanically. He had not formulated another coherent thought apart from fury before Mary appeared in a towelling robe and asked him to fix her a drink from the liquor console.

He complied grumpily, aware that he must not let his anger show through, yet incapable of putting on a cheerful expression. Mary asked him, as was inevitable, "Who were you talking to on the phone?"

"I called Bristol," Victor said, more or less without lying. "I've been thinking about that housing development over there, and wondering if it would be worth our while to sell up and go somewhere a bit more isolated."

"What did they say?"

"I didn't get any joy."

Mary sipped her drink, frowning. She frowned a lot nowadays, and it was turning her once-pretty face into a mask of aging wrinkles. Victor noticed the fact and thought with detachment of how that brief phone-call had altered the reaction it had conjured up in him only an hour ago.

Then, drunk on the memory of Karen, he had been thinking: *I could leave her, if there are young girls available, I could have a grand fling before I finally lose the urge . . .*

Such thoughts at his age seemed ridiculous in modern terms, but he had never adjusted to modern terms. He realised now with resignation that he never would. "Celebrating his twenty-first" was a privilege time had stolen away.

"This drink tastes terrible," Mary said. "Are you sure you set the machine right?"

"What? Oh, damn it! Of course I'm sure! It's been mucking

me about the past few days and nobody can come to fix it
before the weekend."

"Talk about progress!" Mary said with a scowl. "Our head
boy in Lagos would have died rather than make a mess of a
cocktail like this."

She gulped the rest of it down anyhow, with a grimace,
and set aside the glass. "I'll go and get dressed, then," she
added. "What time are the Harringhams expecting us—noon,
or half past?"

"Noon," Victor said. "Better hurry."

When she had gone, he fixed himself a drink too—
manually—and stood gazing out the room's window-wall at
the encroaching hordes of interchangeable houses across the
valley. Thoughts flickered in his mind like a series of project-
ed slides that had been shuffled out of coherent order.

*Over a hundred million people in this damned island and
they let these blacks come and go as they want.*

*She seemed like a decent girl and suddenly it turns out that
she . . .*

*Bloody machine cost a fortune and doesn't work properly.
Have to send for repairmen and they make you wait. Back
home it was done by servants and if one of them didn't work
there was always another to be hired and trained.*

*Decadent, dirty-minded, obsessed with sex like the black
brutes we tried to get some sense and civilisation into!*

*Try telling that to Karen and make her understand, try
explaining the spaciousness and real leisure in the life I had
to leave behind. Mary understands; she comes from the same
background. We can at least share our grouses if nothing
more.*

Which, he realised dully, meant that there could never have
been any substance in his brief dream of leaving her and
going off for a few wild-oat years before he ran out of
energy. His marriage to Mary had lasted; his others, to
English-born girls, hadn't. And the same on her side, too: she
had been married before to someone who didn't understand.
A row between himself and her didn't have to be explained
away and excused—she felt the same aching disappointment
with the world as he did.

Some people had adjusted, come home after having well-paid jobs in Africa or Asia tugged out from under them, accepted inferior posts at home and worked their way back up. He'd tried and tried, but it never suited him—sooner or later there was a crisis, a loss of temper, a complaint, and an interview with the management ... He wasn't poor, they had enough to live on. But they had no purpose, and almost no occupation.

He wanted to turn back time, and could not.

At least, though, he and Mary had not been allowed children—he had used up his permitted maximum of three in his second marriage, and the two boys and the girl were in their middle twenties now, which meant they had probably just escaped the full impact of the decadence claiming Karen.

If they hadn't ...

But that he would rather not know. If he couldn't get from life the only thing he desired—return to the colonial society he had been brought up in—he preferred that the world turn its back on him and leave him to mope undisturbed.

continuity (21)

MORE HASTE

Arrayed like a tribunal on one side of the vast palatial office: G. T. Buckfast, face like thunder; the skeletal Dr. Raphael Corning from State; Hamilcar Waterford and E. Prosper Rankin.

Grouped like victims of a trial where they were denied both counsel and knowledge of the charges: Norman House and Rex Foster-Stern.

"It's been leaked," Old GT said, and the three others flanking her nodded in comical unison.

Victoria?

The thought crossed Norman's mind like a shooting-star, and although he stamped on its traces— *the hole, that's impossible!*—it left a charred streak.

He said, "Sorry, GT, I don't understand. I'd have thought the first inkling of a leak would come from a buying wave in MAMP stock, and that hadn't happened up to this morning."

"The fact remains," insisted Old GT. "Isn't that right, Prosper?"

Rankin scowled and repeated his nod, his eyes on Norman.

But the past few days of solid and surprising achievement had lent Norman a heady sense of his own capability. He said, "Who's supposed to be in the secret and how?"

"Common Europe," Waterford said, biting the name off like crunching a candy-bar. "As a whole, to judge by what our informants are passing along."

"Accordingly," said Old GT, "we're going to have to reconsider everything about the project, which was predicated on secrecy. The costings, the estimated time, the returns, the—"

"The people," Rankin cut in. "Much more important, GT. We shall have to turn our entire personnel upside-down and shake out their pockets."

"Which is your responsibility still, Norman," GT confirmed.

"Now just a second," Norman said, feeling reckless. *Victoria? A search like that would not only waste time, it'd be bound to bring me under scrutiny too, because this case involves not millions but billions.*

"I agree with Norman," Foster-Stern said unexpectedly. "I don't appreciate statements like this without adequate evidence to back them, GT. You realise you're calling in question the discretion of my entire department? We're the ones who have handled the hypothetical data."

A vision of endless reams of green printouts from Shalmaneser blinded Norman for a second. Facing the whole thing again from the start, the hypothesis being amended to assume loss of secrecy, appalled him.

Also, despite everything, Victoria had existed in his life.

He said fiercely, "GT! I tell you something straight—shall I? I think you're doing something you've never done before in your business career, overlooking the obvious."

GT bridled and flushed. Norman had admired her ability for years; finding that she didn't know one of her own VP's was a Muslim and hence a non-drinker had breached that wall of unalloyed respect and implied that she preferred to put up with, rather than actively promote, the modern standards that encouraged brown-noses in industry.

But he was surprised at himself, even so; telling off the founder of General Technics was a step clear outside his old patterns of behaviour.

"In what way?" GT demanded frigidly.

"I've been too preoccupied with the specifically African

aspect of the project to follow what other departments were doing," Norman said, thinking fast on his feet. "But now I think of it, the data which were fed to Shalmaneser must have been gathered by somebody. Ah ... Yes, here's an example. Our market costings include items like transportation of raw materials once they're landed from MAMP. Was the information in store or did we have to go look for it?"

GT and Rankin exchanged glances. After a pause, Rankin said, "Well, the African market has been a very minor one for us up till now."

"In other words we had to send someone out to make inquiries," Norman snapped. "Add another thing: we're comparatively ignorant of African attitudes, so we're anticipating recruitment of former colonial advisors to help us avoid silly mistakes. Shalmaneser had an estimate of the number of potential recruits. How was it arrived at?"

"We had it from our London office," GT grunted.

"And how did they get it? I'll wager they commissioned a survey, and somebody noticed that General Technics was interested in something they hadn't previously considered. Add still another point: who do we have on the spot in Beninia?"

"But—" began Waterford.

"Nobody," Norman said, without waiting for him. "We have agents in Lagos, Accra, Bamako and other main cities in the West African region, but Beninia is a piddling little hole-in-corner country we've never cared about. Bamako is in a former French territory, Lagos and Accra were formerly British—where do the former colonial territories get their commercial and governmental data processed?"

There was a blank expression on GT's face which was pure joy to Norman.

"I see what you're setting course for," Dr. Corning said slowly—the first words he had uttered during the discussion. "The ex-colonial powers offer a discount on computer-time to their former dependent territories, which is substantial enough for them to have relied on the Fontainebleau centre rather than developing their own."

"Thank you, doctor," Norman said in triumph. "Do I have to spell it out, GT? This corporation of ours is like a state within a state—as Elihu said to me when he first mentioned the Beninia project, we could buy and sell a lot of the underdeveloped countries. Any move we make is going to attract the attention of European rivals, and you may lay to it that corporations like Krupp and ICI and Royal Dutch Shell have bought themselves codes for the Fontainebleau computers that make a nonsense of attempts at secrecy. In any case, the Common Europe Board has a vested interest in seeing that big profitable projects go to their firms and not ours. They might have passed on the information their intelligence services picked up, quite legitimately; as to the whole of Common Europe knowing about the Beninia project, I think you're understating the case. I'll wager it's already been evaluated by Sovcompex and by now there's a good chance the data are going to K'ung-fu-tse in Peking!"

Foster-Stern was nodding vigorously, Norman saw with pleasure.

Stunned, GT said, "But if you're right—and I admit you probably are, blast it!—we might as well cancel the whole idea!"

"GT, I said you're overlooking the obvious," Norman exclaimed. "We have one thing Common Europe hasn't and never can have, and the Russians can't have and the Chinese can never dream of having. We've *got* MAMP, it exists, and it's sitting on a strike of raw materials adequate to underpin the Beninia project. Where is Common Europe going to get competitive quantities of ore? They're the oldest industrialised area of the world; their seams of coal and iron are played out. The only possible competition I've been worried about is Australia—the Outback is the last mining region in the world which hasn't been fully exploited. But Australia is notoriously underpopulated. Where can they find ten thousand spare technicians to move *en masse* to Beninia for even the preliminary stages, let alone the actual development phase?"

"They couldn't," Dr. Corning said with authority.

There was a pause. At length GT said, looking down at her hands to avoid meeting Norman's eyes, "I owe you an apology, Norman. I immediately jumped to the conclusion that we'd hit a case of conventional industrial espionage. It's a strange thing for me to admit, but—well, I guess I just am not used to handling projects of this colossal size. At least I can offer by way of excuse the fact that Raphael didn't correct me on behalf of State, which *is* used to such mammoth undertakings."

"State," Corning said with grim humour, "is also used to highly effective and systematic spying."

Hamilcar Waterford had been brooding to himself in silence. He said now, "If what Norman says is correct—and especially as regards the ability of big European corporations to penetrate the security of information processed at Fontainebleau, I'm inclined to think he's on to something—then what can we do to minimise the impact of it? My impression is there's nothing we can do except accelerate the project to the greatest possible degree."

Corning nodded. "While Common Europe, Russia and Australia can probably be discounted, the Chinese might just consider it worthwhile to starve their people for another generation in order to buy the Beninian bridgehead. They've had notoriously poor luck on the continent lately, but they're indefatigable in trying."

"I'd suggest," Norman said, savouring his ascendancy, "we ask Shalmaneser for the optimum plan out of those so far examined, and take that to Port Mey at once. Meantime, while negotiations are continuing, we can ask him to assess the likelihood of the competition getting to know the details. The Fontainebleau set-up is pretty good, but Shalmaneser is still ahead of any other computer in the world, which is a further ace we have in the hole."

"That sounds sensible," GT approved. "Will you find out from Elihu whether he can make the trip on short notice, Norman?"

"He can, I can say that straight off," Norman declared. "Ever since President Obomi made that public announcement about his failing health, Elihu has been on emergency standby."

GT slapped the desk. "Settled, then. Thank you, gentlemen, and once again my apologies for blasting off into an unjustified orbit."

In the elevator car which they shared going down, Corning said to Norman, "GT's not the only one who owes you an apology, by the way. When Elihu said you were the right man to hold the reins on the Beninia project, we checked what we had on you and our computers said he was probably wrong. I was in two minds about you for that reason. But today you've demonstrated you have a sense of proper proportion, and that's a rare talent nowadays. Just goes to show, doesn't it? There's no substitute for real-life experience even in the age of Shalmaneser."

"Of course not," Foster-Stern muttered grumpily from the other side of the car. "Computers like Shalmaneser don't deal in realities. Something like ninety-five per cent of what goes through that frozen brain of his is hypothetical."

The car stopped and the doors opened for Norman's floor. Corning reached past him and held them to prevent the automatic controls cycling. He said, "You play chess, either of you?"

"No, go is my game," Norman said, and thought of the infinite pains he had taken to master it as the pastime to match his abandoned executive image.

"I like the L game myself," Corning said, in a standard one-up ploy. "But the same applies in all of them. I mention chess simply because I ran across the phrase in a chess handbook. The author said that some of the finest melodies of chess are those which never actually get played, because the opponent sees them coming, of course. And he called one entire chapter 'Unheard Melodies', showing combinations that would have been masterly had the other player done what was expected of him."

He gave a faint smile. "I suspect that GT is frustrated at the non-co-operation of our opponents."

"Or else maybe lives ninety-five per cent of her life in imagination, like Shalmaneser," Norman said lightly. "It sounds to me like an easy recipe for bumbling through life. One can hardly accuse GT of that, though—*si monumentum requiris,* and all that dreck." He gestured at the magnificence of the GT tower surrounding them. The Latin tag, of course, also belonged to the period when he had been erecting his carefully designed image.

Somewhat to his surprise, he discovered that Foster-Stern was gazing at him in open-mouthed wonder.

"Is something wrong?" he demanded.

"What? Oh—no!" Foster-Stern recovered and gave a dazed headshake. "No, you've just given me an idea. And what's more, one that none of our psychologists has ever brought to my notice, which is saying something. The stacks of half-baked theory they keep routing to my office—!"

Puzzled, Norman waited. Foster-Stern was hardly an expert in computer theory, or he would have been too busy in his own speciality to accept the appointment he held on the GT board, but since Projects and Planning Dept relied entirely on computers he could scarcely be ignorant about the subject, either.

"Look!" Foster-Stern continued. "You know we've been trying to get Shal to live up to what theory promises for a computer of his complexity and behave like a conscious entity?"

"Of course."

"And—well, he hasn't. Detecting whether he had would be a subtle problem but the psychologists say they could spot a personal preference, for instance, a bias not warranted by facts programmed in but by a sort of prejudice."

"If that happened, wouldn't Shalmaneser become useless?" Corning objected.

"Oh, not at all—the element of self-interest is absent from most of the problems he's given. It would have to appear in some programme which directly affected his own future, putting it very roughly. He'd have to say something like, 'I don't want you to do that because it would make me uncomfortable'—that kind of thing, catch? And I'm beginning to wonder whether the reason he hasn't behaved the way we expected is because of what you just instanced, Norman."

Norman shook his head.

"What intelligent *living* creature could live ninety-five per cent of his existence on the hypothetical level? Shalmaneser is all awareness, without a subconscious except in the sense that memory banks don't preoccupy him before they're cued to help solve a problem to which they apply. What we shall have to do is try running him for an extended period on *nothing* but real-time and real-life programmes. Maybe then we'll get what we're after."

Foster-Stern sounded really excited by now. Carried away by his enthusiasm, the others had failed to notice that two more GT staffers were patiently waiting for the brass to finish with the elevator and let them take a turn.

Suddenly perceiving them, Norman said, "Well, it's a fascinating possibility, but way off my orbit, I'm afraid. Ah— you wouldn't think of trying it out before we've set up the big one, would you?"

"Oh, of course not. We might have to clear down hypothetical stuff for a month or more, and that would take about a year to arrange, what with the schedules we already have contracted. Nonetheless . . . The hole, we're blocking people, aren't we? See you later, Norman, and congratulations on what you did upstairs just now."

Norman stepped out into the corridor, feeling a little adrift. Something had happened to him that felt as though it repaid the hard work, the loss of sleep and even the indigestion he had suffered in the past few days. But the aftermath of outfacing GT had left him no energy to work out what that something might be.

The one thing which was clear undermined the sense of elation: he was now, very definitely, going to be pitchforked into the middle of Beninia while he still regarded himself as inadequately prepared.

context (18)

ZOCK

Aud	*Vid*
Trackin hiss	White-out screen
Pick up 7-beat bass below aud threshold	Face of group leader negatived white-for-black green-for-red BCU
Synch in five-beat	
WAH YAH WAH YAH WAH	Lips move
Sitar picks up 5	BCU sitar PU
7 beats express takeoff	White-out, shade to pink
Octave up bass	Blur to grey on beat
Bass up 2nd octave	Star-out purple, gold, orange
Bring in at 4-beat intervals tympani, Lasry-Bachet organ, pre-cut speech tape	MLS full group with spots blue shading yellow then pink
MANCH/total recall/ SHIFT/man that's really someth/WHIP/ah whoinole cares anyway/GARKER/ garker/GARKER/garker (ad lib)	XLBCU leader's uvula, negged
	Super sitar on Las-Bach organ
Snatch of Hallelujah chorus Leader talks over gp: YOU GOT THE OFFYOUR-	BCU pigeon's wing, white feathers

ASS FOR BOTH OF US MY
SPAREWHEEL AND ME
AND SHIGGY MAKES
THREE
Las-Bach FFF waltz-time

Acceleratube passes by
Resume speech tape
I GOING BUST MY
SKULL
Kiss loudens synch with
Resume bass, sitar

Rpt with leader over:
LEAVE this WORLD to
ROT
GONE to BUST my SKULL
SHIFT this SCENE on POT
TRIP on TINE and PULL
HEAVen ON my HEAD
MIGHT as WELL be DEAD
MAGine ALL we COULD
DO if WE was FREE
SHEETing HOLE we're
NOT
YAGinOL is GOOD
ALL i CAN is BE!
(etc.)

$ *
====

Shiggy fondles own breasts,
green over shading blue

BCU shiggy's hands as each
taken by male right hand and
pulled apart
Interior tunnel
Hold
Green bars shift on black
VLS zooms in to BCU kiss
Track thru head of shiggy to
face of gp leader XLBCU

Shiggy walks along front of
Las-Bach org watching player
stroke glass columns and
produce sound, then bends
over and begins to suck longest (bass) column

BCU tympani beater
Street scene negged w shiggy
arm-in-arm w leader and
sparewheel
White-out
(etc.)

$ *
====

* Total in both columns: another planetary-collision-size smash hit
for the Em Thirty-Ones, not permitted to be broadcast over any channel serving the Pacific Conflict Zone.

continuity (22)

THE PRICE OF ADMISSION

It occurred to the seething Donald after a while that he had foreseen the indignity due to be inflicted on him. The idea was irrational, but that didn't concern him; he was content to feel that his curious state of mind on the express, when he had thought those wild thoughts about Odinzeus, stemmed from a prevision of this gesture to deprive him of manhood.

Phrasing it that way was absolutely stupid, of course. He had not infrequently considered a reversible sterilisation operation, but the need had never arisen; all the shiggies he had to do with were fitted with their tiny subcutaneous progestin capsules, secreting a year's supply without risk of pregnancy. But he was away from home and familiar things, and what he had deemed familiar had turned and rent him, and in any case his subconscious was not amenable to persuasion. It clung with animal obstinacy to the reassurance that in the ultimate resort a man could make a man.

He was, however, in Yatakang. He had passed through the expressport building, crouched low under its protective roof of concrete capped with thick earth and trees, and here he was outside and being assailed by scores, hundreds, of Yatakangis, some of them addressing him in pidgin that included Dutch and English words. A porter with a wheeled electric barrow had brought his belongings out, too, and was standing by awaiting payment for the service.

I forgot to change some money. Did they give me any along with my papers?

There had been an envelope with credit-cards in, he remembered that, but was there any cash? Looking, he discovered half a dozen crisp ten-tala bills, worth about—hmmm—sixty cents each. He gave them to the porter and stood by his bags for a while, occasionally scowling at the youths and girls who clustered around offering to find him a cab, tote the bags, sell him souvenirs and sticky-sickly sweet-meats, or merely staring because he was a round-eye. All the youths were in off-white—sometimes dirty—jackets and breeches, mostly barefoot, and the girls in sharengs of twenty different colours from black to gold.

Across the parking lot paralleling the expressport building, where stood a number of electric and many more human-powered cabs—rixas—along with two or three modern Chinese-built buses, there was a whole rank of gaudily-decked booths made of light waterproof fabric on frames that were either natural bamboo or plastic imitations. A policeman was marching up and down in front of them, frowning at their keepers and receiving bland smiles in response. Donald struggled to put them in perspective. The Solukarta régime discouraged superstition, he knew that, but according to the signs over these little booths they were places where one might make a propitiatory sacrifice to whatever god one favoured before leaving on a journey, or to acknowledge a safe return home from abroad. They were doing good business, too—he saw five or six people approach them in the short time he stood watching. Each took a cone-shaped lump of incense and set it burning with much touching of hands to forehead and heart, or lit a streamer of paper printed with a prayer and watched until it had fizzled smokily into nothing.

Glancing sidelong at Grandfather Loa's looming bulk, more clearly visible because the rain was lightening, he found he could hardly blame the Yatakangis for keeping up their old customs.

"Ah, my American friend," a soft voice said alongside him. "Thank you again, Mr.—?"

He turned, speaking his name mechanically, to greet the Indian girl. In her flowing full-length sari she looked even more graceful and delicate than before, though it was clear from the way she kept adjusting its hang she was unused to anything that so encumbered her legs. .

"You're waiting for a cab—? No, I see there are plenty. What, then?"

"Taking stock. I've never been here before." He uttered the words with mere forced politeness, though he was intellectually aware she was both pretty and emancipated; the impact of what the Yatakangi doctor had just done to him seemed to have numbed his male reactions for the moment.

"Yet you speak Yatakangi, and apparently very well," the girl said.

"I wanted to learn a non-Indo-European language, and it came handy because not many people were studying it . . . Are you going into Gongilung?"

"Yes, I have rooms booked at a hotel. I think it's called the Dedication Hotel."

"So have I."

"Will you share a cab with me, then?"

No surprise at the coincidence. Why should there be? The Dedication Hotel was the only hotel in Gongilung catering for a Westernised clientele, an automatic choice if rooms were available.

"Or would you rather ride in a rickshaw? I don't believe you have them in America, do you?"

Rickshaw—of course: the root from which the modern Yatakangi word "rixa" must derive. Donald said, "Have we not too much baggage?"

"Of course not. These drivers look just as strong as the ones we have at home. Yes? Hey, you there!"

She waved energetically at the first rixa-man on the line, and he pedalled his curious five-wheeled conveyance over to them. He made no objection about the amount of baggage, as she had promised, but loaded it up on the rear platform until the springs sagged, then held the low doors for them to get in.

The seat was narrow and pressed them together, but if his companion didn't mind Donald didn't. He was beginning to regain his normal mood.

"I'm Bronwen Ghose, by the way," the girl said as the driver hoisted himself up on one leg to exert maximum pressure on his pedal and get his heavy load moving.

"Bronwen? That's an Indian name?"

"No, Welsh. There's a complicated story behind it involving my grandfather going to sea as what they used to call a Lascar and having his heart broken in Cardiff by a Welsh girl." She laughed. "It puzzles everyone until I explain. What are you doing in Gongilung, Donald, or am I being inquisitive?"

"Not at all." Donald scanned the stream of traffic into which they were now merging; most of it consisted of pedal-driven miniature trucks, interspersed with electric gadabouts carrying either passengers—in incredible numbers, five or six to a vehicle no larger than this rixa—or bags and bales and boxes of indeterminate goods. Over the roadway bright streamers hung, a little faded from the rain, some of which praised Marshal Solukarta and some of which exhorted the Yatakangis to free themselves of European preconceptions.

"I—ah—I'm covering the genetic optimisation story for Engrelay Satelserv," he added.

"Really? How interesting! Are you a specialist in that area?"

"To some extent. I have a degree in biology, that is."

"I see what you mean—'to some extent'. What Sugaiguntung has done isn't, obviously, something one would cover in a college course, is it?"

"You know something about genetics yourself?"

Bronwen gave a wan smile. "Believe me, Donald, in a country like mine you can't be a woman of child-breeding age and not know something about it—unless you're illiterate and stupid, that is."

"I suppose not." Donald hesitated. "What brings you here, by the way? Business or pleasure?"

The answer was a long time delayed. Eventually she said, "Illness, to be frank."

"Illness?" he echoed in astonishment, and looked her over as best he could, crowded into the rixa's narrow seat.

"Nothing contagious, I promise. I wouldn't repay your kindness with such a nasty trick." She forced a laugh which made the rixa-man turn his head and narrowly miss a gadabout crossing his front wheel.

"No, it's something you'll perhaps know about if you're a geneticist. I have— Ah, the English word escapes me!" She snapped her fingers, and he caught at her hand.

"Don't do that in Yatakang!" he said, showing an apologetic face to their driver as he again turned around, this time looking suspicious. "It's bad luck except on certain specified days of the year. It's supposed to be a signal to call back the ghosts of your ancestors!"

"Goodness!" She put the knuckles of her other hand to her fine white teeth, pantomiming dismay. Belatedly Donald realised he was still holding the hand he had caught at, and let it go.

"It's a complicated country," he said. "You were just going to tell me—?"

"Oh yes. When the bones make too many of the blood-cells that kill germs, what is that called?"

"Leukaemia."

"Leukaemia, that's the word I wanted."

"But that's terrible," Donald said, genuinely concerned. In this day and age one thought of any kind of cancer including cancer of the blood as being a disease of old age, when the regulating mechanisms of the body began to break down. In youth, there were cures, and a whole body of legislation governed the production and use of carcinogenic substances.

"In America, I believe, it's now rare, but there is a lot of it in my country," Bronwen said. "I am lucky—my husband died, as you know, and I inherited enough money to come here and take a treatment which cannot be had in India."

"What kind of treatment?"

"One which that same Dr. Sugaiguntung invented. I don't know very much about it."

They had reached the top of a long incline diving towards the heart of Gongilung, and the road was flanked with low-cost warren-like tenements, several of them decorated with the ubiquitous political slogan-streamers. Their driver, alarmingly, removed his bare feet from the pedals and crossed them on the handlebar, using both hands to extract and shield a cigarette which the rain threatened to damp out. But Donald saw that all the other drivers were doing the same, so he resigned himself.

"I remember reading about this," he said, frowning "If I recall rightly, what has to be done is in two stages. First, you infect the bone-marrow with a tailored virus that substitutes for the uncontrolled natural genetic material. Then, when it's brought leucocyte production back to normal, you have to displace the tailored material in its turn and complete the job with a facsimile nucleus—"

"I wouldn't know about that," Bronwen said, shrugging. "I know two things about it: it's expensive, and it's painful. But I am glad to be here."

There was silence except for the hushing of the wheels on the roadway and occasional angry shouts from drivers who thought their right of way had been infringed. Donald could find nothing to say; he could only look at Bronwen's pretty face and read the unhappiness there.

"I am only twenty-one years old," Bronwen said finally "I could live for a long time. I *want* to live for a long time."

"And you're a widow already?"

"My husband was a doctor," she said stonily. "He was killed by a mob who found out he was using vaccines made from pig-serum. He was thirty-three."

The distant thunder of an express roaring down towards the port drowned out any attempt at an answer Donald might have made.

At the Dedication Hotel one of the staff spoke both English and a little Hindi, so Donald could relinquish his job as interpreter. Frowning over the elaborate computer-form he had to punch to describe himself, he hardly listened to what Bronwen was saying to the reception clerk. At the back of his mind he was reviewing what he had to do for "professional" reasons: call at the International Press Club, to which he had been given a temporary admission card, and rendezvous with the Engrelay Satelserv stringer; check in at the government information office and make sure of receiving their official releases; and grease as many palms as he had to in order to secure a personal interview with Sugaiguntung. That was going to be a long, expensive and quite possibly fruitless task. Since the news broke, no foreign journalist had managed to see the Professor Doctor alone, only at press-conferences masterminded by government spokesmen.

Despite being round-eyed, Indians were comparatively acceptable in Yatakang at the moment; they were regarded as fellow sufferers from the legacy of colonialism. Europeans were liable to encounter the dislike engendered by the former governors, the Dutch, and some of it was bound to rub off on Americans owing to the continuing strain in diplomatic relations; Bronwen had already vanished to an upper floor before Donald's bags were collected and he was led to his own room. It was a typically Yatakangi assembly of paradoxes—fine old hand-woven silks in glass frames filled with helium to prevent decay, a low tray full of cushions to serve as a bed, a shower compartment panelled in mock-marble alongside a bidet, a toilet, and a large plastic basket full of smooth round stones for the benefit of orthodox Muslim visitors who declined to do otherwise than the Prophet ordered when cleaning themselves after having their bowels open.

A bellgirl in a blue shareng silently and efficiently put away his clothes, showed him how to operate the paper clothing dispenser and the shoe-weaver, and apologised for the fact that the TV was out of order, "but it will be fixed very soon." There was dust on the knobs; that promise had probably been made to the last twenty guests.

At least, though, the phone was working. When he was alone he sat down at it, feeling vaguely uncomfortable about not having a screen so that he could see his correspondent and looking at the wall-mounted mirror instead.

In that mirror, just after he had punched his first number, he saw a door—not the one he had come in by, the one leading to the adjacent room—and it was creeping open.

He rose to his feet with as little sound as possible and

darted across the narrow room, taking his stand where the door would shield him. A glance at the mirror showed that whoever was entering could not see him by reflection—nor, by the same token, could he see the intruder. But a dusky hand came around the corner of the door, and a foot, and—

He pounced, his newly acquired eptification in combat making his movements sure and economical. In the next second he had the intruder by wrist and neck, ready to lift into the air and drop across his knee in a disabling blow to the base of the spine.

Also in that second he said with horror, "Bronwen!"

"Let go, you're hurting!" she panted past the grip he had taken on her slim throat.

"I'm terribly sorry!" Frantic, he helped her to regain her balance, steadied her with a hand on her arm as she swayed. "But you shouldn't have come in like that—one never knows what's liable to happen nowadays!"

"I certainly wasn't expecting that," she said wryly. "I thought I heard your voice and realised you'd been put in the room next to mine. I'm sorry. I only wanted to surprise you."

"That you managed," he said grimly. "Oh—that must be my call. Sit down. I'll be with you in a moment."

He darted back to the phone, which was making ill-defined grunting sounds in Yatakangi. The speaker was not, as he had hoped, the local stringer he was to visit, but the stringer's partner, who didn't know when his colleague would be back and declined to do more than take a message.

Donald told him where he was staying and cut the circuit. Swivelling his chair, he looked at Bronwen and gave a wry grin.

"Know something? For a sick girl, you're strong."

"It's only in the preliminary stages," Bronwen muttered, looking at the floor. "My husband diagnosed it immediately before they killed him."

Now he had a chance to take in her appearance. She must have gone straight to the paper clothing dispenser and fitted herself out with a set of Yatakangi garments; she was in a pale grey shareng and a short stiff yellow coat.

She noticed him looking, and fidgeted, plucking at her waist. "These things are awful," she said. "Worse than what we get at home, and that's bad. I was only going to ask you if you could spare a little while to help me buy some cloth dresses instead of paper like this."

Donald made some quick mental calculations. Coming to Yatakang, he had picked up time; it was local morning, evening back in California. Yatakangi custom decreed a sort of siesta between noon and three poppa-momma; he would not be able to make his appointments for earlier than three, therefore, and that left a couple of hours free.

"Sure I can," he said. "Just let me make a few calls and I'll be with you."

"Thanks very much," she said, and returned to her own room without closing the door.

In there, the closet swung open instead of sliding as his did. He noticed this almost at once, because on resuming his seat at the phone he could see the reflection of a reflection in the mirror which had shown him the silently opening door. He kept his eyes on the glass absently as he waited for his call to the government information office to go through.

In that fashion, he saw her pause and glance down at herself in the drab grey and yellow paper and make a moue.

"Yes?" said the phone.

"Overseas correspondents liaison section, please."

"Wait one minute."

She put her hands up to her breast as though to tear off the offending garments, but the paper was too tough, being reinforced with plastic against Yatakang's frequent rain. Defeated, she slipped off the little coat and balled it up angrily, tossing the crumpled remains on the floor.

"Overseas liaison," the phone said.

"My name is Donald Hogan and I'm accredited to you by Engrelay Satelserv. You should have had notification of my arrival from my head office."

"Please repeat the name and I will see if that is so."

The upper part of the shareng, automatically pre-pleated by the dispenser into a rough approximation for her size and height, unfolded from her with a rustling noise. Donald caught his breath. She was wearing nothing under it, and her breasts were like small brown pears with nipples of bright carnelian.

"Yes, Mr. Hogan, we have been notified about you. When will you wish to come and register with us for official journalistic status in Yatakang?"

"If three this afternoon is not too early—?"

She had unwound the three turns of the shareng from her waist and was bending over to sort out the complicated slots and tags that made up the portion between her legs. Her breasts hardly moved as she doubled over.

"I will consult the appointment schedule for the appropriate official. Hold on, please."

She must have managed to put the garment on, but it was taking her a great deal of trouble to get it off. She turned, still bending, as though to get a better light on what her hands were doing, and her small shapely buttocks loomed round in the square of the mirror. Light caught the tuft of black hair at their parting.

"Yes, three today will be acceptable. Thank you, Mr. Hogan," the phone said, and clicked off. Donald rose, his mouth a little dry and his heart hammering, and went through the doorway.

With her back to him, she stepped aside from the ruin of the paper shareng and said, "I knew you were watching, of course."

He didn't say anything.

"I think sometimes I'm mad," Bronwen said, and there was a slight high edge of unborn hysteria on her voice. "And then again sometimes I think I'm not mad, but very sensible. He taught me to love my body—my husband. And there may not be very much time left for me to show that love."

She turned at last, slowly, pivoting on one delicate foot of which the sole, Donald saw now, was tinted with pinkish dye to match the paint on the nails.

"I'm sorry," she said abruptly. "It's no special compliment to you. It's just . . . Well, I've never had an American, so I'd like to. While I can. That is, if you want to." The words came out with a strange flatness, like a machine talking. "I'm quite—how does the pun go? I'm quite impregnable, isn't that it? They sterilised me just in case leukaemia of my sort is hereditary. I'm absolutely and *completely* sterile."

"So am I," Donald said in a tone that shocked him with its gruffness, and tugged loose the comb that held her long black hair, spilling it down her in a tressy waterfall of forgetfulness.

tracking with closeups (19)

SMALL WANTS AND THOSE EASILY SATISFIED

When his TV went wrong and would show nothing but a field of irregularly wavering grey lines interspersed with dots which moved like dust suspended in liquid and examined under a microscope to demonstrate Brownian motion, accompanied by a white-noise hiss from the speaker, Bennie Noakes thought about having it repaired. After an hour or two, however, he discovered that the random patterns and the noise were themselves psychedelic. What was more, reality didn't intrude those annoying and disgusting bits about people killing people. Digesting himself down to a unit of pure perceptivity, he continued to watch the screen. Occasionally he said, "Christ, *what* an imagination I've got."

continuity (23)

HE STUCK IN HIS THUMB

The Bight of Benin! The Bight of Benin!
One comes out where forty went in!

There was no direct express service to any point in Beninia. The country could not afford to build one of the huge
five-mile concrete pans that the planes required, let alone
the ancillary services. From the sleek modern womb of the
express Norman was decanted at Accra and put aboard a
tiny, ancient, wobble-winged Boeing that ran the local services via Port Mey to up-country Nigeria. It could not have
been built more recently than 1980 and it was serviced by
trucks carrying not lox and hydrazine but kerosene. Their
hoses leaked, as he could smell, and he thought wildly of
outbreaks of fire.

The Bight of Benin! The Bight of Benin!
The chiggers burrow beneath your skin!

The pressure-cooker heat of Africa pasted his clothes to
his skin with a mixture of sweat and steam.

The Bight of Benin! The Bight of Benin!
Blackwater fever and pounds of quinine!

Arrogant officials in what he did not at first recognise as
uniforms—the xenophobia of the end of last century had
eliminated European rank-symbols like peaked caps and Sam
Browne belts, to replace them with militarised counterparts
of tribal dress—welcomed the chance to show their contempt

for their black American cousins, children of Africans who hadn't had the sense or skill to hide from the slavers.

The Bight of Benin! The Bight of Benin!
The rain never stops and it waters the gin!

Passed through alleys of wire-mesh like cattle on the way to the slaughter-house, the party from GT with Norman and Elihu at its head proceeded to join the line waiting for transfer to the Port Mey flight. Five centuries blended into a confused stew of impressions: fat matrons swathed in gaudy cotton with matching turbans, progressive young girls in the pre-European garb of skirtlet, beads and earrings who sometimes looked on Norman with vague approval, businessmen probably from South Africa whose Western clothes contrasted with their negro colouring, a doctor—local style—carrying a vast bundle of ritual objects each with its precisely defined function in remedial psychiatry and most possessing their own distinctive aroma, an imam from Egypt in friendly professional conversation with a dog-collared Episcopalian priest . . .

The Bight of Benin! The Bight of Benin!
Godforsaken since God knows when!

The announcements about arrivals and departures which were uttered at intervals over booming loudspeakers were in English of a sort, but it took Norman several minutes to realise that fact. He had known intellectually that the language left behind by the colonial government was breaking up as Latin had done after the fall of Rome, but he had thought of it as happening more in Asia than Africa, to which despite everything he had certain emotional ties. Between the spoken announcements there was a never-ending susurrus of recorded music. Out of curiosity he counted the beat-pattern of one of the numbers and identified it as being in seventeen-four time, the ancient Dahomeyan rhythm of *hun* against *hunpi*, child against mother drum. He mentioned this to Elihu for want of anything else to say.

The Bight of Benin! The Bight of Benin!
You go in fat and you die there thin!

"That's something we wished on the paleasses, anyhow," Norman said.

"No," Elihu contradicted. "Complex rhythms like that

were among the things that the Europeans took away from us along with the rest of tribal culture. Jazz rhythms were from military marches and French dances. Modern rhythms are from Europe too—five-four from places like Hungary, seven-four from Greece and the rest of the Balkans. Even the instruments they've naturalised in the West are things like the sitar, from India, rather than the cora."

"Whatinole is a cora?"

"Half a gourd with a skin stretched over it as a resonator, and a frame carrying harp-strings and bits of metal that vibrate in sympathy at the correct frequencies. You will see it around here but it hails from further east; the best players are still Sudanese, as they've always been."

The Bight of Benin! The Bight of Benin!
Made us beasts instead of men!

"Did you check up on the African side of your ancestry?" Elihu inquired. "You said you were going to, I believe."

"Never had time," Norman muttered. But he looked at the people around him with sudden interest, thinking: *maybe some of these people are my relatives—they took a lot of slaves from here.*

"You won't be able to tell by looking," Elihu said. "Can you tell an Ibo from a Yoruba, an Ashanti from a Mandingo?"

Norman shook his head. "Can anyone?"

"There are types, the same as there are among people of European extraction. But there are black-haired Swedes and blond Spaniards, and here you don't even have those nice obvious traits to go by."

The Bight of Benin! The Bight of Benin!
Godamercy on a child of sin!

"They're calling our flight," Elihu said, and moved forward as the gate they faced was dragged open squealing on its hinges.

During the flight to Port Mey, a man carrying a musical instrument made from a stick, an old wooden box and some tongues of scrap metal tuned to a pentatonic scale, struck up a song in a wailing voice. Norman and his companions, except Elihu, found it embarrassing, but everyone else liked the idea of some home-made music and joined in.

"He's a Shinka," Elihu said. "From Port Mey. Telling everyone how glad he is to be going home after visiting Accra."

A fat woman carrying a child of less than a year had taken maximum advantage of the duty concession on liquor and passed a quart bottle of arrack around among her seat-neighbours. Norman refused her offer, trying to smile, saying very slowly and clearly that he was a non-drinking Muslim—whereupon she insisted that he take a piece of majnoun instead, from a box she had tucked into the folded cloth at her bosom. That much he consented to, thinking that the hashish it contained would not be much different from the pot he was accustomed to at home, and before they landed he was in a far more cheerful mood. The man with the musical instrument rose and went from seat to seat inviting improvised contributions of a verse for his song: Elihu, obliging after some thought, did so in good Shinka and the man fell on his neck with joy. Norman was almost disappointed at the loss of a chance to do the same himself, in English, and felt a sudden wave of astonishment at what had happened to him.

Worried, he whispered to Elihu when he had the opportunity, "Elihu, I feel very odd. Would there have been something in that candy apart from—?"

"They're Shinkas," Elihu said, as though that explained the entire universe, and went back to the discussion he had started with the musician, in the language of which Norman was totally ignorant.

At a loss, Norman pulled out an advertising leaflet for the airline from the pocket beside his seat, and found he was staring at a conventionalised map of West Africa which made the various countries look like slices of pie wedged into the northern coast of the Bight. Narrowest of all was Beninia, a mere sliver compared with RUNG or Dahomalia.

"Jack Horner," he murmured, half-aloud, and Elihu cocked an eyebrow at him inquiringly.

"Nothing."

But the idea seemed very funny, and he giggled without intending to.

Pulled out a plum! Right, too: no one in history ever pulled a plum like this one out of anybody's pie!

Bit by bit, he began to develop a curious sense of dual personality. Despite Elihu's offhand dismissal of the possibility, he concluded that something must have been added to spike the majnoun he had eaten. Nothing in his experience had ever induced in him this bipartisan reaction he was now undergoing.

On the one hand, his intellect remained exactly as it had been before leaving New York earlier today. When the official reception party met them at the miniature Port Mey landing-ground—Embassy staff of assorted colours and an honour guard of the toy Beninian Army in garb ideal for a parade but absolutely ridiculous for warfare—he was able to look about him and formulate corresponding ideas, such as that this was a silly place to pull financial plums out of. This wasn't mere poverty. This was downright squalor. The road along which the Embassy cars hummed and bumped towards home was maintained, after a fashion, by gangs of labourers with pick and shovel, but it was flanked by hovels, and the only sign of official intervention in the unhampered process of human degradation consisted in a banner saying, in English, that Beninia welcomed foreign investors. He had never expected to see, in this brave new century, naked children playing in mud with squealing piglets; here they were. He had never expected to see a family of father, mother, grandfather and four children on a pedal-driven conveyance made from three antique bicycles and two large plastic crates; they were held up at the airport exit to let one pass ahead. He had never expected to see one of the pioneer Morris trucks, the first fuel-cell design to achieve commercial operating cost, full to the brim of children aged between nine and fifteen waving and grinning over the tailboard; he saw no fewer than six during the journey, decorated with pious signs stating MORE HASTE LESS SPEED and THERE IS NO GOD BUT GOD and DO AS YOU WOULD BE DONE BY AMEN.

The air was heavy with unspilled moisture even worse than

he had experienced during the wait at Accra, which added to his inclination to be cynical.

Yet, at the same time as he was noting all these signs of backwardness and poverty, he was possessed of a sort of exhilaration. The road gang engaged on maintenance were accompanied by a group of four singers and musicians, making a rhythmical worksong out of the monotonous beat of the picks and counterpointing it with drums made from empty cans of different sizes. At the gaping, rag-curtained door of one of the hovels he saw a proud mother showing off her new baby to admiring neighbours, beaming with infectious delight. And standing outside another he saw a truck marked with a red cross, whose driver, dressed in a plastic coverall, was meticulously spraying himself with disinfectant from an aerosol can prior to getting back in the cab—slim proof, but proof, that the twenty-first century had made contact with Beninia.

Elihu was engaged in discussion with the gaunt young negro who had been holding the reins of office during his absence—the Embassy's First Secretary. He was at least eight years younger than Norman. Watching him, Norman wondered how it felt to be responsible for one country's relations with another, even on so small a scale as Beninia represented, at that age. He glanced over his shoulder, seeing the two other cars following with the remainder of the GT team—a girl from Rex Foster-Stern's Projects and Planning Dept, an expert in African linguistics specially recruited for the visit, and two economist-accountants from Hamilcar Waterford's personal advisory group.

Fishing in recent memory for the First Secretary's name—Gideon . . . something? Gideon Horsfall, that was it—Norman leaned forward.

"Excuse me breaking in," he said. "There's something I'd like to ask you, Mr. Horsfall."

"Ask away," the gaunt man said. "And please call me Gideon. I hate being mistered." He gave a sudden chuckle that ill-matched his rather skeletal look; he was a sort of parallel to Raphael Corning, though shorter and much darker, which threatened to send Norman's wandering mind off down a side alley concerned with the involvement of thin nervous types in modern politics.

"I used to save mistering for paleasses," he added when he recovered from his amusement. "But having been here a while I think I have that problem in perspective for a change. Sorry, you were going to say—?"

"I was going to ask whether you feel the same way about Beninia as Elihu does," Norman said.

There was a pause. During it, Gideon looked around at the suburbs of Port Mey closing in on either side. Apart from the fact that the ground was not compact enough to carry high buildings—as Norman's research had informed him, much of Port Mey had been swamp before it was drained by the British and partially reclaimed—it bore a striking resemblance to pictures of slums in Mediterranean Europe a century ago, with narrow alleys across which lines of washing were strung up, debouching onto the adequately wide but badly pot-holed street they were following.

At length Gideon said, not looking at Norman, "I can tell you this much. When they decided to post me here, in spite of the nominal promotion—I'd been Third Secretary at the Embassy in Cairo, you see—I was furious. I thought of this as a hopeless backwater. I'd have done anything to get out of it. But they made it clear that if I didn't swallow my pride I could look forward to a future at attaché rank, indefinitely.

"So I said yes, at a sheeting awful cost to my mental stability. It was touch and go whether I actually got there or whether I went under care with a shrinker. I was practically living on tranks. *You* know how it is to be brown-nosed in a paleass society."

Norman nodded. He tried to swallow, but his mouth was so dry there was nothing under his palate except air.

"I've been running things while Elihu was away," Gideon said. "Not that there's much to run, I grant you. But—well, two years ago being faced with that much nominal responsibility would have caved me in. I wouldn't have been able to help it. Nothing else has happened to me apart from coming here, yet somehow"—he gave a shrug—"I'm back in one piece, and nothing fazes me. We could have had a RUNG-Dahomalian war and I'd have kept going through it. I might not have coped very well, but I could have made the effort and not felt I was helpless and useless."

"That's right," Elihu nodded. "I'm pleased with you."

"Thanks." Gideon hesitated. "Elihu, I guess you'll understand this. Time was when I'd have licked the ambassador's boots for praise like that. Now it's just—well—nice to have. Catch? This is part of trying to explain things to Norman here, I mean, not personal."

Elihu nodded, and Norman had a disquieting sense of shared communication between him and Gideon which he, as a New York-bred stranger, could not hope to eavesdrop on.

"Elihu here," Gideon resumed, turning in his seat to face Norman, "could do anything short of telling me I was a sheeting fool and *proving* it, and I'd still stand up and back my judgment. If he had proof, I'd say so and start over, but I wouldn't feel stupid because I'd been wrong. I'd feel there was a reason—I was misinformed, or some back-home preconception undermined me, or something. This is being confident, which is the same as being secure. Catch?"

"I guess," Norman said dubiously.

"Obviously you don't. Which means I probably can't tell you." Gideon shrugged. "It's not a thing you can isolate and show off in a jar—here's the reason why. It's something you have to experience, get through your skin and into your belly. But . . . Well, some of it is in the fact that there hasn't been a murder in Beninia in fifteen years."

"What?" Norman jolted forward.

"Truth. I don't see how it's possible, but it's a matter of record. Look at those slums!" Gideon pointed through the car window. "You'd think that was the sort of place designed to breed gang-rumbles and muckers, wouldn't you? There's *never* been a mucker in Beninia. The last murderer wasn't even one of the majority group, the Shinka—he was an Inoko immigrant aged sixty-some who caught his second wife cheating."

I'd love to bring Chad Mulligan here and shoot down some of his precious theories, Norman thought. Aloud he said,

"There's no doubt in that case that Beninia does have something."

"Believe me, codder," Gideon said. "Another thing, religion-wise. I'm a Catholic myself. You?"

"Muslim."

"Not a Child of X?"

"No, orthodox."

"Me too, in my own Church. But did you ever hear of a country where Right Catholics weren't the target for recriminations?"

Norman shook his head.

"Now myself, I'm fully appreciative of the benefits of contraception; I have two fine prodgies and they're bright and healthy and the rest of it, and that's sufficient for me. But I used to rail against the heretics until I started to take in the logic of the Beninian attitude."

"Which is?"

"Well . . ." Gideon hesitated. "I don't, even yet, know if it's cruel of me, or simply sound sense. But, you see, when the schism happened there was a good strong element of dogmatic fanaticism among the Catholics here, who are only a tiny proportion of the people—most of them are heathen or of your own persuasion. It was inevitable that a lot of them would regard the Bull *De Progenitate* as repugnant. However, you can't even get an argument started about Right versus Romish over here! People say well, if they don't plan their prodgies a high enough proportion will be sickly to make them non-competitive in the long run, and what's more they'll tend either to bankrupt themselves with too many children or else they'll get so many psychological hangups from enforced continence they'll handicap themselves in later life. And the people here don't just believe this, they act on it! And to cap the lot—!"

"What?"

"The figures show they're right," Elihu said unexpectedly. "There's not much available here in the way of social analysis apart from what's run as a commercial venture by the United Africa Company and the Firestone people, who've been using their Liberian bridgehead to sound out new markets now automobile rubber is a shrinking outlet. But I don't need to tell you about that, I guess. Fact remains, though: the percentage of economic influence exerted by Right Catholics has gone down by twenty-odd per cent since the schism and will certainly go further."

"When both groups were running with the brakes on," Gideon said, "the competition was loaded their way, thanks to their relative degree of Europeanisation. Now one side has dropped its handicap, and it's going ahead like an accelera-tube entering the vacuum stretch of the tunnel."

The car swung sharply off the road and along the driveway of the U. S. Embassy building, a somewhat decayed but still handsome relic of the colonial period with tall pseudo-classical porticos on three sides of it.

"What would happen to Beninia if we didn't intervene?" Norman said as the wheels crunched to a stop on gravel. "I know what Shalmaneser says, but I'd like an on-the-spot answer from you, Gideon."

About to leave the car, Gideon checked his movement. He said after a pause for thought, "Depends."

"On what?"

"On how many Shinkas the Dahomalians and the RUNGs left alive when they'd carved up the country."

"I just don't catch," Norman confessed, having turned the statement over in his mind.

"You won't until you've made the acquaintance of a good few Shinkas. It took me a while to realise the truth, but I finally got there." Gideon paused again. "You're a Muslim, you say. Have you read the Christian gospels?"

"I'm a convert, raised as a Baptist."

"I see. In that case, I don't have to explain the context of the bit about 'the meek shall inherit the earth.' The Shinka are the only living proof I know of that promise. Sounds crazy? You wait and you'll see. They digested the Holaini, who wanted to ship the whole tribe off to the east as slaves. They digested the British so well they were almost the last British colony to be forced into independence. They digested the Inoko and the Kpala when they fled here from the neighbouring countries. Give them a chance and I swear they'd digest the Dahomalians and the RUNGs too. And what's more—!" A sudden unaccountable fierceness entered Gideon's tone.

"What's more," he concluded, "I think they're going to digest you. Because they've done it to me."

"And me," Elihu said lightly. "And I approve. Come on, Norman—I have to take you to see Zad this evening, and we lost a lot of daytime on the flight."

HOW TO

"Hydroxy fuel-cells of the type used to power GM trucks up to 2½-ton capacity and certain foreign imports, notably the Honda series 'Fuji' and 'Kendo', can be turned into either a flame-gun or a bomb. In the case of the GM version, a file-cut should be made at base of valve A (see diagram) and pipes B and C re-routed to follow the dotted lines. A slow-match attached to a piece of string should be placed at point D, suspending a carborundum whetstone. When this falls into contact with brake-disc E it will spark the leaking gas and . . .

"The plastic insulation marketed by General Technics as 'Lo-Hi Sleevolene' is recognisable by its pink-pearl colour. Macerate each pound weight of the stripped insulation in 1 pt. absolute alcohol. The resultant doughy sludge is heat-stable up to 20° below the average flashpoint of commercial butane but thereafter dissociates with release of approx. 200 times its original volume of gases . . .

"A large number of recent manufactured products employ honeycomb aluminium sheet bonded with a European adhesive sold here under the name 'Weldigrip'. This tends to fail when exposed to gamma. Radio Test Sources Inc.'s catalogue item BVZ26 incorporates a cobalt-60 emitter designed for inspecting high-carbon steel castings up to 9″ thick. It should be placed close to a critical joint . . .

"GT's catalogue item RRR17 is a heavy-weather sealant applied to the underside of public transport vehicles. A little battery acid held in place with a sac of tackythene will cause it to attack the metal it's in contact with . . .

"Minnesota Mining's new sulphur-reclaiming bacterium, strain UQ-141, can be caused to sporulate simply by withholdng sulphur compounds. The organisms can then be kept in a domestic freezer for up to two months. Suggested uses include . . .

"GT is currently offering lox in quart flasks at a price 10% below its competitors. Wind the flask with magnesium flashwire (16 turns/inch) and connect suitable igniter and timer. Applications will be numerous . . .

"Japind's LazeeLazer monochrome unit can be modified as shown in the diagram. Depending on what grade of multiplier plug is incorporated in the circuit, voltages of up to 30,000 can be obtained. At full load the unit burns out in 1.5 sec., but careful pre-sighting will . . .

"A tailored bacterium from the British ICI list, catalogue ref. 5-100-244, is exceptional in that it can be mutated at home. A solution of 1/1000 HCl in distilled water breaks one of the RNA bonds. Application of the modified form leads to rapid plasticisation of virtually all thermo-setting plastics . . .

" 'Sterulose', Johnson & Johnson's new medical wadding, makes an ideal stabiliser for home-brewed nitroglycerine. Wrap each wad in paper soaked and dried in a solution of potassium nitrate or use fulminate caps for detonators . . .

"The soles of Bally of Switzerland's new 'Stridex' shoes are made of a compound that, ignited, emits dense clouds of choking black smoke. Certain grades of pot burn with a hot enough tip for the roach to start the process, to wit . . .

"Wrap a piece of flexion (preferably blue, as the dye helps) around 1 carton of 12 compressed-air bulbs of the type used in a General Foods whipped-cream dispenser. Coat with 'Novent' plugging compound to make a ball about 7" diam. The covering prevents the detectors at the garbage plant from reclaiming the metal of the bulbs. On a test run at Tacoma the resulting shrapnel put the disposal furnaces out of action for six hours . . .

"You probably heard the Bay Area Rapitrans was stalled for a full day. The diagram shows what did it. Placed on the track-bed, the device emits signals that tell the line computer a train is permanently stuck in that station . . .

"A signal injector powered by two dry cells can be left in a public phone-booth and *without interferring with normal operation of the phone* (thus delaying detection) will cause up to 250 random calls per hour over the area served by the local exchange . . .

"A parasite emitter light enough to hang under a child's kite or 2-ft. diam. hot-air balloon will repeat a 10-sec. slogan for up to 1 hour on regular TV sound wavelengths. See schematic . . .

"Empty one self-heating 'Camp with Campbell' soup-can by perforating it at the point shown in the picture, NOT conventionally at the top. Refill with any explosive or flammable compound flashing below 93° C. Close hole with surgical waterproof tape. On puncturing the can will become a grenade with a delay of 7 to 12 sec. according to contents . . .

"The adhesive used to seal capsules containing GT aluminophage is vulnerable to acetic acid. A delay-timer can thus be made by mixing water and vinegar in suitable ratio . . .

"United Steel's monofilament reinforcement yarn V/RP/SU is magnetosensitive. A timer activating an electromagnet could give the stuff applications e.g. on power-lines or in computers, inducing random cross-connections . . .

"An aerosol suspension of Triptine in peanut oil acquires interesting electrical properties. Try smearing it on a dust-precipitator . . .

"There are static-dischargers on the metal frame of the bridge at Kennedy Loading Point, Ellay. There should be a use for two or three hundred unwanted volts . . .

"The missile-bombardment doors on the North Rockies Acceleratube are sensitive to gamma. The sensor is in a large black container at the eastern entry and at the western it's in a green conical thing. Those doors weigh over a thousand ton apiece . . .

"Near the junction of Eleazar Freeway with Coton Hudson Drive the computer cables serving the traffic signals over 120 sq. mi. pass within a foot of the surface. There's a hydrant sign . . .

"Eastman Kodak is offering an interesting new collapsed-benzene compound. Wherever there are strained bonds there's energy waiting to be tapped. Pass the word when you find out how to spring the poor captives . . .

"Don't scrap your last-year's model Frigidaire! Units 27-215-900 through 27-360-500 employed a coolant liquid that was quietly withdrawn when they discovered it was capable of being mixed with Vaseline to make a gel—and the gel burns at over 500°. We suggest using it for paint. It turns a nice pale green colour and will sustain its own oxidation in films thinner than .001 inch . . .

"If you have re-evacuation facilities, note that the electron gun in current Admiral TV sets can be modified to deliver a linear instead of a fanned jet. What it does to a sensitive circuit is nobody's business, but it ought to be . . .

"Table salt in GT's solvent 00013 does very interesting things to copper, aluminium and brass . . .

"Try cross-connecting leads 12 and 27 on a Wontner electroplating unit. But make sure you're not in the building when the power goes back on. Cyanide is fierce stuff . . .

"They've precautioned most traffic-carrying tunnels out this way against smoke, aerosol radio-sources, control-circuit jammers and incendiaries. They still haven't coped with Minnesota Mining's strain RS-122, which turns concrete into a fine powder, nor GT's 'Catalight', an oxidising catalyst for asphalt and related compounds. Thought you'd like to know . . ."

—*From a selection of duplicated, photocopied,
holographed, offset, lithoed and printed
leaflets on file at Ellay police HQ*

context (19)

A FREE RENDERING OF TWO NATIONAL ANTHEMS

It is expected as a matter of course that every household in Yatakang should have the audivid recording of this, as prepared live during a mass rally in Gongilung on the Leader's birthday, 2006:

"We are the descendants of Grandfather Loa.
Blood runs in our veins as hot as lava.
Our united voice shakes the world.
We can build mountains and take them away.
      Together with our beloved Leader
      We will shape a new destiny for our country.

"There are a hundred beautiful islands.
There are millions of powerful people.
There is one right path for all of us.
Praise the Leader who expresses our common will.
      Together with our beloved Leader
      We will shape a new destiny for our country."

On the other hand, even though somebody pointed out to Zadkiel Obomi during his first term of office that Beninia had no anthem and he told the officious busybody to go and write one, the only time the Beninians were thoroughly exposed to it was when Jacob Fikeli and his Black Star Marimba Or-

408

*chestra took a fancy to the tune and put it on the West
African pop-parade:*

"Land of peace and brotherhood
To thee we pledge our love.
We value thee all other good,
All earthly wealth, above.

"Freedom came within a year
We never shall forget.
Our love for thee, Beninia,
Shall grow still greater yet."

(Fikeli's version was in Shinka. It went approximately:

"You ask why I'm in Port Mey
When my home is up-country.
Listen and I will tell you
The whole ridiculous story.

"I went to visit my uncle.
My uncle had a lot of palm-wine.
Everybody was helplessly drunk.
I met a girl relieving herself in the bush.

"My uncle had got married a third time.
I didn't know the girl was my aunt.
She wants to divorce him and come to me.
I can't afford to pay compensation!")

continuity (24)

THIS SCENE NOT SHIFTED

When Bronwen said in a matter-of-fact tone that she believed she had been one of the temple girls at Khajuraho in a previous incarnation, Donald was not at all surprised.

The centre of Gongilung had gradually been redeveloped from its original higgledy-piggledy layout until it approximated an H, the verticals and crossbar being the main avenues (Dedication, on which their hotel was located, National and Solukarta, respectively), the spaces between the legs being parks and recreation areas. Closing off the inland end were the government buildings and the university; closing off the other end was the port. On either side the city straggled for miles in an irregular arc paralleling the shore, a fringe of resorts and expensive villas shading back into the shabby overcrowded slums fledging the hillside.

The rain having ceased, the clouds having drawn aside, the cone of Grandfather Loa could be seen brooding over the Shongao Strait with a wreath of mist around his head like a halo.

When they dressed and went out to see what stores were open they at once picked up a gaggle of followers. Bronwen seemed able literally to ignore them, and Donald reasoned

410

that perhaps, coming from a country as grossly overcrowded as India, she would not have expected anything else. But he himself found that he hated the sensation of being watched and followed, no matter how openly.

Moreover, though the curious bystanders confined themselves to staring and whispering, he fancied he could detect hostility in their manner. It might be illusion. If their interest was due to no more than fascination at his strange white-skinned appearance, though, why were there so few smiles among those sallow Asian faces?

At every intersection there were collapsible booths almost buried under the load of goods they offered for sale: papers and journals, records, reefers, cigarettes made of a strain of tobacco alleged to lack all carcinogenic compounds—Donald didn't feel inclined to put the claim to the test—telescopic umbrellas, sun-glasses in cheap Japanese photo-reactive plastic, busts of Marshal Solukarta, sweetmeats, sandals, brooches, knives . . .

One of them, facing a wall-mounted shrine, made a speciality of devotional objects and displayed a more-than-ecumenical tolerance: from luminous St. Christophers through miniaturised Korans sealed into bracelet charms and guaranteed to contain the entire authentic text to traditional Yatakangi incense volcanoes. At this one Bronwen insisted on stopping for a thorough inspection, while Donald fretted and fumed because their halting allowed their followers to close in and surround them. Most of them were teenagers, with a sprinkling of older folk: some pushing bicycles, some carrying packages, interrupting their shopping or delaying an errand to gaze at the foreigners.

And yet . . . their presence wasn't the only thing that made hm uncomfortable. He looked up, over their heads, and there was the volcano looming.

The impulse was ridiculous; nonetheless, he made an effort of will and gave in to it. He pushed his way to the window of the booth and bought one of the incense cones. The seller naturally assumed he wanted it for a souvenir, and tried to persuade him to take a Solukarta bust as well. Only slapping down a two-tala coin, the exact price of the cone, made him shrug and desist.

"What do you want that for?" Bronwen asked, putting back a pair of bright yellow sun-glasses which were far too big for her.

"Tell you later," Donald said curtly, and shoved the Yata-kangis aside so that he could get at the wall shrine.

As they realised what he was doing, they exchanged looks of surprise and their chatter died away. Embarrassed by their intent scrutiny but determined to go through with what he had started, he placed the cone on the shrine's brass tray, crusted with the ashy traces of a thousand such. Having lit it, he made the proper ritual gesture—a bow and hand-move-ments akin to the Indian *namasthi*—and wafted a wisp of the smoke towards Bronwen.

The reaction of the natives was all Donald could have hoped for. Puzzled, but not wishing to fail in the proper procedure, members of the crowd moved towards the shrine, each placing his or her right hand in the smoke for a moment and muttering a short conventional prayer More courageous than the rest, a boy of fifteen or so thanked Donald for buying the cone, and the remainder copied his example. After that, they dispersed with many backward glances.

"What was all *that* about?" Bronwen demanded.

"I couldn't explain without giving you a course in Yata-kangi sociology," Donald grunted. "It merely proved that something I read about nine years ago hasn't been changed by the current government."

"Governments don't change things," she said. "Only time does that." The statement had the glibness of a proverb. "*I know the pig is a cleanlier animal than the sheep, but try telling that to a yelling mob . . . There's a dress-store, on the next block. Perhaps I'll get what I need there.*"

With maximum patience, Donald sat through forty minutes of trial and error while she paraded before him in a succes-sion of Yatakangi clothes to ask if this one or that one suited her better. He began to grow annoyed. Honesty compelled him to wonder if it was at her or at himself. For years he had enjoyed the comfortable, no-questions attitudes of the prosperous modern bachelor working the New York shiggy circuit, but something—contact with Gennice, maybe, or simply the disruptive intrusion of real life into his placid existence—had made him discontented. Ordinarily it would not have bothered him that Bronwen was clearly very vain. He had had an astonishing amount of pleasure from her slender brown body; moreover, someone suffering from leukaemia was to be pitied and allowances ought to be made.

Yet, when the choice was made and her gorgeous evening sari had been packaged in a plastic sachel and she herself in a shareng of peacock brilliance and she asked him whether it wasn't time for lunch because she was hungry, he hesitated over his response.

He said finally, "You're taking a lot for granted."

"What?"

"I am here on business, you know, I have other obligations besides helping you to find your way around Gongilung."

She flushed. Her pale brown skin mottled with the darkening effect of the underlying blood.

"So am I," she said after a pause. "Though mine, of course, is the kind of business where it's pleasanter to pretend that one is merely amusing oneself. Do you not have to eat, though?"

He didn't answer. After a moment, she put out her hand and took the bag containing her sari, which the saleswoman in the store had given to Donald automatically.

"In bed," she said, "your American crudity has a certain exciting quality. Out of it, it's merely bad manners. Thank you for giving me so much of your *valuable* time!"

She tucked the package under her arm and spun on her heel.

Donald watched her go, wondering just how much of a fool he had been.

With a little trouble, he found his way to the press club, a State-run organisation which was inevitably plastered with testimonials to the beneficence and unalloyed Asiatic thinking of the Solukarta régime, but which, he decided after wandering around its facilities, was going to prove very useful. As well as a restaurant, recreation-rooms and a bar—with a special section for Muslims offering only coffee, soft drinks and huqahs—there were phone and telefax rooms, a large library with a selection of a hundred or so prominent Asian journals, and a series of TV sets tuned to all the most important services covering the area, including the satellite relays in English, Russian, Chinese, Japanese, Arabic and the major European languages.

On a California time-base it was about time for his evening meal. Served by waiters as obsequious as if the colonial period had never ended, he ploughed his way through a huge dish of ristafl, the Yatakangi counterpart of paella but bearing a corrupted Dutch name cognate with the Indonesian *rijstaafel*. There were not many other people in the restaurant, but literally everyone else stared at him for the same reason that had drawn a crowd around him in the street: he and a mannish woman with Slavonic features, whom he assumed to be a Russian, were the only white people among Asiatics and Africans.

Having an hour to kill before his three o'clock appointment, he went to the library to digest his food. While he was patiently reading the day's issues of the three major Yatakangi papers—here, the impact of TV's instant news had not yet abolished the ancient influence of the printed press—he grew aware of someone looming over him.

He glanced up to discover a tall, dark-skinned woman of early middle age, her hair drawn tightly back on the crown of her head and lending her a severe expression. Guessing at once that this must be the Gongilung representative of Engrelay Satelserv, the one Delahanty had warned him to be tactful with, he rose to his feet.

"Donald Hogan," the woman said, with the typical slight Afrikaner accent of the modern South African. "My name is Deirdre Kwa-Loop. I found your message at my office when I called back an hour ago, and guessed you'd be here since you weren't at your hotel."

She offered him a blunt-fingered hand which he shook as cordially as he could.

"I gathered from some of the things they said over the past few days that Engrelay wasn't exactly overjoyed with what I'd been doing for them on the optimisation story," she went on, dropping into a chair that faced him. "I'm sorry they took it quite as far as sending out a biology specialist, though. That's what you are, correct?"

Donald, settling himself back in his own seat, gave a wary nod.

"Why sorry?"

"Putting it simply, friend, you've been sent after a non-story. I've seen a few in my time, but this is the *baas* of them all."

Donald looked blank. During the pause, a waiter passed and inquired if they wanted anything; Deirdre ordered coffee.

"Come off it!" she continued as the man moved away. "You must know what the set-up's like in this country—it positively breeds non-stories!"

"I don't really," Donald said. I've never been here before."

"But they said something about you speaking the lingo."

"I do—just a little. But this is my first visit."

"Why, those blockbottomed . . . ! No, that's unfair. I guess there can't be too many people around who know genetics and Yatakangi both—it's the son and daughter of a bitch of a language." Deirdre sighed, leaning back in her chair and putting her fingers together.

"Better fill you in on the scene, then—clear away some of the crazy ideas they seem to keep at Engrelay HQ. Let's begin with me, since they probably didn't advertise the full details of my status. I'm here primarily for the Cape Broadcasting Commission. Since Cape doesn't yet stretch its funds to satellite relay stations they don't object if I act as stringer for one—maximum one—beam agency that does have satellites. I used to represent the Common Europe Satelserv, but a year or two ago I managed to change horses in midstream. Didn't expect much to come of the new status. Like any other country where the government keeps a tight rein, most of what you pipe through is handouts and your own stuff has to be carefully tailored to avoid offending the censors.

"Then suddenly the only big story in five years breaks, and here I am. For a bit I thought *wow*. But what have I had since the first day? Official propaganda and official brush-offs. For a reason I cannot figure out but can make some educated guesses about, the lid is on and the pressure is rising."

"What sort of guesses?" Donald demanded. "Do you mean Sugaiguntung can't do what—?"

"Sugaiguntung's tinkered with genetics here before. Moving him over to people instead of rubber-trees is a change of quantity, not quality. But if rumour's to be trusted this place is going to be turned over and shaken." Deirdre let her voice drop almost to a whisper after a quick survey of their neighbours in the library.

"I hear Jogajong is back."

Donald stared.

"Do I have to tell you what that means? If it's true, Yatakang is going to go up in a fashion that makes the Singhalese Revolution look like the Wars of the Roses!"

There was a pause. Eventually Deirdre said, "Okay. Before you ask why I told you that, I'll explain. Don't kid yourself you can stick to your brief and cover nothing but the Sugaiguntung story. Scientific expert or not, if anything does blow, you'll be Engrelay's man on the spot and I'll be what I've always been—a local stringer. I want to strike a bargain with you."

"Such as . . . ?"

"Share leads. A four-hour beat on any genuine new story either of us picks up solo."

Donald thought that over. He said at length, "I can't think of any reason why not, except I don't see that I'm likely to pick up much that you can use."

"I'm no expert. I may be wrong about the optimisation programme. What I have to go on is political, not scientific."

The waiter delivered her coffee, and she poured a cup before resuming what she was saying.

"You see, I've been here long enough to recognise the typical official smokescreen. Solukarta is generating window for all he's worth. This genetic programme is supposed to be developed from Sugaiguntung's work on apes, right? In every country people are clamouring for the process because they've been forbidden to become parents, right? Yet no foreign correspondent, not even the Chinese and Japanese, has managed to get at Sugaiguntung without some 'interpreter' or other. I *speak* Yatakangi—what's more Sugaiguntung studied in your country and wrote his scientific papers in English before the government hinted that it was—ah—'unpatriotic'. For me he needs an interpreter?"

"Editing," Donald said.

"You're on the orbit." Deirdre poured the first of her coffee over her large lower lip and set the cup down with a chinking noise. "Right—your turn to do some talking. I want to know about the scientific side. Far as I can figure out, the only part of the optimisation process which has been properly discussed is a cloning technique—that the right word? Thought so. But as I understand it . . . Well, Sugaiguntung's a genius and nobody says otherwise, but for this you'd need not genuises but assembly-line technicians."

"That's pretty well right," Donald agreed. "But how about all these doctors and nurses from outlying islands, coming to Gongilung to be taught the method?"

Deirdre gave a coarse laugh. "They came, all right. But they haven't been sent up to the university for instruction. They've been told to go home and await receipt of a *printed manual*."

"It sounds as though I'm chasing shadows," Donald said.

"We think so. Of course, the people don't, and that's where trouble may arise. If they decide they've been deceived—boom!"

Donald pondered. He had no doubt that this was exactly what the people who had sent him wanted to hear: that the optimisation programme was a fraud mounted for political reasons. But surely a man with an international reputation like Sugaiguntung's wouldn't allow his government to let itself be caught out in a flagrant lie? Sugaiguntung was at least as much of a patriot as any member of the world-wide confraternity of science could be. Besides, he'd be blamed along with Solukarta if the calamity occurred.

"Come on!" Deirdre said. "I want to hear your view. There isn't an expert on genetics in this country who'll talk freely to a foreign reporter—they just roll their eyes as though Sugaiguntung was Grandfather Loa incarnate."

Donald drew a deep breath. What he was going to say could have been found as easily through an encyclopedia connection over the phone, but laymen possibly wouldn't have known the right questions to ask.

"Well, there are three main ways of optimising your gene-pool without diminishing your population. Solukarta seems to be trying to keep it steady—I recall seeing that his planners were assuming a plus two per cent value for the year 2050—so we can disregard culling."

"What's that?"

"Selective eugenic extermination of bad hereditary lines."

Deirdre shuddered. "They were talking about that in my country before the War of Independence—but never mind. Go on."

"One way is what's now generally adopted in countries with a suitable enforcement agency: eugenic legislation. Without actually killing off the bad heredities, you make it difficult or impossible for them to reproduce. That's not much more than a directed version of natural selection, and people have grown used to it.

"Another technique is the one you mentioned—cloning. You implant a sound cell-nucleus in an ovum in place of the faulty one which results naturally from conventional fertilisation. This has drawbacks—it costs a fortune because it takes skilled tectogeneticists to do the job, and it's susceptible to unforeseen side-effects. Even if you make the transplant with apparent success you may induce recessive mutations that crop up in a future generation. The child is necessarily of the parent's sex. It takes anything up to twenty attempts before you get a viable ovum. And so on.

"The third way is the easiest. You deliberately breed from sound lines only, as you do with domestic cattle. This can be simple—you merely send the mother to bed with a healthy partner—or it can have luxy elaborations, up to and including external fertilisation by AID and reimplantation in the mother."

"I've been wondering," Deirdre said, "whether the outcome of all this is going to be no more than a national sperm bank, so people can have cubs by Solukarta and other prominent figures."

Donald hesitated. But what he had in mind to say was far from restricted knowledge, and would at least give the impression that he was keeping the bargain he'd struck.

"I think not," he said.

"Why?"

"Solukarta daren't have prodgies. He's carrying the gene of a rare disease called porphyria—the one that sent King George III of England out of his skull."

"I didn't know that!"

"He doesn't like it noised around. And being recessive it's easy to cover up. But if you check on the relatives he's managed to—ah—*lose* since coming to power, you'll find clues."

Deirdre gave a thoughtful nod. "Well, anyhow," she resumed. "My guess is that with the available resources—no matter how many pupils Sugaiguntung has trained at the university—Yatakang can't afford anything better than some sort of selective breeding."

"If they try it," Donald said, "they're headed for trouble."

"Why?"

"It limits the gene-pool. If we have any claim to be boss species on this ball of mud, it's founded on the fact that we have the largest available gene-pool of any animal or plant whatever. We can cross-fertilise from one pole to the other. And the ability to cross our lines out is the thing that really entitles us to vaunt our supremacy over creatures that vastly outnumber us, like ants and nematodes."

He noticed that Deirdre stiffened a trifle at that. Small wonder. Just as Israel had become almost fascist in its racialism during the last century, black South Africans had become fanatical on the subject during this one. He thought of Norman and hurried on.

"Well, take it as read that we don't possess enough information to optimise our genetic endowment on a simple breeding basis. We're more likely to run into the kind of trouble which turned the Afrikaners paranoid." That relaxed Deirdre again, he noticed with amusement.

"But in the second part of the programme Solukarta's proposing a fourth method, and this is where the crunch comes. Actually tailoring the genes in a fertilised human ovum so that the resulting baby will have specified talents, some of them—by implication—unprecedented in human history. That's what's excited the public's imagination in my country. How about you?"

Deirdre sighed. "Same is true in Asia. Most of the people around here are still conditioned by ancestor-worship, in spite of the propaganda against it. They like the idea of having two or three healthy, long-lived children instead of a crowd of sickly ones, because they're more likely to survive and take care of their old helpless parents, so they're amenable to eugenic legislation. But the promise of having children with brand-new talents fascinates them. It would mean—by implication, as you just said—that those children would be exceptionally grateful to the ancestors who endowed them with their special abilities."

"How about back home, among your own people?" Donald ventured.

"I'll be frank, as much as I can," Deirdre said after a moment's hesitation. "Despite having taken our country back from the white *baas*, despite having run it far more efficiently, we tend to nurse a suspicion of our own inferiority. To be able to prove scientifically that our children would be not only the equal of anyone else's but actually ahead of them . . ."

She let the words die away and gave a shrug.

Graft on to that the European reaction, especially in countries as densely populated as Holland and Flanders which lack the spillage zone enjoyed by the French-speaking Walloons . . .

Donald sighed. Somehow, the entire human race seemed momentarily united in a single entrancing dream—the hope that the next generation they would bequeath to Mother Earth would be whole, healthy, sane, capable of making amends for the rape they had inflicted in olden days.

The tantalising promise had been made. And it looked as though the promise was a lie.

Abruptly, awareness of the time shattered his musing, and he jumped to his feet.

"I shouldn't worry about being punctual for appointments here," Deirdre said sourly. "They've kept me hanging around often enough—they deserve some of their own medicine for a change."

context (20)

THE PROS AND CONS OF A LUNATIC SOCIETY

"Thank you for that kind introduction, Madam Chairman. Well, ladies and gentlemen—you will forgive me for sitting down while I address you, I'm sure, because coming home from Moonbase Zero after a long stay is rather like getting up after being bedridden for a month and carrying one's own weight under six times the lunar gravity is a tiring task.

"I thought I might begin by answering some of the questions which people most commonly ask me, and to which I assume the answers aren't very widely known or else they wouldn't crop up so often. As you know, my speciality is psychology, so people very often say to me, 'Isn't it a terrible strain living up there on the Moon—isn't it a hostile, terrifying environment?'

"They're always surprised when I say no, not nearly as bad as right here on Earth. But that's the literal truth. You see, on the Moon you know exactly how the environment can be hostile to you. You know that if you puncture a tunnel-wall, or snag your suit, you're in danger of death, or at least of losing a limb to dehydratory gangrene when the sphincter at the next joint inwards seals off the empty section of the suit. You know that if you forget to switch your suit to reflecting before crossing a patch of open ground in full sunlight you'll bake before you return to shadow, and if you don't cut in your heaters when you go out at night your feet will be frost-bitten within fifty metres.

"More important than that, though, you know you're in an environment where co-operation is essential to survival.

"There are no strangers on the Moon. I've had my life saved three separate times by people I'd never met before and one of them was a Chinese. I've done the same—and this is not in any sense boasting because it's a fact of lunar existence—for two people, one a professional colleague and one a novice I hadn't even spoken to since his arrival a week earlier.

"Living-space is at a premium, of course, and we're all jammed together in a sort of immobile submarine, but we're hand-picked for our ability to make allowances for the failings of our fellow human beings, and anyone who doesn't measure up to the intensive demands of the lunar base is shipped home fast. Perhaps some of you have seen a play called 'Macbeth of Moonbase Zero', Hank Sodley's remake of the Shakespeare original, in which this paranoid establishes contact with aliens who can predict the future? The whole thing's a nonsense, because paranoia loses its meaning on the Moon. You *are* being threatened, and you can learn and control the forces threatening you.

"Down here on Earth, though, you may walk around the corner and find yourself confronting a mucker with an axe or a gun. You may catch a strain of antibiotic-resistant germs. You may—especially here on the West Coast—run into one of the little pranks invented by the funny people who treat sabotage as an amusing hobby. You have absolutely no way of telling whether that innocuous stranger over there is about to haul out a weapon and attack you, or blow a disease your way, or explode an incendiary bomb in your disposall tube.

"In short, life on the Moon is much more like Bushman society prior to European contamination, or the basal culture of the Zuñi, than it is like life here in California or Moscow or Peking.

"That's why we Lunatics don't regard our environment as intolerable. Muckers don't develop where people feel that everyone else is on their own side rather than out to undermine them. Diseases can be controlled almost down to single organisms because we have the finest sterilisation facilities imaginable—just let a little space and raw sunlight in, and you've cooked every known terrestrial germ to a faretheewell. Lunar-native organisms, of course, can't infect human bodies. And as for playing dangerous pranks with sabotage gadgets, this is literally unthinkable.

"Now when I've explained that, people usually say how odd it is to find the staff of one of mankind's most advanced scientific projects behaving more like Bushmen than modern Americans. That is, if they've seen the point of my earlier explanation.

"So I have to say no, it's the reverse of odd, it's a simple consequence of the fact that the lunar environment contains a fixed number of variables. Human beings can cope with big plain facts like seasons or lunar night and day, like drought or vacuum, like a pestilence among the game animals they feed off or a rocket going astray and crashing a load of provisions into a mountainside. What we *can't* cope with is seven billion competing members of our own species. You have too many incalculable variables to make a rational response when a crisis occurs.

"And one more thing, too. There's no one on the moon who doesn't know that he's making a contribution to the whole. Not a day goes past but you can point to something you've done and say, 'I achieved that today!' It may be physical, like adding an extension to the living accommodation, or it may be intangible, like adding to our stock of stellar observations, but it's indescribably satisfying. These days, an urban psychiatrist here on Earth thinks twice about handling a case with a rural background, but up there I've been responsible for the mental welfare of people not only from different countries but of different religions and different ideologies, and I've never had a major problem from it.

"When I get this far people usually flinch and inquire nervously whether that includes the little red brothers. And I can say nothing else except that trying to subvert vacuum or a solar storm will get you *one* place and that's a grave.

"Of *course* I'm including Chinese! Like I said, I owe my life to a Chinese colleague, a man we'd exchanged with the staff of the communist observatory at Aristarchus. And down here in the middle of the Pacific, which apart from Antarctica is the only part of the planet that you can compare to the Moon for loneliness and lack of life-supports, all you can think of doing is blasting each other. It makes me sick. Madam Chairman, somebody had better get me a trank, and maybe then I'll be able to get on with the cosy tourist-type gossip I have down here in the rest of my notes. Right now I don't think I could read it wthout vomiting."

continuity (25)

DADDY OF THEM ALL

There was one local touch in the suite they assigned to Norman for his stay at the Embassy: a sixteenth-century mask of carved wood stained in shades of stark red, black and white, mounted on the wall at the head of his bed. Otherwise he might still have been in the States, apart from the fact that occasionally the power seemed to fluctuate and the lighting grew momentarily yellow.

He was instructing one of the servants—a local boy of about fourteen who spoke a minimum of usable English— where to stow his bags, when the intercom sounded and he found it was Elihu calling.

"There was a memo from Zad in my mail-tray," the ambassador said. "We're to dine at Presidential Palace at eight-thirty; he'll have the ministers of finance, education and foreign affairs to meet us. Can you present a preliminary brief?"

"I guess so," Norman shrugged. "Does he want the whole GT team or just me?"

"He doesn't specify, but I think it might make sense to establish the maximum of personal contact right away. Will you inform the others? And I'll warn him there will be six of us—no, seven, come to think of it, because Gideon should be there too. He speaks pretty good Shinka, and we may need that."

"I'd assumed anyone of cabinet rank would speak English here," Norman said after a pause.

"African English and American English are going separate ways," Elihu grunted. "You'd be surprised at some of the changes that have taken place. Be ready to leave by eight-fifteen, then, please."

Norman nodded and cut the circuit. He turned to the boy, who was hanging up his clothes, almost relieved to be able to give him something else to do. Personal service in the States had grown to be a thing you confined to the business field; to have it done in a domestic context was vaguely unsettling.

"You know which rooms the other Americans have been put in?"

"Yessah!"

"Go and ask them to come and see me as soon as possible, please."

"Yessah!"

He had finished the unpacking himself by the time the first of his colleagues entered: Consuela Pech, a pretty girl of mainly Puerto Rican extraction whom Rex Foster-Stern might have chosen for his representative either because she was the optimum candidate or because he'd been sleeping with her and grown bored and seized the chance to move her out of his way. Norman had barely had time to exchange a greeting with her when the three others came in together: the economists delegated by Hamilcar Waterford largely because they were both brown-noses, Terence Gale and Worthy Lunscomb, and the linguist whose acquaintance Norman had made only just before leaving, Derek Quimby, a chubby fair man with an air of perpetual bewilderment.

"Sit down, all of you," Norman invited, and took a seat facing them as they grouped in a semi-circle. "We're being kicked straight into orbit this evening—having dinner with the president and three of his ministers—and I thought we should review our initial presentation. Derek, you won't be particularly involved at the first stage, but I gather you have some specialised local knowledge which may indicate weakness in our thinking now and then, so I'd be pleased if you'd point out any such difficulty, right?"

Derek nodded and swallowed largely.

"Fine. Consuela, if I know Rex, your dept has armed you with everything we'd normally use in putting over a project at home. How much of it can be scaled down for an over-dinner discussion?"

"I insisted on them giving me material for three different levels of presentation," Consuela said. "I can tackle this easily. Also I can tackle a delegate committee with up to twenty personalised approaches, and I can tackle a meeting of the Beninian parliament with the full complement of sixty-one members present, on a screen-and-speaker basis."

"Excellent!" Norman said, amending his previous guess about the girl's aptitude for this job. "Now the minister of finance is going to be there, and he's the man most likely to jump to our side. It can't be any fun at all handling the budgetary problems in a country like this which is permanently on the verge of bankruptcy. Terence, I want you and Worthy to sweeten him right at the start with some costings. Don't worry about precision, just get it into his head that this chunk of ground has suddenly acquired colossal economic potential. Now there's a good chance, remember, that we know more about the economics of this area than he does—we have the benefit of Shal's analyses and in accordance with the old saw about the high cost of being poor I doubt if Beninia has ever been able to afford comparable service from the Common Europe computers. Don't lean too heavily on superior information. Ease him into thinking that it's his, not our, local knowledge that's making the scheme viable. Clear?"

Worthy said, "Can be tried. What do we know about him as a person, though?"

"I'll arrange for Elihu, or Gideon perhaps, to let you have a character-sketch while we're on the way to the palace. Consuela, let's go back to you. The minister of education is your first target because so much of the scheme is predicated on bringing up the literacy and skilled-labour level in under a decade. I want you to begin by seeing if you can get her to macluhan the local situation. Bring her around to the subject of how traditional attitudes condition people's reaction to local information. She'll probably react well, since she must have been educated abroad—there isn't a centre of higher learning here worth the name apart from this privately owned business college you presumably know about."

"I can give you some tips," Derek put in, addressing Consuela. "Some highly suggestive things have happened to the English vocabulary the colonial régime left behind here."

"Thank you, Derek," Norman said. "That's exactly the kind of thing I'm looking for from you. Now let's look at a question we haven't faced as yet. What's our biggest single obstacle to acceptance for this scheme?"

There was a moment of silence. Terence said at length, "Well—ah—the risk of not getting back the return we're looking for! I mean, before we conduct our on-the-spot surveys we can't be certain that—"

Norman was shaking his head vigorously.

"It's not a monetary problem. It's a personal one."

"Whether we can sell it to the president," Consuela said.

"Correct." Norman leaned forward, injecting his voice with urgency. "I've said this before and I'm saying it again. You can't regard Beninia as a modern, Western, administrative unit. Elihu has dinned this into me until I think I've got the image, but I want to be certain we all share it. This is more like a colossal family with nearly a million members than it's like a nation in our sense. Let me refresh your memories about the way Elihu put it to the GT board. What President Obomi is looking for is a heritage to leave his people that will save them from being swallowed up in their powerful neighbours. He's not going to look at this in terms of hard cash, except insofar as economic security will contribute to general welfare. Talk to him about food, not money; talk about building schools, not processing prodgies into mechanics and technologists; talk about healthy children, not about mileage of sewer-pipes. You get the image? You're certain? Because what's important is to fulfil the president's hopes, not underpin the failing stocks in MAMP!"

He saw their nods, but knew it wasn't for their benefit he had added that final emphatic warning. It was for himself.

I haven't seen or sensed the proof of it yet, but Elihu swears to it and I think I have to believe him. It's only fair and just that sometimes making a fat profit should coincide with doing long-term good, and chances come too seldom for us to miss even one of them.

Now that he had finally seen Beninia, though, he was irrationally afraid that he had built himself an illusion at long range, and next week or next month he might cease to be able to accept that he was doing good. And if that happened there would be no other handy prop with which to underpin the shattered parody of purpose that justified his life.

A short while later he was terrified to realise that when he spoke that apparently clear injunction to himself and his colleagues all he had done was mouth the words. He had not, even he himself had not, taken in the full implications of the statement.

At the Presidential Palace a magnificently robed major-domo nearly seven feet high ushered them into an ante-room where black servants were bringing apéritifs and trays of tiny African hors-d'oeuvres to the assembled company: Mrs. Kitty Gbe, education; Dr. (Econ.) Ram Ibusa, finance; Dr. (PPE) Leon Elai, foreign affairs; and President Obomi.

Upon seeing whom, Elihu strode forward unceremoniously and embraced him. Drawing back, he said, "Zad! My God, this is terrible! You look ten years older and it's only been a couple of months!"

"I have no more gods," the president said. He drew back from the embrace and forced a smile. "It's wonderful to see you back here, anyway, Elihu. There was a moment when I feared—but never mind that, I have good doctors and they keep me going somehow. Will you not introduce me to your distinguished fellow countrymen?"

He blinked his surviving eye at Norman and his companions.

"Why—ah—of course," Elihu said. "Let me present first Dr. Norman Niblock House, of General Technics' board ..."

Norman held out his hand. "I'm honoured to meet you, sir," he said. "And I hope very much that we've worked out a way to solve some of your country's problems, and that you'll find it acceptable."

"Is it, Elihu?" President Obomi inquired, glancing at the ambassador.

"I've done my best to get you what you asked for," Elihu said.

"Thank you," Obomi smiled. "You must explain it to us over dinner, Dr. House. I know it's a shame to spoil good food with business, and my chef will be infuriated, but time is running out for me and—well, I'm sure you'll appreciate my plight."

He turned to Consuela as Elihu named her and ushered her forward, while Norman stepped back in a daze. Automatically he waved aside a tray of drinks that a servant held before him.

The matter can't be settled that easily! Surely there will have to be argument, persuasion, a selling job? . . . How about these ministers of his? Are they as prepared as he is to take someone else's word when the whole future of their nation is at stake?

He stared at them, the one plump woman and the two medium-sized men with their cheeks scarred in traditional designs, and could not detect anything less than satisfaction in their expressions. The truth began to sink through the sluggish water of his mind.

When Elihu compared Obomi to the head of a family, I thought he was just invoking an analogy. But this is how a family welcomes friends with a proposition to make—offers food and drink, deals first with personal matters, gets around to the irritating questions of business later. They aren't looking on us as foreign delegates: ambassador, representatives of a giant corporation. It's more as though . . .

At that point he almost lost track of the inspiration that was slowly emerging to awareness. He got it back in the voice of Chad Mulligan, asking whether anyone knew an interior decorator he could tell to do up an apartment for him with the latest modern gewgaws.

That's it.

He took a deep breath.

A country or a super-corporation had behaviour-patterns distinct from smaller groups, let alone individuals. Needing something done, they briefed diplomatic missions, or put out a contract to tender, or in some other fashion formalised and ritualised their action, and if they failed to prepare thoroughly enough there was calamity.

The President of Beninia, needing something done, had acted just the way Elihu described, but until this moment Norman had failed to grasp the exactness of the comparison—like a paterfamilias he had turned to an old friend whom he trusted and explained his needs, and when the friend came back with his expert proposal . . .

It was settled.

But it took him until the time of their departure, after midnight, to convince himself that he was right, and most of the following day to make his colleagues understand.

LETTER

"Dear Norman: This must be the first letter I've written in over three years. Talk about old habits dying hard ... I guess what I really want to do is set down some notes for an article, but addressing a mass audience I'm *sick* of. I've done it in books and journals and over TV and at lecture-meetings and I'll probably revert to that eventually because my skull threatens to burst with all the pressure inside, but the time I spent down in the gutter got me used to talking to *a* person, one at a time, and what I really need is to be able to turn into a million of myself and go out and have a million separate conversations because that's the only way you ever establish communications. The rest is just exposure to information, and why should anybody look at one wave on a sea?

"I really appreciate your loaning me the apt. Some people called up who hadn't heard you were due to leave, and if my books did nothing else they got me a modicum of notoriety, so I'm invited to sundry forthcoming events in your place. I'll try not to disgrace you, but by God it'll be tough.

"It's very curious coming back, at one blow, from the bottom to the top of this society we've constructed. It doesn't look any better from this angle. I remembered that opinion, but I guess the melancholia it generated when I first reached it is alien to my temperament. I know it was what inspired

Hipcrime—I felt getting outside the regular conformist orbit was the only route a sane man could take.

"But there isn't an outside. Talking about 'society's outcasts' or 'opting out' is so much whaledreck. The fact that we generate huge quantities of waste is all that allows people to go outside; they're benefiting from the superficial affluence which conformists use to alleviate boredom. In essence, using the term 'out' is as meaningless as trying to define a location outside the universe. There's no place for 'outside' to *be*.

"Where, for example, would your fellow Aframs, of the type who disclaim paleass-style living, find themselves if the society they so despise fell to bits? Hypothesise a plague which affects only people of Caucasian descent (as a matter of fact it exists, and the Chinese field-tested it in Macao about three to four years back, but the news was quietly stifled and I only heard about it by accident). Getting rid of us with our damnable arrogance wouldn't cure the human race of its hereditary diseases.

"I'm beginning to wonder whether I ought not to copy the example of those people out on the West Coast who seem to have taken up sabotage as a kind of hobby. Something is horribly wrong with our setup, and they're adopting a proper scientific technique to determine what. (I don't know if anyone has pointed this out before—I suspect not. I have a disgusting habit of jumping to private conclusions which makes me wonder if I'm really living in a fantasy world not shared by anyone else.)

"Said scientific technique is to alter one, and only one, of the variables at a time, to see what effect the change has on the total interaction and hence deduce the function of the force you're tampering with. Trouble is, of course, the impact is randomised, and no one is in a position to analyse the results.

"I guess maybe I'll try and do it, since there are no other volunteers. I'll head for California and start a study of the consequences of disorganising a city.

"No, that's a hitrip-type illusion, to be honest. I never will do it, nobody will do it. I'm too scared. It would be on a par with climbing down the shaft of a fusion generator to watch the plasma whiz around the bottle. Somebody send us a Martian anthropologist, for heaven's sake!

"Did you ever wonder how a doctor feels, faced with a disease he can't cure, which he knows is so contagious he's liable to catch it off the patients he can't help? That's me at this minute. Christ, I'm a rational being—of a sort—rational enough, at least, to see the symptoms of insanity around me. And I'm human, the same as the people I think of as victims when my guard drops. It's at least possible I'm even crazier than my fellows, whom I'm tempted to pity.

"There seems only one thing to do, and that's get drunk.
"Regards—Chad Mulligan"

continuity (26)

HERE COMES A CHOPPER

The government maintained its press liaison bureau on the top floor of a fifteen-storey block well towards the inland side of Gongilung. Having presented his papers of accreditation to a bland, unsmiling official, Donald wandered across the reed-mat flooring towards a window that give him a fine view over the city.

To his left, crowning a hill, rose the white towers of the university. He stared at them, wondering in which of them Sugaiguntung worked. What could have happened to a man like that to make him a mere stalking-horse for a propaganda claim? Long pressure, no doubt, was capable of caving in even a genius whose independence of thought had laid the foundations for his country's continuing prosperity.

And speaking of pressure . . .

From here, for the first time, he could see the physical evidence for something he had intellectually been aware of and never digested into his emotions—a parallel to the feeling he had had the night he walked out into the city he thought of as home and discovered he could trigger a riot by his presence.

With only a hundred-odd scattered islands to contain them, Yatakang boasted a population of two hundred and thirty millions. At an average of over two million people per island that meant this was one of the most crowded areas on the face of the globe. And from here he could see the crowding.

Even the sides of Grandfather Loa himself were dotted with huts, and winding paths linked them and led down to the shore.

He thought of Chad Mulligan's dictum about the pressure which made citizens of ancient Rome think that joining the eunuch priesthood of Cybele was an easy way out, and shuddered. Here was a modern counterpart: what pressure made people feel that scratching a living from the slopes of a live volcano was better than moving to a safe distance from its possible eruption?

A voice from behind said softly, "Mr. Hogan!"

He turned, to find the same official as before confronting him.

"Director Keteng will see you now," the man told him.

Director Keteng was a portly man with a chill manner who sat behind a rampart of communications equipment, as if he had decided to frame himself in every possible attribute of his rôle as patron of the transmission of information. It seemed to Donald that Bronwen had been right; the Solukarta government, for all its policy of eliminating superstitious attitudes, had managed only to transfer their scope from inanimate idols to living—and fallible—human beings. This office was a shrine, effectively, dedicated to a god not of news but of what the people were allowed to hear.

At a curt gesture, Donald sat down facing Keteng.

"You speak Yatakangi?"

"A little."

"It is not a popular language among American students. Why did you learn it?"

Donald repressed a desire to strangle this pompous fool in the cables of his own innumerable phones. He said in as mild a tone as he could muster, "I had the chance to learn a non-Indo-European language and chose Yatakangi because it was said to be very difficult."

"You had no special interest in Yatakang?"

Ah.

Lying fluently, Donald answered, "My college training was

in genetics, and the greatest living geneticist is one of your compatriots. That was one of the important reasons."

But flattery was not something this man reacted to. He shrugged. "You have never come here before. Now you do come, you are not exactly—shall we say?—in a great hurry. As a specialist in genetics, it is doubtless news of our genetic optimisation programme which attracts you."

"Yes, that's so. The public interest which the announcement has created in my country surprised my employers, so it was quite a long time before they took the decision to send me here. But—"

"Your countrymen do not believe the truth of our claim," Keteng said flatly. "Do you?"

Donald hesitated. "I hope that what you say can be done," he said at last. "It's been some years, though, since Professor Dr. Sugaiguntung published full details of his current work, so—"

"He had been engaged on secret research for the government," Keteng said. "Research of that kind in your country is mostly of two types: first, it is done so that one corporation can make more profit than its rivals, and you have spies who make a living out of uncovering company secrets and selling them to competing firms; or, second, it is concerned with more efficient ways to kill people. In this country it has been concerned with more efficient ways to have people born and grow up as intelligent adults able to make important contributions to their native land. Have you any opinion on these contrasting attitudes?"

"As a geneticist I cannot help admiring the programme you've announced and Professor Dr. Sugaiguntung's reputation is not the least significant warranty for its future success."

Donald hoped that equivocal reply did not betray the fury which Keteng's contemptuous tone had inspired in him.

"It is clear that you, like all Americans, do not approve of the existence of people who can do better than you at anything," Keteng grunted. "However, since your people have finally deigned to pay attention to this major breakthrough, it behoves me to facilitate your conveyance of the facts to them. I shall give you now a card of authorisation entitling you to the rights legally accorded to foreign reporters, a letter for the surgeons at Dedication University so that you may have your sterilisation operation conducted without charge, and a schedule of the press conferences arranged for the coming week. Is there anything else you wish to inquire about before you leave?"

"I was instructed to seek a personal interview with Sugaiguntung at the earliest opportunity," Donald said.

"The Professor Doctor is far too busy to spend time chatting with foreigners," Keteng snapped. "If you look at the programme I'm giving you, however, you'll see he is scheduled to make a public appearance at the press conference the day after tomorrow. You will have a chance to question him then along with other correspondents."

Donald's temper, fraying steadily under Keteng's purposeful gibes, now threatened to give way entirely.

"What keeps Sugaiguntung so busy?" he demanded. "No reasonable scientist would have allowed his programme to be made public until all the preliminary work was finished. This kind of thing makes people suspect that the work *isn't* finished—that the announcement is exaggerated, if not worse."

"No doubt," Keteng said with heavy irony, "that is the report you have been instructed to send back for the edification of your compatriots. You Americans lack subtlety. Go up to the university clinic and you'll see what keeps all of us 'so busy' in Yatakang! We haven't subsided into decadence of the sort that allows you to think in terms of finishing a job and then relaxing. We have plans that will occupy us for the next generation, because we don't accept the idea of 'good enough'. We aim at perfection. And the Professor Doctor shares that view. Is that all?"

No, it's not even the beginning. But Donald swallowed the words unuttered and rose obediently to his feet.

For the time being, in fact, it would make sense to treat all official suggestions as orders. Keteng had told him to go to the university and look it over for himself while he was there for the compulsory operation. He hailed a rixa immediately he left the building and told the driver that was where he wanted to go.

It was an uphill pull for the slim and wiry pedaller, but the journey would have had to be slow even down a one-in-three incline. All the approach streets in the vicinity of the university were cramfull of people. With a student body of over sixty thousand, Dedication University was an academic foundation of respectable size, but these people, Donald noted with interest, were not all students. They were of assorted ages from teens to borderline senility; one could tell where there was a particularly ancient member in the crowd because those surrounding him or her formed an ad-hoc bodyguard to keep away the press. Honouring old age was still a live tradition here.

After a while, as the rixa crept through the throng, he began to wonder whether any of these people were students. What few remarks he caught clearly—he did not want to lean out from the rixa and show himself off, drawing attention for his Caucasion features—made him think that they were visitors from other islands. If that was true, since at a rough guess there were ten or twelve thousands of them in the mile and a half he had traversed, there was a good solid basis for the official claims about a public welcome for the genetic programme.

For, dotted about here and there, he saw tired and dispirited youths and girls carrying slogan-boards, and all of them made reference to Sugaiguntung.

Hmmm . . . Going to the university in the hope of catching a glimpse of the great man?

Ahead loomed the wall enclosing the university precincts: a seven-foot barrier of pure white ornamented with the stylized whorls and strokes of Yatakangi calligraphy—widely employed, like Arabic script in Egypt, as a frieze-motif on all public buildings. In weatherproof enamels of red, blue, green and black, durable testaments to the greatness of Yatakang and the wisdom of Solukarta shut out the crowd of intending sightseers.

At the only gate he could see, there were not merely police on duty, their buff uniforms patched with sweat and the holster-flaps turned back from the butts of their bolt-guns, but also a number of young people wearing armbands of the national colours, red, blue and green, who seemed to be trying to address the surging visitors ranged all along the wall, pushing and exhorting. Straining his ears over the hub-bub, he thought he distinguished a few comprehensible phrases: "You must be patient—the doctor in your village will be told what to do—work hard and eat well or your children won't be healthy whatever we do . . ."

Donald gave a nod. This must be the kind of evidence on which Deirdre Kwa-Loop had based her statement about the consequences of disappointing the people of Yatakang.

The rixa-driver finally managed to deposit him close to the gate. To the policeman who came to investigate he showed his passport and the letter from Keteng authorising him to attend the university clinic without charge. The policeman read the document slowly and summoned two of the brassarded youths who passed nearby. With their aid, the eager crowd was kept back from the gate while it was briefly opened to pass Donald inside the wall.

A shareng-clad girl carrying a folded umbrella greeted him as he stepped out across a tiled platform. He was in a court with a fountain and a sand-garden in the middle, and cloisters all around it under pagodaed roofs. The cloisters were ramped so that on this, the entrance side of the court, their continuation was on a level below the street he had left; from under the platform he could hear a jabber of voices and many walking feet. Standing, or shoving a way through, there were at least a hundred students in his field of view.

"Good afternoon, sir," the girl said, using a stock Yata-kangi honorific from the root meaning "senior".

"Good afternoon," Donald replied, looking her over and noting that she also wore a brassard. "I am to go to the clinic here." He held out Keteng's letter.

"I will escort you, sir," the girl said. "I am on stranger guidance duty today. If at any time you need information ask someone wearing a band like this." She recited the words with a bright, forced smile, but her tone suggested tiredness. "Please come along."

She led him down a short steep flight of stairs to the cloisters passing beneath the platform, opening her umbrella as she did so. It served, apparently, as a gangway warning;

Donald saw several students tap their companions on the shoulder and move them aside.

The walk was a long one. He had arrived on the wrong side of the precinct. Without a guide he could have got hopelessly lost five or six times. Their route took them past more than a score of separate buildings, which the girl identified for him.

"Asiatic languages section—history section—oceanography section—geography and geology section . . ."

Donald paid little attention. He was far more interested in the young people he encountered. Keteng was right, he admitted reluctantly. There was an air of almost frantic busyness unlike the atmosphere at any American university he had ever visited. Even the few students he saw who were just standing about were talking—he heard them—about their studies, not about shiggies or what to do at the weekend.

"Biochemistry—genetics and tectogenetics—and here we are at the clinic!"

He came back to the here and now with a start. The girl was holding a door open for him; beyond it, he glimpsed the international pastel décor and sniffed the international disinfectant odour of a hospital.

"You said that that was the genetics department?" he demanded, gesturing to the last building they had passed.

"Yes, sir."

"The department in which the famous Dr. Sugaiguntung works?"

"Yes, sir." This time the girl's smile seemed not to be forced; there was genuine pride in her voice, too. "I have the honour to work in that department. I am studying directly under him."

Donald framed a flowery phrase including gratitude for her help, admiration of her beauty and a good deal about the plight of a foreign stranger. Contacting one of Sugaiguntung's own students would be an incredible stroke of good fortune!

But before he could speak she had folded her umbrella and marched briskly away. Twenty students had crowded between him and her by the time he reacted.

And there was a nurse eyeing him from inside the clinic's door, about to address him. He sighed. All he could do was mark down the salient features of the genetics building in his mind's eye, in case he got the chance to return here.

Making this quick final survey, he noticed something that struck him as strange about the passing students. There were many fewer smiles than one might expect among people who felt they were achieving great things. Nodding or waving to friends, they maintained looks of serious concentration.

And the girl who had brought him over from the gate had sounded tired.

Exhausted from being driven too hard? That would fit. Dedication was the outstanding one of all Yatakang's many centres of higher education; competition to get in must be fierce, with millions of families uging their children on.

The thought made him nervous. He wasn't used to being among people who admired dedication to the degree where they would wear themselves out. At home, it had become unfashionable. He turned to speak to the nurse and explain his reason for calling here.

Just as he did so, there was a scream. Jerking his gaze back, he saw a ripple run through the students closer to the genetics building, and something rose above the close-packed dark heads. Light glinted on it. He recognised its unique shape at once: a phang, the Yatakangi scimitar to which these people were so fond of comparing their sword-sweep of islands.

The single scream blurred into an unvoiced howling and a boy stumbled weeping out on to the immaculate face of the sand-garden that here too separated the white towers and the pagodaed walks. He was bleeding brilliant red from a slash across his chest. After two yards he fell and began to leak his life into the ground, writhing.

In sick amazement Donald envisaged himself as the carrier of a new and strange disease: the infective agent for riot and slaughter. He had only arrived in this city today, and . . .

One didn't have to have previous experience of this phenomenon. One knew, instantly. It was a fact of modern life—or death. Just a few yards from him, past a barrier to vision composed of abruptly panicking students, was a person who had gone over the edge of sanity and decided to run *amok*.

The demand it made on his perceptions was too great for him to take the whole scene in. He saw single facets of it: the bleeding boy, the fear-stricken survivors, and then a girl in a slashed shareng who stumbled out as the boy had done, making deep footprints in the sand-garden, holding one of her own small breasts against herself with her hand and staring down at the monstrous gash which had almost separated it from her body—too stunned to cry, able only to stare and suffer.

The mucker had chosen a perfect site to gather victims. Cramped into the walkway at the point where people leaving the high genetics building were hampered by doors, there was no need to seek targets, only to chop and chop. The blade swung into sight again, sowing spatters of blood on walls and faces and backs, and slammed down butcher-wise, cleaving meat and bone. Overhead, faces appeared at windows, and a long way off a buff-uniformed man with a drawn bolt-gun came in sight, fighting his way through the press of fright-crazed students. A third victim collapsed off the walkway like a jointless dummy, this one a youth with his brains spilling out to the day.

The mad yelling turned to a word, and the word was a name, and the name was—Donald didn't understand why— "Sugaiguntung!" Why should he be sent for? Was the mucker not human, but one of the modified orang-outangs he'd produced? The possibility seemed wild, but no wilder than the idea that he should have walked into a mucker directly upon his arrival.

Without realising what he was doing, he found himself trying to get a clear sight of the killer, and because he stepped away from the clinic door his retreat—available, not yet used—was cut off. A pack of terror-blind students crushed past him, one of them falling and unable to rise for an eternal moment, knocked back and back to sprawl on the pavement as careless legs and feet battered him.

Not a student. The fact impressed itself on Donald at the same instant as another, far more urgent. The person who had fallen was a man of middle age, growing stout, and—a rarity among Yatakangis—bald at the crown of his head. But that was a snapshot, meaningless. What counted was that the mucker had come after him.

Donald's mind chilled as though someone had cracked his skull like that of the dead boy a few yards distant, then poured it full of liquid helium. He felt a control and detachment like a cryogenic computer, and time ceased for a while to be linear and became pictorial.

This is a classic portrait of the mucker phenomenon. The victim is a thin youth a little above average height for his ethnic group, sallow, black-haired and dressed in conventional garb spotted with fresh blood. His eyes, which are black-irised, are fixed wide open, and the pupils are doubtless dilated though the contrast is too low for me to see them. His mouth is also open and his chin is running with saliva. There is a little froth on the left cheek. His breathing is violent and exhalation is accompanied by a grunt—haarrgh ow haarrgh ow! His muscular tensions are maximised; his right sleeve has split from the pressure of the biceps. He has a convulsive grip on his phang and all his knuckles are brightly pale against his otherwise sallow skin. His legs are bowed and his feet planted firmly apart like a sumo wrestler's when confronting an opponent. He has a conspicuous erection. He is in a berserk frame of reference and will not feel any pain.

With that realisation, a question came—what in God's name am I to do?—and time re-started.

The phang whistled and stung Donald's face with drops of blood hurled at him so fast he could feel them like gale-driven needles of rain. He jumped back, the man on the ground made another attempt to get up, the mucker almost lost balance cancelling the violence of the blow he had aimed at Donald and diverted the blade to the man on the ground and with the very tip of it managed to write a line of pain across his bumping buttocks.

Weapon.

Someone had said that to Donald Hogan: a variant Donald Hogan, the Mark II man who had learned nearly a thousand different ways to end a human life.

Never go against an armed man without a weapon if there's one in reach. If there's not one in reach, get in reach of one!

There was nothing to snatch and wield. There was a solid wall, a tiled pavement, pillars anchored to carry a heavy roof, and a sterile oriental garden without a living tree from which to tear a whip-like twig.

And the mucker was about to kill the prostrate man.

The phang rose in a high energy-profligate arc to be slammed down and divide the body like a pig's dead carcase. Through the glass door of the clinic whitened faces paler than any Asiatic's ought to be gazed fascinated, hypnotised, frozen to stillness with horror.

Donald was alone on a fifty-foot stretch of the walkway, and no one was close bar the man on the ground, the injured in the sand-garden, and the mucker.

The sword was at the apex of its swing and he launched himself off the balls of his feet. He hit the mucker with his shoulder and it was like charging a wooden statue, the flesh was so rigid with insanity. It was too late to countermand the decision to slash, but the man went off balance as Donald passed behind him, one hand cushioning his collision with the wall and diverting him like a bounced ball to a point out of reach. The phang met tiles, not flesh, and rang with a metal scream and turned in the mucker's hand and lost him his dry grip, making the hilt slippery with blood, and shed some of the sharpness of its edge. Also the jar made the steel-stiff muscles of the man's arm disobey him for a second.

Weapon.

In the middle of the sand-garden, five rocks smoothed by water into curves and holes. He went for them, remembering where the mucker had been and trying to calculate so that he could throw without aiming when he got to the little pile. The nearest was heavier than it looked and that wasted his calculations. The flung rock passed the mucker at shoulder level and fell to the floor and the mucker raised the phang again and made to spring straight at Donald—

And his foot landed on the rounded stone and slid from under him.

There was only one other rock he could hope to throw: a whitish one with a hole to hold it by weighing seven or eight pounds. He lobbed it at the mucker's groin, exposed by the parting of his legs in a skidding fall, and it and the mucker landed on the floor together, hammering his testicles against the pavement.

Incapable of feeling pain in his present state, the mucker was not immune to the reflex consequences of a blow in the genitals or on the coccyx. His breath stopped from the latter, and there seemed to be universal silence, for Donald had lost the power to recognise anything but that ghastly gulp and grunt.

Yet he was superoxygenated by now, of course. He would not miss the ability to fill and empty his lungs . . .

He clawed the sword back from where it had fallen and Donald threw a handful of sand in his eyes while he was spending time on that. The blade whistled again, and this time touched Donald on the right forearm with a sting like a bee.

Weapon.

He had used up what there was: two rocks, sand. The sand had blinded only one of the mucker's eyes and losing parallax would not bother him. He was up on his feet, armed, about to jump at Donald from the foot-higher vantage of the walkway.

Weapon.

Donald saw it. And damn them.

The mucker made his leap and Donald fell sideways and the phang bit into sand and was slow in recovery. (It was as though the man were an extension of the weapon, not the weapon of the man.) He rolled and kicked and his shod foot met the mucker's elbow just above the joint and opened his fingers, making him release the phang. A second kick, badly aimed but helpful enough, put the hilt out of reach and the mucker recovered his breathing reflex and was able to scream a curse and went for the weapon without caring what part of it he grasped and took the blade, not the hilt, and cut open two of his own fingers and picked it up and threw it at Donald who had to duck the whirling arc of steel and threw himself after it and Donald got one leg under him and put his head down and met the mucker's nose and mouth with the crown of his own head and chopped inwards with both hands at the sides of the mucker's waist and used all the strength in the leg which was beneath him to lift himself off the ground with the sand shifting and threatening to betray him and pitch forward with his head still down and butt the mucker's nose flat against his face and his head against the providentially placed rocks in the middle of the sand-garden.

But that's not my weapon.

He felt momentarily stupid. The mucker wasn't fighting back. He was underneath and gone limp and at his nape, which was in Donald's field of vision about as close as he could take a proper focus, there was a big rock that he must have hit as he tumbled backward.

But I had a weapon, didn't I?

A little foggily he remembered what it was, and rose to his feet and brought the mucker with him and got up over the edge of the walkway and ignored the man with the cut buttocks lying near the glass door of the clinic and likewise the people behind it who were scattering backwards with exclamations of dismay and used his weapon.

Which was, as he had been taught, a sheet of glass that could be smashed to make cutting edges.

He saw without interest as he turned the mucker over that there was already a smear of blood on his nape from the contusion the rock had caused. Then he used the head as a hammer and broke the door and cut the man's throat on one of the pieces that remained in the frame.

He said in Yatakangi to the frightened little people beyond the door, "You pig-fucking yellow cowards. You shit-eating children born from a buggered arsehole. You piss-coloured piles of carrion. You dung-flies. You prickless and ball-lacking catamites. You street-walking widows who never had a man except for money. You cock-sucking blood-licking arse-kissing defilers of sacred shrines, you brainless heartless gutless cockless offspring of an imbecile and a deformed cow, you flea-bitten child-robbers who poisoned your fathers and raped your mothers and sold your sisters to the Dutch and carved up your brothers for sale in a butcher's shop, you gutter-hugging traders in second-hand excrement, why didn't *you* do anything about this?"

And after that he realised that he was carrying a corpse and he had cut both his hands so that he could not tell whether the blood dripping down his chest was his own or the mucker's and he understood what he had just done and he let the body fall and crumbled on top of it and began to cry.

the happening world (12)

THE GENERAL FEELING

"You do realise what it means, don't you? In effect, all
"You do realise what it means, don't you? In effect, all
"You do realise what it means, don't you? In effect, all
our children are going to be handicapped!"
our children are going to be handicapped!"
our children are going to be handicapped!"
"What good are all our gadgets going to be when we're up
"What good are all our gadgets going to be when we're up
"What good are all our gadgets going to be when we're up
against people who can think better than us?"
against people who can think better than us?"
against people who can think better than us?"
"You know what you can do with the Eugenics Board, don't
"You know what you can do with the Eugenics Board, don't
"You know what you can do with the Eugenics Board, don't
you? You can—"
you? You can—"
you? You can—"
"It's going to reduce us, relatively speaking, to being
"It's going to reduce us, relatively speaking, to being
"It's going to reduce us, relatively speaking, to being
morons and cripples."
morons and cripples."
morons and cripples."

"Did you see that Engrelay Satelserv decided to send an
"Did you see that Engrelay Satelserv decided to send an
"Did you see that Engrelay Satelserv decided to send an
expert in genetics to Yatakang?"
expert in genetics to Yatakang?"
expert in genetics to Yatakang?"

"Well, if a company like that is taking it so seriously
"Well, if a company like that is taking it so seriously
"Well, if a company like that is taking it so seriously
there must be something in it."
there must be something in it."
there must be something in it."

"But the government seems to be trying to convince people
"But the government seems to be trying to convince people
"But the government seems to be trying to convince people
it's a lie."
it's a lie."
it's a lie."

"What that means is that they haven't got the skill to
"What that means is that they haven't got the skill to
"What that means is that they haven't got the skill to
do the same for us."
do the same for us!"
DO THE SAME FOR US!"

"DO THE SAME FOR US!"
"DO THE SAME FOR US!"
"DO THE SAME FOR US!"
"DO THE SAME FOR US!"
"DO THE SAME FOR US!"

(UNFAIR   Term applied to advantages enjoyed by other
people which we tried to cheat them out of and didn't manage.
See also DISHONESTY, SNEAKY, UNDERHAND and
JUST LUCKY I GUESS.

—*The Hipcrime Vocab* by Chad C. Mulligan)

continuity (27)

MANSCAPE

Near the road, high grass flushed green with summer wet, set with low bushes, punctuated with trees. Tethered on expensive chains because they could gnaw through rope or leather, goats strained to crop the tree-bark and kill the trees though there was plenty of grazing closer to the pegs they circled. Chains apart, the road seemed like the only human intrusion into a beast-plant universe, and not the road as such because wild nature was reclaiming it, pitting its surface with holes that held bowlfuls of mud, but its idea of straightness.

Yet the manufactures of man came into view and went again. Every mile or two there were plots of ground trenched for vegetables surrounding a hamlet built in traditional Beninian style of timber and thatch. Some of the wealthier families' homes were turtle-plated in a riot of colours, the owners having taken old cans, oil-drums, even sheets of metal from abandoned cars, and after flattening them with mallets lapped them together as carefully as medieval armour to protect the wood against wet, rot and termites.

Maps of the district had been kept up to date by a makeshift system involving as much gossip and rumour as actual surveying, but even if they had been revised last week by a team of UN geographers Norman would still have found it hard to relate that out there with this flapping on his knee.

He had to say painfully to himself, "Those two hills must correspond to these markings, so this is where they would mine river-clay and bake it into porous filters for the plastics plant at—where?—Bephloti . . ."

The insect humming of the engine beneath their vehicle's floor droned down to a grumble. Steering, Gideon Horsfall said, "Sheeting hole, I hoped we'd make it clear to Lalendi before I had to swap cylinders. I'll pull down off the road when we get around the bend."

Around the bend there was another of the interchangeable hamlets, except that this was one of the fourteen per cent of the country's villages which possessed a school and a clinic. It was the wrong day for the clinic, a plain white concrete hut with large-lettered signs in English and Shinka, but the school was busy. As yet, in this region, the summer rains were only intermittent; the full drenching flow would follow in three weeks. Accordingly the teacher—a fat young man with a fan and spectacles of an old-fashioned pattern—was conducting his class under a grove of low trees. They were boys and girls from about six to twelve, clutching UN-issued plastic primers and trying not to let themselves be distracted by the appearance of the car.

It wasn't yet raining, but it was horribly humid. Norman, clammy from head to toe, thought about the energy required to get out and stand up. He asked Gideon whether he needed help in swapping cylinders. Twisting around to take a pair of fresh ones—one hydrogen, one oxygen—from a crate on the back seat, Gideon declined the offer.

But Norman got out anyway, and found he was looking at the verandah-like frontage of a house on which a small group of women were assembled, and one man, middle-aged, very thin, who lay among them on a low trestle-table. They were wringing cloths in buckets of water and wiping his skin, and he seemed to be making no effort to co-operate.

A little puzzled, he asked Gideon, "What's the matter over there? Is the man ill?"

Gideon didn't look at once. He dropped the cylinder-tray at the back of the car, unclipped and reconnected the gas-hoses, and gathered up the empties for return to store before following Norman's gesture.

"Ill? No, dead," he said absently, and went to put the cylinders inside the car.

One of the older pupils of the school, squatting cross-legged at the back of the class, raised his hand and asked something of the teacher.

"Is something wrong?" Gideon demanded, realising that Norman had made no move to get back in the car.

"Not really," Norman said after a pause. "It's just that I . . . Well, you see, I've never seen a corpse before."

"It doesn't look any different from a living person," Gideon said. "Except it doesn't move, and it doesn't suffer. The hole, I was afraid of that. Do you mind being a visual aid to the schoolmaster for five minutes?"

The women had finished their task of washing the corpse; they poured out the dirty water on the ground and a piglet came over to lap at a puddle it formed. From the long poles supporting the thatch over the verandah, a few chickens solemnly looked down. One of the women fetched a galvanised tub full of something sticky and white and began to daub the corpse's face, using a bundle of hen's feathers tied on a twig.

"What's that for?" Norman asked Gideon.

"What? Oh, the white paint? Relic of early missionary interference, I gather. All the pictures of saints and angels they saw when they were being converted to Christianity had white skins, so they decided to give their dead a better chance of admission to heaven."

The entire class of children rose to their feet and waited for the teacher to walk past, take station at their head, and lead them over towards the car.

"Good morning, gentlemen," the fat young man said affably. "My class has requested permission to put a few questions to you. Since they have little chance to travel about themselves, perhaps you'd indulge them."

"Certainly," Gideon said with only the trace of a sigh.

"Thanks awfully. First, may we know where you come from?" The teacher turned and held out his hand expectantly to one of the older pupils, who gave him a rolled map in bright colours and simplified outlines. Those children who were not too much attracted by the car or the preparation of the corpse craned to see whereabouts in the world Gideon would point to.

When his finger stabbed down in the area of New York, there was a concerted sigh.

"Ah, you're American!" the teacher said. "Sarah, we learned about America, didn't we? What do you know of that great country so far away?"

A serious-mannered girl of thirteen or so, one of the oldest pupils, said, "America has over four hundred million people. Some of them are brown like us but most of them are Cock . . ."

She hesitated.

"*Cauc* . . ." corrected the teacher.

"*Caucasian*," Sarah managed. "The capital is Washingham—"

"Washing—?"

"Washing*ton*. There are fifty-two states. At first there were thirteen but now there are four times that number. America is very rich and powerful and it sends us good seed for planting, new kinds of chickens and cows which are better than the ones we used to have, and lots of medicines and disinfectants to keep us healthy."

She suddenly smiled and gave a little skip of pleasure at her own success in the brief recitation.

"Very good," Gideon approved.

A boy next to Sarah, about her own age, raised his hand. "I should like to ask you, sir—"

Norman felt inclined to let his mind wander. No doubt this was one of the regular public-relations jobs Gideon had to cope with when he went about the country in this incredibly informal manner—which struck Norman as absurd: the First Secretary of the U. S. Embassy stopping off at random in an isolated village and chatting with children! But he had his mind too full trying to organise his perceptions.

He had discovered why organising them was so difficult a few seconds ago. The sight of a corpse being made ready for burial, matter-of-factly in the view of everyone, was a shock to him. In sterile modern America one was intellectually aware that death could be a public event, from heart-failure or more messily through the intervention of a mucker, but hardly anyone had actually seen a mucker on the rampage, and emotionally and for all daily purposes one assumed it was something that took place tidily in a hospital out of sight of everyone except experts trained to handle human meat.

But people do die.

In the same way, Beninia was a continuing shock. Taken in by eye and ear, the canned information supplied by Shalmaneser and the GT library was manipulable, digestible, of a familiar sort. Confronted with language, smell, local diet, the sticky hot early-summer air, the clutch of mud around his shoes, he was in the same plight as a Bushman trying to make sense of a photograph, exhausted by the effort to bridge the gap between pre-known symbol and present actuality.

Yet it had to be done. Isolated in the air-conditioned GT tower, one might juggle for a thousand years with data from computers and pattern them into a million beautiful logical arrays. But you had to get out on the ground and see if the data were accurate before you could put over the programming switches on Shalmaneser from "hypothetical" to "real".

His attention shot back to here and now as though a similar switch had been pulled in his own mind. He had heard, in memory, the rest of the boy's question.

"—how the Chinese can do so much damage in California!"

Gideon was looking baffled. "I'm afraid I don't quite follow you," he said after a moment.

"You must forgive the child, sir," the teacher said, plainly embarrassed. "It's not the most tactful subject—"

"I'll answer any question, tactless or not," Gideon said. "I didn't quite follow, that's all."

"Well, sir," the boy said, "we have a television set here, and teacher makes us older ones watch the news programme after school before we walk home, so we see a lot about America. And there's often a piece about damage done by Chinese infiltrators in California. But if Americans are either like you, or like English people, and the Chinese are like what we see on television, with their funny eyes and different skins, why can't you recognise and catch them?"

"I get the point," Norman said gruffly. "Like me to handle that, Gideon?" He pushed himself away from the roof of the car where he had been leaning and approached the group of children, his eyes on the questioner. Not more than thirteen at the oldest, yet he had phrased his inquiry in first-class English with a slight British inflection. Learned off one of the Common Europe news-commentators, probably. Still, it was an achievement at his age.

"What's your name, prodgy?"

"Simon, sir. Simon Bethakazi."

"Well, Simon, you're probably old enough by now to know how it feels when you do something silly you wouldn't like other people to find out about. Not because you'd be punished, but because people would laugh at you—or because they thought of you as one of the cleverest boys in the school and a clever boy oughtn't to have done such a stupid thing. Catch?"

Simon nodded, face very intent.

"Only sometimes things happen which are too big to hide. Suppose you—hmmm! Suppose you knocked over a jug of milk and that was all the milk in the house? And it was your fault but you'd been doing something silly to make it happen, like seeing if you could hang by your feet from the rafters."

Simon looked blank for a second and the teacher, smiling, said something in Shinka. His face cleared and he had to repress a grin.

"Well—you might try and put the blame on someone else . . . No, you wouldn't do that, I'm sure; you're a good boy. You might try and blame it on a pig that tripped you up, or a chicken that startled you and made you fall over.

"The Chinese would have to be very clever indeed to do all the damage they're supposed to. But because America is a big and rich and proud country we don't like admitting that there are some people who aren't happy—who are so unhappy, in fact, they want to change the way things are run. But there are only a few of them, not enough to make the changes happen. So they lose their tempers and they break things, same as people do anywhere.

"And there are some other people who would also like to change things, but who haven't got around to using bombs yet, or setting houses on fire. If they thought there were many more like themselves, they might decide to start too. So we like to let it be thought that it's really someone else's fault. Do you understand?"

"It may be a trifle sophisticated for him," the teacher said aside to Norman.

"No, I understand." Simon was emphatic. "I've *seen* somebody lose his temper. It was when I went to stay with my cousin in the north last year. I saw an Inoko lady and gentleman having a quarrel."

Incredulous words rose to Norman's lips. Before he could utter them, however, Gideon had coughed politely.

"If you'll excuse us, we have to get on our way," he said.

"Of course," the teacher beamed. "Many thanks for your kindness. Class, three cheers for our visitors! Hip hip—"

Back on the road, Norman said, "And what would State think of that—uh—presentation?"

"It was honest," Gideon said with a shrug. "It's hardly what they'll hear over the TV, but it's honest."

Norman hesitated. "There was something I wanted to ask, but it seems foolish ... The hole! Why was young Simon so eager to stress that he'd seen someone lose his temper?"

"That's a very bright kid. And sophisticated."

"Anyone could see he's no simpleton! But I asked—"

"He could say that in English. He couldn't have said it in Shinka, which is his native language, and that's good for a boy barely into his teens, isn't it?"

Norman shook his head in bewilderment.

"Ask this linguist—what's his name? The one you brought with you."

"Derek Quimby."

"Ah-hah. Ask him if you can express the idea of losing your temper in Shinka. You can't. You can only use the word which means 'insane'."

"But—"

"I'm telling you." Gideon guided the car around a wide curve, seeking a route between potholes. "I don't speak the language well myself, but I can get along. Facts are: you can say 'annoyed' or even 'exasperated', but both those words came originally from roots meaning 'creditor'. Someone you get angry with owes you an apology in the same way you're owed money or a cow. You can say 'crazy' and put one of two modifiers on the front of it—either the root for 'amusing' or the root for 'tears'. In the latter case, you're talking about someone who's hopelessly out of his mind, sick, to be tended and cleaned up after. In the former, you're inviting people to laugh at someone who's lost his temper, but will return to normal sooner or later."

"They regard anger as being literal insanity?"

"They don't regard it as being important enough to have a separate word to label it, that's all I can say."

"But people must lose their tempers occasionally!"

"Of course they do. I've even seen Zad lose his temper. But that wasn't *at* anybody—it was the day his doctors told him he must retire or die. Did him a power of good, too, like any catharsis. What they don't do is go crazy-mad and smash things that they'll regret later. I've been here more than two years and I haven't seen a parent hit a child. I haven't seen a child hit another child. Trip him over, yes, or jump out at him from around a corner and pretend to be a leopard. You know what the Mandingo used to say about the Shinka in the old days?"

Norman gave a slow nod. "They were magicians who could steal the heart out of a warrior."

"Right. And the way they do it is by dodging passion. I don't know how they manage it, but there's the record. A thousand or more years in the same spot, not bothering anyone, and like I said the day you arrived they swallowed up the Holaini and the Inoko and Kpala immigrants . . . Shall I tell you something you really won't believe?"

"You already did."

"I mean *really*. Laying out that corpse and painting its face white reminded me. The first Christian missionary to come here was a Spanish friar called Domingo Rey. You know the Spanish had a trading post not far from Port Mey, an outstation for Fernando Po? There's a marker on the site you could go and look at if you have time.

"Anyway, this friar did a very un-Christian thing. He went out of his mind and drowned himself after he'd been here seven years. He was convinced he'd been trapped by Satan. He'd learned enough Shinka to start preaching, and started off with some of the parables and highlights of the gospel, and to his dismay the people he talked to said no, you've got that wrong, it wasn't anyone far away called Jesus but our own man Begi who did that. You know about Begi?"

"I don't think I do," Norman said after a pause.

"Any briefing on Beninia that leaves Begi out of account isn't worth having," Gideon grunted. "I guess you'd call him a folk-hero, a sort of Jack character, or maybe like this Anancy that you find in the West Indies. His name apparently means 'winter-born', and they say he always used to carry a blunt spear and a shield with a hole in it—to look through. And as you might expect the stories about him were more to the Shinka taste than those about Jesus.

"The one which allegedly drove the poor friar out of his skull—want to hear it?"

"Sure, go ahead."

Gideon eased the car down a particularly rutted stretch of road, avoiding potholes. "Well, the stories say he'd reached a ripe old age and enormous popular eseem because he'd made wizards look foolish and overcome a sea-monster and even got the better of his grandfather's ghost, so everybody used to bring problems to him. And one time the boss Holaini, the Emir—which the Shinka turned into 'Omee', incidentally, meaning 'indigestion'; they love bad puns—the Emir, anyway, got sick of the way the Shinka kept outsmarting their lords and masters. Like for instance they'd imposed a swingeing tax and people went to Begi and complained, and he said why don't you drive your fertile cows into the Holaini bull-pens and give them back their own calves when you pay the tax? Which sort of tickled their sense of humour. And, by the way, he said, according to the story, 'Give the Emir what belongs to the Emir!' "

"Render unto Caesar?" Norman muttered.

"You've hit it. So finally the Emir sent messengers to demand who was playing these underhand tricks, and Begi owned up and off he went, and the Emir pegged him out on an anthill in the traditional style. And when his old blind father the chief came to visit him in his last moments, he said the Shinka shouldn't hold his death against the Holaini because they were too stupid to see the point of what he had said to them."

"Father, forgive them, for they know not what they do?"

"Your being raised as a Baptist saves me explaining a lot of things to you, doesn't it? I guess if Friar Rey had been a bit more sophisticated he'd have thought of the possibility that some Christian legends had reached here on the grapevine, like the story of Buddha is supposed to have got to Rome and led to his being canonised as St. Josaphat—you heard that one? But I guess the climate of ideas wasn't on his side in those days.

"Well, what it boils down to is that Begi already enshrined the Shinka concept of a perfect man, tolerant, level-headed, witty—the whole shtick. It wasn't till some more broad-minded missionary hit on the notion of saying that Begi was a prophet sent to the Shinka that Christianity made any progress here. And nowadays you'll hear Shinkas saying that Begi had better sense than Jesus because he brought his teaching to people who understood it, while Jesus over-reached himself and preached to people like the British who can't have understood or they wouldn't behave as they do."

There was a period of silence except for the humming of the motor and occasional complaints from the suspension. At last Norman said, "I told you I'd never seen a dead body before. I don't know how I could have said that." He swallowed enormously, his throat seeming to be blocked against the admission he was trying to make. "Because . . . Well, the other day I *killed* somebody."

"What? Who?"

"A Divine Daughter. She took an axe to Shalmaneser. She'd already chopped the hand off one of our technicians."

Gideon thought that over. He said eventually, "There's a Shinka proverb."

"What?"

"You have many years to live—do things you will be proud to remember when you're old."

THE OLD LADY UNDER THE JUGGERNAUT

The decision to schedule it for clearance and development
Was taken at a meeting with all the due formality
By the people's democratically elected representatives
None of whom had been inside—only to the doorstep
Briefly during canvassing for the last election
Which was when they smelt the smell and knew they didn't
   like it.

A junior executive from the Health Department
Said it was unthinkable that children and old people
Should nowadays exist in such Victorian squalor.
He named fires with open flames, he named splintered
   wooden floorboards,
Windows with single panes, toilets without airtight lids.
Committee members shuddered and agreed on the removal.

Notices were sent to sixty-seven heads of families—
The list compiled from records of electoral returns.
A date was fixed for transfer to brand-new accommodation.
Objections could be entered as the law demanded.
If the number of objections exceeded thirty-three per cent
The Minister of Housing would arrange a public hearing.

Not included in the data was a woman called Grace Rowley.
In accordance with instructions the electoral computer
Having failed to register her form for three successive years
Marked her as non-resident, presumed removed or dead.
However, to be certain, it did address her notice.
No answer was recorded before the scheduled date.

*

It happened to be the morning of her seventy-seventh
   birthday.
She awoke to noises that she had never heard in her life.
There were crashes and landslide sounds and engines
   roaring.
When she got up, frightened, and put on her greasy coat
Over the unwashed underclothes she always slept in,
She found two strange men going through her other room.

The passing years had filled it with mementoes of a lifetime:
Shoes that had been fashionable when she was a pretty girl,
A gift from a man she had often wished she'd married,
The first edition of a book that later sold a million,
A cracked guitar to which she had once sung lovesongs,
A Piaf record bought during Piaf's heyday.

A voice said, "Christ, Charlie, this is worth a fortune."
Wrapping an ornament, a newspaper informed him
Of the triumphant success of the first manned Moon-
   landing.
A voice said, "Christ, Charlie, did you ever see such junk?"
Names were strewn broadcast: Dylan, Brassens, Aldous
   Huxley, Rauschenberg, Beethoven, Forster, Mailer,
   Palestrina . . .

Like silt deposited by the river of time in oozy layers
The sludgy heritage of passing fashion-generations
Testified to the contact of Miss Rowley with her world.
And somehow the strain . . . old age . . . the contact broke,
   anyway.

Looking up and suddenly discovering her staring at them,
The men, who were both young, thought, "Oh my God.
  Oh my God."

*

With the authority of the committee, democratically elected,
They took away Grace Rowley and they put her in a Home.
By authority of the committee, democratically elected,
They auctioned her belongings apart from her clothing
And prosperous antique dealers purchased some of it
And sold at huge profit to collectors and even museums.

When the question next came up of excessive public outlay
On the maintenance in council accommodations of senior
  citizens,
It was explained that Miss Rowley's belongings when sold
Had more than defrayed the cost of accommodating her
Because she had lived for only another month, and
  moreover
A medical school had saved them the price of a funeral.

continuity (28)

FROM HERE ON DOWN IT'S UPHILL ALL THE WAY

Someone fetched a diadermic syringe and shot through the blood masking Donald's wrist, wishing on him a premature night. When he awoke it was real night; darkness lay on the windows of the room where he found himself, as complete as if the glass had been magicked to an ebony mirror. His cut hands had been dressed and his bruises swabbed with something to reduce their ache. Watching by him in the glow of a self-luminous wall-panel was a very small girl in nurse's coverall and sterile mask.

It was raining again. He heard the sound of it on the walls, soft as a slack drum. He moved his hands and felt the faint remaining sting from all the many gashes he had inflicted on himself, and his vision turned the pure red of new blood and he moaned.

Prepared, the girl gave him another shot, into the muscles of his exposed upper arm, presumably a trank of some kind. It left him with a dull ache, but the horror declined to the bearable intensity of nightmare. She counted his pulse while it was taking effect and he lay there not objecting. He could feel the pulse himself against her fingertips. When it was down to a rate he judged to be in the middle seventies she rose and went to the door.

Through it he heard raised voices, a man's and a woman's, harshly arguing. The man said he wanted to go in and the woman said he would have to wait no matter who he was. Eventually she won and marched into Donald's room.

She was big for a Yatakangi, about five feet seven and solid, not wearing a shareng but a man's tunic and breeches and boots that thumped on the plastic floor. Her hair was cut short and she carried a recorder with a pistol grip. Behind her followed two buff-uniformed policemen who combined to close the door and shut out the nurse and the other, unseen speaker.

"You're feeling better?" the woman asked.

Donald nodded.

"Good. Our medical treatment is of the highest standard, of course." She gestured to one of the policemen, who seized a chair and placed it where she could face the bed. "I am State Police Superintendent Totilung. It is necessary for me to ask you some questions."

"Before charging me with murder, I suppose," Donald said.

"If that is an American joke please take notice that I cannot spare the time for social chatter." Totilung settled her big firm buttocks on the narrow seat and pointed the recorder at him like the muzzle of a blunderbuss.

"Who was he?" Donald said suddenly.

"What?"

"The man I killed—who was he?"

Totilung bit back a sharp retort, probably scheduled to have been along the lines, "I'm asking the questions, not you!" She said with ill grace, "A student who had been overworking. His family expected too much of him, they say."

I thought it must be something like that. Donald knuckled his temples with his bandaged fists. "Go ahead, Superintendent," he sighed. "What can I tell you that the witnesses can't? There were plenty of people watching."

"True. Constable Song was among them"—she gestured at one of the policemen accompanying her—"but the crowd prevented him getting a clear shot at the man who ran *amok.*"

"I remember," Donald said. "I caught a glimpse of him trying to get along the walkway." The trank kept his voice under control; without it he thought he would have screamed.

I didn't have to kill him. He was already unconscious!

"All this is wasting time," Totilung said. "Now! You are Donald Hogan, a reporter working for English Language Relay Satellite Service?"

"Ah—yes."

"You came to the university ostensibly to undergo the sterilisation compulsory for foreigners?" She didn't wait for an answer, but added, "That has been attended to, by the way."

Donald's hand, against his will, leapt to his genitals. Unsmiling, Totilung said, "There will be no scar or discomfort. And they assure me that an operation to reverse the effect would definitely be successful."

Donald withdrew his hand like a guilty child caught playing with himself. He said angrily, "Why bother to question me? You know things about me that I don't know myself!"

Totilung ignored that. She said, "We examined your papers and other belongings. Also your body. You are physically in good health with some trace of a stimulant drug no doubt taken to counteract the time-gain on your flight from America—correct?"

Donald gave a wary nod. Luckily there was a jar of just such a drug in his baggage at the hotel. But he had taken none of it; the trace they had detected must be the last residue of what he had been given during eptification.

"In our records there has never been a case of an unarmed man overcoming a mucker before," Totilung said. "Of course, we have very few muckers, and the enlightened system under which we now live is helping to reduce the number still further." She included that assertion without much conviction, as though it were a required propaganda claim. "However, we have made theoretical studies of such people, and our experts conclude that the reaction of a mucker, not being subject to rational judgment, are faster than those of a person in a normal state of mind. Yet I have to accept what many witnesses tell me: you defeated one much younger than yourself and what's more armed with a phang. So what I want to know it this—what makes you such an efficient killing machine?"

Nobody had told Donald how to answer that question. It had apparently not occurred to those who had trained him that his talent might be revealed at a time and place he had not chosen. He said weakly, "I—I don't know."

"Are you a trained athlete? Some of our psychologists believe that athletes who break records can voluntarily enter a berserk state."

"No—uh—no, I'm not. I keep myself in good shape, but that's all."

"And you were not drugged, and you were not in such a blind rage that you might be regarded as *amok* yourself. This—"

"I think I was," Donald said.

"What?"

"I think I was in a blind rage. I saw all these people running away from one boy just because he had a sword. And there was this man lying on the ground who was trying to get up and couldn't make it and in another minute he'd have been dead as well." He forced himself to an upright position and glared at Totilung.

"It made me ashamed—*that's* what did it! It made me ashamed to see them running to save their own skins and not one trying to help the man on the ground!"

Hurt by the gibe because it came from a foreigner, and worse yet from a round-eye, Totilung said stiffly, "But when a mucker—".

"Yes, someone had told them you can't cope with a mucker! But I did it, didn't I? I got so furious at seeing this herd of cowards, I went for him. I *must* have been mad with rage, or . . ."

He checked himself. Totilung said, "Go on. Say what you were going to say."

"Or else I wouldn't have pushed him through the glass door." Nausea boiled up his stomach at the memory.

Totiling sat quite still for a good thirty seconds, her square masculine face giving no clue to her thoughts. At last she switched off the recorder and rose.

"There is a lot more I should like to know," she said. "But

as things are ..." She shrugged. "I will add only a word of warning."

"What?"

"We in Yatakang do not much care for expert assassins who drop in from other countries. From now on until you leave I shall make sure that you are watched—partly because of what you have done, much more because of what you may be going to do."

She turned on her heel and Constable Song leapt to open the door for her. Across the threshold as she went out Donald heard her say to someone, "All right, you can see him now."

Yatakangi medical treatment might have helped Donald's abused body; it couldn't reach in to salve his horrified mind. Thirty-four years of easygoing existence had not pepared him to hear someone call him an expert assassin and realise it was a true description. Distracted, he barely paid attention when his new visitor came in accompanied by the same nurse he had found by his bed on waking.

"Mr. Hogan?" the man said, and repeated, "Mr. Hogan ...?"

Donald forced his head to turn, and recognised the man with the bald crown whose life he had saved from the mucker. Upright instead of sprawling, he now had a tantalising air of familiarity, as though long ago his face had appeared on a TV screen.

He uttered a mechanical greeting in Yatakangi. The man responded in good English. "Please, let me speak your language—it's a long time since I had the opportunity. English is—ah—out of fashion here these days ... Well! Sir, I wish first of all to express my gratitude and admiration, but I think words are too feeble to do that."

It's the last thing in the world I'd want to be admired for, and as for thanks I don't deserve them.

But it was too great an effort to explain that. Donald sighed and gave a nod. He said, "Ah—I don't believe I know your name."

"My name is Sugaiguntung," said the man.

I believe in logic, the sequence of cause and effect, and in science its only begotten son our law, which was conceived by the ancient Greeks, thrived under Isaac Newton, suffered under Albert Einstein ...

That fragment of a "creed for materialists" which a friend in college had once shown to him rose through Donald's confused mind. Simultaneously he seemed to be thinking *I don't believe in coincidences like this* and *it was right outside the building where he works* and *Christ what a time to find myself face to face with him.*

The situation was so absurd he found himself having to repress a hysterical giggle, and Sugaiguntung looked alarmed, as though suspecting that he might be choking. He gestured at the nurse to come forward, but Donald mastered his fit of idiot amusement.

"I feel like laughing at myself for not recognising you," he mumbled. "I'm very sorry—won't you sit down?"

Very cautiously—presumably because of the sword-cut across his buttocks—Sugaiguntung lowered himself to the chair Totilung had vacated. Leaning forward with an earnest expression, he said, "Sir, I understand you're a reporter. Since you might now be writing my obituary ..." He hesitated. "Well, such a debt can never be repaid. But possibly there's something I could do that would be of professional use? An exclusive interview, a guided tour of my laboratories? Ask as much of my time as you like. But for you, I'd have no time at all."

Like a man on the border of drunkenness trying not to give away the state he is in, Donald fought to order his chaotic thoughts. Helped by the trank, he grew calm. Reviewing in memory what Sugaiguntung had just said, he was struck by the curious turn of phrase he had employed, and a relay closed in that part of his mind where he stored tiny details noted long ago, about such matters as not snapping one's fingers in Yatakang.

Christ, that would be a dirty trick to play on him! But I'm soiled already, and it would short-cut me out of this hateful, horrible country ...

He studied Sugaiguntung from the corner of his eye. He knew the scientist was in his middle fifties. Perhaps that made him old enough to adhere to some of the ancient ways which the Solukarta government was propagandising against. It was worth taking the chance.

There was, or had been, a Yatakangi belief that if one man saved another's life, the man saved must put himself—once only—absolutely at his rescuer's disposal, to do something if need be which would cost the life the rescuer had earned. Not until he fulfilled this obligation could he call his life his own again.

He said suddenly, "All right, professor. There is one thing I want from you."

Sugaiguntung cocked his head alertly.

"Professor, I'm not just a reporter." *I'm an expert assassin—STOP THAT!* "I took my degree in biology and wrote my doctorate thesis in palaeogenetics. The reason I was sent here—the reason why it was so ridiculous for me not to have recognised you at once—well, I'm here to cover the genetic optimisation programme, of course. As I understand it, your government has pledged itself to do two things, and used your name as a guarantee that they will be done. First they're going to clean up Yatakangi heredity and ensure that only sound stock survives. And then they're going to breed an improved model of man.

"Experts in my country find it hard to believe that with its present resources of trained geneticists your government can keep even the first part of its promise, and nobody at all except yourself could bring about the second.

"So let me ask you straight out whether it can be done. Because if not—well, sure I'd like to have an exclusive interview, sure I'd like to tour your labs. But it would be a waste of time."

Hearing himself speak, he wondered if he was being a fool. As Keteng had said, Americans lacked subtlety, and that was about the crudest possible approach.

There was a silence which seemed to drag on towards eternity. He could hardly credit his senses when at last he saw Sugaiguntung move his head once from side to side: *no*.

Forgetful of bruises and cuts, he jerked himself into a

sitting position. He ignored the nurse as she darted to adjust the head of the bed.

"Professor, do you mean—?"

Sugaiguntung leapt from his chair and began to pace back and forth. "If I don't confide the truth to someone," he snapped with un-Yatakangi fierceness, "I shall myself go out of my mind! I shall turn mucker like my miserable student today! Mr. Hogan!" His voice dropped almost to a whisper. "I'm a loyal and patriotic citizen of my country—this is my home and I love it dearly! But is it not a man's responsibility to save what he loves from the stupidity of someone else?"

Donald nodded, astonished at the reaction he had called forth, like peering down the crater of Grandfather Loa and finding that the mists had parted to show bright lava, red as flowers.

"Someone has been a fool!" Sugaiguntung said passionately. "I have seen the success of our government, the change and the benefits it has brought—are they to be thrown away and with them everything *I* have struggled for? Mr. Hogan!" He halted and faced Donald. "You'd heard my name before this—this announcement was made?"

"Of course, hundreds of times."

"In connection with what?"

"Tailored bacteria as good as any in the world. A strain of rubber-tree which is the envy of competing countries. A mutated *Tilapia* which feeds millions who would otherwise be sick from lack of protein. A—"

"Thank you," Sugaiguntung cut in. "Sometimes, just lately, I have come to imagine that I dreamed it all. But did you hear any mention of four apes which killed themselves?"

"*Suicide?* By an ape? But I thought your work on apes was the basis for—"

"Oh, there's one who still survives." Sugaiguntung dismissed the remaining specimen with a wave of his hand and resumed his pacing. "But I judge that you know something of psychology as well as biology, yes? An ape which can conceive a way to kill itself is already sharing part of what sets man aside from other animals. If I do not have to explain that fact to you, perhaps I can make clear to you something else which I've failed to convey to—to certain persons in authority here."

He clenched his fists on the air, as though physically attempting to mould words out of nothing.

"Forgive me if I express my thoughts clumsily. I hardly know myself what I'm afraid of, but I do know very definitely that I'm afraid. I say without pride, Mr. Hogan—believe me, without pride at all, because what I thought of as a divine gift has turned to an intolerable burden—there is truly no one else in the world who has done what I have done. Consider! One of the other things which is ours alone is language, the power to grasp symbols and associations in the mind and conjure with objects and events that are not present to real perception. I amended the genes of an orangutang, and I made five infants who could share that with us, too. But we made language, we—men! These were apes, and the world they grew up into was human, not belonging to them. I think that is why four of them found ways to leave that world. The fifth is alive. You can meet him if you wish, talk to him—he can speak a few hundred simple words . . ."

"But this is fantastic!" Donald burst out, thinking of the scores, the hundreds of gene-moulded pets he had seen, miserable proxies for thousands more which had proved non-viable, less fitted for life after human tampering than their natural progenitors.

"You're impressed? Then let me ask you this: what would you have done if they'd come to you as they came to me and said, enough trials with apes which are inferior, your country demands that you work with human germ-plasm and if there are failures you must put them aside like any experiment which has gone wrong?"

"You mean you haven't yet succeeded with human material?"

"Success—what is success?" Sugaiguntung countered bitterly. "I suppose in some sense I've succeeded. Many times I've taken the nucleus from a donor cell and transplanted it to an ovum and it grew; sometimes I've touched, bent, altered a chromosome, and people have had healthy children of their own flesh and blood which might otherwise have been sickly or insane . . . They were satisfied, I think. Perhaps you can call that success."

"Have you tried to mend Solukarta's gene for porphyria?"

"That too," Sugaiguntung admitted, not surprised to hear that Donald knew of the well-guarded secret. "It has a side-effect. There would be a cleft palate."

"It could be repaired surgically—"

"With a Cyclops eye and a permanent fontanelle."

"I see. Go on."

"I hardly know how to." Seeming not to look at his environment, but to stare beyond the walls into the unguessable future, Sugaiguntung seated himself again by touch. "The code for a man is more complex, but not essentially different from that for a bacterium; it says divide and combine instead of divide and diffuse, but nonetheless it says *divide*."

He paused. Aching with impatience, Donald said, "But if you can endow an ape with the ability to use language, it sounds as though you're in reach of exactly what your government has promised!"

"Hm?" Sugaiguntung started. "Oh yes—with the knowledge we now have, using cloning techniques and tectogenetic alteration of faulty genes, Yatakang could be more or less free of congenital disorders in another century."

"But that's not what they're laying claim to!"

"Mr. Hogan, don't you understand? I'm not *interested* in what claims have been made! They're political, not scientific." Sugaiguntung drew a deep breath. "Mr. Hogan, what *is* a man? Some of him is the message passed down the centuries in a chemical code—but very little. Take a human baby and let it grow among animals as a feral child. At puberty is that a human being, even though it can mate and breed its physical form? No, it's a bad copy of the animal it was raised by! Listen, there is a point on a chromosome which I can touch—I think I can touch—and after fifty, a hundred failures, I can give a baby forebrain development which might be to ours as my orang-outangs' to their mothers'. Who is going to teach that child? When four out of my five apes killed themselves because we could not teach them how to live except as humans—and they weren't human! I could touch another place where certain muscles and bones are coded and make a man who stands three metres high with bones thick enough to bear his weight and muscles to run and jump and throw. I am less sure of this because huge strength was not required in my apes. But I think I might do it. Perhaps he'd have pink eyes and no hair, but . . ."

A chill permeated Donald's body. He said, "But then you could breed supermen."

"I can read the pattern of your nuclei like a street-map of this city," Sugaiguntung said without conceit. "Give me a million cells from your body—breed them in cultures from a shaving of skin you wouldn't miss, wouldn't feel—and I will tell you why, in chemical terms, you are the height you are, why your hair is that colour, why you are pale-skinned and not dark, why you are intelligent and have good digestion and the life-line in the palms of your hands forks a centimetre from the root. I haven't looked—they're under bandages. But your type has a galaxy of associated characteristics, as does anyone's.

"I could transplant a clone-nucleus from one of these cells and give you an identical twin who was your son. I could with luck say there was a good chance of making him taller than you, stronger, more agile, conceivably even more intelligent by a few per cent. If you insisted on a blond I could probably make him a blond. I'll go further: if you wanted a girl I could make you a fair imitation. It would have some male attributes—a flat chest, a moustache. But it would not have a penis."

"If you can do this already, though, in twenty-five more years—"

"After that time, who will have taught my government not to make claims it cannot justify?" Sugaiguntung cut in.

Donald leaned back in the bed, his head beginning to ache. He said, "I'm sorry, I'm hopelessly confused. By the sound of it, you can carry out the *second* part of the optimisation programme, the one everybody thinks is far-fetched, while the first, which is based credibly on present knowledge, is the one that can't be managed . . . Have I understood you?"

Sugaiguntung shrugged. "I know what level of intelligence is required to make a good tectogeneticist. The Yatakangi gene-pool won't provide the—the *army* of them which the programme calls for in less than a century. Not if anything else in the country is to be kept going in the meanwhile."

"Does the government realise this?"

"I have said it openly and often, and they answered that they were the best judges of political expediency, I should go back to my laboratories and do as I was told." Sugaiguntung hesitated. "In this country, as I'm sure is true for yours also, one inclines to believe the specialist. But to specialise is to be ignorant, and there are certain inflexible facts . . ."

"If they run into those facts," Donald suggested, "they're likely to soft-pedal the first part of the programme, and emphasise the second—mount a crash project to produce modified and improved human beings!"

"Which they must not!" Sugaiguntung said, marking each word by pounding fist into palm. "Out of my five apes four killed themselves. We took very great care. But for our precautions they might have killed a man. You can pen and guard a super-ape. Which among us humans will try to control a super-human? It will not be stopped from killing if it desires to kill."

Almost inaudibly he added, "You of all people should understand. It is only a few hours since you yourself killed."

He should not have said that. Donald had been within arm's reach of his old self: accustomed to accepting information dispassionately, organising it like pieces of a puzzle until new patterns emerged. He had barely even worried about the fact that he was not recording—like a genuine reporter—what the scientist said to him; he relied on his long training to sift and absorb the salient points.

Faced with a reminder of what he had done, however, there was only one way he could digest the circumstances and remain rational—to accept himself anew as Donald Hogan Mark II, the eptified killer to whom murder was all in the day's work.

He knew he must exploit the vital and unique admissions Sugaiguntung had made. Against that, he felt pity for the genius scientist whose love of country had led him to complicity in a lie, blessing a propaganda stunt, and infringement of his most dearly held ideals. The strain of reconciling them was intolerable. Part of him folded away to the subconscious level, like atoms in a strained molecule awaiting the opportunity to release their stored energy at the compound's flashpoint.

He said, "What do you think of your government now, Professor?" His tone lent barbs to the words.

"I am afraid for my country if it remains in power," Sugaiguntung whispered.

"What do you want? What would you most like?"

"What would I like?" Sugaiguntung blinked. "I should like—I should like to be free of this pressure. I am becoming set in my ways, I am fifty-four years old, but I have ideas I've not yet tried, I can teach younger people what I know and cannot write down ... I should like to be what I trained to be, a scientist, instead of a political figure-head!"

"Do you see any chance of getting what you want so long as this government remains in power in Yatakang?"

There was a long silence. At last Sugaiguntung said, "I have hoped, and gone on hoping. Now ... Now I have to pretend that there is still hope."

"You must give me a letter of authority," Donald said after some thought. "You must write that I can come to your private address for an interview—put down where I have to go. You can have what you want. I swear it, I will make sure that you can have what you want."

context (22)

MOTHER AND BABY DOING WELL?

"Hello, you out there, furious at the Eugenics Processing Board for denying you the right to parenthood! Wouldn't be so bad if paternalism were out of fashion altogether, would it? But it's inner than in. You put up with a hundred and one things that are forbidden 'for your own good', and if there's anything you *are* allowed to do it's probably for the good of the people who could forbid it and don't.

"I'm lucky, since they tell me I have a couple of good healthy prodgies—matter of fact, they've both called me recently since they learned I hadn't returned my phosphorus to the planetary pool. Their calls set me thinking about the chances I took when I started them on their merry way, and some of the facts I've dug up are kind of scary. I mean, without a computer analysis would you ordinarily do something that gave eight chances out of a hundred of saddling you for ten, fifteen years—maybe for life—with a greedy, demanding and stupid animal?

"Right. I'm talking about a subnormal child.

"Digging around, I came up with an estimate given to a reporter in Stockholm in 1959 by Professor Linus Pauling, the man who hung a name and identity on a disease called phenylketonuria. That's the earliest place I've found the hard, cold figure of eight per cent, and I'm too lazy to look any further right now.

"Pauling said: approximately two of every hundred babies born in communities for which records existed suffered from some kind of congenital disorder, and the few studies which had at that time been continued to puberty suggested the eventual total might run as high as eight. This would include speech defects, alexia, colour-blindness and assorted other handicaps not detectible by inspection of a new-born infant.

"Not all these, naturally, were hereditary. Many were the result of intrauterine or natal trauma. The genotype of a spastic might be admirable.

"However, a barrel of dreck has been thrown down over the neat dividing line between hereditary, due to the genes, and congenital, due to accident. None of the experts, let alone members of the lay public, that I've talked to has been able to agree on the cause of the difficult cases without an expensive and time-consuming study of the parental germ-plasm.

"You see, traumata—which is Greek for 'bruises' but means outside interference in this case—include the consequence of excessive exposure to X-rays in the womb, infection of the mother with German measles, ingestion of a carcinogenic or mutagenic substance which gets to the gonads, hitripping on Yaginol while you're pregnant—and that's so addictive there are some mothers-to-be you could write on with a hot iron, 'It'll deform your baby!' and they'd say get off my orbit, you're crowding me down—and additionally the gradual deposition in body-tissue of long-life radioactives such as radio-strontium, radio-iodine, radio-caesium and radio-carbon . . . *et caetera.*

"And these things have just about counteracted the advances in medical science which have eliminated the traditional causes of spasticism. You decide to have that kid, you're still bucking an eight per cent risk that if he reaches puberty he'll suffer from a congenital disorder.

"Mark you, some of them are pretty minor. For instance, pollen-allergy is hereditary, not congenital even, but modern antidotes make it possible for a child with pollen-asthma to lead a fairly normal life. Sounds like nothing, doesn't it— these days?

"Except that before he dies that child will likely have spent seventy-five thousand bucks on antidotes!

"Now if you've been turned down by the Eugenic Processing Board, what's happened is that they've assessed the risk of you having a handicapped child not at eight but at eighty per cent. You may disagree with them on the definition of a handicap—this recent row over dichromatism, for example. They have solid achievements to their credit, though. Fifty years ago Pauling said it would take twenty generations for all the recessives due to radioactive fallout to appear; now, they have tabs on enough of them to say they'll be eliminated in fewer than twelve. That ought to cheer up your ten-times-great-grandchildren, if any!

"But I tell you this, having looked at you for a good many years with the maximum cynicism I could contrive. There's nothing so good about *you* that it deserves to be physically perpetuated in the body of your own born child. You're hiding behind that Eugenics Board decision to conceal the fact that you're really evading the responsibility of looking after a person who's eventually got to go and face the world alone. You don't want to risk him coming back and saying it was your fault he didn't emerge a winner in the game of life. I know some people, even, who are lying about their clean genotype, pretending to a hereditary handicap to excuse their childless state.

"Why can't they be honest about it? I'm in favour of people who don't breed, mostly. But not because I prefer dogmatic homosexuals, or because I favour religious fanatics like the Divine Daughters, who put on celibacy to mask their borderline hysteria. No! Only because a person who doesn't insist on the expensive luxury of being a parent frees himself, or herself, to become a parent for one of the underprivileged children we already have.

"If you've been forbidden to start a prodgy, you *know* there are potential adoptees around who are superior to anything you could breed. Wouldn't you like to raise a child to be brighter than you are, more successful, handsomer, sexier, healthier?

"No, you sheeting well wouldn't. You'd prefer it to stay in a public orphanage where substandard nutrition will reduce its intelligence and lack of maternal affection will turn it into an unsuccessful neurotic.

"When a species becomes terrified of its own young, it appears to be scheduled for the grand disposall down which went the dinosaurs. Some of us, as I've just demonstrated, are afraid in case their prodgies will prove inferior to themselves, which is halfway rational, but some are afraid they'll be the opposite, and that's insane. Now you're erecting an Asiatic scientist you'd never heard of before a couple of weeks back into a Messiah-figure. All right, suppose Sugaiguntung *can* do as they maintain and tailor a baby to specification? What are you going to ask for?

"Cleverer than you? But you don't want to spend your old age feeling you're a drag on your prodgies.

"Stupider than you? But you don't want to waste the rest of your life looking after a fool.

"What you want is one which is guaranteed to behave itself until it's old enough to run away from home, so that forever after you can complain about the ingratitude it displayed. But I doubt whether even Sugaiguntung can build that into an ovum with warranty of success."

> —*From an article which an over-eager journal commissioned Chad Mulligan to write when they realised he wasn't after all dead*

tracking with closeups (21)

THE DRY CHILD

Linguistic evaluation suggests the earliest form of the name "Begi" is transliterable rather as "Mpengi" and in consequence it is generally rendered "winter-born". The more close rendering would be "child of dry season". December and January in northern Beninia (where he was supposedly born) are both least humid months of every year.

It has been suggested the name was originally "Kpegi" (i.e. "foreigner") but this would not give rise to the "Mpengi" form mentioned above. In any case Shinka superstition has it that a child conceived at the breaking of the maximum summer rains (hence born in midwinter) is likely to be livelier than average. Attempts to show that Begi was in fact a solar myth originating in latitudes where seasons are marked enough to foster concepts of death and rebirth of the sun are tantalising, but fruitless in the absence of any other than oral evidence, though it is highly possible that prehistoric cross-cultural interaction provided some elements of the Begi myth which has descended to us. On the other hand . . .[1]

[1] Preamble to doctorate thesis submitted by Mrs. Kitty Gbe of Port Mey, Beninia: Univ. of Ghana, Legon, Accra, 1989 (xii + 91 pp., 3 illus., map).

BEGI AND HIS GREEDY SISTER

One day Begi was lying on the floor near a basket of fried chicken his mother had made for a festival. His sister thought Begi was asleep and took the largest chicken-leg and hid it under the roof.

When the family gathered to eat Begi refused what he was offered from the basket. He said, "There is a bigger bird roosting under the roof."

"You're silly," said his mother, but his sister knew what he meant.

He climbed up and got the chicken-leg and ate it.

"You stole it and put it there," his sister accused. "You wanted to have the biggest piece."

"No," Begi said. "I dreamed that wanting to have the biggest piece was the best way to get the smallest."

And he gave her the gnawed bone.[2]

BEGI AND THE FOREIGN MERCHANT

Once Begi went to the big market in Lalendi. There he saw a merchant from another tribe. The man was selling pots he claimed were made of gold, but Begi went behind him and took a knife and tried to cut the metal. It would not cut like soft gold although it was shiny and yellow.

So Begi picked up the biggest pot and pissed on the ground underneath and put it back.

Then he went around to the front and there were many people wanting to buy those gold pots which Begi knew were only made of brass.

Begi said, "That is a fine big pot there. I need a pot like that to piss in at night."

And everybody laughed, thinking he was a fool to put that liquid in a pot fit to hold the chief's finest palm-wine.

"Piss in it and show me if it leaks," Begi said. The merchant laughed with everyone else and did so, saying what a shame it was to defile such a valuable pot with urine.

Begi lifted it up when the merchant had finished and the

[2] *Op. cit.* p. 4.

ground underneath was wet with piss. He said, "I will not
buy a pot no matter how fine it looks if it leaks when you
piss in it."

So all the people beat the merchant and made him give
their money back.[3]

BEGI AND THE SEA-MONSTER

After he had left the house of the fat old woman, Begi
walked along the trail through the forest whistling the tune
he had learned from her and plucking the five wooden
tongues of the *kethalazi*—what the British nicknamed the
"pocket piano" when they came much later to Begi's part of
the world.

A little bird heard him and fluttered down to the side of
the trail, eager to listen to this fine new tune but a little
afraid because Begi was a man.

Seeing how timid the bird was, Begi stopped on the path
and sat down. He said, "Do not be afraid, little cousin. Do
you want to learn my song? I will teach it to you if you will
teach me one of yours."

"That's a good bargain," said the bird. "But I can't help
being afraid of you. You're as much bigger than I am as the
monster from the sea is bigger than man-people."

"Certainly you're smaller than I am," Begi said. "But your
voice is far sweeter than mine. I have heard you make the
whole forest echo with your melody. By the bye, though," he
added, "what is this monster you just mentioned?"

The bird told him that at a village near the sea, a day's
walk distant, a huge monster had come out of the water and
caught two children and eaten them, and everyone had run
away to hide in the bush.

"I am bigger than you are," Begi said. "But I can't sing
better than you. Perhaps the monster is bigger than I am. It
remains to be seen if he can think better than I do. I shall go
there and find out."

The bird said, "If you are not afraid of the monster I will

[3] *Ibid.* p. 18.

try not to be afraid of you." He perched on Begi's head and dug his toes into the woolly hair there.

So Begi walked all day carrying the bird and teaching him to sing the old woman's song. After many hours' journey he came to the village where everyone had run away from the monster.

"Little cousin!" he said. "What is that I see on the horizon, where the dark blue water meets the light blue sky?"

The bird flew out over the sea to find out. When he came back, he said, "There is a storm coming. There are clouds and lightning."

"Very good," said Begi, and went to look for the monster.

There he was lying in the market square, as much bigger than Begi as Begi was bigger than the little bird, and the bird had all he could do not to fly off in terror. But he clung to Begi's hair with all his might.

The monster roared at Begi, "Hey there, weakling! You come at the right time! I have finished digesting the children I had for breakfast and I'll have you for my supper!"

"I'm hungry too," said Begi. "I haven't eaten today."

"There's something to eat sitting on your head," the monster exclaimed. "You'd better make the most of it before I gobble you up!"

Privately to the bird, Begi whispered, "There's no need to be afraid. I would rather hear you sing than make a meal of you. But I don't believe this monster cares about music."

Addressing the monster more loudly, he went on, "No! I'm saving this bird for the time when I'm so weak I cannot go and hunt for food."

The monster laughed. "If I eat you, when will the day come which finds you so hungry you must eat your pet?"

"I don't know," answered Begi. "Any more than you know when the day will come when the giant whose back you ride on will need to eat you."

"I don't ride on anybody's back," declared the monster.

"In that case," said Begi, "whose are the jaws I see closing on you? Whose is the voice I hear making the welkin ring?" He raised his blunt spear and pointed.

The monster looked out to sea and saw the black clouds looming down on the village and the waves rippling like the tongue of a hungry beast licking its chops and heard the sound of thunder like the grumbling of hunger.

"There is the giant whose back you have been riding on," said Begi. "It's called the sea. We men are like fleas compared to it, so we are usually safe—we would not even make a mouthful for such a colossus. Even so, sometimes it hurts us when we annoy it and it scratches. But you are as much bigger than I am as I am bigger than this bird on my head. And by the sound of it the sea is *very* hungry."

The monster saw the flash of lightning like the gleam of white fangs in the mouth of the ocean, and he jumped up howling and ran away. He was never heard of again.

When the people came back to the village from where they had been hiding in the bush, they asked Begi, "Are you not a mighty warrior, to have driven away that horrible monster?"

So Begi showed them his blunt spear and the shield with a hole in it which he always carried, and they said, "What does this mean?"

"It means," he explained, "that you cannot use a spear to kill a flea which is biting you, and a shield is no use against a monster that could gobble you up shield and all. There is only one way to win against both a flea and a monster: you must think better than either of them."[4]

BEGI AND THE GHOST

Once the people were much troubled by a *tlele-ki* (ancestral spirit) which terrified the women going to fetch water and made the children have bad dreams.

Begi's father the chief called together the *kotlanga* (council of adults), and Ethlezi (lit. "sorcerer, medicine-man") told him, "It is the spirit of your father, Begi's grandfather."

The chief was very upset. He asked Begi, "What can grandfather want with us?"

Begi said, "There is only one way to find out what a ghost

[4] From "Tales of Our African Brethren: Folklore of Beninia and the Gold Coast" by The Rev. Jerome Coulter, DD: London 1911 (vi + 347 pp., col. frontis., 112 line drgs. in text).

wants. We will go and ask him. Or if you won't, I will by myself."

So he learned from Ethlezi the right way to speak politely to a ghost and went out at night to the dark lonely place where it had been seen. He said, "Grandfather, I have brought you palm-wine and goat's blood. Eat if you will but talk to me."

The ghost came and drank the wine and took the blood to make itself strong. It said, "Begi, here I am."

"What do you want with us?" Begi asked.

"I keep watch on the village. I see that everything is going badly. The law-suits are not judged as I would have judged them. Young people are disrespectful to their elders. The girls go with boys they do not intend to marry. There is too much food so that people grow fat and lazy and there is so much palm-wine that they get drunk and sleep when they should be hunting."

"My father the new chief judges law-suits differently because he is dealing with different people," Begi said. "The young people learned how to talk to their elders from their parents, who were taught by you. The girls choose their own husbands now and when they marry they are happier than their mothers. As for being lazy and sleeping, why not, when we know that spirits like you keep watch over the village?"

The ghost had no answer to that and it went away.[5]

BEGI AND THE WICKED SORCERER

Begi came to a village where everybody was afraid of a sorcerer called Tgu. He could make cows and women miscarry, he could set huts on fire without going near, he could make witch-dolls and if he stabbed with his special knife the footprint someone left in a muddy path the person would fall sick or die.

Begi said to Tgu, "I want you to help me kill a man whose name I cannot tell you."

The sorcerer said, "Pay me. But you must bring something

[5] From "Begi, an African 'Jack the Giant Killer'" by Roger F. Woodsman in *Anthropological Communications*, vol. XII, no. 3.

of his—a hair or a scrap of nail or some of the clothes he has worn."

"I will bring you something of his," said Begi. He went away and came back with some excrement. Also he gave the sorcerer a mirror and some valuable herbs he had gathered.

The sorcerer made a witch-doll and roasted it at the fire singing powerful magical chants. When it was dawn the people of the village came to see because they were afraid to come at night, the magic was so strong.

"The man will die," said the sorcerer.

"Now I can tell you his name," said Begi. "It is Tgu."

The sorcerer fell on the ground in a fit, shrieking that he had been tricked. He said he was sure to die at once.

Begi took the chief of the village apart and said, "Wait one more hour. Then you can tell him the excrement belonged to a friend of mine called Tgu in another village. I am going away to laugh with my friend at the foolishness of the sorcerer."[6]

BEGI AND THE STEAMSHIP

(*Author's note: this must be a very late accretal to the mythos.*)

Begi went to the seaside and there he saw a big ship with smoke coming out. A white man from the ship met him on the shore and talked with him.

Begi said, "Welcome. Be my guest while you are here."

The white man said, "That is a foolish offer. I am coming to live here."

Begi said, "Then I will help you build your hut."

The white man said, "I will not live in a hut. I will live in a house of iron with smoke coming out of the top and be very rich."

Begi said, "Why do you wish to come here?"

The white man said, "I am going to rule over you."

Begi said, "Is it better living here than where you come from?"

[6] Gbe, *op. cit.* p. 80.

The white man said, "It is too hot, it rains, it is muddy, I do not like the food and there are none of my own women."

Begi said, "But if you want to come and live here it must be better in some respect. If you don't like the weather, the food or the women, then you must think it is better governed than your own country, and my father the chief rules us."

The white man said, "I am going to rule you."

Begi said, "If you have left your own home you must have been sent away. How can a man who has been sent from home into exile rule better than my father the chief?"

The white man said, "I have a big steamship with many strong guns."

Begi said, "Let me see you make another."

The white man said, "I cannot."

Begi said, "I see the way of it. You are good at using what other people have made and nothing else." (*Author's note: it is an insult in Shinka to say that a man cannot make anything, as a self-respecting adult is expected to build his own house and carve his own furniture.*)

But the white man was too stupid to see Begi's point and he came and lived here anyway.

However, after a hundred years he learned better and went home.[7]

continuity (29)

I BEG TO REPORT

The doctor in charge of Donald wanted to keep him in the hospital overnight. It took him an hour's arguing and the threat of reporting to his agency that he had been incarcerated before they reluctantly sent him back to his hotel in an official car, with escort. By now, scores of reports based on rumour must have been circulated telling how Sugaiguntung had been rescued from the mucker; Engrelay Satelserv might well have had the story from Deirdre Kwa-Loop. He didn't care. On the first day of his mission he had succeeded more completely than those who sent him—let alone he himself—could ever have dreamed. What counted was not getting the story on the beam, but his discovery that the man on whom the whole Yatakangi optimisation programme pivoted was afraid as much of its possible success as of its probable failure.

For fear that his identity and rôle in saving Sugaiguntung might have become widely known, he insisted on being sent up to his room by a back route avoiding the main lobby. They found a baggage elevator and no one saw him except an incurious porter. Having got rid of his escort, he made sure that the door between his room and Bronwen's was bolted on his side, and opened his communikit.

One of its circuits could be adjusted to detect bugging devices. He found one sunk in the wooden surround of the closet. Not caring about subtlety, he played the flame of his pocket lighter on it for a minute or so. A cautious reporter, he reasoned, would be expected to want to keep his exclusive stories to himself. There was also a tap on the phone, but that he didn't worry about; it was inactive except when the instrument was in use.

Effortfully, he composed two messages, one in writing, to be read over the phone, the other whispered into the hidden device which would impose it, scrambled, as a parasite modulation on the phone signal. The former badly recounted that a mucker had attacked Sugaiguntung and he had dealt with him. The latter said that if anybody cared the scientist was riper than a plum and ought to be picked.

He put in for a call to the nearest available relay satellite and was told he would have to wait. He waited. Eventually the connection was made and he sent the double message. While he was thus occupied he heard Bronwen's door open and shut and the door between the rooms was tried, very gently.

The job done, he shut off the phone and put the communikit away. They had fed him at the hospital before letting him go; he wasn't hungry. He thought about a drink or a joint, and lacked the enthusiasm. He undressed and climbed into bed.

Lying in the dark, ambushing him, was a young man with his throat bleeding a river.

In a short while he got up. There was a rim of light around the door to Bronwen's room. He unbolted it and pushed it open. She was sitting on the bed, naked, in the full lotus posture, as composed as if she had been waiting for him.

"Forgive me," she said. "I was very rude to you earlier." She began to unfold her limbs like a flower opening its petals to the sun. "You must have sensed that you were needed."

Donald shook his head blankly. By now she was off the bed and approaching him with a slight sway of her hips.

"Is it true what I've been told—that you saved Dr. Sugaiguntung from a mucker?"

"Yes, that's true."

"You sensed that you were needed for that, didn't you? It

was why you left me all of a sudden. You have the power we call"—he didn't catch the word, which was long and assonantal, more likely to be Sanskrit than modern Hindi.

"No," Donald said. Standing unclothed in the middle of the floor, he began to shake. He had thought it very hot tonight, but he was chilled to his marrow, shivering and shivering. "No," he said again. "The only power I have is the power to kill, and I don't want it. It makes me terribly afraid." His teeth came together after the last word and started to chatter.

"It is always like this when you are used as the channel for a divine force," Bronwen said, as though she had spent her entire life studying the question. "It overloads the body and mind. But you are lucky. It could have burned you out."

Not burned, frozen. Wouldn't it have been better if the mucker had killed Sugaiguntung, perhaps me too? What am I going to make him do?

But that had passed out of his control.

Bronwen was reaching up with professional detachment to place her palm on the crown of his head. After that she touched him lightly on the forehead, throat, heart, navel, pubis and coccyx: the seven chakras. She said, "The force has gone from your belly to your head. You are thinking of things that never happened. Let me draw it back."

She dropped gracefully on one knee and addressed his body with her mouth.

Eventually the phone's buzz, which at first he did not recognise, it being shriller and shorter than its counterpart at home, dug him from the sleep into which Bronwen's violent love-making had driven him. He clambered out of bed and stumbled into his own room, hand groping for the switch.

Muzzy, he looked at the instrument blurred in darkness and waited for the screen to light. It was long moments before he realised there was none, and he should have said something to indicate the connection had been made.

"Uh—Hogan," he muttered.

"Delahanty!" an excited voice exclaimed. "Congratulations, Hogan! Engrelay Satelserv never expected anything like this big a story!"

"Christ, was that all you wanted to say? It's two-thirty anti-matter here."

"Yes, I realise that. Sorry. But I thought you deserved to be told at once how delighted we are. Of course, what you filed will require some editing, but . . ."

He paused. Donald waited passively for him to finish.

"You got that? I said it'll require editing!"

Oh. Donald made a long arm and picked up his communikit, setting it alongside the phone. There would be a message coming through blipped and scrambled, which the machine would play back afterwards in comprehensible English. But things like the code phrases he had been taught seemed childish and irrelevant in the wake of the mucker's death.

"I catch," he said. "Sorry. I'm exhausted."

"That doesn't surprise me," Delahanty said. "Taking on a mucker—it's incredible! And of course it was a complete beat for us because the day's official releases haven't included it. Gone to top level for a decision, probably. All we had was a third-hand rumour before your story hit. We're playing it for all it's worth—and you will be too, naturally."

"I asked for a private interview," Donald said absently.

"Excellent! Make sure you get film, too—our regular stringer will set that up for you, I'm certain." He wandered off into a welter of fulsome praise until eventually he cut the circuit.

Relieved, Donald altered the controls of the communikit and listened to the clear-language version it had automatically deciphered from the incoming signal.

Delahanty's voice, reduced to bare recognisability by the frequency-chopping effect of the blip process, said, "Hogan, I took it straight to Washington to be computed and the verdict is that he must be got out as fast as possible. There's never been a whisper of disaffection concerning him before, and he might change his mind.

"Get him to Jogajong's camp. We run a submarine courier service up the Shongao Strait—that's the way we got Jogajong himself in and out. Aquabandit activity is maximal at the moment, but it'll drop back in a few days.

"We're relying on you. There'll be medals in it if you fancy them. Good luck—and by the way! If you can handle a mucker, the experts say, you can handle *anything*."

The thin whisper died away. Donald sat in the darkness staring at nothing, thinking about Sugaiguntung and maybe having to kidnap him and getting him across the Strait to the jungle cove where Jogajong was lying low under the very noses of those who most dearly wanted to put him to death, then escaping by submarine with Chinese hunter-killers in pursuit . . .

I want out. I want out. I want OUT!

A hand touched him on the shoulder. He jumped and whirled and it was only Bronwen come to see what had become of him. She moved so silently he had not heard her approach.

"It was my head office," Donald said. "Pleased with what I've done."

The words tasted filthy on his tongue.

context (23)

TO BE AVOIDED

Dr. Corning (at State)	We have Scramble A on, don't we? Good, yes, we do. Dick, sorry to bother you.
Mr. Richard Ruze (Engrelay)	No trouble, Raphael. What can we do for you that we aren't doing already?
Dr. Corning	Yes, we are asking a lot of you just now, aren't we? I have to ask something else, though, I'm afraid. You're carrying this tremendous story filed by the man you sent to Gongilung, Donald Hogan—
Mr. Ruze	Yes, it's wonderful, isn't it? We're extremely grateful to you for giving him to us—we didn't expect to get anything out of him, let alone a sensaysh like this.

Dr. Corning	I'm sorry, I didn't quite follow that. It unscrambled as something about giving him to you and I think it must—
Mr. Ruze	You mean you don't know about that?
Dr. Corning	(inaudible)
Mr. Ruze	He's one of your own people. We're giving him his cover for the trip—hired him as a special correspondent. That was what I thought you had in mind when you said we were doing a lot for you at—
Dr. Corning	No, Dick, I was thinking of something else entirely. A matter I guess is uppermost in my mind. Well, look, this means you're going to feel I'm applying leverage, but—
Mr. Ruze	Lever away, Raphael. We show a sheeting great profit on the Hogan scene so far and we can afford to be generous.
Dr. Corning	I'll go straight to the point, then. You know we run trend-studies on all the big media. Our computers say you're liable to involve Mr. and Mrs. Everywhere in the Yatakangi scene soon. (*Pause of 8 sec.*) All right, you didn't say yes, but we were right last time and the time before.
Mr. Ruze	You want it not. Tell me why?
Dr. Corning	Yatakang means one thing to the audience right now, and

we're taking that subject straight and slow.

Mr. Ruze

I have Shalmaneser time booked for SCANALYZER as usual in an hour or so. I put in a Yatakangi programme for evaluation. Think he'll tell me the details? I'd like a sight of that, if you don't mind, to see if it agrees our own study.

Dr. Corning

Mr. Ruze

Which said . . .

Dr. Corning

Gave them a sixty-forty chance of bringing it off when we first checked. We programmed in some new material about Yatakangi human resources and dragged it down to fifty-fifty. Since then we've been re-evaluating every forty-eight hours and currently it's seventy-three to twenty seven against. (*Pause of 11 sec.*)

Mr. Ruze

I see. You think it might raise false hopes.

Dr. Corning

The impact of Mr. and Mrs. Everywhere would give the claim sort of automatic cachet. It would save you possible later embarrassment and us a lot of definite problems if you—

Mr. Ruze

I read you. Guess we can send them back to MAMP . . . By the way, Raphael, when you asked us to lay that on heavy you hinted there was a big breakthrough due shortly. It's a long time and no roughage.

Dr. Corning
On that, we have eighty-two to eighteen in favour. When it breaks ninety the whole story will bust loose.

Mr. Ruze
It'd better be worth the wait.

Dr. Corning
I so testify. Well, thanks very much, Dick—glad you saw what I set course for.

Mr. Ruze
Don't I always? I'll call you the results from Shal when I have them. 'Bye.

Dr. Corning
'Bye.

continuity (30)

TURN HER ON AND LET HER ROLL

At the head of his cabinet table, in the rather mean and ill-maintained Parliament building, President Obomi struggled to focus his surviving eye on those who had joined him. There was a small patch where vision blurred into meaningless dots and swirls; the doctors said something about a retinal trauma and talked of optic nerve regrafting and regretted that it would take a month to heal if they did operate. There might, now, be a month to spare. He hoped so.

Immediately to his left were Ram Ibusa and Leon Elai; beyond them, Kitty Gbe sat next to Gideon Horsfall. Facing the president from the foot of the table was Elihu Masters. And on the other side were the representatives from GT led by Norman House.

"Well?" said the president at length.

Norman licked his lips and pushed across the shiny top of the table a thick pile of green printouts from Shalmaneser.

"It'll work," he said, and wondered what he would have done if he had not been able to utter that simple phrase.

"Have you any reservations, Norman?" Elihu inquired.

"I—no. None. I don't believe anyone else has."

Terence, Worthy, Consuela, all shook their heads. Their faces had a uniformly dazed expression, as though they found it impossible to accept the evidence of their own judgment.

"So we think it will work," the president said. "Ought it to be done? Leon?"

Dr. Leon Elai also clutched a thick file of Shalmaneser printouts. He said, "Zad, I've never had material like this to work with before. I've barely had time to read it, there's so much! But I've extracted a kind of digest, and . . ."

"Let me hear it, please."

"Well, first there are the problems with our neighbours." Dr. Elai extracted a handwritten white sheet from among the stack of green. "The probabilities are high that for about two years there will be accusations against us for submitting to neo-colonialism. By that time the economic pressure to co-operate in the subsidiary aspects of the project such as placing contracts for manufactures which will by then show signs of being cheaper here than anywhere else on the continent will tend to reduce their violence. Also there will be a chance for them to buy cheap power from us. Within a decade at most, it says, they will become reconciled to the idea.

"Chinese and Egyptian interference is likely to be worse and go on longer. However, we can count on South African support, Kenyan, Tanzanian—shall I read the list?"

"Tell us how it comes out on balance."

"There appears to be no chance of outside intervention halting the project unless some country is prepared to launch a major missile attack on us. And the probability of United Nations retaliation for such a crime is ninety-one per cent." A trace of awe coloured Elai's voice, as though he had never expected to be talking of the foreign affairs interests of his country in such terms.

"Very well. We may expect to be safe from other people's jealousy, then." Obomi's eye switched to Ram Ibusa. "Ram, I have worried about the impact of so much money on our precarious economy. Are we going to suffer from inflation, unjust distribution of income, a top-heavy tax-structure?"

Ibusa gave an emphatic headshake. "Until I saw what this computer Shalmaneser can tell us, I was afraid of that too. But I do now believe we can cope with all those problems, provided we can continue to rely on General Technics' assistance in processing the information. What it comes down to is that we have here the first-ever chance in history to control a country's economy directly. There will not *be* any taxes in the traditional sense!"

He leafed through his own set of Shalmaneser printouts.

"There will first be the loan in which the American government will take its fifty-one per cent share. From it we will make a series of loans of our own, some of which will be into investment funds the interest on which will pay for the following: a subsistence ration of food, an issue of clothing to all working people and children of school age, and medical care of an improved standard. There will also be a building allowance to heads of families which will by law have to be spent on domestic improvements such as house-repairs.

"But the cost of the project will *at once* be of the order of three times our present GNP. Simply by controlling what the computer says we shall be controlling directly a higher proportion of the money circulating in the country than is possible anywhere in the world.

"At the worst possible reading of the factors concerned, the gain to Beninia will consist in the removal of starvation and the improvement of personal and public health. That is, if returns from the markets we intend going into do no more than pay for the guaranteed interest on the original loan.

"Much more likely, we shall also enjoy a very high standard of literacy and technical skill, the fruits of better housing, transport, harbour facilities, housing, school buildings, everything. Especially we shall have power in every house for the first time ever."

His voice dropped away to a whisper and his eyes went out of focus as though he were staring at a dream.

"When you say there will be no taxes, Ram!" Obomi said sharply. "You mean there will be fixed prices and deductions of income at source? There will have to be a great deal of enforcement, and I have always hated enforcing regulations on my people!"

"Ah—it should not be necessary," Ibusa muttered.

"Why not?"

"Suppose inflation actually runs at the probable level of five per cent in the first year," Ibusa said. "We shall withhold the amount of purchasing power corresponding to what would cause a ten per cent increase. There will be a real rise in the standard of living anyway because of the free issues and the loans; the pinch will not be felt. We shall then have surplus purchasing power to release in the year following, when people are growing accustomed to their new prosperity. But in the meantime we shall have loaned out the money we withheld and it will have grown, giving us the power to withhold a further portion, and so on. At the end of twenty years, when the groundwork of the project is complete and everything is in operation, that fund of reserved purchasing power will be used to buy back for the country whatever item still mortgaged is judged most essential to our independent development. It might be the new harbour facilities, it might be the power-system, it might be anything, but there will be enough to let us make the right choice."

He suddenly gave a broad grin.

"Kitty?" Obomi said.

The plump minister of education hesitated. She said after the pause, "I made the best guess I could of what we might need to turn our people into the sort of skilled labour force our American friends are talking about and asked them to have their computer look at it. The machine says we can have everything I asked for three times over, and I can't quite see how!"

"As I recall," Norman said, "you suggested trebling the number of teachers, increasing school accommodation to the best modern standards, and expanding the business college here into a national university with a student body of ten thousand, the rest of the training to be left to trade instructors on an on-the-job basis. Well, according to what I gather from Shalmaneser's report, you don't know yourself what you have to play with. You have a feedback element you left out completely. If the average runs no higher than one in ten, then in any class of forty children you have four who are capable of additional training so that they can relieve part of the teacher's duty in respect of the class next below but one. Your thirteen-year-olds can spare an hour a day to supplement the instruction the ten- or eleven-year-olds are getting. The other day I met a boy called Simon Bethakazi at a hamlet on the Lalendi road. I met him at random—remember him, Gideon?"

"The one who gave me that nasty question about the Chinese in California," Gideon nodded.

"Right. If he gets the chance, that boy will be teaching his own class of forty sub-teenagers in three years' time *and* because he's not teaching them anything he hasn't already learned backwards he's going to be able to study—perhaps more slowly than in Europe or America, but it'll only add one year to a standard three-year course—he'll be able to study a subject at college level.

"Additionally, we envisage bringing in foreign advisors and teachers at generous rates of pay who will cost your taxpayers nothing—they'll be GT staffers—who will combine a job for the project with a compulsory course-leadership assignment. Some of them won't like the idea, and we'll weed them out fast. Others will take to it because their skills are the kind which are being automated away from them at home and they'll react favourably to the chance of handing on their knowledge to human successors. Shalmaneser's been fed the results of surveys we've done in Europe and estimates we can hope for a minimum of twenty-five hundred of suitable calibre.

"And there's one other thing you left out of your own calculations, Kitty." Norman hesitated. "I guess it was owing to modesty, but there are times when modesty has drawbacks. Mr. President, may I address you a compliment which will probably sound fulsome but I assure you is quite sincere?"

"Elihu will tell you I'm as vain as the next man," Obomi said, and chuckled.

"Well, it made me very sceptical when he told me about this country for the first time," Norman said. "I didn't see how a broken-down hole-in-corner place like Beninia could be as good as he claimed. I *still* don't see how! All I know is this—here's a place where there aren't any murders, there aren't any muckers, there aren't any tempers lost, there aren't any tribal squabbles, there aren't any riots, there's nothing of what people in supposedly more fortunate countries have come to take for granted. Yet your people are poor, sometimes hungry, pretty often sick, living in leaky huts and scratching up the ground with wooden ploughs hauled by scrawny oxen ... Prophet's beard, I can't even hear myself say it without thinking it's ridiculous! But what I wind up thinking is—is that I half-wish the slave-traders hadn't steered clear of Beninia. Because I'd be rather proud to think my own African ancestors came from Shinka stock."

There: it was out. Breathing heavily, Norman sought for a response among the people gathered at the table. Elihu was nodding like a benign Buddha, as though this was precisely what he'd expected, and the cabinet ministers were exchanging embarrassed grins. Of his own team, the only one he could see without twisting his head and staring was Derek Quimby, at the end of the line, and the little tubby linguist was apparently nodding violent agreement, not a reaction one would look for from a Caucasian in Beninia.

Obomi said finally, "Thank you, Norman. I appreciate that. It's the way I've always felt about my compatriots, and it's good to hear visitors agree with what I might otherwise mistake for parochialism. Well, are we decided, then?"

Everyone signified assent.

"Excellent. We shall present the project to Parliament for ratification as soon as possible, and then you'll go right ahead with the loan and with your campaign to recruit the foreign advisors. That's correct, Norman?"

"Yes, Mr. President," Norman said.

Going out of the room, Gideon Horsfall drew him aside with a conspiratorial air.

"Didn't I tell you?" he said. "Beninia would digest you! And here you are—digested!"

the happening world (13)

RÉSUMÉ

Shalmaneser is a Micryogenic ® computer bathed in liquid helium and there's no sign of Teresa.

When Eric Ellerman tried to get at the Too Much cultivating section of the Hitrip plant, they asked some very awkward questions.

They gave Poppy Shelton clearance when they karyotyped the embryo and she celebrated with a party. Roger caught some bleeder trying to slip her a cap of Yaginol and knocked him arse over eyebrows.

Norman Niblock House is in virtually sole charge of the Beninia project.

Guinevere Steel is wondering how to reconcile that metallic name she adopted with the trend towards a more natural look that is going to dominate the fashion scene by fall.

Frank thinks Sheena has become quite unreasonable. After all, in a little while the baby will start to show and it's simply not legal.

Arthur Golightly found something else he'd forgotten he owned.

Donald Hogan proved to be the right man for the job just as the Washington computers promised.

Stal Lucas has pretty well made up his mind about the shiggy Eric Ellerman was supposed to have had in Ellay. Her name was Helen and she was a blonde of five foot five.

Philip Peterson has just lost another girl-friend.

Sasha Peterson thought she was *quite* unsuitable.

Victor and Mary Whatmough had a row after the Harringhams' cocktail party but they're used to that.

Elihu Masters is delighted at having been able to do his old friend the right sort of favour.

Gerry Lindt's first offence became the second. And the third. And . . .

Professor Dr. Sugaiguntung is afraid for his country.

Grace Rowley is dead.

The Right Honourable Zadkiel F. Obomi is under sentence of death from his doctors.

Olive Almeiro is in serious trouble with the Spanish authorities for advertising genuine Castilian ova for sale.

Chad C. Mulligan couldn't give up being a sociologist after all, but since he hates the idea he's mostly drunk these days.

Jogajong is encamped with a small group of loyal followers waiting for the current mood of wild enthusiasm in favour of the Solukarta régime to die away.

Pierre Clodard has mentioned the idea of divorcing his wife Rosalie, but so far only to his sister Jeannine.

Jeff Young sold that batch of GT aluminophage, and it did very satisfactory damage.

Henry Butcher is in jail.

There's a new Begi story. Nobody knows where it got started. It's called "Begi and the American".

Mr. & Mrs. Everywhere have not yet been to Yatakang. If they go, áll hell will break loose.

Occasionally Bennie Noakes says, "Christ! What an imagination I've got!"

Meanwhile, back at the planet Earth, it would no longer be possible to stand everyone on the island of Zanzibar without some of them being over ankles in the sea.

(POPULATION EXPLOSION Unique in human experience, an event which happened yesterday but which everyone swears won't happen until tomorrow.
                    —*The Hipcrime Vocab* by Chad C. Mulligan)

tracking with closeups (22)

THE CLIMAX OF MORE THAN A LIFETIME OF ACHIEVEMENT

It was not a good day for Georgette Tallon Buckfast. It had begun with her weekly checkup and the doctor had said she was over-exerting herself again. She told him he was a liar, and when he pointed to the mute evidence of her body—high levels of fatigue-products, excessive blood-pressure—she cursed it and him.

"I'm putting through a deal bigger than you could even think of!" she snapped. "Bigger than even I have handled before! All you have to do is keep me going!"

The body was becoming a burden. She would have liked to trade it in for a new model. But all the medical experts could do was add to it, supplement it, furnish it with props.

She could not accept that with the funds that sufficed to buy a whole country she could not buy health.

It's not as though I'm being greedy. I'm not asking for youth and beauty.

Why should she? She had never been beautiful; gradually she had come to feel beauty would have been a handicap, put a brake on her ambitions. As for youth, they called her "Old GT" and she found it flattering. It put the creation whose initials she shared on the same footing as other "old" concepts—Old Faithful, Old Glory . . .

Now, today, with the culmination of her greatest ever gamble, it was right that there should be some ceremony, some formality. If only it didn't have to be here, in this chilly computer shrine . . .

Alert, an attendant saw to it that she was more warmly insulated, and the irritation passed. Waiting for the exact, pre-set moment, her mind wandered.

I worried about Elihu's recommendation, never thought too highly of young House, but in my time I've learned to recognise when a man digs in his heels. And we could have pulled him out if we'd had to. But instead he's managed to sell the entire Beninian government and tomorrow I shall no longer be running just a corporation but a whole country I've never seen!

"Ready now, ma'am," a soft voice advised her, and she stared at the enigmatic shape of Shalmaneser, which she had made possible and did not understand.

I wonder if God sometimes feels that way about His creatures.

She liked speech-making and show because she fed on tributes to herself, but the mood of the times was against it. She rationed it, warily, to people who might appreciate it: meetings of stockholders who liked to sense the majesty and solemnity of a multi-billion dollar enterprise. This was only a gathering of staffers, most of whom were scientists not connected to the big scene of real life. Down there, a man in white moving some switches, watched attentively by his colleagues and the assembled members of the board. Consultations. It all seemed to be taking an appallingly long time.

Surely one of those reports said something about Shalmaneser reacting in nanoseconds?

"What's going on?" demanded Old GT.

Her secretary went to inquire, and spent another long time in whispered discussion, and eventually came back with a man who looked very worried indeed.

"I hate to have to tell you this, ma'am," he informed Old GT. "But something appears to be slightly wrong somewhere. I imagine we'll sort it out soon but it'll require a bit of work."

"What?"

"Well, ma'am . . ." The man's face grew actively unhappy. "As you know, we've run scores of programmes through

Shalmaneser in connection with this Beninia project, and he's functioned perfectly in all of them. It just so happens that today—"

"Come to the point, you fool!"

"Yes, ma'am." The man wiped his face with the back of his hand. "All those other programmes were run on a hypothetical basis, the entire group of assumptions being 'given' and derived from our own researches. What we've done now is to switch over the optimum programme, the one we've decided to put into practice, so that it enters Shalmaneser's real-world consciousness and interacts with everything else he knows about the world."

"And—?"

"He's rejected it out of hand, ma'am. Says it's absurd."

Black fury flooded up from the bottom of Old GT's mind, engulfing first her belly, where it made her guts seem to twist into knots and pull tight, then her lungs, which gasped air and strained to fill with gases suddenly turned to sluggish pitch, then her heart, which thundered and battered at her ribs as though it would break out of their cage, her throat and tongue which grew stiff, cracking like old dry paper folded and pressed, and at last her brain, which composed the thought:

"!!!!!"

"Get the doc!" someone said.

"Xx xxx xx," said someone else.

"_____"

". . . . ."

"   "

.

continuity (31)

GROUNDWORK

The phone went again. Cursing, Donald stumbled to the switch. At first there was only a loud background noise, as of many people hurrying to and fro. Suddenly a woman's voice blared at him, charged with anger.

"Hogan? You there? This is Deirdre Kwa-Loop! Engrelay head office just called me. There was a bargain, remember? Four hours on a beat!"

Stunned, Donald stared at the phone as though he could look along the cable despite the lack of a screen and see the face of the person he was talking to.

"Nothing to say, huh? I'm not surprised! I should have known better than to trust one of you bleeders! Well, I've been around this scene a while. I'm going to fix it so you never get—"

"Fasten it!" Donald snapped.

"The hole I will! Listen to me, paleass—"

"Where were you while I was tangling with a mucker?" Donald roared. In the mirror adjacent to the phone he saw the light in Bronwen's room go on, a peach-coloured glow.

"Whatinole has that got to do with it?"

"A hundred people saw that mucker nearly kill Sugaiguntung! What did you want me to do—count off four hours and call you by a critonium clock? The word must have been all around the press club within five minutes!"

Heavy breathing. At length, reluctantly: "Well, after about four poppa-momma things are usually quiet, and—"

"So what you did you went out on the town, hm?"

No answer.

"*I* see," Donald said with heavy sarcasm. "You thought I'd hire a gang of messengers and tell them, 'I made a promise to this woman who can't cover her own stories—you have four hours to find out where she's hiding herself!' Know where I was four hours after it happened? Drugged into coma at the university clinic! Will you take *that* as an excuse?"

Silence.

"The hole with you, then—I'm going back to bed!"

He cut the circuit. Almost at once, the phone buzzed again.

"Sheeting hole! What is it?"

"Management, Mr. Hogan," said a young man's voice, very nervous. "Is very many persons wish talk with you. Is saying most urgent, sir."

Donald changed to Yatakangi and spoke loudly enough for the sound at the other end to carry if it wasn't directional-ised.

"Tell them to go peddle their grandmother's urine. If there is another call on this phone before nine o'clock I shall have you—you personally—wrapped in the hide of a gangrened cow and hung up for the buzzards, do you understand?"

One thing I never appreciated before I came here: Yatak-angi is a very satisfying language to invent insults in.

He thought for a while. Eventually he gathered up his clothes, his communikit and anything else that looked as though it might come in handy in the morning, carried them through into Bronwen's room, and bolted the door from the far side before rejoining her.

This time, however, he did not manage to go back to sleep. It was as though his mind had sent unpleasant information garnered from Delahanty's earlier call and the events of the day down echo-delay circuits of varying lengths, and all the echoes had coincided at this point in time.

He only vaguely noticed what he had been half-expecting: footsteps in the corridor, a thunderous knocking on his own room's door, chinking and scratching sounds as someone tried a pass-key. But he had remembered to put over the dead-lock. The would-be intruder cursed and went away, probably regretting the bribe he had given the reception clerk for the room number.

That, though, was less important than the conflicting thoughts and images reverberating in the gong of his skull. Ten years of behaving like a sponge, doing no more than absorb second-hand information, had not equipped him for action of the kind now expected of him. Even the new version of himself produced by eptification could not cope with the demands on him.

Beside him, Bronwen whispered invitations to lose himself in animal sensation, but he was drained of the capacity to respond. He told her to be quiet and let him think, and at once regretted it because out of the darkness a moron-face emerged, slack silly mouth reflected in a gash below. He repressed a moan and rolled over on his side, terrified.

There's got to be a way—think, think!

Gradually possibilities developed towards plans. The mucker's image faded, taking with it his sense of sick dismay, and it was replaced by a vague pride in what he was being relied on to do—an act that could determine the course of history.

I know how to get at Sugaiguntung. I know how to contact Jogajong. Between the two it's just a matter of . . .

His body relaxed, and was rested even as his busy mind shaped and patterned the events of the day.

At eight o'clock he sent for breakfast and picked his way through many small dishes of cold fried and pickled delicacies—fish, fruit, vegetables. Gulps of scalding tea washed down the food. Bronwen, as naked as she had been all night, served him silently and made sure he was replete before taking any herself.

He found he liked that. It was sultanesque. It was foreign enough to match the strange country he had wandered to.

Couldn't imagine Gennice doing it . . .

"I have to go out," he said eventually. "Perhaps I'll see you again this evening."

She smiled and embraced him while he was thinking that if

he did see her again something would have gone disastrously wrong. But it was bad to imagine such catastrophes. He put on his clothes, equipped himself, slung his communikit over his shoulder and went down brazenly to the main lobby.

It was morning-busy, but there were, in addition to the staff and clients, people of every possible colour who were simply sitting around until they spotted him. Then they closed in like sharks approaching a wounded swimmer, raising cameras, recorders and voices.

"Mr. Hogan you must—Mr. Hogan let me please—listen and I will—"

A fat Arab woman who had reacted faster than the others put a camera practically under his nose. He snatched it away and threw it in the face of a Japanese on the other side of him. When a burly turbaned Sikh got in his way he hit him with the side of his hand and stepped over his falling body. At the side of the main door there was an indoor palm in a pot, which he jumped at and pulled over, delaying all of the reporters except a persistent African whom he had to kick in the shins. The man stumbled and tripped up the next person coming after him, which gave Donald the chance to get out on the street and signal an empty cab.

A car with two impassive men in it followed him: proof of Totilung's promise, he guessed. He offered his driver fifty talas if he could lose them, and the man took him through a series of narrow alleys half-blocked by bazaar-stalls, contriving eventually to get a herd of goats between his own vehicle and the one following.

Well pleased, Donald paid the man off and changed to a rixa next time they passed one. He could do nothing to make himself wholly inconspicuous, owing to his complexion and appearance, but at least for the moment no one knew for sure where he was.

Three rixas later, he reached the vicinity of Sugaiguntung's home. He had no expectation of finding the professor in, unless his doctors had insisted that he rest following the attack by the mucker, but he wasn't here to take advantage of the promised interview.

Scouting the district on foot, he found it to be much as he

had guessed from the city-maps he had seen—quiet, prosperous, aloof from the bustling life of the centre of the city, having a fine view of the Shongao Strait. There were houses here, not apts, each one enclosed by a wall and surrounded by gardens—either set with flowers and shrubs in the Western style, or paved, gravelled and ornamented with water-worn rocks. Only three wide roads traversed the area, to allow taxis and delivery-trucks access. For the rest, especially on the seaward, lower side, there was only a maze of paths which he explored with his ears always open for the approach of a curious stranger.

Fortunately, he had picked a quiet time. The heads of families would mostly be at work, the children in school, the servants cleaning house or away marketing.

Sugaiguntung's own home was in the shape of a very short-legged T, set in a garden of pentagonal form with its shortest side fronting a road. He walked all around except along that short side, where there was a bored policeman swinging a truncheon, noting certain interesting facts such as the location of a stunted tree which overhung the wall and the presence in the house—silhouetted against a window-wall—of a dumpy woman busy at her chores.

Wife, housekeeper? More likely the latter. Donald recalled a report that Sugaiguntung's wife, a woman older than himself to whom he had been married almost twenty years, had drowned while boating four or five years ago, but no mention of a second marriage.

He was about to make one more tour when the peace of the morning was interrupted by the appearance, trudging up the main road, of a party of dedicated-looking youths and girls carrying slogan-boards praising Sugaiguntung and Solukarta. Their intention was clearly to gawp at the great man's home. Although it provided a distraction for the policeman, who ran to meet them and engaged in fierce argument with the leaders, their arrival meant that thirty or forty curious pairs of eyes were staring in Donald's direction. He melted away behind the wall and began to work towards the seashore, along the route by which he would have to take the professor if he persuaded him to leave.

He lunched in a reed-thatched inn and watched a juggler with a tame monkey while the other patrons—who had seen many more monkeys than Caucasians—watched him. Beginning to grow alarmed, he abandoned his last glass of local rice-beer when he decided that the proprietor was spending too long staring at him.

He doubled away inland for a bit before returning to the waterfront during the siesta period. Apart from fishermen dozing in the shade of their beached praus, there were few people about, but nonetheless he wandered along to a totally deserted stretch before he discreetly produced a compass which had been included in his equipment. By its aid he determined which of the six or seven dark indentations he could see in the green shoreline at the foot of Grandfather Loa must be the one leading to Jogajong's secret encampment.

About then it began to rain again, and he made his way back into the city, heading for the office of the man on whom he must rely to get across the Strait, the so-called freelance reporter Zulfikar Halal. He found him on the third floor above a carpet importer's warehouse, fast asleep amid the pungent scent of hashish.

Christ. This is my contact with Jogajong?

Halal himself was shabby and unshaven; the room was littered with old newspapers, labelless tape-spools and packets of holographic photos. Obviously this was not merely his office but his home, for a screen in the corner failed to hide a heap of tumbled clothing and shoes. However . . .

Donald woke him with some difficulty. Startled, Halal forced his eyes to focus and looked first bewildered, then scared. Scrambling to his feet, he said, "*Hazoor!* Is your honour not the reporter, the American reporter?"

"That's right."

Halal licked his lips. "*Hazoor,* forgive me, I was not expecting you to come here in this fashion! I was told—" He recollected himself, darted to the door and peered out. Satisfied there was no one eavesdropping, he nonetheless continued in a whisper.

"I thought your honour was not supposed to contact me until much later, until—"

"There isn't going to be a much later," Donald snapped. "Sit down and listen hard."

He outlined what he wanted, and when, and Halal's eyes rolled.

"*Hazoor!* It is risky, it is difficulty, it is expensive!"

"The hole with the cost. Can you do it?" He produced a roll of fifty-tala bills and fanned them with his thumb.

"Your honour," Halal said fawningly, fascinated by the money, "I will do my best, by the grave of my mother I swear it."

Donald felt a little frightened. For all that Delahanty had vouched for this Pakistani, he neither looked nor acted like a trustworthy agent. Still, there was no one else. Short of stealing a boat to cross the Strait, he had to put himself in Halal's hands.

He said toughly, hoping to impress the other, "I don't want you to do your best. I want you to do what I've told you to do—understand? If you let me down ... Well, you heard how I tackled that mucker at the university?"

Halal's mouth gaped open. "That is true? I thought it a piece of bazaar nonsense!"

"With these hands," Donald said. "And if you fail me I shall take you and wring the blood from you like water from a wet washcloth. I promise that on *my* mother's grave."

He was back, now, in the bazaar quarter where his taxi of the morning had lost his pursuers. There was one more thing to attend to before the city re-awoke from its siesta, and he would have to hurry.

He picked his way between rows of merchants' stalls closed up while their owners slumbered, until in a little side-alley he spotted a phone-booth well concealed from passers-by. Someone had voided his bowels on the floor, but that was a minor nuisance. He kept a careful watch all the time he was composing his two messages on the communikit, his disguised gas-gun in his hand. He was very much aware that the moment he put in his call to the nearest Engrelay satellite someone might realise he was the caller.

But he thought he had got away with it until, gathering up his equipment and making to open the door of the booth, he recognised Totilung standing on the far side of the narrow alley.

tracking with closeups (23)

BEGI AND THE ORACLE

Begi came to a village where the people believed in omens, signs and portents. He asked them, "What is this about?"

They said, "We pay that old wise woman and she tells us what day is best to hunt, or court a wife, or build a new house, or bury the dead so that ghosts will not walk."

Begi said, "How does she do that?"

They said, "She is very old and very wise and she must be right because she has become very rich."

So Begi went to the house of the wise woman and said, "I shall go hunting tomorrow. Tell me if it will be a good day."

The woman said, "Promise to pay me half of anything you bring home." Begi promised, and she took bones and threw them on the ground. Also she made a little fire with feathers and herbs.

"Tomorrow will be a good day for hunting," she said.

So next day Begi went into the bush taking his spear and shield and also some meat and a gourd of palm-wine and rice boiled and folded in a leaf and wearing his best leopard-skin around him. At night he came back naked without anything at all and went into the wise woman's house.

He broke a spear on the wall and with the head he cut in half a shield that was there and gave away half the meat she had and half the rice she had to the other people and poured out on the ground half her pot of palm-wine.

The old woman said, "That is mine! What are you doing?"

"I am giving you half of what I brought back from my hunting," said Begi.

Then he tore off half the old woman's cloak and put it on and went away.

After that the people made up their own minds and did not have to pay the old woman anything.

continuity (32)

FIRST WITH THE NEWS

Still a little dazed, having been called from bed, Norman stared at the face in the phone-screen. It was that of E. Prosper Rankin, the company secretary of GT.

"Norman, I thought I'd better call you at once and tell you the news before it breaks over the TV. You may have to take some urgent precautionary measures. Old GT has had a cerebral haemorrhage and isn't expected to last the day."

The identity of initials between creator and creation filled Norman's mind briefly with a vision of the GT tower bursting apart in its upper storeys and pouring dark red blood from its windows. He said after a pause, "What should we do here, then—slack the tempo?"

"The exact opposite," grunted Rankin. His manner indicated that he had not expected Norman to mouth any conventional professions of regret. Georgette Tallon Buckfast, all her life, had been a person to admire but not to love. "The first effect is bound to be a wave of panic selling in GT shares and all the subsidiary companies. Our estimates are that prices will drop by thirty to forty million today regardless of what we do. We desperately need something to kick them back up again as soon as possible."

"And you're counting on the Beninia project to provide the rebound." Norman frowned. "Well, I don't see why it shouldn't—we secured our parliamentary ratification yester-

522

day, on schedule, and Dr. Ram Ibusa is making arrangements to fly to New York with me and sign the contracts on behalf of the government."

"I see a reason why it shouldn't," Rankin countered grimly. "I haven't told you what the shock was which caved in Old GT."

Premonition filled Norman's mind with the sound of earthquakes.

"When we switched Shalmaneser's own programme for the project from 'hypothetical' to 'actual', he rejected it. And the technicians can't find out why."

"But—!" Norman groped for words. "But Shal must have some sort of grounds for the rejection!"

"Oh, the first thing they did was ask him pointblank why. He spat back everything he'd been fed about Beninia and its people and announced that it was inconsistent with the larger mass of data already in store." Rankin pounded fist into palm. "And that's absurd! Every last item has been checked out on the ground by you and your team . . . Any ideas?"

Norman shook his head, numbed.

"Well, you'd better start thinking hard. My feeling is that we're going to have to launch the project anyhow and pray for a miracle to save us from calamity. If we don't get out the grand slam publicity in forty-eight hours at the latest, a calamity of a different kind is due beyond doubt. According to a digest of data about Beninia which I viewed the other day, the people there were alleged by their neighbours to be pretty competent wizards. You're on the spot—go see if they can conjure up the miracle we need!"

He cut the circuit and the screen died slowly into dark.

the happening world (14)

THE BENINIA CONSORTIUM
(General Technics Inc.
General Technics (Great Britain and Commonwealth) Ltd.
General Technics (Australasia) Pty.
General Technics (France) SA
General Technics (Deutschland) GmbH
General Technics (Scandinavia) Aktiebolaget
General Technics (Latin America) SA
General Technics (Johannesburg) Pty.
Mid-Atlantic Mining Inc.
and all subsidiary companies and corporations of the above)
TOGETHER WITH THE GOVERNMENT AND PEOPLE
OF BENINIA

announce the flotation of a substantial PUBLIC LOAN
FUND yielding a warranted FIVE PER CENT PER AN-
NUM with excellent prospect of a yield approaching EIGHT
PER CENT (fully computed by General Technics' "Shal-
maneser")

The term of the loan to be in the first instance 20 YEARS
with option of reversion or continued participation for a
further 30 YEARS making 50 YEARS IN ALL

Prospectus and certified true copies of the above-mentioned computer analysis available on request from . . .

*

THE BENINIA CONSORTIUM

invites applications for contracts of employment in the country of Beninia from persons having experience of West African conditions particularly in the former colonial territories. Salaries will be generous. The term of employment will depend on circumstances but is expected to average five years. Round-trip allowance; one month home vacation and two months local vacation per two-year period; removal and resettlement expenses; generous weighting for sub-standard conditions of accomodation. Write, giving details of time spent in West Africa and full description of posts occupied, to . . .

*

THE BENINIA CONSORTIUM

requires staff preferably but not necessarily having experience in West Africa, in the following specialities:

Architecture	*Education*
Transportation	*Communications*
Civil engineering	*Mechanical engineering*
City planning	*Medicine (esp. tropical)*
Law	*Economics*
Cybernetics	*Power, light and heat*
Plant erection	*Human ecology*
Water purification	*Public health & sanitation*
Textiles	*Agriculture*
Ore refining	*Production planning*
Plastics synthesis	*Electronics*
Mining, mineralogy	*Printing & publishing*

—and literally EVERY OTHER DISCIPLINE involved in the running of a 21st-century nation! Applications to . . .

*

WANT TO GET OUT AND SEE THE WORLD BEFORE YOU SETTLE
DOWN?
WANT TO HELP OTHER PEOPLE?
WANT TO ENJOY TOP PAY AND UNIQUE EXPERIENCE?
The Beninia Project is one of the most exciting ideas ever
conceived and YOU can be part of it!
Call us at . . .

*

Stock cue VISUAL: white boy age appx. 17 lifts up negro
child to see handsome tall new building under blue sky.
Stock cue SOUND: "Thinking about . . . Beninia?"
Stock cue VISUAL: BCU child's wondering face.
Stock cue SOUND: "That's the part of the big scene
where more things will be happening . . . more marvels will
be wrought!"
Stock cue VISUAL: cliptage splitscreen—jungle with animals, building in course of erection, children running, river
with boats, etc.
Stock cue SOUND: "Beninia Theme" specially recorded
by the Em Thirty-Ones.
Stock cue VISUAL: Mr. & Mrs. Everywhere walk across
village square with tame deer following towards (pan) fine
new sky-line of buildings and people of village fall in behind,
children playing with deer and trying to get on for a ride.
Stock cue SOUND: "Beninia Theme" down and speech
over—"You too could be part of this fantastic, magnificent,
unprecedented twenty-first century venture! Note the number
of the nearest agency hiring volunteers!"
Live cue SOUND: local station reads in call-code as appropriate.

*

"Mary dear, I've been thinking about these advertisements
for Beninia."
"Yes, Victor, I know you have. But things must have
changed out there, you know."
"They're changing here, aren't they? Faster and less palat-

ably! I've made up my mind. I'm going to send them an application."

"T'avais raison, Jeannine. T'as parlé au sujet des Américains qui allaient s'intéresser à la Béninie, et voici une réclame que je viens de trouver dans le journal. Tu l'as vue?"

"Montre-le-moi ... Ah, Pierre! C'est épatant! Moi, je vais y écrire sur le champ! Toi?"

"Je leur ai déjà donné un coup de téléphone."

"Mais ... qu'est-ce que pense Rosalie de tout cela?"

"Sais pas."

"Tu n'as pas demandé à ta femme si elle veut—?"

"Heu! Je m'en fiche, Jeannine. Je te dis franchement: je m'en fiche!"

"Frank, do you suppose they have eugenic laws in a backward country like Beninia?"

"What?"

"GT is hiring people to go there. And they've established an office right here in the city to interview candidates."

*

Teach: mathematics, English, French, geography, economics, law ...

Train: teachers, doctors, nurses, engineers, meteorologists, mechanics, agronomists ...

Build: houses, schools, hospitals, roads, docks, power stations, factories ...

Process: iron, aluminium, wolfram, germanium, uranium, water, polythene, glass ...

Sell: power, antibiotics, knives, shoes, television sets, bullsperm, liquor ...

Live: faster, longer, higher off the hog.

*

THE BENINIA CONSORTIUM WANTS—WANTS—WANTS—!

continuity (33)

GOT IT AND GONE

The rain had ceased while Donald was making his phone-call, but water was still running in the gutters. It seemed for a short eternity that the only sound anywhere was the trickling of it as it drained through the grating of a sewer.

At last Superintendent Totilung spoke.

"Mr. Hogan, I believe Professor Dr. Sugaiguntung has been expecting a visit from you. He told me he had offered you a private interview."

"That's right," Donald said, his voice creaking like an old iron gate. Still half inside the phone-booth, gas-gun in hand, communikit slung over his shoulder, he glanced sidelong towards the mouth of the valley. It was blocked by a police-man with his bolt-gun drawn.

"And a personally guided tour of his laboratories."

"That's right too."

"You're full of contradictions, Mr. Hogan. Any number of foreign reporters would have given their arms for the privilege you've been accorded. Yet you haven't been in touch with the professor all day. Will your head office be as pleased with you tomorrow as they were this morning?"

Totilung's eyes, bright, sharp, dark like currants in a suet roll, fixed him. Mere shock began to cede place in Donald's mind to honest fear; he felt the agonising prickle of sweat inside his clothes.

"I propose to call on Dr. Sugaiguntung this evening, at his home."

"You expect to find there all the information you want—his experimental animals, his charts and graphs, his computer analyses, films, instruments?" Totilung's manner was deliberately scathing.

"You let me plan my work and I'll be pleased to let you get on with yours," Donald said tightly. "In my judgment the interview comes before the guided tour of the labs, so—"

"You've wasted your chance, then," Totilung shrugged. "I'm carrying a warrant for your arrest on charges of assault and battery, and of damaging a camera the property of Miss Fatima Saud." She added in Yatakangi to her companion, "Bring those handcuffs over here—but keep your gun ready! This man's a trained killer."

Wary, not taking his eyes off Donald, the policeman drew the cuffs from his pocket and approached Totilung.

I've been tricked. I've been conned. I've been driven down a blind alley of life. I never wanted to be herded into corners where I had to kill or be killed. To be back where I was, bored and ordinary and dull, I'd give anything, anything!

But he could not afford to be arrested and waste time and perhaps be deported. Tonight he must pull the plum from the tree and carry it home.

He forced himself towards calm with a deep, controlled breath. Assuming Totilung had been hunting him when someone reported that he was calling an Engrelay satellite from this booth, she would have come straight here. The street on which the alley debouched was too narrow for a prowl car; it, and the driver, must be waiting at the end of the block. With luck he had only Totilung and one man to contend with for the moment.

He let his shoulders slump in resignation as she took the cuffs and stepped up to him, making sure her body did not block her companion's fire. The latter followed close behind her, gun levelled. Donald held up his hands as though meekly preparing for the cuffs to be put on and fired the gas-gun—not at Totilung, but at the man.

The searing jet struck his cheek, blinded one eye, poured

into his mouth as he gasped, scalded his lungs and doubled him over, choking. Reflex triggered his gun and a bolt went to ground with a sizzling noise in a pile of rubbish twenty feet away. Donald wasted no time on him, though. He accelerated the upward motion of his hands and drove the fingers that did not hold the gas-gun into Totilung's fleshy jowl. Distracted by the handcuffs, she was slow in bringing up her arms to cover her face. He kicked her leg below the kneecap and as she twisted sideways in agony he dropped the gas-gun, grasped her arm and tripped her.

She fell backwards, sprawling, mouth open to scream, and he jumped on her belly with both feet, driving all the wind out of her. The man was recovering: choking and weeping, he was waving the gun as though mortally terrified of shooting his chief instead of Donald.

Donald leapt off Totilung and butted the policeman back against the opposite wall of the alley. His soft cap was no protection as his head slammed into the brickwork. He howled and let the gun fall.

Donald caught it before it hit the ground, turned it over in his hand as he stepped aside, and shot first the policeman and then Totilung to death.

It's the thing we know best how to do to a man. We're marvellous at it, wonderful, unparalleled.

Working fast, he pulled the bodies together, his hands becoming sticky with the melted fat on their crisp skins, turned to the consistency of pork-crackling by the energy bolts. He wiped them on an uncharred portion of the policeman's uniform and unslung his communikit. He placed a book of matches inside the lid as he had been shown. Hand on the control knob, he forced himself to review the layout of the streets nearby and decided that if the prowl car which had brought Totilung had come as close as possible it must be on the right of the alley. There seemed to be more noise than a few minutes ago; the siesta was at an end.

He turned the control knob to its unmarked final setting and ran.

Coming in sight of other people after leaving the alley, he had to force himself to walk with deliberate slowness, his right hand in the side-pocket of his shirjack to disguise the bulge of the gun. After twenty paces like that he heard the dull crumping sound behind him. All around him people started and looked and pointed. He copied them, for fear of seeming more conspicuous than his complexion made him, and saw that two whole buildings extending right the way from the alley to where he stood had abruptly leaned back with a cloud of smoke and dust. The air was full of screams.

Shortly, the screams were drowned out by the noise of the buildings as they folded up wet cardboard fashion and slumped into rubble and corpses.

From then until sunset time was sliced into disconnected images that might be not visual, but internal. Once he was in a corner of two walls bringing back the lunch he had eaten at the reed-thatched inn by the sea, wondering with detached curiosity at the way his stomach had altered the colour of the food. Another time he was leaning over the counter of one of the ubiquitous street-corner kiosks, pretending to argue with the proprietor over prices because there was a police car passing. But there was no sequence in the experiences. There was a fixed, due moment at which he must return to contact with the world, and until then he preferred not to perceive.

Darkness came, and triggered the command he had given himself. Shaking with the weakness that stemmed from terror, revulsion and vomiting, he made his way like a man in a dream to the district where Sugaiguntung had his home.

By half past seven he was within a block of it, and regaining his self-control. Concealed from a prowl car by a little clump of scented bushes, he felt his awareness mesh anew with exterior events. He re-learned how to frame coherent thoughts.

There's a lot of activity around here. They can't have dug out Totilung's body yet, surely? But it wouldn't take a genius to deduce what I did.

He fingered the gun in his pocket. It still had almost the full charge with which he had left the police-station armoury. He tried to find comfort in telling himself that he had been trained with the most advanced techniques to use such a weapon and win. It was no good. The only escape lay in action.

Action, distraction, fraction—I'm less than a man.

Circumspectly he moved on. A little way, and he had to throw himself flat in the shadow of an ornamental hedge to escape notice by a man on foot carrying a gun.

They're waiting for me. Has Sugaiguntung repented of the confession he made, changed his mind about wanting out? I won't let him. I daren't.

It took him another half-hour to establish exactly how the premises were guarded. Apart from the prowl car, which was moving quietly back and forth along each of the three roads that served the area, there were seven police stationed around Sugaiguntung's pentagonal garden, one sentry responsible for each side and paired men at the gates. Otherwise, he was relieved to discover, life seemed to be going on as usual. He caught snatches of sound from TV sets and in one of the nearby houses a group of people seemed to be rehearsing a scene from a traditional opera, singing in high forced voices and beating gongs.

At least he ran small risk of having to cope with inquisitive neighbours as well as the guards.

On leaving the hotel this morning, he had brought one trank with him to steady himself in the final emergency. He choked it down, praying that his stomach would not reject it before the capsule dissolved.

When it had taken effect, and his teeth no longer threatened to chatter, he made his way to the ornamentally deformed tree he had noticed this morning, which overhung the wall of Sugaiguntung's home. The man responsible for guarding this side of the house always seemed to pass directly beneath it.

On his next tour, he did as previously, and Donald's feet took him at the back of the neck, toes together. His whole weight followed and slammed the man face foremost into the ground, muddy from the rain. He struggled for only a few seconds before fainting, nose and mouth blocked against breath.

Donald shorted out his gun by tossing it into a puddle, where it discharged in a cloud of hissing steam, and clambered back into the tree. Edging along the stoutest of the branches which overhung the wall, he was able to drop on the far side where a flowering bush would break his fall. He was in sight of the main gate from here, where the two guards stood side by side in the glow of a lamp, but they were looking the other way.

On this side, the house's windows were all in darkness except one, which was screened by wooden slats. He headed for it, avoiding the pool of light cast by a lamp over the front door, and stole a glance inside. He saw Sugaiguntung sitting alone on a low pouffe before a table laden with empty bowls and dishes, just finishing his evening meal. The door of the room opened and the woman he had seen this morning came in, to ask whether she should clear away.

He dodged around the nearest corner of the house and went to the opposite side, hurrying at the expense of silence because it could not be long before the policeman's absence was noticed by his colleagues. At the back of the house there was a pair of sliding glass doors leading into the garden. He peered in, but saw nothing because the room beyond was so completely dark. He made to move on—and brilliant light leapt up in his face.

He was dazzled for an instant, too startled to move. Then his tortured eyes told him that the man who had put on the light was Sugaiguntung, and Sugaiguntung had recognised him and was coming to open the door.

He fell back, hand hovering by his gun, and hoped desperately that no one was looking in this direction from outside the grounds.

"Mr. Hogan! What are you doing here?" Sugaiguntung exclaimed.

"You invited me to call," Donald said dryly, his moment of shock obliterated by the swift assistance of the trank he had taken.

"Yes! But the police say they want to arrest you, and—"

"I know. I hit someone with a camera this morning and because Totilung would dearly love to deport me she's using it as an excuse. What's more, she'll have the chance if you don't put out that light!"

"Come inside," Sugaiguntung muttered, drawing back. "In the house is nobody but my housekeeper, and she is growing deaf."

Donald darted past him. Sugaiguntung closed the door and let slatted blinds fall over it, blocking the view from outside.

"Professor, do you still want what you said you wanted yesterday?" Anxious for the answer, Donald kept his hand close to his gun.

Sugaiguntung looked blank.

"Do you want the chance to get away from being used as a political tool?" Donald rapped. "I said I could give you that. I've risked my life to make it possible. Well?"

"I have been thinking about it all day," Sugaiguntung said after a pause. "I think—yes, I think it would be like a dream coming true."

In the distance there was a shout and the sound of running feet. Donald suddenly felt as limp as a rag.

"Thank God. Then you must do as I tell you. At once. It may be too late even now, but I think not."

Down the back pathway to the other gate, at which there were two more guards stationed, Sugaiguntung running on the path itself, Donald parelleling him noiselessly on soft ground. The guards looked behind them and turned a hand-lamp.

"Quickly!" Sugaiguntung panted. "Your sergeant wants you to go to that side of the house!" He pointed to his left. "Someone has knocked out the man who was on guard there!"

The policeman stared in the indicated direction. They saw the swivelling beams of handlamps and heard a voice bark an order. At once they took it for granted that Sugaiguntung was telling the truth and doubled away.

The moment they had rounded the corner of the wall, Donald flung open the gate and herded Sugaiguntung through. The gate gave on to the series of winding paths which he had scouted this morning. To the right and down-slope lay the sea.

If that bleeder Halal has let me down, what shall I do?

But it was too soon to think of such terrible possibilities. He hurried Sugaiguntung along as much as he dared, listening over the sound of his own breathing for any noise of pursuit. None had arisen before they emerged from the end of the path on to a quiet residential street. Now they had to walk without hurrying, occasionally crossing over to escape recognition by an evening stroller.

After an interminable time they saw a taxi at an intersection, which they were able to hail. In it, they rode to the waterfront and left it at a place popular with tourists where there were several restaurants specialising in grilled fish and Yatakangi folksongs. Mingling with the crowd but taking every advantage of awnings, screens and corners to avoid showing themselves directly to the curious, Donald led the way to a stretch of beach where during the day there had been thirty or forty fishing-boats.

His heart was in his mouth on the last lap. He nearly fainted with relief when he saw that—in keeping with Halal's promise—although many of the praus had already put to sea, their lights bobbing against the looming bulk of Grandfather Loa, a few were still nosed into the sand, their crews assembling one by one and laughing together, passing bottles of arrack and cigarettes.

"A man is supposed to have arranged for one of these boats to take us across the Strait," Donald explained to Sugaiguntung in a low voice. "Wait here. I'll go and find him."

Sugaiguntung gave a nod. His face was mask-like, empty of emotion, as though he had not yet had time to digest the implications of what he was committed to. Leaving him on his own worried Donald, but there was no alternative: that face was far too well known to be shown to all these fishermen.

Halal had said he would arrange to have a blue lamp hung from the mast of the boat assigned to carry them. There was no such lamp on any of the boats, Donald discovered with renewed dismay. But there was one with a lamp on the mast even if it wasn't blue. Growing desperate, he tried to persuade himself that the colour did not matter—perhaps they had not managed to find the necessary blue glass for it.

Three men were readying the boat for sea, coiling the typical Yatakangi seine-nets on the bow thwart and sluicing them down so that they would sink at once when they were tossed overside.

Gambling everything on guesswork, Donald hailed the man who appeared to be the skipper.

"I seek the man from Pakistan, Zulfikar Halal!"

If that kief-sodden coward caved in on this job, I'll . . . But I wouldn't have the chance. I'll be jailed, or dead!

The skipper paused in his work and turned his head. He gazed for a long moment. Then he picked up a handlamp and flashed it directly at Donald.

He said, "Are you the American, Hogan?"

For an instant Donald failed to understand the question—the man had given his name a Yatakangi inflection. Directly the words sank in, the world seemed to capsize. Thinking that at any moment police might emerge from the hold of the prau, he jumped back, tugging his gun free from his pocket.

"No need for that!" the skipper said sharply, and laughed. "I know you. I know where you want to go. To Jogajong. He has many supporters among us fisherfolk. The word went around today that if you asked for help we should give it. Come aboard."

context (24)

PROGRAMME REJECTED

Q reason for rejection

ANOMALIES IN GROUND DATA

Q define Q specify

DATA IN FOLLOWING CATEGORIES NOT ACCEPT-
ABLE: HISTORY COMMERCE SOCIALINTERACTION
CULTURE

Q accept data as given

QUESTION MEANINGLESS AND INOPERABLE

THERE LIVES MORE FAITH IN HONEST DOUBT

Norman should have been at the grand official ceremony when Ram Ibusa signed the contracts with the Beninia Consortium, at the press conference thereafter and at the formal banquet in the evening. Instead, he handed Ibusa over to the GT hospitality department and fled.

He had seen and heard and sensed too much. For all the cheering news about the market, where GT stock had already bounced back to the level it had left on the founder's death and seemed set to go higher; for all the false gaiety and the excited PR releases and the loudspeakers relaying the specially commissioned "Beninia Theme"—he could not stand the atmosphere in the GT tower. There were so many grey faces, so many blithe masks slipped when the owners of them thought they weren't being watched.

The feeling in the air was of the kind that might have reigned over a Hebrew encampment the day Jehovah declined, for His own inscrutable reasons, to perform a miracle and wipe out the high priest of Dagon.

And that, Norman judged, was not merely a comparison but a definition. The omniscient Shalmaneser had let his faithful disciples down, and with half their minds they were afraid it might not be his fault, but theirs.

Curse computers for a trick of Shaitan! Of all the times

Shalmaneser might choose to fail us he picks now, now, when my life and hopes are committed to his judgment!

He bought a pack of Bay Golds and went home.

The Watch-&-Ward Inc. key slipped smoothly into the lock. The door moved aside and showed him the interior of the apt, untidy, some of the furniture in different places, the liquor console surrounded by dead men not carried to the disposall, but otherwise not changed.

He thought at first the place must be empty. He looked into his own bedroom and saw that the bed was rumpled but only because someone had lain on the cover, not because it had been slept in. Shrugging, he lit one of the reefers he had bought and went back into the living area.

A faint snore came to him.

He strode over to Donald's old room and flung the door open. Chad Mulligan was asleep on the bed, not in it, his hair and beard unkempt and not a stitch on him, only shoes.

It was just after four poppa-momma. What in the world was the man doing asleep at this time of day?

"Chad?" he said. And a second time, more loudly: "Chad!"

"Wha . . . ?" Eyes blinked open, shut, open again and this time stayed open. "Norman! Sheeting hole, I didn't expect to see you back in New York! Uh—what time is it?"

"Gone four."

Chad sat up and forced his legs over the side of the bed, knuckling his eyes and trying to stifle a monstrous yawn. "Ooh-*ah!* Sorry, Norman—*wowf!* Welcome home. Excuse me, I shan't be fit company until I've showered."

"Since when have you taken to sleeping in the daytime?"

Chad managed to rise to his feet, and kept rising until he was on tip-toe, thrusting out with both hands to stretch his stiff muscles. He said, "It's not a habit. Just last night I was thinking and thinking and thinking and couldn't sleep at all, so I got drunk at breakfast time and that was that."

"What were you thinking about? And didn't you know there's an inducer in the pillow there? That would have put you to sleep."

"Inducers make me dream," Chad said. "Liquor doesn't."

Norman shrugged; neither he nor Donald had ever been

affected in that way by a sleep-inducer, but he remembered that one or two of the shiggies who had stayed here had complained of the same trouble—a risk of nightmares.

"Go ahead and take your shower," he said. "Don't be too long. I want to talk to you."

A sudden idea had come to him, which was probably a vain hope, but any chance no matter how slim was worth taking in the present crisis.

"Sure," Chad muttered. "Do me a favour, though—have some coffee sent up."

Five minutes later, dressed, hair and beard still wet but combed into orderliness, Chad collected the cup of coffee waiting for him and sat down in Donald's chair facing Norman in his own favourite.

"I envy you that Hille chair," Chad said absently. "About the only thing in the place I do envy you, to be candid. Comfortable. And you know it's going to remain a chair, not suddenly turn into a cosmorama unit . . . Okay: talk to me!"

"Chad, you're rated the most insightful living social analyst."

"Whaledreck. I'm rated a drunken sot. I've reached the stage where I get too drunk too fast to bother going out to look for shiggies, and I *like* women." He gulped down his coffee and wiped his moustache with the back of his hand.

"I want to hire you," Norman said stonily.

"Hire me? You must be hitripping. On the one hand, I'm too rich to have to work. I figured out I can exhaust myself just about twice as soon as I can exhaust my money. I'm trying to get that down to a fifty per cent margin and going to work would screw me up. On the other hand, I can't make anybody listen to me so what's the good of my working? That's settled, I hope. Have a drink—no, have a joint. Come out with me and collect some shiggies and we'll celebrate your return. Anything!"

"I have an almost completely free hand on the Beninia project. I want you, at a salary you can name yourself."

"Whatinole for?" Chad's astonishment seemed genuine.

Norman hesitated. "Well—you've heard Elihu singing the praises of Beninia, haven't you?"

"You were there at the time. Sounded like he had his private pipeline to Paradise."

"Think I'm the sort of codder who's easily persuaded?"

"You mean do I think you're a hard case? Uh-uh. But you like to come on as one. What are you working up to—understudying Elihu's PR job?"

"Exactly. Chad, that is a country which just seems to have been getting on quietly with its own business in the middle of all kinds of chaos. There used to be others, but they've all been caved in by outside interference—Nepal, Tahiti, Samoa—gradually reduced to Jettex Cursion status."

"What else would you expect? Like I keep telling people, we're a disgusting species with horrible manners and not fit to survive." He added irrelevantly, "Did you get the letter I sent you?"

"Yes, of course I did. I didn't reply because I was too sheeting busy. Now *listen* to me, will you? Outside interference or not, the Beninians haven't had a murder in fifteen years. They've never had a mucker at all, not even one. They talk a language in which you can't say that a man has lost his temper except by saying he's gone temporarily out of his skull. Thousands of Inoko and Kpala poured over the border as refugees only a generation ago and there's never been any tribal disorder between them and the people who were there already. The president runs the whole shtick—a million population, which is piddling by modern standards but a lot of people if you try and count heads—he runs it like a household, a family, not a nation. Is that clear? I don't think I can explain what the difference is, but I've seen it going on."

He was beginning to get through. What he could see of Chad's face above the beard and moustache expressed concentration.

"One big happy family, hm? Okay, so what do you want me to do about it? Sounds as though they're getting along all right by themselves."

"Haven't you caught any of the news bulletins where the need for the Beninia project was explained? I saw a replay of what Engrelay Satelserv is carrying while I was down at the GT tower just now, and all it left out was the risk that Dahomalia and RUNG may fight over Obomi's grave."

"Sure I've been catching the news. Been following the progress of your old beddy Donald."

There was a moment of blank puzzlement. "What about Donald?" Norman demanded.

"It was in the same bulletin where I saw about the Beninia project!"

"I guess I didn't catch the whole bulletin, only the extract they were replaying at GT . . . What did he do?"

"Saved Sugaiguntung from a mucker, is all. Killed the man with his bare hands."

"*Donald?* Chad, are you orbiting? Donald could never in a million years—"

"All human beings are wild animals and they're not fit to roam around loose." Chad got to his feet and approached the liquor console. "I'd better have a hair of the dog."

Norman shook his head, dazed. Donald? Coping with a mucker? It seemed so fantastic he dismissed it from his mind and switched back to what he had been saying before.

"Chad, I'm going to keep hammering at you until you cave in, understand?"

"About going to Beninia?" Chad measured out a generous helping of vodka and began to compose a whistler manually, as though he distrusted the programmed mixing instructions. "What for? You want a sociological advisor, you go get someone with the proper background. What do I know about West Africa? Only what I've read and seen on screens. Go hire some specialists."

"I *have* specialists. I want you, Y-O-U."

"To do what that you think they can't?"

"Turn Beninia upside down and shake out its pockets."

Chad tasted the whistler critically and added another shake of angostura. "Uh-uh, Norman. You just leave me to rot myself into my grave, there's a sweet codder. And I promise I'll comfort my premature old age with the idea that there really is a place somewhere on the pocky face of Mother Earth where people don't kill each other and don't run *amok* and generally behave like decent people should. I don't want to go there because at the bottom of my mind I guess I just don't believe in such a place."

"Nor does Shalmaneser," Norman said.

"What?"

"Shalmaneser has rejected every single attempt we've made to integrate the facts about Beninia into his real-world awareness. He says he won't accept what we tell him about its history, its commerce, its culture, or its social interactions. He claims there are anomalies in the data and they get spewed back."

"Can't you order him to accept the data?"

"If he refuses, you can no more order him to compute with them than you can make him act on the assumption that objects fall upwards. We're going out of our skulls, Chad. The whole Beninia project was predicated on our being able to process every step of it through Shalmaneser—not just the hardware of it, but the educational programmes, the probable diplomatic crises, the entire economy of the country practically down to the prodgies' pocket-money for half a century from now. And he keeps on about these anomalies which I know from my own experience aren't there!"

Chad stared at him. After a pause he began to chuckle. "Of course they're there," he said. "You've just been telling me all about them. Don't catch, hm? Norman, you must be suffering from brain-rot, I guess. Okay, you win—never let it be said I refused to help a friend out of trouble. Hang on until I finish my drink and I'll come along and pay a call on Shalmaneser with you."

Still baffled, yet convinced from Chad's manner that to him there was a solution of transcendental obviousness, Norman was about to reply when the phone sounded. He swivelled his chair and reached for the switch.

The screen lit to show Rex Foster-Stern's agitated countenance. "Norman!" he burst out. "Whatinole are you doing there? Prosper is going into orbit with fright—when we couldn't find you for the press conference he practically fainted!"

"That's okay," Norman said. "Tell him I've been arranging to hire a special advisor." He glanced at Chad, who gave a shrug and spread the hand that wasn't holding his drink.

"Sheeting hole, couldn't you have picked a better time to worry about recruitment?" Rex demanded. "Who is this advisor, anyhow?"

"Chad Mulligan. I'm bringing him down to talk to Shalmaneser now. Have him cleared for vocal interrogation in half an hour, will you?"

"Half an hour? Norman, you must be—"

"Half an hour," Norman repeated firmly, and cut the circuit.

"Y'know something?" Chad said. "It might be quite interesting, at that. I've often thought I ought to get acquainted with Shal."

tracking with closeups (24)

NO REASON, PURPOSE OR JUSTIFICATION

The sergeant kept 019 262 587 355 Lindt Gerald S. Pvt. to the last and when handing over his pass accompanied it with a scowl.

"I sheeting well hope you behave yourself better outside than in, Lindt!"

"Yes, sergeant," Gerry said, woodenly at attention in spite of having reclaimed his civilian clothes, eyes fixed on a point in space above the sergeant's shoulder. He had lost five pounds during recruit training and had had to draw in the belt of his slax.

"Shouldn't wonder," the sergeant said with contempt. "You're a softass at heart, aren't you?"

"Yes, sergeant."

"You've learned something in the army, at least, hm? Well, don't take it for everlasting gospel. Before you're through here we'll have had that heart out of you and made it over in a different design. All right, shift the scene."

"Permission to dismiss, sergeant?"

"Dis-miss!"

He was a week later going into Ellay on pass than the rest of his intake. Last time he had been on thirty-six hours' punishment drill. He was beginning to get an insight into the technique now: any recruit who wet his boots, as the current phrase went, immediately on reporting was marked as a scapegoat. It saved the noncoms the trouble of choosing one by their own judgment. The rest of the squad saw the treatment meted out to him and were supposed to quake in their boots and behave themselves.

He had done rather better than average in every instruction session so far, being brighter than average and also in better physical condition. Most of the other men in his squad were brown-noses from states where they were still at an economic disadvantage and had neither the funds nor the imagination to dodge the draft; there was a sprinkling of whites from the same states and not a few Puerto Ricans had also been grabbed by the computers. Underlying the singling out he had experienced, he suspected, there might possibly be a lean-over-backwards official directive aimed at encouraging his companions: pick out the tall good-looking blue-eyed fair-haired one and hit him because he can't complain it's prejudice.

He was the only blond in the whole squad.

Being better than others hadn't saved him from worse treatment.

Thesis, antithesis—synthesis.

Along with everyone else he climbed aboard the hoverboat running shore-pass parties from Boat Camp to the mainland. He felt no particular enthusiasm about being turned loose. He felt no particular enthusiasm about anything except keeping his nose clean. But for the risk of appearing odd, he would probably have preferred to sit in the barrick-room and write home.

At the point where the hoverboat ran up the concrete slip and on to the road, someone had managed to stretch a single strand of GT-manufactured monofilament wire between two posts. The driver was in a hurry—he had seven more runs to make this evening before he could use his own pass—and hit the wire at nearly forty miles an hour. It sliced through the cab with hardly any drag at all, breaking inter-crystalline and not the tougher molecular bonds, barely leaving a mark on metal and plastic because they re-welded themselves on the

Johanssen principle before air could get at the interfaces and cancel out their natural adhesion.

A force that tended to separate the parts, however, was capable of opposing the reunion.

Gerry Lindt happened to be turning to look at someone who had put a question to him. The twisting force was adequate to prevent his neck from bonding back together when the wire sliced through. Perhaps it was as well; he could have been paralysed from the neck down by the damage it did to his spinal cord. But the last horrible sight of his own torso as his eyes rolled along with his head towards the floor of the vehicle was nearer to eternal torment than even his sergeant would have wished on him.

It was obviously partisan work, not random sabotage. There was a grand roundup of suspected partisans organised immediately, and out of the two hundred and some they arrested they actually caught no fewer than four people in direct Chinese pay.

It was no special comfort to Gerry Lindt.

continuity (35)

For a fearful moment after he had brought Sugaiguntung to the boat, Donald thought the scientist was going to balk. There were so many things he did not know about this man whose life he had altered like an act of God. Was he afraid of the sea, was he a claustrophobe who could not be hidden in the hold?

But the reason for Sugaiguntung's hesitation became apparent with his next utterance.

"You did say—Jogajong?"

"Right!" Donald snapped. "Who else in this country could be trusted to keep you away from the gang in power?"

"I—I hadn't realised." Sugaiguntung licked his lips. "I don't involve myself much in things like this. It's all so strange and such a shock . . . Captain!"

The skipper looked attentive.

"Do you truly have faith in that man?"

Christ, we're going to have a political debate now! Donald sharpened his ears for the drone of a police helicopter or the chug of a reaction-powered patrol-boat.

"Yes, sir," the skipper said.

"Why?"

"Look at me, sir, and my friends here—half in rags. Look at my boat, which needs painting and a new engine. Marshal Solukarta tells us fisherfolk that we are the bedrock of our country, bringing in the precious food that keeps us healthy and improves our brains. Then he fixes the price of fish at twenty talas a basket and when we complain he tells us we are committing treason. I am not even allowed to leave my work and try and make more money on land. Saving your presence, sir—you are Dr. Sugaiguntung, aren't you?—what this country needs is not better children but better adults, who could raise their children better anyway."

Sugaiguntung gave a shrug and approached the side of the boat. He looked for a way to clamber over the gunwale, but there was no ladder or step. Donald, giving a final nervous glance behind him, put away his gun and helped the skipper hoist the scientist aboard.

"You will have to hide in the fish-hold," the skipper said. "It is stinking and dark. But the patrols are certain to stop us at least once if we approach the far shore. We shall have to make the trip very slowly, and before we can risk being searched there must be plenty of fish in the hold to deceive them."

They must have done this kind of thing before, Donald realised, as with quick efficiency the two crewmen brought old tarpaulins and wrapped him and Sugaiguntung in them to protect their clothes. They were instructed to lie at the furthest end of the hold where there was a vent bringing in fresh air. Then they were left to themselves while the boat was put out to sea. Shortly, its whole fabric was shuddering with the irregular chug of the reaction-pumps.

In darkness alleviated only by a grey patch where light from the mast-head lamp soaked through the slats over the air-vent, Sugaiguntung uttered a whimper.

"Don't worry," Donald said, unable to prevent it sounding like a forlorn hope.

"Mr. Hogan, I don't know if I've done the right thing. I—I may have fallen into a pattern of habit instead of taking a decision."

"I don't understand." The scrap of anthropological information read years ago leaked back to consciousness. "Oh—yes, I think I do. You mean there's a custom. Someone who saves your life buys a lease on it."

"It is what I was taught as a child, and there is a great

deal of irrationality left in us moderns. I have never been near to death before except once from a virus I caught. And that was while I was still a boy. One was supposed to buy back one's right to free will by doing something at the—oh!— the behest of the one who saved you, is that right?"

"Yes, that's good English for it. A bit antique but good English." Donald spoke absently; he had just caught the sound of seine-nets splashing into the water. Any minute now the filling of the hold with fish would begin, and would have to be repeated heaven knew how often before the boat could head for the far shore of the Strait.

Sugaiguntung went on, like a recording: "I know as a scientist that burning a cone of incense can do nothing to appease a volcano, yet when my wife lighted one for Grand- father Loa I smelt its smoke in the house and somehow I—I felt better for it. Do you understand that?"

Donald thought of Norman sending away to his string of Genealogical Research Bureaux and gave a sour chuckle. "I guess so," he admitted.

"But, you see, I had been thinking: what would they remember me for if the mucker had killed me? Not for the things I am proud of, my rubber-trees and my bacteria that I tailored to suit human needs. They would have remembered me for something I myself did not promise to do, which I myself could not have done! They would have grown to think of me as an impostor, wouldn't they?" There was a pleading tone to the words, as though Sugaiguntung was desperately seeking justification for his own decision.

"Very likely," Donald agreed. "And it wouldn't have been fair."

"No, precisely, it wouldn't have been fair." Sugaiguntung repeated the words with a kind of relish. "Nobody has the right to steal the reputation of someone else and use it to prop up a false claim. That is definite. I shall have a chance to tell the truth now, shan't I?"

"You'll have every facility you could possibly want."

Abruptly a hatch squealed open and the first of the netfuls of fish came squirming loathsomely down into the hold, to die gasping in a foreign element. More followed, and more, until they were a mass that screened the two hiding men from anyone merely peering in at the hatch.

What unexpectedly turned Donald's stomach was that they made a noise as they died.

The world reduced slowly to a dark stinking nowhere.

He had almost drifted into sleep because that was the only available escape-route when the skipper called very softly from the hatch.

"Mr. Hogan! We have been lucky—the patrol-boat on duty here is going the other way and we can watch her lights. Be quick and we can put you ashore now!"

Stiffly Donald forced his way over the slippery mounds of fish, their scales clinging to him and giving him patches of phosphorescence like a Yatakangi ghost in a temple painting. When he had levered himself out of the hatch—by touch, because the skipper had extinguished the masthead light—he turned and helped Sugaiguntung out. Soaking from the water which had puddled on the floor of the hold as the fish drained, they stood together shivering on the flimsy deck.

"I have made a signal to the sentries who hide in the trees over there," the skipper whispered. "They know we are friendly and will not fire on us."

"What are your crew doing?" Donald asked, seeing that the two other men were leaning over the bow and groping into darkness.

"There is a cable on the sea-bed," the skipper said. "We do not want to make any noise with the engine and the wind is too light to move us quickly . . . Ah!"

With a faint splashing the crewmen recovered the cable. To it, they attached a grapple; then, straining their muscles, they began to haul the boat inshore. The sky was heavily clouded, but even so Donald could make out the difference between black sky and black land. A few lights on the slopes of Grandfather Loa, away to their left, flickered mockingly.

The boat jolted and Sugaiguntung caught at his arm, almost knocked off balance.

"Quickly—go ashore now!" the skipper urged. "I see the patrol-boat's light coming back this way."

To Donald, there was no way of distinguishing between

one and another of the many boat-lights dotting the Strait. He was not inclined to argue with an expert, however.

"What reason can you give for coming here if you're challenged?" he asked.

"We shall say we wanted to get rid of a *latah*-fish."

"What's that?"

"It's poisonous. It has spines that make a man mad if they prick him. They would not dare to walk ashore and look for it in the dark because it is dangerous after it is dead." The skipper thrust at his shoulder, pushing him forward. "But be quick—if they are going to come and talk to us they will wonder why it took so long to throw a small fish into the bushes!"

Donald scrambled down over the side away from the patrol-boat, as the skipper advised. Up to his ankles in the soft sand, he turned to help Sugaiguntung down. He felt the scientist trembling uncontrollably as they touched.

"Straight inland!" the skipper whispered. "Someone will come to meet you. It won't be a ghost!"

And with that bitter Yatakangi joke he at once had the boat freed from the sand and turned about.

Trying not to make too much noise, Donald guided Sugaiguntung on to dry land. There was only a fringe of sand before their legs were clutched at by stringy grasses and then by shrubs. Casting about, Donald found what might be a path and headed along it, Sugaiguntung two paces behind.

"Stop!" someone said very quietly in Yatakangi.

Donald obeyed, so quickly that Sugaiguntung bumped into him and clutched at him. Now Donald distinctly heard the scientist's teeth chattering.

Christ, can't he take it a little smoother? At least this is his own country—he hasn't been picked up and dumped half a world away from home.

But home had proved as hostile as any jungle, of course.

One—two—three sentries emerged from concealment. It was just possible to see that their heads were misshapen; they all wore black-light glasses. Two of them carried guns and stood back warily while the third, holding only a black-light projector, studied Donald and his companion. Satisfied about their identity, he said, "Follow us! Make as little noise as possible!"

Then there was a time of blind walking down a tunnel that twisted and turned like the intestines of a snake. It must have been cleared out, shaped and reinforced from the actual greenery hiding it, and very efficiently—Donald never caught a glimpse of the sky beyond. Eventually it began to rise.

Sugaiguntung sobbed with exhaustion and the man leading the way slackened his pace a trifle, for which Donald was glad. His sense of direction had lasted almost this far, but was beginning to let him down for lack of external data to supplement his judgment. As far as he could tell, they had headed towards Grandfather Loa—was it his slopes they were now breasting? He towered to nine thousand feet and it would be ridiculous to try and make Sugaiguntung go very far up such a mountain.

Abruptly the man ahead gestured for them to halt. Panting, they did so. There was a half-heard exchange with another hidden sentry. Given the chance to think about something other than walking too fast uphill, Donald realised that the temperature had dropped sharply from its daytime peak, yet ahead there was warm air—he could feel it on his face.

"Go past me," said the man who had answered the sentry's challenge. Donald and Sugaiguntung complied.

Within another ten yards they found themselves in a small roofed-over clearing, half-walled by two outcrops of sloping ground. At the far side of it was a dark patch which appeared to be a cave, no more than four feet high. Sitting on the stumps of the trees which had been cut down to make the clearing, then—Donald's darting eyes spotted clues that could never have been seen from overhead—grafted to standing trees and bent together to provide a camouflage screen, were about eight or nine men and women wearing drab clothes and slung about with weapons. The warm air which he had noticed blowing against his face emanated from a heater in the centre of the group.

One of them rose.

"Mr. Hogan?" he said in a good English accent. "My name is Jogajong. Welcome to my headquarters. You have struck a great blow for freedom in Yatakang tonight. Dr. Sugaiguntung, we are honoured by your presence."

The scientist mumbled something Donald did not catch.

"While this is not a luxury hotel," Jogajong said, "I believe we can offer adequate hospitality while you are waiting for the submarine to come and collect you. You need not be afraid that the heater will attract infra-red detectors—in that cave there a hot spring sometimes bubbles up and gives off warm gas. The nearest peasant habitation is nearly a kilometre away. I have more than a hundred loyal guards on the approach paths. And, as I imagine you know in view of the way you were brought here, I have many good friends among the common people. Sit down, please. Are you hungry, thirsty, wishing for a cigarette?"

Donald sniffed the air. As though reminded of its duty by Jogajong's words, a puff of brimstone-scented gas wafted from the cave-mouth and made him think of hell.

But there was something reassuringly confident about the rebel leader's greeting. It gave him time to review what he had just lived through, and at once the moment of greatest terror—greater even than when Sugaiguntung put on the light inside his house and revealed him at the glass door—claimed his attention.

He said, "What happened to Zulfikar Halal?"

There was a pause. Jogajong only shrugged.

"He told me it would be expensive to buy transport across the Strait!" Donald insisted in a voice tinged with shrillness. "I gave him a thousand talas, and the bleeder didn't show up!"

"He lied anyway," Jogajong said without emotion. "We have good communications with your countrymen here, and as soon as we heard what you hoped to do we made arrangements of our own. There were six boats waiting beyond their usual time of sailing tonight, and any of them would have brought you to me—not because they were bribed, but because I asked it of them."

"You mean I never need have gone to him at all?"

"That's correct."

Donald clenched his fists. "Why, that dirty—!"

"Yes, he is a weak link in my chain," Jogajong nodded. "I

prefer always to rely on my own countrymen. But of course your people feel that espionage is a filthy business and it is better to put the dirt on someone else's hands. I shall make a report; he will not have the chance to deceive anyone else."

"What will you do?" Fury made Donald eager to hear of torture: slow fires, nails pulled out by the roots.

"A word in the right place will ensure his arrest," Jogajong murmured. "And the jails of Gongilung are not the next thing to Paradise ... Don't concern yourself. You have done more than enough, and his treachery did not in the upshot mean that your bravery was wasted."

Donald sighed and relaxed. What the rebel leader said was obviously true. He glanced around the clearing again.

"How long do we have to wait—have they told you?"

"Until the level of activity among the aquabandits has dropped enough to give the submarine a chance of coming through unmolested."

"Major Delahanty said something about that. How long?"

"I would estimate three to five days," Jogajong said equably. "If necessary we can mount a certain—ah—distracting event to lure their forces away, but it would be better not to. The disappearance of someone so eminent as Dr. Sugaiguntung is going to give a great deal of trouble to the Solukarta régime anyhow. I hope they are prevented from concealing the truth; the suspicion that he may have left of his own free will could do incalculable good for my cause."

Donald rubbed his chin. "Hmmm! Are you sure it would be better if the news leaked out?"

"Definitely, sir."

"Could you get an anonymous message to someone at the Gongilung press club?"

"Easily. I had in fact thought of doing that, but I would need the names of people who would take such information seriously, not write it off as mere rumour."

"I can give you a name," Donald said.

"Excellent!" Jogajong hesitated and glanced at the other people in the clearing, silent on their tree-stump stools. "But for this moment you will excuse me—I must complete the staff conference I'm holding. Later we can talk more fully, yes?"

Donald gave a dull nod.

Staff conference? Why not? Things must have been like this in more countries than I could count—Russia, China, Cuba, South Africa ... A handful of men and women meeting in a secret lair, and then suddenly coming out and turning as though by magic from fugitives to cabinet ministers! Who should know better than I do how quick and easy such a transformation is?

And to plot Yatakang's next revolution on the threshold of a volcano seemed perfectly, inexpressibly apposite.

THE MAN WITHOUT CONVICTIONS

When Jeff Young read about the trap set for the party of soldiers coming ashore from Boat Camp he put two and two together. The same partisan who had bought the alumino-phage from him had asked for monofilament wire of a type which happened to be in store at the metalworking shop. One of the gossip sheets had circulated his way recently, apparently, and drawn his attention to some uses for the stuff based on traps which Maquis used to set in World War II for dispatch-riders on motorcycles, except that in those days they had to use piano-wire and because it was thicker and easier to see its employment was generally confined to twilight.

He was a little sorry about the eleven dead and thirty-one seriously injured soldiers. His preference was for sabotage that did no more than stir people up, like ants whose nest has been kicked—in essence, a sort of joke.

Granted, there had been nothing funny about the episode that left him with one short leg . . .

The beauty of this wire stranded together out of single, immensely long molecules was, of course, that it cut almost anything as readily as a cheese being sectioned, and its breaking-strain was closer than any other sort of wire to the theoretical maximum. Handling it, naturally, was a problem— one had to wear gloves of monofilament mesh, or tugging on it would slice flesh cleaner than a razor.

Thinking about it, he came up with an entirely new way of putting a rapitrans train out of operation, a means of exploding a town-gas pipe at a distance not exceeding two miles, and the device which later caved in the North Rockies Acceleratube.

context (25)

A FAVOURITE STORY OF CHAD MULLIGAN'S

"This very distinguished philosophy professor came out on the platform in front of this gang of students and took a bit of chalk and scrawled up a proposition in symbolic logic on the board. He turned to the audience and said, 'Well now, ladies and gentlemen, I think you'll agree that that's obvious?'

"Then he looked at it a bit more and started to scratch his head and after a while he said, 'Excuse me!' And he disappeared.

"About half an hour later he came back beaming all over his face and said triumphantly, 'Yes, I was right—it *is* obvious!' "

continuity (36)

MAKESHIFT

The moment Norman and Chad appeared in the lobby of the GT tower an anonymous staffer dashed over to them and announced that Rex Foster-Stern wanted to see them. A second came up and said that Prosper Rankin had been looking everywhere for Norman, and a third caught sight of him and came to let him know that Hamilcar Waterford was asking where he had got to.

Rankin and Waterford could stew, but Rex was a different matter. Norman said, "Where is he?"

"Down in the Shalmaneser vault."

"That's where we're going."

"Er ..." The staffer was plainly flustered. "Who is the gentleman with you, sir?"

"Chad Mulligan," Norman said, and brushed the staffer aside.

GT's image-maintenance was excellent, but Norman could detect the subtle clues that indicated it was breaking down. It meant nothing that there were two parties of visitors in the huge lobby waiting to be escorted on a tour of the building— proof that rumours of the corporation being poised on the edge of catastrophe hadn't managed to outweigh the impact of the Beninia publicity. It meant nothing that a team from Engrelay Satelserv was bringing in cameras and other equipment on air-trolleys to cover the formal banquet scheduled for this evening. It meant nothing that reporters of all possible skin colours and probably also the Alexandrian five sexes were coming and going with one eye on the current release-sheet and the other on the way ahead.

The real situation was reflected in the staffers who whispered together in corners, in the refusal of a board member heading for the exit to even smile at a foreign journalist, in the scent of tension Norman could practically take a grip on with his hands.

Down, directly to the lower level of the Shalmaneser vault. Someone must have called to warn Rex that Norman had arrived, for the man's agitated face was the first thing revealed when the elevator door slid back.

"Norman! Have you any idea of the trouble you've—?"

"Did you do as I asked?" Norman cut in.

"What? Well, yes, but the trouble it's cost to do it, and the money! Why, we had to postpone contracted time worth half a million on your say-so!"

"A little trouble is a fair exchange for a disaster, isn't it? And how much does the Beninia project involve?"

Rex wiped his face with the back of his hand. "Norman, I know you're pretty well in charge of that, but—"

"The hole! I *am* in charge of it, Rex, and I have more to win or lose on it than anybody except the Beninians themselves and maybe Elihu Masters. What have you arranged for us?"

Rex swallowed and let his hand fall to his side. "He's due to clear for direct vocal interrogation in about—ah—six minutes. But fifteen minutes was the most I could fix for you; after that there's the regular SCANALYZER contract time and that I *dare* not monkey with."

"And I see you're keeping the tourists away for the moment."

"It's driving your old dept out of their skulls, but what else could I do? *I* don't know what company secrets are going to be idly chatted about, do I?"

"Chad!" Norman turned. "Fifteen minutes be enough, or do you want me to go up to Rankin and cancel the SCANALYZER slot?"

Chad had walked forward as curious as any casual sightseer off the street and was surveying the whole apparatus of Shalmaneser from one end to the other. Some of the staffers at work on the equipment looked uncomfortable at his intense interest in them.

"What? Oh! Yes, if I can't hit it in a quarter of an hour I obviously didn't draw the right conclusions."

"Mr. Mulligan, are you claiming to be able to solve in fifteen minutes a problem that's been blocking our best technicians for days on end?" Rex sounded as though an affirmative answer would make him explode with sheer fury.

Chad finished his study of Shalmaneser's exterior and leisurely faced Rex. "And who are you?" he inquired.

"Foster-Stern, VP in charge of projects and planning. This whole scene comes under my dept."

"Ah-hah. In that case you can spare part of these remaining few minutes to check me out on the data Norman gave me, see if he overlooked anything significant."

This is a new Chad Mulligan. Norman realised the fact with a start. He'd heard contempt in that voice before, but it had always been searing, edged with the passion born of frustration. Now it seemed cold and deliberate, such as might be used by a man in charge of subordinates whom he could only rule by sarcasm and insult. The overtones rang loud and clear, saying: *I'm a better man than you are!*

Additionally, Chad's stance had altered. Gone was the slumped posture of the man resigned to defeat, promising he would debauch himself to death and abandon his ambitions. There was a tension in his body and a light in his eyes as though he were bracing himself for a terrific contest and fifty-one per cent sure of coming out the winner.

As though he has always been trying to make an impression ever since I first met him, and now he's forgotten about that and gone back to being himself.

And Chad Mulligan being himself was a far more impressive sight. The curled lip, the hands that jabbed the air as if to carve out by the handful the substance of words uttered in his barking voice, the aura of authority gathering around him as one by one he added more staffers to his audience. Question and answer; question misunderstood, answer cut short with a glare; staffers tripping over their own tongues in their eagerness to be helpful . . .

Norman was barely listening. He felt dazed. He had wagered his entire hopes on a man whom he could scarcely claim to know, and the idea that he was holding a ticket for a won bet was hard to digest.

Where have I seen this kind of transformation before . . . ?

The thought "man I can scarcely claim to know" showed him the association that led to the answer, and it seemed ridiculous: Donald Hogan.

But there was the fact. In just this way Donald had revealed the occasional, much curtailed trace of excitement at a scrap of amusing or potentially significant information, capable of being matched like a missing piece from a jigsaw puzzle into a fascinating new pattern.

And in just that way also Donald had shattered Norman's view of him as though the real man had reached past him and broken the distorting mirror in which he had always previously preferred to look.

Killed a mucker with his bare hands? Not Donald. Never placid nonentity Donald whose temper I risked a score of times in petty domestic rows!

He shied away from the vision of his body lying on the floor after trying his roomie's patience too far and forced himself back to the here and now. Chad was saying, "One minute to go, right? Check me out one more time on the procedure, then: I say cue for question and that switches in the gadget which limits the reply to manageable proportions, but if it doesn't work I have to say either hold or cancel according to whether I want to revert to the same subject or change to another."

His listeners nodded in unison.

"What do I say if I want to make him accept new data?"

Blank expressions. Eventually Rex said, "Well, Mr. Mulligan, I don't think you ought really to—"

"Fasten it. *What do I say?*"

"You say 'postulate'," Rex said reluctantly.

"That's hypothetical! What do I say to *make* him take it?"

"Well, you see, we didn't really envisage programming him with fresh material verbally, so—"

"Mr. Foster-Stern! If you keep me hanging about, I'm quite prepared to tell Norman over there he's got to arrange cancellation of the SCANALYZER slot, and you don't want that, do you?"

Rex swallowed enormously, Adam's apple bobbing. He said in a faint voice, "You have to say, 'I tell you three times.'"

Chad stared, and broke into a grin. "The hole! So someone in this monstrous ziggurat must have had a sense of humour at one time! I bet whoever dreamed that one up didn't last here, though."

Someone standing close to Shalmaneser's printouts called, "Cleared down now, sir—ready for vocal interrogation!"

I have told you once, I have told you twice—
What I tell you three times is true . . .

That snatch of doggerel from *The Hunting of the Snark* went around and around in Norman's head as he watched Chad approach the readin mike with maddening slowness. His comparison of the man to a champion preparing for a fight had been exact, he realised. To Chad, this was a challenge of unique quality—perhaps the only one that would have forced him out of his self-imposed rôle of disillusioned cynic.

"Shalmaneser?" he said to the mike. "Hi, Shal. My name is Chad Mulligan."

Norman had heard Shalmaneser's voice before, but it always made him shiver a little—not because it had any intrinsic eerie quality, but because of the associations it conjured up. In fact it was derived from the speaking voice of a celebrated operatic baritone and was rather pleasantly inflected.

But the baritone was dead—suicide—and knowing that made it almost intolerable.

"I know your books, Mr. Mulligan," Shalmaneser said. "Also I have stored several TV interviews with you. I recognise your appearance and voice."

"I'm flattered." Chad dropped into a chair facing the mike and the battery of cameras trained around it. "Well, I gather you don't have much time for idle conversation, so I'll come straight to the point. Cue: what's wrong with the Beninia project?"

"It won't work," Shalmaneser said.

Norman stole a glance at Rex. It was impossible to tell by looking whether the man's agitated condition was due to Chad's nonchalance or to the knowledge that using Shalmaneser in this fashion slowed his lightning reactions to a level close to the human, wasting precious time. Giving a machine the power to talk in ordinary English had meant funnelling everything through subsidiary installations which worked at less than a thousandth of the speed of light-writers.

"Cue: why not?" Chad said.

"The data given to me include unacceptable anomalies."

"Cue: would it be fair to say you don't believe in what you've been told about Beninia?"

There was a measurable pause. Rex took half a pace forward and started to say something about anthropocentric concepts compelling Shalmaneser to search his entire memory-banks.

"Yes. I don't believe it," the artificial voice announced.

"Hmmm . . ." Chad plucked at his beard. "Cue: what elements of the data are unacceptable? Be maximally specific."

Another, longer pause, as Shalmaneser examined everything he had ever been told which referred to the subject and discarded all but the most essential items.

"The human elements concerned with social interaction," he said at length. "Next, the——"

"Hold!" Chad snapped. Once more he tangled his fingers in his beard and tugged at it. "Cue: have you been taught the Shinka language?"

"Yes."

"Cue: is its given vocabulary among the anomalies that cause you to reject the data?"

"Yes."

All around, technicians began to exchange astonished stares. One or two of them dared to sketch a smile.

"Cue: are the living conditions described to you as obtaining in Beninia of a kind which lead you to expect different behaviour from the people there from what you've been told?"

"Yes."

"Cue: is the political relationship between Beninia and its neighbouring countries another of the anomalies?"

"Yes." Immediately—no delay.

"Cue: is the internal political structure of the country also anomalous?"

"Yes."

"Cue: with maximal specificity define your use of the term 'anomalous'."

"Antonym: *consistent*. Synonym: *inconsistent*. Related concepts: congruity, identity—"

"Hold!" Chad bit his lip. "Sheeting hole, that was a bad choice of approach ... Ah, I think I see how I can .. Shal, cue this one: does the anomaly lie in the data given to you with direct reference to Beninia, or does it only become apparent when you're dealing with Beninia in relation to other countries?"

"The latter. In the former case the anomaly is of the order which I am allowed to accept for the sake of argument."

"Whoinole is that codder, anyway?" someone asked in hearing of Norman.

"Chad Mulligan," someone whispered back, and the first speaker's eyes grew wide.

"Evaluate this, then," Chad said, frowning tremendously and staring at nothing. "Postulate that the data given you about Beninia are true. Cue: what would be necessary to reconcile them with everything else you know? In other words, *what extra assumption do you have to make in order to accept and believe in Beninia?*"

Rex jerked forward another half-pace like a marionette, his mouth open. All around the vault, which was now in dead silence except for the echo of Chad's voice and the soft humming of Shalmaneser's mental processes, Norman saw jaws drop correspondingly.

Obvious!

The pause, though, stretched, and stretched, until it was intolerable. One more second, Norman thought, and he was going to scream. And—

tracking with closeups (29)

WHILE THE BALANCE OF HIS MIND WAS DISTURBED

"Mary!"

Standing by the window, staring with a bitter expression at the advancing tide of repetitive suburbs cresting the far side of the pleasant English valley, Mary Whatmough heard her husband's voice calling her excitedly. She swallowed half the gin that was in the glass she held—she felt somehow guilty about pouring herself large drinks—and turned just as he entered the room, holding up a letter like a flag of triumph.

"It's from the Beninia Consortium! Listen! 'Dear—etc.'— where are we? Yes, this is the important bit. 'While we cannot hold out the hope of remuneration as generous as we would accord to an applicant with more specialised skills, we do believe that experience such as you described in your letter would prove valuable to our staff in the preliminary stages of the project. Please let us know when it would be convenient for you to call at our London office and discuss the matter personally.' "

Articulating carefully—the draught of gin had hit her rather harder and very much more quickly than she had expected—Mary said, "It sounds as though some of those blacks have finally seen sense, doesn't it?"

"What do you mean?"

"Isn't it obvious? They never were fit to run their own

affairs, and now they've realised it and asked somebody in to help them who can."

Victor folded the letter. Then, looking down at it, he began to pleat it into parallel strips. He said without raising his head again, "Ah—I don't believe that's exactly the thinking that underlies the project, my dear."

Across his mind there flashed a brief vision of a pretty girl's face in a phone screen. In the background, a dark human shape.

Things have changed. It's no good looking for a rebirth of my world or Mary's. But I did have a lot of pleasure out of Karen. Perhaps there's a chance . . .

"It may not be the thinking," Mary said. "But it's the fact, isn't it?"

"Possibly, of course," he agreed uncomfortably. "But I hardly think it would be—uh—politic to talk in those terms. It might give offence. Mightn't it?"

"You're beginning to sound like my father," Mary said. That was always—had been for twenty years—the prelude to an argument. "And look where such talk got him! Thrown out on his ear by an ungrateful bunch of upstarts!"

"Well, dear, we wouldn't be responsible to the Beninians directly, you see—our employers would be an American company working under contract to them."

"I haven't any time for Americans. I've told you so a thousand times. Trust them to put some snotty brown-nose over you, half your age, who'll insist on you calling him 'boss' and bowing every time he speaks to you! What are you doing?"

Victor had taken the letter and torn it meticulously into four.

"It isn't any good, is it?" he said. He was addressing the air, not his wife. "She's bound to get drunk at a party some time and start talking about the prime minister or somebody as a 'brown-nose', and then where would I be? Back here, or somewhere worse, so . . ."

He turned on his heel.

"Where are you going?"

"Oh, *shut up,* will you?"

She shrugged. Victor was always getting these fits of bad

temper. At the Harringhams' party the other week, for instance. It was a wonder Meg Harringham hadn't smacked his face. But he'd get over it, same as usual, and probably by this time tomorrow he'd be denying he ever said it. And he only tore the letter into four so it could still be read and it was reassuring after all these years that those stupid Africans had realised which side their bread was—

When she heard the shot, at first she couldn't believe it had come from inside the house. Even after she had opened the door of Victor's den and seen his brains splattered all over the zebra-skin rugs she didn't believe it.

OF THE GREATEST SIGNIFICANCE

There had appeared to be a problem: where to accommodate the staff supervising the earliest stages of the Beninia project. Short of building a new suburb to Port Mey, delay had seemed inevitable until someone thought of asking Shalmaneser and from his incredible mass of data he sifted out a solution. There was an obsolete aircraft-carrier up for sale.

GT had beaten out a bid from New Zealand, and the fact was currently the subject of violent argument in the Parliament out there. However, if they still wanted it in say a year's time they could have it and welcome. Meantime it afforded several advantages, besides symbolising the fact that the project would scarcely begin to move inland for another six months. The initial work concerned MAMP and Port Mey's harbour facilities: expanding the former to supply as much ore as the project would absorb, and dredging out the latter to cope with the largest ocean-going vessels.

Norman's respect for Shalmaneser had gone up yet another notch as a result of that suggestion. He approved anything which hastened the project; it had become almost a hunger in his mind to see it succeed.

He walked out across the carrier's flight-deck, busy as usual with copters for both passengers and freight, said hello to Gideon Horsfall descending from one of them in a great hurry, and leaned on the rail facing the land. Just at the moment it wasn't actually raining, but if anything he detested this condition of saturated air still more. It made his clothes clammy and his scalp itch.

Absently rubbing his head, he stared towards Africa. A coaster was easing past into Port Mey, her reactor-fed jets giving one pulse every two seconds or so, pop . . . pop . . . pop . . . Lining the deck, several dark figures yelled and waved at the carrier. Norman waved back.

It was several minutes past the due time when the copter from Accra came down the ladder of the air. Norman was at its door directly it settled and felt a stir of impatience when the man he was expecting turned to say good-bye to a couple of his fellow passengers.

But at last here he was, jumping to the deck and holding out his hand to be shaken.

"Good to see you here," Norman said. "Took you long enough!"

"Don't blame me," said Chad Mulligan. "Blame GT's staffers. Everyone from Prosper Rankin down seems to regard me as some kind of a miracle-worker. Though part of it was my fault, to be honest. I decided I could study up the background better in New York than here—library facilities aren't too good in Africa, they tell me." Gazing around the deck, he added, "It's great to see one of these antiquated arks being put to some practical purpose. What's her name?"

"Hm? Oh, she was formerly the *William Mitchell*, but they told us to change it right away, and—" Norman chuckled. "Nobody could think of a better name than the *Shalmaneser*."

"Both male names, hm? I don't mind bivving in principle but this is doing it on altogether too grand a scale." Chad mopped at his forehead, which had begun to glisten with perspiration the moment he emerged from the copter's conditioned air. "What's the climate like down below?"

"Better, by a fraction." Norman turned towards the nearest elevator. "Who were those people you were talking to in the copter, by the way? The man's face looked familiar."

"You probably saw a picture of them. They're a young couple from the States that you've hired. Going up-country to get some new school off the ground. Frank and Sheena Potter were the names."

"Yes, I remember them. Their application was a borderline case which came to me for adjudication—something about an illegal pregnancy. But they seemed satisfactory otherwise, so I said take a chance, we can always pull them out later if we have to."

"I noticed the pregnancy—by now you can't help it. But they seem very attached to each other and that's a good sign. How's your recruiting going, by the way?"

"We're not getting former colonial officials of the quality we expected. Or maybe we are and I'm being too rigid." Norman ushered Chad into the elevator. "The same day I dealt with the Potters' case, I remember, I was sent another which I'm still sitting on. Can't make up my mind."

"What's the difficulty?"

The elevator stopped and they emerged into the bowels of the beast. Norman fingered his beard and studied the direction signs, then started left along the corridor.

"It was an application from Paris," he said. "I don't know if I'm being too doctrinaire, but—well, they're a brother and sister whose parents were both *pieds-noirs,* and the Algerian legacy isn't what you'd call a good reference."

"Don't take them even if they come on bended knees. Also don't take any Portuguese or Belgians or wooden nickels. Christ, listen to me generalising. Where are you taking me?"

"We got here." Norman opened a steel door and led the way into a large, well-furnished, air-conditioned lounge, the former wardroom of the officers' mess. "I thought you'd probably want a drink after your long trip."

"No thanks," Chad said curtly.

"What?"

"Oh, maybe a cold beer, then. Nothing stronger. I owe you a lot, you know, including wringing out the alcohol from me." Chad dropped into the nearest vacant chair. "I couldn't go on drinking and study up on Beninia at the same time."

"Well, that's good news," Norman said. He hesitated. "Ah—you haven't reached any conclusions, have you?"

"Conclusions? You mean hypotheses, I hope. I got here five minutes ago and so far I haven't set foot on Beninian ground. But . . . Well, speaking of recruitment as we were: did you get me the people I want?"

"You asked for a sheeting lot of them," Norman grunted. "What was it you said? 'Psychologists, anthropologists, sociologists and synthesists not hopelessly straitjacketed by adherence to an ism'—is that right?"

" 'Glutinous adherence', to be exact. But did you *get* them?"

"I'm still working on the synthesists," Norman sighed. "That's a discipline which doesn't attract as many people as it ought to—seems people have this idea that Shalmaneser is automating them out of a job, too. But I turned in an application to State and Raphael Corning said he'd see who he could find. For the rest—well, I've short-listed a dozen possibles for you to interview, all well recommended by their current employers."

"Sounds discouraging." Chad scowled. "I prefer people who've ruffled their employers' tempers so many times . . . But that's prejudice. Thanks, it sounds fine. Incidentally, I think I will have that beer after all."

"It's on the way."

"Splendid. How's everything else here—how's Elihu?"

"He dropped in this morning with Kitty Gbe, the education minister, to talk over the selection programme we're mounting to choose the first wave of student-teachers. I think he's at the palace this afternoon."

"And the president—how's he?"

"Not good," Norman said. "We got here too late. He's a sick man, Chad. Remember that when you meet him. But under the—the veil of senility there's a rare personality."

"Who's going to take over?"

"A caretaker government under Ram Ibusa, I imagine. As a matter of fact Zad signed regency papers yesterday to be used if he does become too ill to continue."

Chad shrugged. "I don't suppose it'll matter much. Shalmaneser is running the country as of now, isn't he? And from personal acquaintance I think he'll make a fine job of it."

"I hope you're right," Norman muttered.

A girl arrived with Chad's beer and placed it on the table

between them. Chad followed her appreciatively with his eyes as she moved away.

"Local recruit?"

"What? Oh, the waitress. Yes, I imagine so."

"Pretty. If they have shiggies of that calibre here I may enjoy my stay even if I don't find what I'm looking for. But I forgot—you have a fixation on blondes, don't you?"

"I don't have any fixations any longer," Norman said stonily. "Fixations and Beninia don't co-exist."

"I noticed," Chad said. "I'm glad you finally did, too." He poured half the beer down his throat and set the glass aside with a contented sigh.

"Speaking of what you're looking for," Norman said, a trifle over-eager to switch subjects, "I take it from the requirements you sent me that you—"

"That I haven't the vaguest notion what I'm after," Chad interrupted. "You'd better be ready for me to ask for something entirely different tomorrow. In fact, on my way over I realised I should have asked for some biochemists and geneticists as well."

"Are you serious?"

"Not yet. Give me a week or two and I very well may be. Also priests and imams and rabbis and fortune-tellers and clairvoyants and—Norman, howinole should I know? What I asked for just seemed like a reasonable basis to start from!"

"Ask for whatever you want," Norman said after a pause. "I have a suspicion there's nothing more important, not even the Beninia project itself."

"There you go again," Chad said. "Feeding my ego. Christ, aren't I vain enough already?"

tracking with closeups (30)

DÉFENSE D'ENTRER

Approaching from the street, Jeannine thought at first the house must be empty, but she soon perceived a glimmer of light from behind the heavy old-fashioned drapes covering the window of the *salon* and heard the soft sound of the piano. It was one of her brother's favourite pieces, *La Jeune Fille aux Cheveux de Lin*.

The front door, curiously, was unlocked. She went inside. By the distant glow of the street-lamps she saw that the hallway was in disorder; bits of a large vase crunched under her shoes and a Moroccan rug had been kicked against the wall in a heap. The air was thick and sweet with the aroma of kief.

The music ended. She opened the door of the *salon* and saw her brother silhouetted by a swinging lamp. A kief cigarette burned on a brass dish and a half-empty bottle of cognac and a glass stood beside it on the lid of the piano.

He spoke her name in a neutral voice and she came in and closed the door. Moving to one of the low cushioned benches she said, "Where's Rosalie?"

"We had a row. She walked out." He began to let his hands wander up and down the keyboard seemingly under their own volition, framing long wailing lines of melody which somehow suggested the Arab songs no piano could imitate.

Jeannine listened for a while. She said at length, "You heard from the American company."

"Yes. You?"

"Yes. They took you on, I suppose, and that started the row?"

"On the contrary." He got abruptly to his feet, shut the piano, drained his glass and brought it and the bottle over to a low table in front of his sister. Sitting down beside her, he poured himself another shot and asked with his eyes if she wanted some. He received assent and made to rise and fetch a glass. She stopped him with a touch on the arm.

"We can share it. Don't bother to fetch another."

"As you like." He stubbed his cigarette and opened the box to offer her one.

"You said on the contrary. Did they not accept you?"

"No. That was why I lost my temper with Rosalie. You?"

"They turned me down as well."

For a long time after that there was silence. Eventually Pierre said, "I don't seem to care very much. I ought to. I remember I hoped very strongly that I would be engaged to go to Africa. Here I am not having secured the post and on top of it having lost my wife—yet I feel numb."

"There's no chance of a reconciliation?"

"I detest the idea. Is it worth having if it has to be cobbled together from the broken pieces? Only the most precious objects deserve that treatment."

"I'm in the same gallery," Jeannine said after a pause. "Raoul did not realise how much the idea meant to me. We disagreed and for the last time. It's not worth the trouble."

"Outsiders don't understand. They can't understand." Pierre emptied the cognac glass and refilled it. His sister took a quick sip at it the moment he let it go.

"What are you thinking of doing now?" he inquired.

"I've not decided. Now my mind is made up to go to Africa again, I suppose I shall look around for an alternative. Even yet there's no hope of going home, but certain other countries are tolerant of Europeans, and perhaps they would be better than a swampy little nation in the equatorial rain-belt."

"Egypt engages many Europeans," Pierre agreed. "Mostly Germans and Swiss, but Belgians too."

"There is something else Raoul told me about: how disturbed the Common Europe Board is becoming over the Americans in Beninia, how they may attempt to counter it with aid to Dahomalia and RUNG."

"That too will need advisors. And yet—" He swallowed hard. "It was such an effort to rein in one's pride and make application to go and serve *les noirs*. To be told after humbling oneself that it was all a waste—it's insupportable."

"Mon pauvre. I know how you feel." She picked up the glass again; over its rim as she drank, she found her eyes locked with Pierre's.

"Yes, you do, don't you?" he said. "If there were not in the whole world a single person who sympathised, I believe I would go mad."

"I too." With what seemed like a great effort of will she detached her gaze from his and put down the glass. Not looking at him again, she said, "I believe—do you know?—it is there, the reason for my chaotic life of disorder. From one man to another, counting it a triumph to remain together for a year . . . Looking for someone like you, my heart. Never finding anyone."

"But at least you had the endurance to continue looking," Pierre said. "I gave up. Only when it was forced on me, the first time and now the second, did I admit my discouragement."

The air seemed heavy not only with the fumes of kief, but with something that needed to be spoken and could not. He pushed himself to his feet as though the atmosphere physically dragged on him.

"Let us have music. I feel the emptiness of the house."

"As empty as my soul," Jeannine said, and filled her lungs with kief again.

"What shall we hear? Triumphal m u s i c? A funeral march?"

"Will you play yourself or put on a recording?"

"A recording. I have no heart for more." He sorted along the rack and dropped a reel into the player. "Some Berlioz for vigour, hm?" he muttered as he put out the swinging lamp. "It is a clever match, the vision on this one. I don't believe you've seen it."

The small screen of the player lit with patterns of white and gold; by its glow he found his way back to her side. Stiff, they watched for a while. The volume was shattering, the master's demand for huge orchestras having found its apotheosis in modern amplification.

"I should get a newer player," Pierre said. "With this one loses the third dimension unless one sits directly before the screen."

"Here, come a little this way. But you're not comfortable. One needs African bones to sit on these accursed things. Will you move to an armchair?"

"No, one cannot fit both the armchairs into the narrow area before the screen . . . We had some arguments over that too, Rosalie and I."

"You can see well there? Let me lean on you. No, with your arm around me. Good, that's comfortable."

A little time passed. There was scent in her hair. It was soft to put his cheek on. The images and colours matched to the music were of the first order, reaching to him even through his depression and apathy, and he was lulled. He felt, but did not react to, her strong slim fingers twining around his hand, and when she stirred slightly he did no more than adjust his own position economically to correspond. It was natural when her fingertips started to caress the back of his hand and his wrist that he should copy the movement and some while before it registered that he was touching the bare skin of her breast.

The screen of the player went to white and sky-blue. In the sudden brightness he looked at her. On her cheeks he saw that there were tears glistening: two shiny little rivers flowing from two dark pools.

He scarcely heard what she said, for the clamouring music, but her lips framed the words clearly enough.

"There will never be anyone else for either of us, will there, Pierre?"

He could not answer.

"It's the truth," she said, a little louder and very wearily. "Shall we stop pretending? I'm sick of everyone, Pierre, except for you. Brother or not, you've been my only friend the whole of my life and I'm no longer young. The Parisians want no part of us, the French ignore us, the rest of Europe is a chaos like the vomit of a greedy dog, and now it turns out the *sales noirs* won't interest themselves in us. Where else are we to go, tell me that?"

Pierre shook his head and raised one hand in a gesture signifying absence of all hope.

"Ainsi je les emmerde tous," Jeannine said. So far she had only loosened her bluzette and parted it to expose the breast she had given him to stroke; it was a very beautiful breast, of a fullness that trespassed over the border of voluptuousness. Now she unzipped the garment completely and threw it aside. He made no move to stop her, but equally no move to co-operate.

Having looked at him from the length of an arm away for a few thoughtful moments, she said, "I've sometimes wondered whether you lost your women because you were less of a man than I imagined. Is that so, Pierre?"

His face suddenly grew dark with anger. "No question of it!" he snapped.

"No question, either, that I'm an attractive woman. It came to me suddenly today, when I received that letter, what I really want. And what you want, too. A dead world. But there must be some of it left. I thought: we understand each other! We could—we *must*—go and look for what we want, the sensible way, in company. There are things that would have to be arranged but I can arrange them. There are places where they value a person more than a piece of paper saying what he was when he was born." She hesitated.

"We could have children together, Pierre."

"Are you mad?" The words were whispered between pale lips.

"Think for a while," she said composedly, and leaned back

on the cushions to continue watching the record. She put her palms on her breasts in a parody of modesty that she knew could be relied on to inflame most men.

When she felt the first touch of his hand she turned her mouth up hungrily to be kissed.

context (27)

"Linguistically Shinka in the pure traditional form exhibited only by extremely old men and women when reciting songs, catches and folk-tales learned as children is a typical member of the sub-family which dominates this area. A number of anomalies have been noted in addition to the ones originally cited, especially significant being the cognate relationship between the words for 'warrior' and 'fool', and the homonymic identity of the words for 'wound' and 'disease'.

"However, 'pure' Shinka has been displaced almost completely. Heavy contamination exists in all urban centres with English, though there is no self-sufficient vocabulary forming a pidgin. The Holaini dialect constitutes a pidgin in that it hybridises a vocabulary mostly of local origin with grammar originating elsewhere and *vice versa*—these two poles often co-existing in the same speaker and varying in his speech according to the degree of communication he has with his listeners. Over the whole of the north of the country where Holaini influence is most pervasive the majority of the people irrespective of origin understand Holaini words and can follow simple Holaini sentences but the predominant domestic usage must be classed as contaminated Shinka.

"Additionally there are the enclaves of Inoko and Kpala each of which retains its parent language (now with heavy Shinka contamination) but is effectively bi-lingual or, in the

case of children educated at schools where in class they have
to speak English, tri-lingual.

"English is the language of government, foreign commerce
and to a great extent of the intelligentsia. TV broadcasts are
made in all five languages including English but entertain-
ment is either locally produced in Shinka or bought in canned
form from abroad in English.

"Languages of which traces can still be detected include
Arabic, Spanish, Swahili, and along all the borders of the
country the various adjacent dialects, which have occasionally supplied the common term for trade-objects.

"A systematic analysis of the vocabulary recorded will be
begun as soon as . . ."

"Physically the inhabitants are negroid with marked incur-
sions of Berber in the north and a substantial minority in the
vicinity of Port Mey with some English or Indian ancestry.
The average height for both sexes is below the average for
adjacent countries (for men ½", for women 1" approx.) and
so is the stripped weight. This is accountable (a) in terms of
dietary deficiencies and (b) in terms of the debilitating effect
of endemic diseases. Trypanosomiasis and malaria are well
known to the inhabitants and they have been efficiently
educated in public health measures for these, but an insidious
and apparently antibiotic-resistant strain of 'blackwater fever' abounds and occasionally provokes infantile mortality
though it does not appear to be fatal in adults. Tuberculosis,
smallpox, and a number of other diseases are held at bay by
an inoculation service well accepted by the populace, but
. . ."

"The median IQ of the school pupils tested by our team
lies nearly 2½ points below the average found in adjacent
territories but it is uncertain at present whether this is statis-
tically significant as the tests were difficult to weight for
background noise. Assuming the difference is real it is probably due to dietary deficiencies over many generations, the
staple diet of mealie flour, sago and other starches being only
lightly reinforced with high-protein substances and fresh veg-

etables. Successful government education in the use of citrus fruits, however, has eradicated scurvy, and fish-meal is now available.

"On the other hand, a small number of outstandingly bright children were found, of whom one tested at approximately 176. Tests are continuing to try and determine whether there are any more exceptional genetic strains cropping out . . ."

"A number of conflicting rituals have been found associated with the standard landmark-events: birth, puberty, marriage, bearing and fathering of children, sickness and death. Some are of local origin while many others can be assigned to Muslim or Christian influence. A table is appended showing the significant features of such ceremonies with areas of highest incidence. NB: the attitude of the people towards these events is essentially celebratory rather than magical or propitiatory but it cannot be established whether this is an indigenous factor or due to gradual de-ritualisation by Europeans of their own religious festivals during the colonial period . . ."

"The structure of the family is typically patrilineal among Holaini and trends towards the matrilocal among the southern Shinka, especially in the cities where maximal movement of male labourers is found. However, both sexes enjoy equal rights before the law and folklore indicates that women of forceful personality were accepted into male councils before the advent of the European. The elaborate familial terms of aboriginal Shinka are giving way to a simplified pattern probably related to the English and much influenced by missionary teaching. However, it has not yet been determined . . ."

"The ideals of the community were examined both in Shinka and English with marked variation between the results. In English targets such as 'wealth' and 'to be President' scored high; in Shinka qualities such as (translating loosely) 'public respect' and 'likable behaviour' scored high. It has not yet been settled whether this is due to a real conflict or is a function of superior availability of the terms . . ."

"As is common in primitive societies there is a high reliance on proverbs and folk sayings in social conversation. However, the content is somewhat idiosyncratic.

"The universal admiration for Begi is well exemplified in the phrase 'You could welcome Begi in your house', a term of praise for someone whose family does him credit.

"Full study of the differences betwen Shinka and Holaini usage, as well as of Inoko and Kpala influence, must await . . ."

"To all study groups from Chad Mulligan:

"You don't yet know! You haven't yet established! You aren't quite sure about!

"How about letting me have something I can take a proper grip on—soon?"

continuity (41)

SEWN ON WITH NEEDLE AND THREAD

An hour after sundown Jogajong shook Donald's hand and gave him into the charge of one of his lieutenants. Escorted by four armed guerrillas and accompanied by four more carrying Sugaiguntung swathed in a sort of cocoon of plastic strips, he set out along a different trail from the one he had been brought in by. On his back, haversack-fashion, were the neatly rolled anti-radar flotation suits in which he and his companion would have to spend perhaps hours of lonely dark waiting before the coast was clear for the submarine.

The trail was rough and the black-light goggles he had been loaned were inefficient. Here, crossing one of the slopes radiating away from the foot of Grandfather Loa, the ground was too warm for the vegetation and the human bodies around him to show up except as blurs. Used to walking soundlessly through the dark jungle, the Yatakangis with him seemed to exude contempt whenever he brushed against a hanging branch or threatened to lose his footing on some lump of mud.

Somehow, though, the distance was covered and they reached the first stage's end at the headwaters of a small river. A crude wooden platform jutted out of the bank, and moored to it was a shabby praheng driven by a stern-sweep. The boatman was waiting immobile, cross-legged on the jetty, smoking a cigarette cupped very carefully between his palms which nonetheless glinted like a firefly when his fingers parted.

Sugaiguntung was placed gently in the bow of the boat and covered with old sacks. Donald stepped aboard next and sat on a midships thwart. Behind him came two of the guerrillas, their bolt-guns across their laps. He could not help wondering how much attention they were paying to him, how much to their ostensible task of watching for spies on shore. With not a word spoken except the password to identify the party, they drifted into the centre of the narrow stream and the boatman began to work his sweep with a faint rhythmical creaking like a cricket's.

The river was like a tunnel floored with water. The trees on either bank leaned together overhead, their crowns trailing strands of creeper and dangling moss. Occasionally a nightbird shrieked, and once some monkeys were disturbed, probably by a snake, and Donald's spine crawled at the unexpected racket.

At the junction where this river joined a larger, they passed a village with not a light showing. In case of someone being wakeful, however, Donald was told to lie down on the bottom boards. When he was allowed to get up again they were well out in the middle of the main stream, riding with the current at a good walking pace, and the boatman had shipped his sweep, holding now a small paddle that served for rudder.

This is the twenty-first century. The thought crossed Donald's mind for no special reason. *This is Yatakang, one of the countries best-endowed with natural wealth and certainly not scientifically backward: witness, Sugaiguntung. And here I am being carried through the night in a rowing-boat.*

Habitation began to become more frequent along the banks. This was one of the trickiest stages of the journey. Donald got off his thwart again and knelt on the bottom boards, his eyes just above the gunwale. A white police launch was tied up at a post facing a village larger than the first one, but there seemed to be no one on board. They passed it without incident and when it was well astern the boatman resumed his sweep. Their progress without it had slowed. Thinking the matter over, Donald deduced that they were approaching the estuary and running against the influx of the sea.

At the river-mouth itself there was a long necklace-strand of buildings, a small port devoted mainly to fishing to judge by the stretched nets on poles which were revealed by a few dim electric lights along the waterfront. Once more, however, no one was in sight; the boats would be out for their nightly expedition and it would be pointless to sit around and await their return before dawn. Donald began to breathe a little more easily.

A short distance from shore the boatman turned his fragile craft broadside to the direction it had been travelling in, and one of the guerrillas took up a flashlamp from the bottom of the boat. He hung it over the side after switching it on. It glowed pale blue. Donald guessed it was radiating mainly in the ultra-violet.

Ten minutes of interminable waiting passed. Then a larger boat, a fishing-prau, appeared from the drifting night mists that shrouded the surface of the water, exhibiting another lamp of the same blue tint as well as its normal running lights. The boatman went past Donald, tossing fenders over the side. Shortly, the two vessels bumped together, almost without noise for the big soft pads separating them.

Awkwardly, Donald helped the two guerrillas to manhandle Sugaiguntung into a rope sling that the sailors on the fishing-prau threw down. They guided him as he was lifted and vanished over the gunwale; then Donald followed and was seized by several hands.

The skipper of the prau greeted him and told him to put Sugaiguntung into his flotation suit right away because they planned to rely on the mist to make their drop closer to shore than they had anticipated. Donald did not question the wisdom of the decision. Everything had gone from him except a certain wan despair at the idea of returning home. The Donald Hogan who had lived in the world's wealthiest country was lost forever, and he could not tell how the stranger who bore his old name would respond to the resumption of his former life.

He complied listlessly, easing each of Sugaiguntung's limp limbs in turn into the soft plastic suit and pressing the valves on the inflation bottles. The scientist should be unconscious for about another hour.

He made a thorough check of the associated survival equipment—water-dye capsules, radio and sonar beacons for dire emergency, lifelines, iron rations, knife ... After a little consideration he removed Sugaiguntung's knife from its sheath and gave it to the skipper. He had said, back at Jogajong's camp, that he had changed his mind. For the sake of insurance it might be as well to have him unarmed—not that an old man weakened by recent illness could offer any resistance to an eptified killer.

He donned his own suit in the same fashion and the skipper detailed one of his crew to rope them together with their lifelines. There must be no risk of them drifting apart while they were bobbing in the water.

He explained to Donald that they were going to be placed in a current that would carry them directly along the deepest part of the channel where the submarine was hiding. Standing by a few miles distant were units from the bases at Isola ready if necessary to mount a distracting raid on a port known to be used by Chinese ships for refuelling and refitment—a gross breach of Yatakangi neutrality, but one which Sugaiguntung's defection would well repay. It was hoped, however, that no intervention would be necessary.

And then—over side in a sort of makeshift bosun's chair, deposited in the water with scarcely a splash, the two of them together, spy and defector.

The crew waved, barely distinguishable for the dark and the swirling mist, and the prau faded into nothing. They were alone in a universe of blurs and ripples.

We must have been here an hour ... No: my watch tells me thirty-five minutes.

Apprehensively Donald strained his eyes and saw exactly what he had expected to see—nothing. The bobbing motion was maddening, threatening to make him queasy; he had not eaten well during his stay at Jogajong's camp although the rebel leader made a point of providing a balanced diet and keeping his followers healthy. The food had been monotonous and untempting. Now he wished he had filled up on something bland like plain boiled rice, for pangs of hunger were starting to quarrel with shadowy nausea in his belly.

Can they really spot us here, rendezvous with us, take us safely aboard?

It was no use reminding himself that this was how Jogajong had been stolen out of the country and sent back, or that Sugaiguntung's value compelled the authorities at home to adopt the safest available route. The rest of the universe felt infinitely far away, as though there could be no contact between this place and any other. The recession of the galaxies had reached its limit; separated from one another by a gulf no light could pass, they too were beginning to disintegrate.

Is it all going to have been worth while? Shall I have saved the people of Yatakang from being deceived by a monstrous lie, as Sugaiguntung assured me?

But that was back in Gongilung. At Jogajong's camp, the scientist had spoken of returning, refusing to co-operate after all.

Why did I not question him to find out his reasons?

He tried to disguise the answer to that from himself, and failed.

Because I was afraid to. If I took unfair advantage of superstition and exploited the traditional reward due to me against his will, I would prefer not to know. I want to believe as long as I can that he came voluntarily.

There was a moan. His blood seemed to freeze in his veins. For an instant his fevered imagination interpreted the faint sound as the wail of a police patrol-launch's siren, far off in the mist. It was an eternal instant before he corrected the idea and realised it was a Yatakangi word in Sugaiguntung's voice.

They had drifted apart to the limit of the lifeline linking their flotation suits. Hastily he hauled on the rope to bring them together. It must be a terrible shock to awaken here; he must offer reassurance before Sugaiguntung could think his mind deranged.

"Doctor, it's all right—here I am, Donald Hogan!"

He grasped Sugaiguntung's arms and peered close under his protective hood. The older man's eyes were open to their limit and he was staring fearfully straight ahead. After a moment he appeared to relax.

"Where am I?" he said in a feeble voice.

"We're waiting for an American submarine to come and pick us up," Donald explained softly.

"What?" Sugaiguntung tensed all over, and the jerk made him bob violently so that Donald almost lost his grip. "You— you *kidnapped* me?"

"You said you wanted to come," Donald countered. "You were very sick from the fever, you weren't yourself, it was better not to overstrain you by making you walk through the jungle and—"

"You kidnapped me!" Sugaiguntung repeated. "I said, I *told* you, I had changed my mind about coming with you!"

"You couldn't have gone back to Gongilung. Once you were committed, there was no turning back. And from here you can't go back. Only onward."

One can't go back from anywhere. One can never, never, never go back!

For a while Sugaiguntung seemed weakened by his outburst. He shook himself free of Donald's hands. Warily, Donald allowed that, keeping a tight grip on the rope instead so that they would remain within arms' reach of each other, and watched as the scientist turned his head to this side and that until he was satisfied that they were truly isolated.

Eventually he spoke again, in a voice thin with weariness.

"What is this thing I'm wearing that's so stiff and hard to move in?"

"It's inflated to buoy you up. That's why it's stiff. It's—I don't know. I guess it's one of the regular survival suits they use for fliers and submarine crews. Jogajong had some ready for use at his camp."

"Oh yes, I've heard of them." There were faint plashing noises as Sugaiguntung inspected the equipment hung about him. "Yes, I see, I understand. There are radar beacons, sonar becaons, to make sure the submarine will find us?"

"Those are only to be used in emergency, when the searchers don't know where to look. Don't worry—they're absolutely sure where to come and collect us." Donald spoke more optimistically than his mood warranted.

"They're not operating?" The words were coloured with alarm.

"The risk is too great. There are Yatakangi patrols all over these waters and there's been a lot of Chinese activity too, they tell me."

"I see," Sugaiguntung said again, and after another cautious survey of the suit fell silent.

That was all right by Donald. Once more he strained his eyes into the mist.

Christ, are they never going to turn up? How long should I allow them—one hour, two, three?

Suddenly, without warning, Sugaiguntung said, "You kidnapped me. I'm not here willingly. I shall not co-operate with your foreign government."

Donald's heart sank. He said fiercely, "You told me you had been tricked by your bosses! You said your people were being cheated! Solukarta had pretended you could turn them into supermen and that was a disgusting lie!"

"But I can," Sugaiguntung said.

The words seemed to hang vast leaden weights on every limb of Donald's body. He said. "You're crazy. The fever—it must be the fever."

"No, it was after the fever." Sugaiguntung spoke without emotion. "It was while I was lying in the cave alone. I had time to think in a way which has not been possible for many years. Always there have been intriguing side-issues that I could not follow up, only assign to some of my students, and not all of them conducted the research properly. Four years ago, or perhaps five, I . . ."

"You what?"

"I thought of something which struck me as promising. A way of adjusting molecular relationships by compressing a signal in time—by programming a computer to perform the alterations so fast the effects of one would not interfere with the others."

"Is that how you think you can succeed after all?"

"No. That is how I half-succeeded with my orang-outangs. But not even your famous Shalmaneser, not even K'ung-fu-tse that they have in Peking, can react swiftly enough to eliminate all side-effects."

"Then how *do* you think you can do it?" Donald demanded. He hauled on the line and brought himself face to face with the scientist, sweat making the interior of his suit clammy.

Sugaiguntung did not answer directly. He continued in the same passionless voice, "Then I tried another method which held promise. I developed a series of template solutions in which one could bathe genetic material, allowing the desired reactions to proceed unhurriedly and avoiding violent deformations of the molecular lattices."

"Yes, I read about that," Donald snapped. "Was that the method?"

"It worked on simple genes, but not on ones as complex as the human. The stability of the template organics tended to deteriorate faster than the process could be completed."

"In God's name, then, what—?"

"Also I had some success with stabilising genes at the temperature of liquid helium. But the return of the frozen material to normal activity took so long it was clearly uneconomic on the mass scale. Besides, unless the increase of temperature was perfectly smooth, at any moment a deviation of a degree or two could induce a dissociation in the genes and waste all one's previous trouble. Discarding that, I next investigated the tuned sonic resonances which—"

He's not telling me anything. He's talking for the sake of talking. Why?

Donald stared all around. A faint stir of breeze touched him on the cheek. Was it his imagination or was the mist lifting? Christ, yes it was! Over there, distinct against the stars, the cone of Grandfather Loa lowering at him!

Unless the submarine turns up right away, we'll be exposed as clearly as if we were—

The thought stopped, kicked aside from his mind by the fearful realisation of the reason for Sugaiguntung's garrulity.

He whispered, "You drecky bleeder! Have you turned on your beacons?"

Not waiting for an answer, he tugged on the line with one hand and fumbled for his suit-knife with the other. He dragged the blade free while his imagination filled the air with the sound of patrol-boats closing in, the hiss of energy-bolts grounding in water and blasting up geysers of steam. He meant only to slash at the thongs holding the beacons on Sugaiguntung's suit, separate the power-leads and drop them to the ocean-bed.

But Sugaiguntung divined his intention and tried to catch his arm. The water hampered him, and the clumsy suit. A movement halfway between a kick and plunge threw him off his aim. The knife went home.

There was a monstrous eruption of bubbles from one of the inflated compartments, and the last of them turned dark. He snatched back the knife, a roaring in his ears and a tingling all over his skin.

"Femoral artery," Sugaiguntung said, now as before without any trace of emotion. "Don't try to staunch it. I won't let you. It is the least I can do to repay my people for the treachery I committed, doubting the word of those who knew better than I myself did. I have been ... disloyal ... but I go to join my ancestors in a way which ..."

His head lolled suddenly to one side, and his upturned face showed a faint, enigmatic smile to the stars the parting mist had now revealed.

There was even yet not enough light to show the colour of the water, but Donald knew it was red. Staring, letting go the knife, letting go the rope, he saw it glow brighter and brighter, the brilliance of lava, and Grandfather Loa erupted in his brain and claimed the latest victim of all the uncounted thousands slain by his wrath.

When the submarine surfaced and he was dragged aboard, he had stopped screaming, but only because his throat was too raw to utter another sound.

tracking with closeups (31)

UNTO US A CHILD

When the girl Dora Kwezi appeared at the door of the schoolroom Frank Potter did not at first notice her. He had his back to the class, writing up a passage on the board and practically shouting over his shoulder because of the drumming of the rain on the roof. She had to call him twice before he heard her.

"Mr. Potter! Mr. Potter sir!"

He turned. She was splashed with mud almost to the knees and her frock was pasted to her handsome young body with the rain. What could have brought her out in this frantic hurry?

"Mr. Potter, please come to your missus!"

Oh my God. But it can't be. Please God, it can't be—it's too soon, another five weeks!

"Go on with what I was telling you to do," he said mechanically to the class, adding to the oldest boy as he passed his desk at the rear, "I rely on you to keep order, Lemuel!"

Then he seized his umbrella, opened it, and dived out into the pouring rain in Dora's wake.

Across the squelching quagmire of the village "square", up the verandah steps and into the small bungalow assigned to them. When they first came here Sheena had looked about her in despair and begun by listing all the things it didn't have which she regarded as essential to mere survival. There wasn't even a piped water-supply; a tank on the roof had to be filled from a water-truck at weekly intervals.

Yet it was a place where they could have their child, legally . . .

"She in the bedroom!" Dora said, pointing, and Frank thrust past her, dropping the umbrella without bothering to close it.

Sheena was stretched out on the bed with her eyes closed, her face very pale, her belly stretched large as a pumpkin under her too-tight dress. Beside her, bathing her face with a rag and iced water, was the nearest approach this forsaken little village could boast to a doctor: Dora's mother Mamma Kwezi, the midwife and layer-out.

"Is it—?" Frank demanded, and could not finish.

Mamma Kwezi said with a shrug, "It is soon, but I have seen early pains before." Her English was good but thick with Shinka consonants.

Frank dropped beside the bed and took Sheena's hand. On his touch, she opened her eyes and gave him a wan smile that almost at once died into a grimace of pain.

He said inanely, "How long since it started?"

"Over two hours, I suppose . . ." Her voice was harsh.

"Why didn't you tell me before, for heaven's sake?"

"But it's far too soon, Frank! It ought to happen next month some time!"

"It is bad to be afraid," Mamma Kwezi said. "I was born, you were born—it is a thing for everyone, after all."

"But if the baby is five whole weeks premature, then—" Frank checked himself, belatedly aware that this was the worst kind of talk to let Sheena hear.

"Yes, it will be weak, that cannot be helped," Mamma Kwezi sighed.

"We've got to get her out of here—to a proper hospital!"

Mamma Kwezi looked at him with big round eyes. She gestured to Dora, hovering in the background, and relinquished to her the task of bathing Sheena's hot face. Drawing Frank aside, she regarded him sadly.

"How will you take her, sir? The road to Lalendi is all mud, and in this rain—"

"I'll phone for a copter!"

But even as he spoke the words he knew they were ridiculous. The pelting rain was practically a solid sheet of water now, the last violent spate before the winter dry period set in.

"No, a hovercraft! That can get through mud, it can get through anything."

"Yes, sir. But can it get here from Lalendi, and back, in . . . well, two more hours?"

"Will it be that soon?"

"It will not be any longer. I have felt a—" Mamma Kwezi put her hand on her own ample belly, at a loss for the word.

"Contraction?"

"Yes. The water will break in a little while, I think."

Frank's world slipped off its axis and spun crazily. Mamma Kwezi put a sympathetic hand on his arm.

"She is a good healthy girl, sir, and you too are a strong father for the child. I am very experienced and careful and I have good medicines and the book they sent from Port Mey with the newest advice which I have read and remembered. It is not like an old juju-woman."

"No, Mamma, I'm sure you're—you're going to do fine." Frank swallowed hard. "But if the baby is going to be so weak and small . . . !"

"We will take good care of it. Now do go and talk on the phone to Lalendi. Have sent a car. Get to help me a good English-type doctor and say what is the trouble. Once I saw in Lalendi a special cradle with very strong air in big cans which is good for babies."

Christ. Long ago and far away before that damned Eugenics Board ruling, I was planning to have Sheena take hyperbaric oxygen therapy during the pregnancy . . .

But techniques like that seemed unbelievable in the setting of this village built of timber and scrap with only a handful of modern houses in the centre: the school, this bungalow, the clinic, the library . . . Even those not modern, slab-sided huts on a grand scale made of concrete in cheap standard panels. Here where TV was something the whole village gathered to watch in a sort of crude cinema, here where there was one phone, no street-lighting, nothing but fluores-